Jane Beeson has been working as a writer since 1978. She has written three previous novels, *Apple of an Eye*, *A Winter Harvest* (which in 1984 was made into a BBC TV series starring Cheryl Campbell) and *About Claire*. She has published, and had broadcast, poetry and numerous short stories, and has written plays for stage, radio and television. In 1993 she received a major Arts Council award for Theatre Writing; her play *Carrington* was produced at the Chichester Festival in 1993 and at the Edinburgh Festival in 1994. She lives and works on Dartmoor.

Also by Jane Beeson

Apple of an Eye
A Winter Harvest
About Claire

Jane Beeson

SCARHILL

Mandarin

A Mandarin Paperback
SCARHILL

First published in Great Britain 1995
by Mandarin Paperbacks
an imprint of Reed Books Ltd
Michelin House, 81 Fulham Road, London SW3 6RB
and Auckland, Melbourne, Singapore and Toronto

A CIP catalogue record for this title
is available from the British Library
ISBN 0 7493 2210 1

Phototypeset by Intype, London
Printed and bound in Great Britain
by Cox & Wyman Ltd, Reading

Author's Note

Scarhill is set during the property boom of the 1980s. Between the time it was first conceived and written and its final publication, many things have altered. Property does not present the investment and development interest it did then; the National Park's policies towards buildings and their conservation have changed vastly over the years – perhaps the change from filling spaces with plate glass to the present desire for leaded or small panes in windows, illustrates this best in the novel.

During the time I have lived here, policy has changed from buying up farmers' land in order to widen lanes for tourist coaches, to re-routing the coaches in order to keep the narrow lanes; from encouraging plantations of softwoods, to approving only the planting of hardwoods; from converting every available building for holiday lets, to refusing planning permission for conversions.

It is in the midst of these changing attitudes that *Scarhill* was written. Policies alter, but the underlying conflicts which I represent in my novel, the conflicts of character under the Pressure of contemporary mobility, remain relevant.

The possibilities that exist between two people, or among a group of people, are a kind of alchemy. They are the most interesting thing in life.

On Lies, Secrets and Silence
Adrienne Rich

Prologue

'Alec, can't we find somewhere bigger? I mean much bigger. I don't think I can stand us all living on top of each other a moment longer, it makes me bad tempered.'

Sophie Deneuve looked round at the heap of books and magazines, the Sunday papers spread over the floors, the videos in slipped-over heaps beside the television.

'This flat is hardly small.' Alec Deneuve looked up in surprise from behind his *Telegraph*.

'But if we can afford it?' Sophie rested her elbows on the table, her chin in her hands.

'Afford exactly what?'

'More space. There's far too much in this living room. You can't even see the furniture beneath all this junk.' She made a sweep with her arm, just missing some dried flowers set precariously on the edge of a table it shared with books, a typewriter, and a heap of clothes.

Alec lowered his paper and looked around. 'It's because the children are like Jane, unnecessarily untidy.'

Jane had been Alec's first wife and was always held responsible by him for any failings in their children, which Sophie found quite as annoying as Jane had done before her. However on this occasion she let it pass, she was too busy making her point.

'What I've been thinking' – she traced her finger along the join in the teak coffee table – 'is that we'd be better off in the country. Scarlet would love it and it would be better for Jude.'

Alec took off his glasses and put them away in their case. A particularly large vehicle passed along the road outside making everything in the flat able to judder, judder. Sophie noticed and made the most of this unexpected support.

'It's noisy too. Very noisy. And Theobald said the one thing essential for Jude was quiet. Peace. You know.'

'My dear Soph,' Alec tried not to feel aggravated, 'we can't change our lives entirely for the sake of Jude. If he can't take undergraduate life, then he'll just have to pack it in.'

'I didn't mean *just* for Jude. But I thought you said after last year when our . . . our assets doubled, that we could afford somewhere in the country if we wanted?'

Sophie kept her eyes lowered and continued to draw patterns on the table top with her finger. Alec was in his mid-forties and could not sensibly be met head on in a manoeuvre concerning property and money. Sophie unfortunately had neither and was only twenty-seven.

Alec glanced at his wrist and stood up. He was meeting a friend at Queen's for his usual Sunday afternoon game of squash. Sophie felt desperate.

'Alec, please. Don't go for five minutes. Can't we talk seriously about what we're going to do?'

Alec picked up his racquet and stood with it under his well-shaved, square, but not too square, jaw. His blue eyes fixed themselves on Sophie.

'Because Jude has been advised to take a sabbatical I cannot see that we need to uproot ourselves and flee to the country.'

'I think I might find it more, sort of . . . rewarding.' Sophie fumbled to qualify her need.

'You wouldn't, you'd be bored, you don't ride. What would

you do? You'd hate the hunting set.' Alec's arguments as always carried weight and a considerable vein of truth.

'I wouldn't be bored. I'd walk and keep chickens and things,' Sophie said hopefully.

'Scarlet will be living up here if she gets a job,' Alec was firm. 'She won't want to spend her weekends driving down the motorway in queues of traffic.' He put on his blazer.

Sophie twiddled a strand of blonde hair, a habit she reverted to under tension. Finally she could contain herself no longer.

'I'm sure it's the right thing for us. I just feel it. You were saying you could sell your partnership, that there was not much point in your staying on, that you'd do better to sell and . . . start up something new, something challenging . . .' She was checked by the expression on Alec's face, then bravely brought out the idea she had been repressing. 'Perhaps we could buy a farm, I think it would be wonderful. I've always dreamt of living on a farm in the South West.'

'If that's what you want, you find somewhere.' Alec let himself out of the door, started down the stairs.

'How?' Sophie hung over the banisters.

'I'm late. We'll talk about it this evening.' The front door opened and closed.

Sophie sighed. She looked at her face in the gilt-framed mirror sunk into the embossed wallpaper. Pale, she thought, pale and lifeless and beginning to get lines on it. London was very ageing, all the traffic and fumes and dirt. Carcinogenic. Back in the living room she looked around her. Alec's pictures on the walls, Alec's possessions, Jane's choice – the wallpapers and curtains, even the fluffy Habitat carpet – but basically Alec's because Jane had taken most of the movable possessions with her. Excepting her children. Sophie had inherited those. She sat down on the sofa, kicked off her shoes and drew up her feet. Then resting her chin on her knees she contemplated her life, and it seemed to her that Alec was unfair in expecting to build her into his existing life like a new gadget. She would be happier, far happier, in a house of her own where there was space – preferably an old house.

She would choose her own furnishings, go round sales buying this and that like Carol Granger had told them everyone did when they'd met her at that wedding ... Sophie's thoughts halted abruptly. Carol Granger. She would ring her, although she was more of an acquaintance than a friend. She would know of any farms for sale in her area – Dartmoor. Sophie's heart gave a thump, it sounded so sort of ... romantic.

'Alec,' said Sophie over dinner, 'I rang Carol Granger. I thought she might know of an agent.'

'Oh?' Alec dug into his melon.

'As a matter of fact she knew of a farm, a farm with a good house.'

'I'm not a farmer.'

'We could have a manager or something, couldn't we?'

'Sophie, this is one of your madcap ideas. Why right down in Devon? Why not Sussex or Hampshire. Wiltshire, even?'

'Jude wants to walk. He'd have all that open space that Theobald talked about. For walks. This farm is beautiful and unspoilt. Please Alec, can't we just *look* at it? It would be fun to accept her invitation for a night anyway.'

'I have no objection to going down for a *night*.' Alec had just bought a new car and the thought of driving it down the motorway appealed to him. 'Yes,' he said thoughtfully, already mentally deciding the route, 'there's nothing to stop us going for a night, having a look at the place.'

Sophie concealed her pleasure. Alec had a perverse streak in him, if she was too enthusiastic he was inclined to become correspondingly less so. She contented herself by ringing Carol Granger to ask for particulars of the farm's agents while Alec watched the *News*.

A week later Alec and Sophie drove down the motorway. The countryside flashed past; Alec drove and Sophie laid her blonde head against the soft headrest and felt the cool breeze blow on her face through the open sun-roof. Now and again she handed Alec an extra-strong mint. They drove mainly in silence, only interrupted by Sophie switching on the radio or playing the cassette. Alec was never talkative, he said he couldn't be when driving. Sophie would have liked to talk, so they swapped over and she drove. But it still didn't make any difference, Alec shut his eyes and went to sleep. Sophie held the wheel, watched the road, ate strong mints and speculated idly on the house they were to see and the big difference it would make to her life, if suitable. She had not got as far as asking herself why her life needed to be different, she simply felt that it did.

Finally they left the motorway, Alec woke up and mapread, and by a succession of tortuous lanes they at last located Scarhill. It had no sign on the gate, which didn't help matters, and they passed it twice before realising that the rusty iron gate framed in nettles and overhung by sycamores was barring Scarhill's entrance. Alec's temper shortened, Sophie grew hot and flushed in the face from reversing and turning the large car in the narrow lane, so it was with great relief that they entered the weed-grown cobbled yard and knocked on what Sophie said was the back door but Alec insisted was the front.

While they waited Sophie had the chance to look round her. She liked what she saw – granite walls, a jumble of roofs with the moor rising across the valley beyond them. She glanced at Alec feeling sure he wouldn't like anything so disordered, but his face was impassive. He stood patiently waiting in his open-necked light blue shirt and navy blazer, and Sophie's heart gave a little leap and flicker of love. After all, he was doing all this for her, it was really wonderfully generous of him.

* * *

'You see,' said Mr Hunter, 'we have pretty well promised Scarhill to Earne Fardon.'

'I know.' Kate Merlin sat opposite him across his desk, her hands folded. 'Is it very dishonourable to change our minds?'

5

Like Mr Hunter she used the plural, making him an accomplice in her proposal.

'Well,' Mr Hunter's voice registered doubt, 'it's not good practice, but as nothing is signed and Earne Fardon has not so far been able to arrange a mortgage, I think it might not be unreasonable to accept the Deneuves' offer.'

'Yes,' said Kate. It was indeed £10,000 more. 'If you think it all right,' she said again, but this time more eagerly.

'I do,' said Mr Hunter. 'In view of your difficult circumstances and the slump in property prices, it seems to me that the price offered by the Deneuves is the fairest of the two.'

'Although,' Kate said, 'Earne Fardon actually offered our asking price?'

Mr Hunter cleared his throat. 'Old Earne knows a bargain when he sees it,' he said. 'I hear he's not purchasing for himself but for his nephew, Gabe Fardon, who is a tenant of the Grangers at present.'

'Oh dear,' Kate's face fell. 'Then perhaps he should have it.'

This was a turn in negotiations Mr Hunter had not expected. 'I advise you to sell Scarhill for its real value, put qualms of conscience behind you, for this is a business deal on which not only your future but your son and daughter's futures depend. And the total sum derived from the sale of the property, you must remember, is to be divided between yourself and Mr Merlin. Leave it to me and I will ring the Deneuves, see if they will pay cash.'

So that is how it was left, and how the Deneuves became the new owners of Scarhill Farm.

I

Kate Merlin stood alone in the midst of the gathering crowd, an anxious expression on her handsome, rather hawk-like face. For today, exactly eight weeks after she had accepted the Deneuves' offer for Scarhill, Hunters and Dobbs, estate agents and auctioneers, were on the premises to conduct a sale of the excess furniture and effects that could not be fitted into the much smaller Bag Down. The furniture had been left *in situ* or strategically placed, and Hunters' man instructed to move from room to room followed by bidders; the most valuable pieces had been put in the old kitchen where Kate now stood as incommoded by the crowd as a beekeeper might be in the presence of a swarm. Had the villagers of Poundsford been bees they might have thought carefully before alighting, or even skirted her. Certainly she was treated with deference, a respect when they spoke, for she had been at Scarhill for seventeen years.

From the beginning there had been much speculation as to the Merlins' suitability, for they were from 'up country'; to be more precise from the commuter-belt suburbs of London, and no one had thought they would 'last'. But as the years passed and first Astra had been born, then five years later, Benjy, the village had come to regard them as permanent – as permanent, that is to say, as human settlements ever are. Kate had the reputation of being strong though vague; that she would become stronger now Donald Merlin had left her, none doubted. His leaving had caused a considerable stir, giving the villagers cause for speculation; some said it was owing to a 'minor breakdown' and referred to it as poor Mr Merlin's 'trouble'; yet others put it down to Kate's failure to keep the books or provide him with regular meals. That she was an artist, a painter, absolved her from more extenuating dissection by her neighbours – if she could be said to have neighbours, for Scarhill was two miles outside the village and isolated from other habitations by its land.

'Have you seen them? They've come.' Astra was at her mother's elbow. Kate, too far away in thought to connect immediately, looked blankly at her fifteen-year-old daughter.

'Who?'

'The Deneuves.'

And certainly there was an indefinable stir in the room, a silence followed by an excited murmur, a raising of temperature caused not only by the increasing numbers, but by the entry of the new owners. Alec Deneuve led the way forward and the crowd unexpectedly parted before him. Sophie, Kate was able to see by unashamedly standing on the bricks of the fireplace, was dressed in carefully faded dungarees as became the new owner of an old farm. As she watched Kate felt a pang, an actual physical sensation of discomfort, for by this time tomorrow the Deneuves would be living in Scarhill – her home.

'She's even prettier than I remembered' – Astra was speaking.

'Oh yes' – but Kate was not fully listening. She was thinking of that day three months back when she had led the Deneuves from room to room, hardly aware of them as people but only as purchasers. Now Astra was forcing her to see them as future neighbours, acquaintances at the very least.

'He looks sort of . . .'

'What?' Suddenly Kate needed to know.

8

'Sort of wax-like. Not quite real – a superman.'

Kate stared over the selection of heads and shoulders before her to the precision of Alec Deneuve's profile, but in the same instant Hunters' man, followed by a seething mass of people, moved to the first lot. She waited for them to pass, then let herself through the door into the salesroom where Hunters' man and his flock had gathered, and would have started across it had not she heard voices discussing her: 'Poor Mrs Merlin – seems a shame so much has to go' – Kate recognised the voice as Mrs Bellamy's from the Poundsford village shop – 'It's hard on the children, that's what Esther was saying. 'Tis a shock for them their father gone.' And before Kate could move out of the doorway and make her presence known, another much younger voice murmured assent. Lucy Fardon's.

Only half listening, Kate pushed forward. Lucy was edging away, moving across the room towards Gabe Fardon who stood slouched uneasily on the edge of a group of locals. Mrs Bellamy also moved away in search of a fresh recipient for her wisdom and Kate was able to follow Lucy along the path she carved through the crowd. Brought to a standstill behind the Fardons, she listened unabashed to their interchange. They in turn were staring at the raised braceleted arm of Sophie Deneuve who was absently pushing back a sliding strand of blonde hair.

'There, Gabe – look!'

'Is that her?' Gabe stared at a short, hatted, dark woman.

'No' – Lucy couldn't believe his obtuseness – 'not that one – that one. The blonde.'

'It don't look to me as though her'll stay long,' Gabe surveyed Sophie with the eye of experience.

'She's ever so smart.'

'Smart? In them old h'overalls? Patched up.'

'That's how they're wearing them now. I like him too.'

Gabe, with the slowness of a countryman used to eyeing stock, turned his attention on Alec. 'Going to farm, is he?' Gabe's expression and the slight quiver of his lip conveyed all. Kate couldn't help but be amused. She pulled herself away only to find herself practically pressed up against Alec Deneuve. It was Alec who spoke first.

'I say, I like your house – ours. I really do. It gets better every time I see it. But the land's its great asset – it's full of possibilities, and a luxury to own that chunk of moor.'

'Yes,' Kate said, aware people on either side were listening and eyeing them; Alec had the kind of voice that carried.

'We had an incredible drive down,' he went on, 'just over three hours from door to door – the Grangers' door. We're PGs there for a couple of nights. I expect you know.' He laughed.

'Yes,' Kate murmured. Roads are the key to our age, she thought. Without them none of us would be here – not people like us and the Grangers and the Deneuves. Only strictly local people, ones who have always lived here and are content to stay. It was the road that opened the countryside up to the middle class, the moneyed class – lanes to the B roads, B roads to the small towns, A roads to the motorways that criss-crossed the countryside to the large metropolises and ports . . . She checked her thoughts, which had a habit of running away with her, looked up furtively at the new owner with the mistrust due to someone taking solid property in exchange for a piece of paper.

'Sophie has gone outside, I believe' – Alec averted his eyes from Kate to the catalogue – 'I know she's anxious for those chairs on the lawn.'

Kate felt herself grow hot. The chairs were nothing to be proud of, Donald would never have let her include them at all, he would have got the local salesroom to collect them privately and sell them incognito. 'Oh but they're rubbish, really,' she explained. 'I had them in the television room for the children.'

'That's one of the indulgences we're looking forward to,' said Alec comfortably, 'a separate television room where the children can be banished. You can't imagine the torture of

10

sharing one's sitting room with teenagers and their friends – and friends' friends.'

'No,' said Kate, and certainly the prospect was awesome. Astra had not yet reached the age of friends, or if she had she did not bring them home, and Benjy's occupations mainly took place outside the house although he often sat tying trout flies in front of the television till he fell asleep.

Alec was still talking. 'We were hoping you'll all come to a housewarming as soon as we're settled in.'

'Thank you – we'd like to. Or I would.' Kate half despised herself for accepting but there was an assurance about Alec Deneuve that made him hard to resist. 'I don't know about Benjy,' she went on, 'but Astra would probably like to come although we've got quite a lot of moving to do ourselves.' As she said it, she felt forlorn. There was so little to move, it could all be done in two days. Heaps and heaps of stuff had gone: the billiard table, the children's old books and games – everything. Even the rocking horse. She lowered her eyes to Alec's olive suede shoes and said, 'I must find Astra' – it seemed her only means to get away. 'There'll be some clearing up to do when everyone's gone.'

'Sophie wants to give you a hand. She was here somewhere.' Alec looked round hopefully but Sophie was nowhere to be seen.

'No, really. It's very kind of her but we can manage.' Kate was definite. She wanted to spend her very last hours alone or with her family in Scarhill, even if only to sweep up. She left Alec Deneuve and went upstairs to check what was left of their own things. Through the open windows voices floated up from the lawn. 'Apparently there's a fantastic amount needs doing, but it's a fabulous house' – Sophie's voice was unmistakable – 'and those chairs are simply delicious, all they need is recovering.' Kate couldn't help smiling; Sophie's way of expressing herself was so exactly as might have been expected.

Her voice was replaced by Alec's: 'It's going to be expensive but, I hope, worth it. I'm told there's a bit of rot got in down

11

the back of the chimney, otherwise I believe it's basically sound. There was no mention of rot in the survey.'

'That's because they can't get in to look without pulling the house down. Surveys are a racket,' another voice answered.

'I hope not entirely,' said Alec. And Kate guessed, not without sympathy, he was thinking of the fee. She crossed to the window and looked out. Her attention was caught by the sight of Dan Callow, renowned as a fencer, who was actually standing in the flowerbed as he leant over the wall talking to Gabe Fardon. She watched in distress as he changed his weight, pressing flat a clump of stocks and marguerite daisies. Finally, she couldn't bear it. She opened the window and called out. They nodded, stood more upright. If only, Kate thought, the flowers could too, but deference made Dan tread all the more firmly.

'Could you move off the flowerbed,' she called down, 'I'm sorry but I can't bear to see plants trodden on.' She knew they thought her mad – it wasn't as though it was her place any longer. They shifted awkwardly, apologised. She thanked them. Dan, she noticed, still had his heel on a sweet-william but she couldn't very well ask him again.

Giving up, she closed the window. I am mad, she thought, what does it matter? But the imprint of Dan Callow's heel crushing the bright green shoots of sweet-william continued to distress her. She made her way down to the salesroom, but it smelt overwhelmingly of hot tweedy farmers and tobacco – she had to get out, and quickly. She went along the back to the outhouse lavatory which, for the day, had a sign with an arrow pointing to it and TOILET in large letters written above the door. Someone was in there. She waited till it was vacant then slipped in and locked the door. She could just as well have gone upstairs but this seemed more impersonal. Better. She looked at her face in the mirror, surprised it didn't look more ravished. She wondered at how little the trials of life showed in the face – or did it simply mark her as unfeeling? She flushed the toilet, rinsed her hands, dried them on the brown roller-towel provided by herself, and returned to the house.

'Aren't you coming in? I'm going to get tea.' Almost four hours later Kate shaded her eyes, not against the sun for the sky was white, but against the light and the blowing of her own hair. Astra stood above her on the yard wall; she could see up her pale legs to her blue briefs. Benjy sat beside her kicking his legs. The final cars with chests strapped to their roofs had gone; the yard had emptied. She lifted the ring of the stove that would be handed on to the Deneuves still burning like an Olympic torch, as indeed the previous owners had handed it on to them. She felt momentarily frightened by the relentless march of time, the imminence of mortality. The boiling kettle comforted.

Moments later Astra joined her mother and sprawled the top of her body across the table, laying her head in her arms.

'You sweep the upstairs and I'll mop the down. Gabe's coming with his lorry to pick up the rest of our things.' Kate looked with distaste at Astra's position, so expressive of the work ahead, her own despair.

'Why all this fuss about sweeping?' Astra raised her eyes if not her head. 'Just for the Deneuves?'

'We can't leave the place dirty.' Kate pushed wisps of hair behind her ears uncertainly, as though under pressure her good resolve might vanish.

Benjy drank his apple juice.

They sat in silence round the scrubbed table for the last time with the window open that looked up to the buzzards whirling over Scardon. Kate had difficulty in swallowing. She gulped noisily and put her cup down, stood visibly bracing herself and held out the broom to Astra.

'What about Benjy?'

'Benjy will find a crate for the hens.'

Astra looked suspiciously at Benjy sitting innocently on the windowseat clasping his mug.

'Get a move on, Benjy,' she said.

13

Benjy remained where he was to assert his own will for a few minutes, then eased himself off the windowseat and sauntered out. He crossed the yard, entered the big barn set at right angles to the house, and viewed with distaste the cobwebby wooden ladder he must climb to the loft above. Once up he looked around him before making his way along beside the wall where it joined the corrugated roof. In two places he found rudimentary nests made of straw and hay, each containing two transparent pearly white eggs. Benjy removed them and put them in his pocket – there were far too many doves and theft was the simplest method of birth control. He wondered how the Deneuves would cope; instinct told him they would not agree to share their loft with the doves in the same way as his own family had done. He reached the far end and finally found what he wanted – the crate. It was mixed with lumps of browning sheep's wool that had been stored in the loft after the sheep shearing each year and, along with his mother's large semi-abstract paintings, was all that now remained. Benjy, who could find a use for most things, stuffed his pockets with the wool and dragged the crate after him towards the trap.

He was still working out how to climb down the vertical ladder which required at least one hand to hold on with and two others to manoeuvre the sizeable crate through the square trap, when the barn door beneath him opened and the Deneuves walked in – or Alec did while Sophie stood in the doorway. Benjy shrank back; he found a hole in the floorboards through which he could look down unseen. Alec stood looking round him with his arms folded. Sophie joined him, stepping gingerly. She shivered as if she was feeling cold but then she wasn't wearing much, he could see her brown freckled skin where her neck joined her shoulders. The light from the open door glinted on her hair. Benjy liked yellow hair; his bird's-eye view was perfect. Alec spoke.

'It's an old original, I should say. Ripe for conversion. With John's help we should be able to make a really roomy extension – self-contained flats if we wanted – taking care, of course, to keep the character of the place.'

'Can we keep the cobbles?' Sophie scraped aside with her toe some of the dried dung, revealing cobbles smooth and worn with age.

Alec frowned. 'It's out of the question if we're going to convert. It'll have to be concreted.'

'I rather love it as it is, though it is awfully dark.' Sophie glanced around her. 'We don't have to alter it too much, do we?' She stared at the arrowslit openings in the barn walls and the worm-eaten joists supporting swallows' nests; Benjy quickly withdrew his two eyes from the convenient hole.

'It won't spoil it, will it? I mean, will it be worth it?' Sophie transferred her wish into Alec's language.

'Oh yes, it's *worth* it. It's a question of telling John what we want and getting estimates in. It really is amazing how it's been let go – you'd have thought they'd have cared about it enough to have done a bit more than they have.'

Benjy wiped his dirty thumb on his trousers and inserted it in his mouth. It comforted him, was a tangible act in his tumbling world – regular, rhythmic. He rocked a little as he sucked and the rocking, though silent, caused dust to fall from the little heaps around the woodworms' holes. Some alighted on Sophie's hair.

'Bits are coming down on me' – she shook her head in consternation, 'Shouldn't we go? The Merlins won't want us hanging around.' They retired from the dark barn into the lighter world of the outdoors.

Benjy made no move till he heard the whine of the Deneuves' car reversing up the drive; he then balanced the crate on his head and shoulders and, guiding it with one hand, lowered himself laboriously down the ladder. Once on the ground, he dragged the crate across the yard to the stable that acted as a chicken house, let himself in and stood gazing up at the chickens perched on top of a hayrack well out of his reach. They huddled up one end, cocking their heads at him and cackling intermittently. In the manger there were three large eggs of a motley hue and one smaller white one. Benjy stretched out his hand to collect them, then paused in the act. Might not the eggs now belong to the new owners in the same way as his farm? His expression grew sulky and he picked the white egg up in his fist and crushed it: the sticky yolk oozed through his fingers. The large eggs he left in the manger; he cleaned his hands on some straw, wiped his nose on his wrist and looked once more at the hens. How was he to reach them?

When Sophie brought Alec unexpectedly on the Saturday morning to look at Bag Down, Astra was reading in the window seat behind the shutters. Inside the room the shutters merged with the panelling so no one could tell there was a window there at all except from the outside. The seat itself was set into the thick wall of the only room large enough and light enough for a studio, and was consequently stacked with her mother's canvases. A solitary easel stood up bravely. Even so the light from the large bowed french windows was still poor owing to a thick box hedge growing on top of a bank opposite.

It was through the french windows that the Deneuves somehow arrived with her mother before Astra could move; then after a few moments it was too late and to emerge would have been altogether too dramatic and startling. So she tried to go on reading, but couldn't.

Sophie said, 'Isn't this quite the most divine place – it's even quainter than Scarhill, isn't it Alec? I can't believe we can stand on ground level here and be upstairs at the other end. It must be unique.'

'On the contrary, I believe it's not uncommon to find these old houses built into the slope of the hill. Am I right, Kate?'

'There are a few around' – her mother spoke unwillingly. It was clear she would have preferred to support Sophie. But she needn't have worried, for Sophie was irrepressible.

'Well, it's special for me because I've never seen one before.

I adore the tiny windows – not these, the others – and the ivy and cobbles. It's absolutely out of this world.'

'The hedge is a nuisance,' her mother said, 'It takes away the light.'

'Oh, but you couldn't touch it.' Sophie was apparently looking out at it for her voice was less distinct, 'it's all so in keeping – it fits. And this room is lovely – lovely and bare,' she said tactfully. 'I hate overcrowded rooms. You're so clever, Kate. You make places sort of ... inviting. It's because you're artistic.'

'I'm going to use it as my studio so it has to be empty,' Kate explained.

'What a brilliant idea. May we look at some of your paintings?'

'Yes,' said Kate, 'but I'm afraid most of them are still in your loft. Gabe Fardon's going to collect them for me, if that's all right?'

'Of course it is. We'd awfully like to buy one. I don't know whether you'd consider it?'

Astra behind the shutters could hear from her mother's reply that she was pleased. Flattered. She heard her say modestly, 'These are not really my best. I should love you to have one but actually I was going to get rid of them and use the stretchers for new ones. I shall have more time now.'

'Oh yes – you'll have masses of time tucked away here. I really envy you having somewhere small. The size of Scarhill *is* quite daunting, but Alec says it's a challenge.'

'Did I?' Alec seemed to have forgotten.

'It is big,' Astra heard her mother agree, and suddenly felt tears pricking at the back of her eyes. She hunched her knees up, clasping them for comfort. She loved Scarhill, she thought she would never again like anywhere as much ... Then Sophie's voice pulled her attention sharply back to the present. 'Jude's just got back from the Greek islands – he's been wandering round with a back-pack – terribly primitive but a marvellous experience for him. He went with a friend of Alec's who used to be a master at his school. He came back yesterday absolutely exhausted. We came really to ask if you'll come over tonight – we're having a rudimentary housewarming. *Very* rudimentary – a barbecue sitting on the rush matting, I've bought tons of it. It's absolutely the only thing for these stone floors. Alec says not having a damp-course is a disaster – hopeless for carpets. So we're leaving most of them in the flat.'

Astra assumed 'the flat' meant London. The way Sophie's mind leaped from one thing to the next she found quite disconcerting. She was used to her mother's mind that progressed with a deadly logic and tenacity and returned to a topic that most others had long since forgotten – 'You will bring Astra, won't you?' Sophie went on. 'I want Jude to meet her. I tried to get him to come with us this morning but he wouldn't get up – Alec and he had a dreadful row.'

'You're exaggerating, Sophie – but I did have to be firm. He's still sleeping off his holiday. Next week there's got to be some kind of mealtime routine, otherwise it's not fair on Sophie.'

'Oh I'm happier not getting meals at all,' said Sophie. 'I like it when they help themselves.'

Astra, from her hideout, got the impression by the silence which followed that Alec didn't agree.

Then the telephone rang and she heard her mother excuse herself and go to answer it at the other end of the house. Astra's alarm increased now she was alone in the room with the Deneuves. Her ankle that was drawn up beneath her was cramped and she held her breath for fear they should hear her as she gradually extracted it. They must have been standing just the other side of the shutters when Sophie said, 'I'm sure all this space – the moor and everything – will be terribly good for Jude, but it *is* rather a responsibility for me, Alec, if you're going to be away a lot.' And at this Astra's curiosity took over, and she listened unashamedly for Alec's reply that never came because at that minute her mother returned and she was left wondering why Jude, who must be at least nineteen, was a particular responsibility for Sophie?

With her mother back in the room she could relax a little; her mother almost certainly knew she was behind the shutters and would ease the Deneuves away from investigating. Sophie was keen to see the entire house but Alec seemed anxious to get back and pointed out that Scarlet was coming down from London and had to be met, so Sophie consoled herself by insisting, 'Tonight, then' – it was clear to Astra that she expected her mother to forget. However her voice went on gaily, 'Astra's quite the most beautiful thing I've seen in years. If I was Jude I'd fall at her feet.'

'It's kind of you to say so,' Astra heard her mother murmur as she moved away with them towards the door.

As soon as their voices receded down the passage, Astra went to the bathroom and sponged her face with cold water. She thought about the Deneuves. She wasn't at all sure that she liked them and she wasn't sure she wanted to go to their party. She was tempted to repeat what she had overheard, but for no exact reason, rather a feeling that her mother might be less anxious for her to meet Jude Deneuve should she know, she decided to keep it to herself.

Alec took half an hour to get to the station and found Scarlet waiting for him.

'I wondered if you'd forgotten me?' Scarlet, who was twenty-one and decidedly unisex in appearance with short frizzed hair and a small but determined chin, got in the passenger seat beside him.

'I'm sorry,' said Alec. 'How was your mother?'

'All right,' Scarlet didn't elaborate. 'She said to tell you Dr Theobald's made an appointment for Jude next week, on the fourteenth. Can you make Jude let him know if he can go?'

There was a silence while Alec steered from the station area on to the main road. Then Scarlet asked, 'Why does he have to keep going? Isn't he better?'

'It's a good idea to have a check-up now and again,' said Alec evasively.

'Mummy wanted to know why he never contacts her.'

Alec kept his eyes on the road. He knew perfectly well that Scarlet, who got on with her mother, was having a dig at Jude and, indirectly, at himself for not encouraging Jude to see more of his mother. But then why should he? Jane had left him, hadn't she? Jane had been the one to go, had behaved thoughtlessly and indiscreetly when Jude was at a very vulnerable age – thirteen, to be exact. What else could she expect? No, if Jude didn't care to see his mother, he'd be damned if he was going to push him. It was not that he found Jude easy himself, quite the opposite . . .

'Daddy, that was a police car you passed' – Scarlet's voice brought Alec sharply back to the present. They drove in silence at a much reduced speed until Alec mentioned the house-warming.

'Who on earth is Sophie asking?' Scarlet demanded, 'She can't know anyone down here yet.'

'Oh there are quite a few she's come across. And Jude's got a friend in Torquay who's coming, bringing some others.'

'What a party.' Scarlet's sarcasm grated on Alec, reminded him of her mother. He wished his children were easier and wondered guiltily if it was the price you paid for divorce. Jude, for instance, had refused to play games, refused to dive for the school, refused to take any interest in Alec's own business, which was manufacturing foam upholstery – and very successful it had been until he'd been offered a partnership in a stockbroking firm and sold out – refused, in short, to take any interest in anything that Alec thought of importance. Alec grew heated even thinking about it. Jude had no idea, absolutely no idea, of the economics of living. Alec had wanted him to read economics at Oxford instead of a futile arts subject in no way orientated towards a career. Jude criticised his – Alec's – values but the way he was going at the moment it looked as though he'd be living off him indefinitely. What mattered, Alec thought, was to stand on your own two feet, not sponge off anyone or be behoven to them. To be fair, Jude was still only a student. But at his age he hadn't been mucking around doing nothing, he'd been a trainee in his father's business. In the end it all came down to enterprise; there was nothing to stop anyone making money if they had imagination and were prepared to work. Alec almost took the direction for Torquay instead of Plymouth, only hastily swerving into the right-hand lane.

'What on earth are you thinking about, Daddy?' asked Scarlet sharply.

'Nothing significant.' Alec lapsed back into a silence that lasted for most of the way to Scarhill.

When the Merlins arrived late at the Deneuves' party Sophie's face was pink and shining and she was wearing an apron. She looked immensely relieved to see them.

'Everything's topsy-turvy. It *would* have to rain. The house is simply not ready for an indoor party but I've had to make the best of it. What do you think?' She led them into the candlelit living room.

'It looks lovely.' Astra was sincere and with good reason, for the old room, with its hefty walls interspersed by niches that glowed with soft light and shadow, looked at its best.

'May I take you to meet Jude?' Sophie laid her hand on Astra's wrist and drew her across the room through the already considerable gathering of drinking people.

Kate, left on her own, looked round for a glass so that she might catch up with the rest, speak and laugh with as much deft ease. With relief she saw Alex coming towards her bearing a tray of drinks.

'You've met all my family, haven't you?' he asked, while waiting for her to select a glass.

'No. I don't think so.'

'We must rectify that. Scarlet?' he caught at his daughter's wrist as she passed, 'this is Kate. The Kate you've heard so much about.' Scarlet smiled politely, shook hands formally, then slithered away amongst her contemporaries. Alec continued his round with the tray leaving Kate again a lonely pillar until Carol Granger, the only face in the gathering she recognised, came over to speak to her.

Normally Kate would have been inclined to avoid Carol who was an acquaintance rather than a friend, but on this occasion she was not sorry to see Carol's distinctive feature, her mane of red hair, wending its way through the crowd towards her. Richard Granger followed his wife, and was unaccountably wearing a thick baggy jersey. He looked hot and uncomfortable, in fact distinctly out of place, Kate thought. Carol, who was quite short, had moved close to her, was looking up into her face. Instinctively Kate took a step back; she found the excessive proximity unnerving, even agitating.

'I see Benjy's with the Fardons. I passed him in the drive earlier. They've borrowed one of my ponies – they're going up on the moor to check their herd – they've got a hell of a lot up there, far too many.'

Kate, who felt both behoven to and guilty towards the Fardons, did not quite know how to reply. She was also surprised at Carol's seeming eagerness to denigrate them, considering they were her tenants.

'Whereabouts are they?' she asked, meaning the herd.

'Out by Finbarrow along the Tramlines. It's good grazing but they don't have "rights" there at all.'

'Doubtless that applies to half the moor ponies,' Kate endeavoured some sort of defence. It was tricky for her with Eddie being Benjy's best friend. 'Who's gone up, do you know?'

'The two boys. I didn't see Gabe.'

'I hope Gabe *is* with them.' Kate, who was the most unfussy of mothers, couldn't help feeling a little uneasy. Eddie and Benjy rode a lot on their own together but out to the Tramlines was a long ride and known for its bogs. Someone barged into her and when she had steadied her glass and again looked up, Carol had gone. Carol, she thought, never wasted much time but told everyone just enough to work them up before moving on to the next person. She immediately felt guilty for the unkindness of her thought, felt unjustified in judging Carol so harshly and yet . . .

'It's so lovely Kate – your dress. I've never seen such exquisite material. Where did you find it?' Sophie was beside her.

'Oh I've had it a long time – it's tie-dyed.' Kate looked down on her dress of burnt sienna and stone. It was quite shapeless but others gathered round her to admire the fabric. While she was being examined rather like an art work, she looked across uneasily to where Astra was holding out her glass to be filled with what looked like orange juice. Kate supposed she should have felt pleased Astra didn't drink, but she did wonder whether alcohol in moderation might not have helped her socially. She was standing now on the edge of the room, slightly drooped like a cold bird. From time to time she nervously shifted her weight from one foot to the other. Her hair was worn straight and loose round her rather pale face, her top lip curled fractionally up at the corners giving her a resemblance to the Mona Lisa. She was wearing a black velvet jacket with a ruched collar over a deep purple antique skirt; round her neck was a high lace collar. Augustus John, Kate thought, might have asked her to model but the average person might well consider her unapproachable if not plain comic. Glancing down at her own dress, Kate asked herself why she who herself dressed unconventionally should desire Astra to conform, and came to the conclusion that Astra was in some sense a parody of herself.

With this telling and unhappy thought Kate looked across to where Astra was being introduced to a boy by Sophie – almost certainly Jude Deneuve. She was looking at the ground. Kate felt Astra's agony of shyness reach out across the room; she willed her to look up, speak. If she could only communicate, that was all Kate asked. No more. But that in itself was a great deal. She quickly turned her back, moved away in case her very presence should in some way inhibit Astra.

Astra stood beside Jude while he fed a cassette into its slot.

'Do you like this?' He turned up the volume. His voice was quite loud. He had fortified himself for the party he dreaded but at which he felt he must shine, by consuming a considerable quantity of orange juice and vodka. Astra, made curious about him by her unintended eavesdropping, was flattered by his attention. He was also undoubtedly goodlooking; his skin sunburnt from his travels enhanced his strange, pale blue eyes. He was tall like his father with a presence of his own and a sort of restless inability to keep still. His fingers twisted and moved over things, or given nothing to move over, clenched and unclenched. But for the time being the vodka had steadied his customary nerves and he compensated for this by going to the other extreme. His apparent confidence was startling, his newly adopted extravagant personality to impress Astra Merlin sat on him uneasily.

'Oh yes.' Astra really knew very little about the group apart from their name.

'You know their last hit?'

'No,' admitted Astra, in deep water.

'They're right at the top – A1.'

'Of the charts?'

'God no – they don't bother. They play at private parties round London. Word of mouth, you know.'

Jude turned up the speaker. A loud, and to Astra alarming, rhythm came up. 'Shall we dance?' He caught Astra's hand and led her into the centre of the room. Astra would have liked to shrink through the floor but couldn't, her face was pink with distress. Undeterred Jude swayed from side to side clapping his hands and giving a peculiar twist of his heel with each shift of weight. Mesmerised, Astra tried to copy. Scarlet and a boy joined them, then another pair she didn't know.

'Come on – let go,' he smiled encouragingly. The music changed and his pace increased.

'I'm really not much good.' But she continued to struggle, making self-conscious jerky vibrations of her hips, half fascinated half repulsed by Jude before her – or she had thought him before her but now he was circling round, disappearing; she was on her own making a fool of herself ... Jude reappeared from behind another couple.

'Let yourself go – get into it.'

Astra flushed. Everyone must be watching her. She tried

but all her movements were too small, understated. Jude was leaving her again. Bobbing, jiggling, totally absorbed in the rhythms – sort of lost, Astra thought. Why couldn't she lose herself, her dreadful conscious self that never let her go? Passing the light switch, Jude pushed it up. Now the only light was from two candles on the piano and one on the window.

'Better?'

'Yes, much.'

The music seeped into her body, her limbs softened, almost she was lost in the movement. Then the track ended and she was herself again, must speak and think. Jude Deneuve was standing very close to her and to her surprise and quite involuntarily, an electric tingle of response passed through her.

'Fill up?' Jude took the glass she still clutched, though empty. 'What are you drinking?'

'Orange juice.'

Kate distinctly heard Astra say orange juice from the other side of the curtain dividing the talking area from the dancers. Poor child, what could she, Kate, have done to make her so inhibited, so . . . puritanical? She boldly held out her own glass to Alec Deneuve.

'Same again?'

'Please.'

'You look almost . . .' he felt for the word, 'absent. Are you all right?'

'I feel absent,' said Kate bluntly. 'I mean I don't feel quite a part of my surroundings. I shouldn't have come. Sophie was quite right – it's too soon after the move. I must apologise. I'm not good at parties at the best of times but I knew Sophie wanted Jude and Astra to meet, and Astra would never have come on her own.' She saw Alec was taken aback, quite unused to people telling the host to his face that they weren't enjoying their situation. 'Don't take any notice of me, please – I'm mildly pissed,' she explained quickly, if less truthfully, to repair the damage honesty had done. No it wasn't honesty, she corrected herself, it was tactlessness, thoughtlessness. It was her worst fault and she knew it . . . Alec, she saw, was edging away from her. 'I'm all right, I promise you,' she said again. 'Don't worry about me.'

Alec, relieved, excused himself and Kate was left on her own, acutely aware of her isolation but lacking the inclination to join one of the talking groups. She felt too old, too incongruous, too sad in short to be standing as a stranger in her recently left home. Over another's shoulder she saw herself framed in the big wall mirror with the back of a younger russet head. The reflection blurred and danced then merged in the shadows of other people who passed and repassed – but not before she observed that she was indeed an older woman and that her dark head glittered with silver. And as she looked a wave of anxiety for Benjy flooded over her. She must go, find out if he was back. She pulled aside the curtain to look for Astra.

'Of course if you've got any rough land you want to get rid of – the sort of stuff you can't do anything with – then I should be very interested,' said Alec. He was talking to Richard Granger.

'I don't *want* to sell but I may be compelled to get rid of my newtake. Twenty-five acres of rough grazing. It's steep but I imagine that's all right for trees.'

'Yes, fine – in fact probably better than flat.' A new business venture was taking shape in Alec's mind. 'Give it a week,' he said, 'and my partners will be down. Think about it.'

'I will.' But Richard had already thought. Arthritis had stopped him in his tracks where farming was concerned, not that he had ever exactly farmed the Warren to its capacity but it had ticked over. Now it was another story and the need for money imperative.

'Give me a ring some time,' said Alec who knew when he had nosed out a good thing.

'I'll have a chat with Carol about it.'

'Do,' said Alec, but his tone was unenthusiastic.

'She's a good businesswoman,' Richard said proudly.

Alec raised his eyebrows very slightly, looked as if he was going to speak, changed his mind and helped himself to whisky.

Jude, sitting on the sofa beside Astra, laid his hand on hers. In an armchair next to them a languid young man perched on the arm beside Scarlet, who sat determinedly smoking. She seemed bored, infrequently responding to her friend's remarks. Astra could only admire her; she looked so cool and composed, as though she had seen it all before and knew where she was going. Astra wondered if she would ever acquire such confidence and thought not; she would never dare *not* to reply if spoken to civilly, and was sure that if she did she would be left at once, rather than courted while she blew bored smoke rings.

Other of the young Deneuves' friends lay on the floor or lolled with their backs to the wall passing a joint from hand to hand. One candle had gone out and two on the piano were dripping and guttering in the draught from the open window.

'I think I'll have to go,' Astra said, 'my mother is waiting.'

'When can I see you?'

'Any time you want.'

'It's really refreshing the way you're quite different – different to all Scarlet's friends. They're all something – punk, or feminists, or carving careers – or just into men and always talking in riddles.' Jude stared intently at Astra as he spoke. Astra felt rather embarrassed; Jude seemed to be overdoing it and she was sure everyone else in the room was listening.

'You mean I'm dull?' she asked, misunderstanding on purpose.

'No – different. Absolutely *not* dull,' Jude laughed. Astra was flattered, pleased. Jude had concealed vodka in her last orange juice and she felt dreamy and relaxed – a part of the party.

'Astra' – her mother was holding back the curtain, beckoning.

'Coming.' The curtain dropped back into place.

'Tomorrow? Can we meet tomorrow? Shall I come to your place?'

'No,' said Astra, thinking of Benjy. 'I'd rather not at home.'

'Then where?'

'I could come over and see you at Scarhill. Some time,' she added.

Jude squeezed her hand. Scarhill didn't strike him as at all a promising rendezvous but he had more sense than to say so. He said instead, 'I won't be able to do any work till I've seen you – it'll be impossible. So come soon.'

'All right,' said Astra, detaching herself from him and making for the impatiently twitching curtain.

Kate was on the other side. 'Thank Sophie,' she murmured. 'Hurry – then we can go.'

Sophie was on the windowseat with Alec's architect who had come down specially from London. When Astra thanked her she stood up and kissed her.

'You must come again and again – now we've found you we shan't let you go easily. I know it's not good for you to tell you, but you are *so* beautiful.' Sophie kissed Astra on both cheeks tenderly. Astra, quite unused to such attention from a comparative stranger, flushed, but the lights were too low for Sophie to see. She slid her arm round Astra's shoulders and walked with her and Kate to the back door. 'It's a heavenly night,' she said, 'and this is the most perfect house for a party. I plan to have at least one a month.'

Carol said to Richard on the way back from the Deneuves' party in their Renault 4, 'He's pretty shrewd, isn't he?'

'Who?'

'Alec Deneuve.'

'I'm in no position to judge.'

'You can tell by his eyes – the way he looks at you.'

Richard didn't answer.

'Oh for God's sake,' said Carol, 'I might as well talk to myself.' It was on the tip of her tongue to jolt Richard out of his apathy by telling him about the ride Alec Deneuve had booked for Sunday; she was to go with him because he didn't know the moor. Instead she said, 'Can't you go any faster?'

'You drive if you want.'

'No thank you – not in these shoes.'

All that were left at the party seemed coupled off except those in a euphoric state behind the curtain. Jude, now that Astra had gone, left his contemporaries and found Sophie sitting alone with a drink in her hand.

'Dance?' he said, and changed the tape.

Sophie stood eagerly. It was the first time anyone had asked her to dance that evening and she loved dancing. She had been feeling rather forlorn in her role as stepmother-hostess and had had to pretend to a greater staidness than was natural to her, so now she flung herself into disco-ing with enthusiasm. She and Jude were both excellent dancers and soon someone drew back an edge of curtain and an audience collected. No one joined in for Sophie and Jude were 'letting go', which meant there was little space. The rhythm was compulsive and soon their audience was stamping and clapping in time to the beat.

Alec had absented himself with John Graves to look at some drawings for the new bathroom. He returned in search of Sophie and opened the door at a moment when she was doing a high kick bent backwards over Jude's supporting arm.

'Sophie!' The disapproval was implicit in Alec's tone. Sophie righted herself, pushed her hair back, laughing, continued for a few moments in a very much more sober fashion, and then told Jude she was exhausted. Meanwhile Alec was going round picking up glasses. Sophie joined him and started to help. Jude came across to them quickly.

'Do you have to do that now?' he said in a low voice. 'It'll make everyone think they've got to go.'

'Everyone's gone,' said Alec coldly.

'*Your* friends perhaps.'

'My friends have manners.'

'Alec,' Sophie reproved.

'This is the last party I come to under this roof.' Jude had gone white.

'*Don't* fight,' hissed Sophie. 'People'll hear.'

'I'd be happy to expose my father.'

Sophie giggled. She was still in high spirits from the dance. 'Come on Alec – leave them,' she said, taking him by the arm. Alec gave in, but had a last shot at Jude.

'See the place is left in order,' he said. 'I don't want to find any burns in the chairs and carpets tomorrow.'

Jude turned his back on his father without replying.

Half an hour later in the bathroom doing their teeth Sophie said, 'Wasn't that very heavy-handed – playing the Victorian father?'

'No – I don't think so. You do make it difficult for me, Soph, flinging yourself about like that. I wish you wouldn't.'

'Do you mean dancing?'

'Like you were – yes.'

'I'm sorry. It was my only dance of the evening.' Sophie felt injured and misjudged.

'I know it wasn't your fault. Jude was making a fool of himself.'

'I can't see why.'

'Scarlet tells me Jane's made an appointment for him to see Theobald next week.'

'Surely that's not necessary?'

'Theobald seemed to think it was.'

'He probably wants the money.'

'Listen Sophie – we've got to face facts about Jude. Look at him tonight, for instance.'

'I think you're one hundred per cent wrong. That was just high spirits – he was enjoying himself. That's what Theobald said he should do, isn't it? Let himself go and be a part of things – not an ... an outsider.' Sophie felt with a greater intensity than she was able to put into words.

'In my opinion he was over the top – not controlled.'

'That's not fair.' Because Sophie felt Alec's criticism of Jude as a poorly veiled criticism of herself she was the more aware of its injustice. 'And anyway, I think he should be allowed to settle down here and forget . . . well, everything. Let being here in the country do him good. It's so beautiful, Alec, all the bats in the twilight yesterday evening, did you see them?'

'Yes, Sophie,' Alec agreed in the patronising tone Sophie had come to dread and which implied her opinion wasn't worth the argument.

Her lip quivered; the evening that had started so well had unearthed the usual tensions. Still, she consoled herself, she had managed to introduce Jude to Astra Merlin and it had seemed as if they would get on. For just a moment a qualm of conscience furrowed Sophie's unmarked forehead, but she quickly dismissed it. She had promised Alec, absolutely promised, never to mention the real reason Jude was on a 'sabbatical'. The college had been very good about it, had retracted their original decision to send him down, given him the option of a year off with psychiatric treatment instead. After all, it would be silly to let one foolish action ruin the rest of his life. So Sophie reassured herself for keeping the secret, and closing her perfectly shaped lips, turned her face into the pillow.

'I wish we hadn't sold Scarhill to the Deneuves,' Astra said to her mother on the way home. 'They may spoil it.'

'So might anyone.'

'I wish we hadn't let them gazump. I wish Gabe Fardon's uncle had got it for them, so it had gone to genuine locals.'

'We're not genuine locals ourselves,' Kate pointed out. 'And as a matter of interest, if you go probing, you'll find a lot of people we think of as locals only came here a few years before we did. Besides, we hadn't actually accepted their offer.'

'They thought we had,' Astra eyed her mother critically, 'and anyway, I'm not trying to prove *we're* local, only that we're less destructive – potentially – to this area than the Deneuves.'

'I don't see that.' Kate felt aggressive partly because of her anxiety over Benjy and partly because she detested it when

31

Astra criticised her. Unfairly. 'We were letting Scarhill fall down because we hadn't the money for repairs. They have.'

'That's just the trouble, they've got tons of money and no sense of . . . of . . .'

'Of what?' Kate felt exasperated and impatient.

'Taste. Or he hasn't.'

'You really are a little snob, Astra.'

'I'm not.' Astra was wounded where she was most vulnerable. She was always being accused of elitism. She couldn't help it, she thought, it was just that she liked things other people didn't.

'If you and Daddy hadn't gone and split up,' she retaliated, 'we wouldn't have had to sell.'

'Astra,' said Kate in a tired voice, 'for God's sake.' Astra felt ashamed, for her mother was almost certainly as attached to Scarhill as she was. That her mother might still care for her father never crossed her mind; Astra didn't much like her father so couldn't see that her mother could either.

'So you don't think they'll spoil it?'

Kate rallied. 'You're being ridiculous. We've sold the place. What the Deneuves do is their affair.'

'You're missing my point completely' – Astra was appalled by what she saw as her mother's dishonesty – 'I'm suggesting it is *our* fault – we should have taken more care who we sold it to. Not let it go to the highest bidder.'

Kate felt hot with rage. Astra was so idiotically idealistic, but then she could afford to be, she didn't have to pay. Keep everyone. 'This isn't an ideal world,' she said obviously, 'and if you go round dealing out "taste" you aren't going to get very far. Everyone has to make a living.'

'But not the Deneuves,' Astra almost shouted. 'They tell you every other sentence how much money they've got. They're talking about building a swimming pool and a hard tennis court – even a sauna in the piggeries.'

'And no doubt you'll use them.' Kate's voice was full of sarcastic derision.

'You've just passed Tinners. Aren't we collecting Benjy?'

32

Kate swore, put on the brakes, and with difficulty reversed the fifty yards by which, in the heat of the argument, she had overshot the entrance.

Benjy had taken his bicycle down to the Fardons' at about four o'clock. He had found Eddie busy with a hammer and nails tacking something with a very nasty smell to the inside of the barn door. He watched for a while then asked Eddie what he was doing.

'What's it look like – knitting?'

'No,' Benjy said, 'it looks like a fox skin you're stretching.'

'Jesus you're a cute one.' Eddie stood back to admire his work.

Benjy asked if they weren't going up top – which meant the moor.

'Sure,' Eddie spat out his gum. 'Gimme time an' I'll have this yere finished.'

So Benjy gave him time. He wandered round Tinners, which was neither old nor new and had a great many sheds and outbuildings although the house itself was quite small. The outbuildings were mainly filled with odd bits of machinery and parts of old cars, but the biggest shed housed a tractor that Gabe Fardon used for any contracting work that came his way. Another shed was full of hens, and yet another, old straw bales and a vast pile of polythene bags. The polythene bags blew away quite often, because torn bits of them were littered round the yard and had caught on the thorn along the hedge. Benjy regarded these ragged adornments with the same interest he accorded to a wild flower or the late May blossom. They were blue like the sky and quite as important – he had a surer painter's vision than his mother, had he known it. He observed without exactly thinking, he kicked objects with his foot, sucked his thumb and absorbed through his eyes. There was no one in the house because Lucy was working and Gabe was not around; the front door was firmly locked and if Eddie wanted to get in he opened a window with a 2p piece kept in his pocket for that purpose. In a few more minutes

Eddie joined him and they went down the field through patches of nettles and docks to the flat ground by the river where the ponies were grazing. Here the grass was scarred by a ring of worn, bare earth. Benjy surveyed it, he hadn't been down the field with Eddie for a long time.

'Carol Granger lungin' er horse,' said Eddie. Benjy made no reply because there seemed no reply to make. He understood from Eddie's tone it was not an activity to be encouraged; he looked back up the hill through the trees and was just able to see the roof of a more substantial building owned by the Grangers and known as the Warren.

Fifteen minutes later Eddie was on a lively black pony called Polly and Benjy on a small bay pony called Theresa. They were to go up to Finbarrow to take a count of Gabe's foals, born this spring and to be left to graze the moor until autumn round-up. Benjy rode like Eddie – in jeans and a jersey and anything he happened to have on his feet. He was used to ponies and, like Eddie, never wore a hat. They despised toffs who wore hats. The fields gradually turned into a sweeping moor valley with a stream running down its centre. Eddie and Benjy followed along a sheep track beside the stream. Up on the top there was bog and cotton grass and bulging grey clouds blowing quickly. Benjy saw some ponies grazing.

He shouted to Eddie.

Eddie stopped.

They changed direction and rode up the steep side of the cleave. They rode to within about twenty-five yards of the ponies, who took little interest in them apart from raising their heads and looking in their direction. Their manes lifted in the wind and their tails blew sideways. They were fat and shiny, life was good, the grazing prolific. Foals lay as though dead outstretched in the sun, or shifted with their mothers, cavorting in circles with tails raised at the sight of Benjy and Eddie.

Eddie reined in.

He counted.

Benjy's pony ate grass. Benjy let the reins slip through his fingers just keeping hold on them so they didn't slip down

Theresa's neck completely. He sat half sideways, dreaming and looking and seeing, and not exactly seeing because he was thinking about flying, hang-gliding, leaping off the side of the cleave.

'You count,' said Eddie, angry because it never came to the same twice.

So Benjy counted.

'Twenty-two.'

'No it's not, it's twenty-four.'

They counted again.

Then a big bay pony came towards them. They expected it to stop when it was close but it came right on. Eddie said suddenly, 'Get goin', Benj – it's the stallion.' And he clapped his heels against Polly's sides. Benjy blinked. He heaved on Theresa's head which was somewhere out of sight at the bottom of her thick grazing neck. The stallion laid back its ears and came for Theresa. Benjy kicked her. She started into a trot. She kicked out at the stallion, Benjy clung to her. Then they were galloping, tearing along the old tramlines which were long and flat and easy to gallop over, but nearly a mile's stretch to the nearest gate off the moor. And all the time the stallion was snapping and squealing and following. Eddie was ahead. Benjy lay tight against Theresa, clinging to her mane, urging and willing her to go faster. Then the stallion reared, striking out with its front feet, missing Benjy's head by inches. He was faster than Theresa and circled round them, snapping and kicking. Benjy had never been so frightened. He called to Eddie who came back. He waved his whip at the stallion.

'Make Theresa go faster,' he said. 'She's in season – that's what's up.'

Theresa couldn't go faster.

'I want to get off,' Benjy said.

'No,' shouted Eddie, 'we'll lose her.'

Benjy saw the stallion out of the corner of his eye, saw it rise up, saw its teeth fasten into Theresa's neck, heard her squeal of pain. He shut his eyes in terror. Then out of the sky came a roar. He thought he was dying, and the shattering noise was the onset of death. As it lessened, another followed almost instantly. Benjy wondered if Theresa was dead too. He thought the stallion had trampled them to death. Then he heard Eddie's shout, 'Come *on*!'

He opened his eyes.

He kicked Theresa.

Eddie was ahead.

'It's gone,' Eddie was screwed half round, looking behind him. 'Whoopee!' he shouted, 'they chased him off.'

Benjy didn't look behind. Ahead, at last, there was a hedge and a gate. They headed for it. Eddie jumped off and undid it. They got the ponies through. The ponies were all of a lather. Benjy was sick. Eddie had a pee.

'He might jump the gate,' Benjy said. 'Let's go on.'

They cantered down the field.

They had a job getting back, the gates were wired up and there was barley growing.

'I think I'm going to be sick again,' Benjy said.

Eddie groaned. 'Tisn't the end of the world,' he said. It had nearly been for Benjy.

'It was the jets done it,' Eddie said. 'Good old jets. I think I'll fly one of 'em later on.'

'Yep,' said Benjy and a bit more sick came up. It spattered down Theresa's shoulder. It was looking at it made them notice the gash in Theresa's leg.

'Jesus 'iself,' said Eddie, 'you'll have to walk.'

So Benjy got off and led Theresa.

They'd come miles out of their way and it had begun to rain. After a bit they both rode Polly, but Theresa didn't like being led. She tugged back all the time and Benjy who had her rein was nearly pulled off.

It was dark when they got to Tinners. The sky was full of dark clouds behind the great ash on the wall. Benjy saw the new moon thin and sharp looking showing through a patch in them. He felt terribly cold. His teeth were chattering and he couldn't stop from shivering. Eddie fetched his father while Benjy held the ponies. Gabe came out and saw to Theresa's leg, and Lucy helped. After they had bathed the leg in disinfectant and observed that the wound was no more than skin deep, Lucy noticed Benjy was shivering. She pushed him ahead of her into the house and sat him on the old chaise. Benjy continued to shiver; his teeth chattered and rattled together in spite of his endeavour to stop them. So Lucy made him lie down and covered him with the usual crocheted blanket. A few minutes later they heard a car.

Slanting rain fell through the beam of the headlights. Kate, her coat pulled up over her ears and face, picked her way delicately through the ankle-deep mud. At the door she didn't knock but entered immediately. Gabe Fardon stood in the lighted hall, commenting on the wicked weather as he ushered her through into the kitchen. Lucy was sitting on the end of the chaise on which Benjy lay.

'Is he all right?' Kate peered anxiously at the prostrate form.

'Fast asleep, bless him!' Lucy looked down on Benjy with a suitably fond expression.

Kate was not surprised to see Benjy on the chaise which was his usual substitute for bed; she was a little surprised he was so soundly asleep, and more so when Lucy hastily thrust heaps of magazines off a chair to enable her to sit. She had intended collecting Benjy without stopping to talk, but it became clear by an unspoken language of signs, that the Fardons were expecting her to stay. Lucy confirmed this by lifting the lid of the Rayburn and pushing the kettle over. Kate sat down and Gabe stood up; he leant against the stove, arms folded, one leg crossed over the other. Eddie sat on the front of an old leather dining chair, knees apart, his boots rolled inwards at the ankle, looking attentive and a trifle sly. Lucy handed Kate a cup of tea and sat on a chair opposite her.

All this time they had discussed commonplaces – Kate's enjoyment of the Deneuves' party; the prices at last Wednesday's market that had been shocking; the EEC's decision to cut back on grant aid; but now Kate recognised the moment had come for which they had been preparing her.

Gabe shifted his weight on to the other leg, refolded his arms. 'Boys had a rough ride today by the sound of it.'

'Sure did,' Eddie confirmed.

'Why, what happened?' Kate made the expected response, allowing for a full description of the ride by Eddie, cross-examined to bring out the desired import by the adult Fardons. All in all, Eddie did a good job and Kate was left in no doubt of Benjy's inadequacies as a horseman and her responsibilities towards Theresa. The gash in the leg was very nasty, all the Fardon faces grew very solemn when it was mentioned.

During the excitement of the story the kettle had got left on and caused condensation, covering the ivory yellow walls and ceiling with small moist drops. The room seemed extremely airless and Kate felt worried about Benjy who seemed in a very deep sleep and was breathing noisily. She stood up and walked across the large room until she could look down on him. Lucy accompanied her, stood beside her.

'Tired out,' Lucy said, smiling fondly. 'Bless him.'

Benjy's visible cheek was very bright, his skin round it blue white.

'He didn't actually get struck by the stallion, did he?' Kate looked at Eddie.

'No' – Eddie smiled at the idea – 'no he was right as rain. It was the pony who was the one.'

Kate made no comment but privately she was convinced Benjy was suffering from shock. She finally accused: 'Was it wise to have let Benjy out on Theresa, knowing she was in season?'

Gabe shifted himself again, took off his cap from the back of his head. 'Us didn't know for certain, you can't always tell. Not until they get with a horse-pony, see . . .' He scratched his head.

'That's the trouble of it,' Lucy looked at Kate with solemn eyes. 'You're never sure. Mind you, if Gabe had been home he would have stopped them going out the Tramlines, but he was away on another job the other side of Meridan and they was gone before I was back from the Co-op.'

Both of them looked gravely at Kate. Eddie plaited some baler cord from his pocket. Kate knew she was beaten.

'Anyway, thank you for having him,' she said. 'I'm sorry I was late coming for him.' And she bent to try to lift Benjy but Gabe was before her. He swung Benjy up in his arms as though he was weightless, and led the way out into the wet night.

On the way home Kate decided she had been mad to apologise when it should have been them. But she didn't want to fight with the Fardons, she liked them apart from situations like this; and she fell to wondering whether or not she had been imagining the hostility she had sensed.

'Pretty maid,' said Gabe, meaning Astra. The car receded and he closed the door behind himself and Lucy.

'Like her mother.'

'No she ain't.' Gabe was decided.

'I don't think Kate Merlin's got any right, keeping us up all hours like she does.' Lucy's resentment grew. Yet she was not sure it was directed against Kate, so much as against her life in general – Kate was just the present target. Lucy, who had plenty of energy and wasn't lacking in potential talent, spent her days working to subsidise the more idle, if attractive, Gabe. It was hard and she felt it. She also resented the fact that she and Gabe were seldom invited to the same parties as the Merlins. It was perfectly understandable, of course, because they had different friends, though Kate Merlin did treat her as a friend . . . or was that only to make use of her when convenient, as a sitter for Benjy who, in Lucy's opinion, was old enough to leave on his own at nights? No, perhaps not, poor little fellow. Lucy had a soft spot for Benjy – in many ways he appealed to her more than her own Eddie, though she wouldn't have admitted it in a million years. It was just that Eddie was like Gabe, he sat down and demanded his meals and never gave her a hand with the clearing up however often she told him off over it . . .

'Tisn't often,' Gabe interrupted her thoughts.

'Tisn't often what?'

'Kate Merlin asks us to have the boy.'

'Too often. I should've said no, since what she done.'

'Earne wasn't quick enough off the mark, see.' Gabe was philosophic.

Lucy looked her resentment. 'It's gone one, and we got to be up by six. All of them can lie in bed till noon if they have a mind to.' And she riddled the stove as vigorously as if she was riddling the Merlins and suchlike out of existence.

'Hey,' said Gabe, 'it won't stay in if you let all the ash down through.'

The following day Alec Deneuve stood on the lawn in front of Scarhill with John Graves; both had an expression of extreme concentration on their faces which were slightly elevated, indicating it was the upper region of the house that held their attention. John Graves took a step back narrowly missing the leat behind him. Alec also stepped back, avoiding the soggy area where a spring oozed up through the grass in all but the driest weather. The sun that had been obligingly warming their backs, now vanished between swollen, white-edged clouds. Immediately the air felt chiller. It was this, rather than any conclusive decision, that made the two men move towards the ancient porch that guarded the entrance to the through passage. They walked up it, heads lowered to prevent a succession of blows from the cross-joists of the ceiling. Once inside the living room they straightened their necks and resumed a normal posture. Houses of antiquity bring with them discomfiture, Alec was daily discovering. The fire, for example, was not yet lit and the much admired chimney and hearth, it seemed to him, was actually sucking cold air down. He looked round rather helplessly for a means of lighting it, but saw nothing to aid him other than rather large lumps of unsplit wood stacked at the sides. Sophie had gone to the shops with Scarlet; Jude had departed early on one of his lengthy all-day walks. Alec felt all at once inadequate. John Graves had seated himself and was spreading out a plan on the round table in front of the sofa. Alec cast a further depressed look at the fireplace, gave up hope, and seated himself beside John Graves. He put on his glasses and, in spite of further draught sucked from under the door round the back of his ankles, endeavoured to concentrate.

'If you take out this partition here and incorporate Bedroom 1 with 2, so making a luxury-sized area for yourselves, it would be perfectly possible to incorporate a bathroom with shower unit in the corner instead of the existing cupboards. The only problem is the beam which, as I understand it, is one of the main supports to the roof.' John Graves broke off and looked at Alec for confirmation. Alec was polishing his glasses; he put them back on.

'I'm afraid,' he said, 'I have no idea what that beam supports. I only know it slopes and is low and that I should not like to take the risk of hitting my head on it every time I exit from the shower without forethought.'

John Graves's face fell fractionally. 'Of course a small bath would be an alternative,' he suggested.

Alec cleared his throat. 'I can't really see,' he said as John Graves had feared he might, 'that the size of the bath will overcome the problem. I shall still wish to stand upright to dry myself.' He was beginning to wonder why he was employing John who, though an old friend, was clearly an ass when it came to this sort of thing. By coming down from London he cost them a fortune and, on top of that, he had to be accommodated in their house at their expense. He was beginning to think they would have been better off with a local architect used to the conversion of old houses. But John was again talking.

'If you were to do away with the area originally designed for the old spiral and now allowing access to Bedrooms 4 and 5, it might be possible to install the bathroom in what is now cupboard area at the top of the existing staircase.'

'Then how should we reach Bedrooms 4 and 5?' Alec, who had a logical brain, grasped the disadvantage.

John Graves studied the plan in front of him at length.

When in a tight corner he usually fell back on confusing his clients by an even more complicated description of the proposed alteration. 'The access to Bedrooms 4 and 5 could be obtained by a further passage running parallel to the existing passage on the alternate side of the chimney breast which now, as it stands, is on the outside of the house but will, eventually, in this plan, be incorporated.'

'Yes,' said Alec. 'Does that mean a new roof?'

'Not a *new* roof,' John Graves was quick to correct him, 'just a small addition to the existing roof – possibly a flat extension that would, so to speak, marry the existing pitched roofs. It would make a most agreeable and private sun-lounging terrace,' he added in a moment of inspiration. After all, Alec Deneuve was that type. From Surrey and used to patios and swimming pools. Later on he might even suggest a sauna in the barn, but the time was not yet ripe . . .

'It seems to me,' Alec was saying, 'an extraordinarily costly way of obtaining a bathroom. Are you really suggesting it is not possible without a new passage, roof and sunbathing terrace?'

'No – no,' said John Graves hastily. 'I was merely suggesting. That would be giving it the whole luxury treatment.'

Alec felt sweat trickling down inside his collar. 'What is wrong,' he said, 'with putting the bathroom here?' He pointed to the plan with his pencil, making a sharp, and not entirely accidental stab.

John Graves surveyed the plan for some moments. 'I think,' he said gravely, 'that would probably need a major reinforcement of the living-room ceiling. I doubt, as it stands, that it would take the weight of the kind of bath you and your wife envisage.'

'But,' interrupted Alec, 'I envisage absolutely nothing extraordinary. Only a six-foot-six enamel bath. Fibre-glass if you like.' He stabbed his pencil right through the plan this time, then regretted the damage to the table.

The door opened and Sophie stood framed as in a picture, surrounded by polythene bags. She stepped down the step,

42

for Scarhill had a step inside and outside almost every door, and deposited her bags in the armchair. Her face radiated health and enthusiasm.

'Taverston is wonderful,' she said happily. 'Terribly trendy shops. I bought a skirt and amazing jacket for Scarlet, and some socks for you. And just masses of fruit and veg. Miles better than in London . . .' she hesitated, 'but actually I think more expensive.' She became aware of the rather stony expression on the men's faces and curbed further description of her enjoyable morning. 'How's it going?' she asked.

'The bathroom is proving difficult,' Alec said, and couldn't refrain from adding, 'though I'm not sure why.'

'It's the drains – the soil pipe evacuation,' John Graves was quick to get in. 'Curiously, like in all old houses, they are situated at the front instead of the back. So to get a bathroom where anyone now would want to put it – at the back – needs major adjustments.'

Alec was incredulous. 'But John,' he said, 'we haven't discussed drains. This is the first I've heard of the drains in any way determining the placing of the suggested bathroom.' He found himself lapsing into the jargon in spite of himself.

John Graves sat back and smiled with a certain sense of triumph. 'I thought,' he said, 'you understood that was the reason for situating the proposed shower complex adjacent to the main beam at the top of the stairs. In this way we could pick up the existing outlet pipe through the airing cupboard – what was the airing cupboard, but is now part of the proposed Bedroom 3. I thought this was understood.'

There was a silence in which Sophie looked from one to another. 'Actually,' she said, 'I had a rather wonderful idea. I thought we'd have a bath like Sharon's – almost circular. They really are rather fun.'

Alec examined Sophie without much love. 'Do you realise we are having a problem fitting even a small bath where you want it – in your bedroom,' – he always said 'your' if a thing was a nuisance – 'without reinforcing the whole of the existing floor structure?' He was off into the jargon again, he could hear himself. 'Now you propose putting in some fancy circular bath weighing I don't know how much . . .'

John Graves interrupted. He had learnt early, very early, that if you wished to see a job through, then it was essential to get on with the wife – or common-law wife, or female person *in situ* as the case might be. He looked considerately at Sophie as he talked, treated her as if her idea was unusual and interesting.

'A circular bath,' he said, 'does not necessarily weigh more than a bath of a more conventional sort. And in point of fact it would solve some of our problems. It could be pushed further back into the cupboard space, thus allowing extra footage between the main beam and sloping ceiling which – and this is an important point – would allow either you, Alec, or Sophie to have room to stand upright.'

'Well if it really would fit,' said Sophie, and she dropped on to the sofa and crossed one knee over the other, 'I do think it would make a change from the dull old conventional baths. Sharon says you can get these new ones in fantastic colours.'

'I'll look into it for you.' John Graves made a note in his diary.

Sophie looked at him pleasantly. 'I don't know if you've finished,' she said, 'but I was going to suggest a drink and an early lunch with us before you have to go back to London. Be a dear, Alec, and make us one of your gin and mint specials.' She lolled back comfortably. Alec stood.

'Isn't it rather chilly in here?' he said, looking with distaste at the grey and fireless fireplace.

'I'll light a fire,' said Sophie. 'I suppose there's some dry wood?'

But the supposed dry wood was in fact wet, and Sophie sat perched on a small stool blowing unenthusiastic embers with bellows whose carved wooden handles were more impressive than their blast of air. Fortunately the gin and Sophie's eternal vivacity did much to compensate for the lack of flames, and by the time all three went through to a cold lunch laid out on

44

the kitchen table, Alec had relented a little towards John Graves – enough at least to be civil.

Carol Granger waited on Kate Merlin's doorstep. She had ridden over, come up the steep lane from the ford beneath for Bag Down was situated exactly two-thirds of the way up the side of a steep cleave. By car it could only be approached from above, but by horse or foot it could be reached by the lane.

Carol made no attempt at civilities or preliminaries but plunged straight in: 'I'm told my pony gashed its leg last night – when Benjy was riding it.'

Kate felt herself grow tense. 'Is Gabe worried about it?' she asked.

'Yes.'

Oh God, thought Kate, I'll have to pay, and what with? Aloud, she said, 'It all seems most unfortunate. I honestly don't think it was Benjy's fault.'

'Nor theirs.'

'If they knew the mare was on heat . . .?'

'They didn't – that's just the point.'

'Then can you blame Benjy?'

'The fact is he was on her when the stallion came for her. He should have used his whip if he'd been quick to guess what was happening.'

Kate felt her stomach turn with anger. She bitterly resented anyone running down a child of hers, especially Benjy, about whom she was doubly sensitive. 'He might have been hurt,' she said.

'Fortunately he wasn't, but my pony was.'

Kate said nothing and Carol went on, 'According to Gabe it may be all right. But if not . . . and anyway it's bound to leave a scar, which means I shan't be able to sell it this autumn . . .' She paused, looked straight at Kate with her small thin lips and determined chin. 'It's up to you,' she said.

Kate said stiffly, 'If you have to have the vet you'd better send me the bill.'

'Thanks,' said Carol briefly. 'I wouldn't ask you but we're in dire straits, financially.'

'I understand,' Kate said. 'I'll insist Donald pays up – he'll have to.' She said it with more conviction than she felt.

'Thanks,' Carol repeated, and they remained for some moments in awkward silence, which Carol finally broke by an abrupt change of subject. 'What do you think of the Deneuves?' She poked with a stick at an ant advancing over the step.

'I like them.' Kate was cautious.

'I like her.'

'Yes – I like her better.'

'I don't envy her taking on those two semi-adult children. It was a very peculiar party – all those odd people down from London.'

'Were they odd?'

'Yes – very. And Jude Deneuve is a case.'

'A case?' Kate was startled.

'Oh I think so. He flits around like a sort of faun and his eyes look quite mad. Apparently he's brilliantly clever. He made a beeline for Astra, I noticed. You'll have to watch out.'

'There's nothing wrong with him, is there?'

'Oh no, not *wrong*. I must go,' she added. And together they walked down to the stable block where she had left her horse.

'Rather a waste, these stables.' Kate surveyed the yard and buildings.

'What will you do with them?'

'Benjy's having the groom's room and Gabe may use the loft for hay. He'll have to put it somewhere.'

Carol secured the throatlash. 'Is that all part of the deal?'

'I imagine,' Kate laughed but Carol didn't join her. She pursed her lips, apparently at the minute orange flies' eggs clinging to her horse's stomach. She poked her foot in the stirrup and hopped on one leg while her horse revolved in circles, wholly absorbing her attention. Once up she pulled it, still cavorting, round and dug her heels into its sides in a determined effort to assume control over at least one untrustworthy creature.

Kate leant over the gate and watched her ride away down the lane. I wish I could like her, she thought, *really* like her. But I don't. I can't, though I admire her energy and courage. She never talks about what she really feels.

She crossed the yard and made her way up towards the house. A cloud of gnats danced before her, showing against the black shadow of a row of cedars that edged the field. The field itself belonged to their neighbour and was a steep watermeadow irrigated by a succession of small leats across the hillside. As she looked rabbits leaped and ran for their holes in the banks. In spite of the move, the problems over money, Kate felt happy. She loved the summer, loved the country. She felt at home in it, not lonely and agitated as she felt in a city, although she had to admit at times to sexual stirrings, which made her long for someone to make her feel the intensity, the passion she had felt not so very many years back. Yet she wondered why she should desire to feel what had seldom brought her anything but an agony of unsatiated need. It was better, much better, she told herself, to keep her emotions uninvolved, to concentrate what intense feeling she still had on her painting and, when necessary, her children. Inside the house she smelt burning. She ran through to the kitchen and saw with despair the saucepan on the centre of the ring. It had been filled with rhubarb for jam. She took off the lid and looked down on the blackened burnt remains. Swearing, she stood it in the sink, turned on the tap and watched the water hiss and spit and leap as it landed on the hot metal.

At the Warren, Carol sat beside Richard watching *Horse of the Year* on television. In spite of being in a valley the house had good reception and often, like tonight, they ate their dinner on their laps. The food was purchased mainly from the delicatessen where Carol worked part time, and consisted of pâté, cheeses and yoghurt that had gone over the date they were safely due to be eaten. The Grangers tucked in happily, their eyes glued to the programme, seldom speaking.

Tonight was an exception. Carol was talkative and Richard, contrary to his masculine image, loved gossip.

'Kate Merlin is becoming battier every day. She's obsessed by how to get enough light in her studio and quite incapable of taking in what's under her nose.'

'What *is* under her nose?' Richard struggled to tuck a piece of well-oiled lettuce into the corner of his mouth.

'That Jude Deneuve is going to make a dead set at her little precious darling Astra. Which is most unsuitable.'

'Why?'

'Well, he's been around, knows what he's up to, whereas Astra's hardly peeped out from the folds of her dear mother's skirts. I can't imagine a worse combination. I heard something about him in the shop from Ma Bellamy too.'

'How do you mean?'

'She didn't go into detail but she did hint he'd been sent down. Mind you, you can't trust her because she exaggerates. Even so, there's bound to be some truth in it.'

Richard's eyes opened wide. 'Oughtn't you to say something to Kate?'

'You can't really, not on hearsay, can you? I have told her straight out I don't think he's suitable.'

'Was that all Mrs Bellamy said?'

'Yes.'

Richard's interest seemed to wane at the lack of explicit detail. 'Astra's growing remarkably pretty,' he commented.

'She might be if she didn't wear all those frightful old rags.'

'She looks all right to me.'

'But then you never look – properly.' Carol screwed the pepper-mill vigorously over her salmon mousse. She sniffed it suspiciously; surely it must be all right? 'The trouble is,' she said, 'Kate is far too dominant. Astra can hardly do a thing without referring to her.'

'Really?' Richard looked puzzled, 'I've never heard her giving orders.'

'Oh no. She's much subtler than that. She never *gives* orders. She just sees everyone does as she wants.'

'I'd never have thought that.' Richard remained unbelieving and reverted to watching the television.

'I'm glad to see you've made the effort. Come up.' Lucien Theobald smiled from his armchair in his London clinic at Jude Deneuve who sat in another armchair on the opposite side of the sham burning coals of the gas fire.

'I thought I ought to,' Jude mumbled. In fact it had only been Sophie's determination that had got him to London; she had woken him, given him breakfast, and then driven him into Taverston to catch the train. Left to his own devices the appointment would have passed and the armchair on Jude's side of the fire would have remained empty. 'Anyway, here I am,' he finished for want of something to say.

'Well how is it? How's Devon?' Lucien Theobald sat back and crossed the ankle of one foot over his knee, clasping his shiny black shoe. He looked at Jude over his gold-rimmed half-moon glasses.

'OK,' said Jude.

'I hope to be down your way in August.'

Jude made no comment.

'Anything to tell me about? Have you come up with any dreams?'

'I haven't been dreaming. Well, only fragments.'

'Have you written anything down?'

'No – the minute I sit up and think, they fade.'

'Would you like some coffee?' Lucien Theobald pushed a bell. A rather glamorous girl arrived, took the order and retired. His secretary, Jude supposed. He wondered what the relationship between them was. Lucien Theobald was an attractive man with thinning, curly dark hair, prominent eyes, and a smile that seemed more sincere than professional. He wore a silk necktie and a gold signet ring; in a way he appeared rather flashy. But Jude felt at ease with him although he didn't consider talking to him of any real benefit.

When Jude's mother had left him, his hair had dropped out overnight which, for a sensitive thirteen-year-old, had been a lasting and humiliating experience; and almost unconsciously from that moment on he had taken against his father. He supposed his mother had gone because she found life with his father intolerable. Whatever the reason, it left Jude in a trauma of love and hate – love for a mother he had never been close to and therefore idealised, and hate for her rejection of him. Though she was friendly with Sophie and still got on with Alec, Jude only tolerated her company and never sought it – in fact he denied himself seeing her as a sort of masochistic torture.

At Oxford he had tried joining societies and clubs, taking part in activities of the theatre group, but his inner misery had not abated. Only when punting under the low willows of the Isis did he gain any sense of release, of calm. He shunned individual friendships, especially with women, until finally, just before the Easter vacation, he had taken himself to a quack analyst. During an hour-long session it had emerged that the analyst considered the root of his troubles to be impotence. At the time Jude seemed willing to talk calmly enough about it to the imperceptive analyst, and even arranged a further appointment, but on leaving the consulting room he had never returned again, and it was shortly after this that the event that Alec and Sophie had vowed never to mention, took place. It resulted in the College sending him down, then, on learning the full history and circumstances behind Jude's action, retracting the order to a year's sabbatical with psychiatric treatment. Jude had agreed, but continued to doubt the benefit of analysis as he sat opposite Lucien Theobald, sipping coffee and looking round the messy but not impersonal room: brocade curtains, sliding heaps of books, two cats moulting hairs, on the walls photos of his daughters rolling about with dogs and laughing – always laughing.

'I think I hate my father.' Jude placed the coffee mug on the bookcase.

'How about your stepmother?'

'Who?' Jude looked puzzled for a moment, 'Oh – you mean Sophie?'

'I expect – yes.'

'She's all right. I like her.'

'A lot?'

'I've never thought. She's just . . . easy. We all like her.'

'Tell me about her.'

But Jude could think of nothing to tell.

'What does she look like then? Tell me that.'

'She's got exactly the looks you'd expect my father to be attracted to. Blonde. She could have been a model but she doesn't have that kind of mentality.'

Lucien Theobald emptied his pipe and refilled it. 'Go on,' he said, wondering what kind of mentality a model was supposed to have.

'I don't think she suits him. I mean they have quite different tastes. In a way . . .'

'What?'

'Well Sophie's more like us. Scarlet and me. She is only twenty-seven. My father is nearly twice her age and set, terribly set, in all his attitudes.'

'But presumably this doesn't put her off him?'

Jude shrugged. 'I think it does,' he said, 'but she won't admit it. Oh fuck – don't let's talk about them.'

They talked some more about this and that but Jude felt he had said enough and withdrew into himself, answering questions but giving nothing until Lucien Theobald suddenly shot at him, 'Are you attracted by Sophie?'

'I've never thought about it,' said Jude easily, and shifted his weight from one arm to the other of the chair.

'I find that rather odd.'

Jude was becoming irritated. What was the point in fishing around for all that long since discarded Freudian stuff? He looked out of the window into the top of a double-decker bus, then back to the gold clock on the mantelpiece. 'I'll have to go,' he said, 'I'm only up for the day on a cheap day ticket.'

'Of course,' said Lucien and they both stood. As they

walked to the door together he said, 'Have you ever thought of getting out of your family, living on your own?'

Jude looked at him blankly. 'Why?' he asked.

'I'm not saying you should,' Lucien Theobald was cautious, 'I'm merely saying it's a possibility you might consider.'

Christ, Jude thought, what is he getting at? Aloud he said, 'I'll think about it.' He took a taxi to Paddington but was so lost in thought that the driver was sitting at the station for several minutes before Jude realised they had arrived. He got out hastily and almost forgot to pay. Trance-like, he walked to platform 5 and got on the train to Exeter. As it pulled out, he gazed at the rows of dreary grey buildings and felt relieved that Lucien Theobald had at last let drop the unhappy incident at Oxford – presumably because he, Jude, had admitted the wrongness of it at the previous session. He settled into his seat and opened his book.

A knock came on the door of Scarhill and Alec Deneuve got up to open it. Two men stood in grey suits in front of two goose-wing grey cars that glittered and dazzled in the back yard.

'Come in,' said Alec affably. 'My wife's out. She'll be back soon.' He ushered them into the kitchen, which was unusually tidy.

They declined refreshment and sat down with Alec at the kitchen table. Alvin Hart, Alec's agent and adviser from London, introduced Tim Miller, from a local firm, as familiar with properties in the area and specialising in finance. A plan of Scarhill's land was laid out between them.

'What we want to get clear,' said Alvin Hart, 'is what area you want to farm and what area is to go under afforestation.'

'The answer to that,' said Alec, 'is I don't actually *want* to farm any myself. I want to put all the land I possibly can, certainly all the rough ground and some of the bottom land along the river, into trees. Of course I want to leave the aspect from the house clear, I want to keep a view, but as I see it most of this land is valueless – except as feed for a few sheep and cattle in the old traditional way – so trees are the answer.'

'Trees are an excellent investment,' said Alvin Hart, 'that's why I've brought Tim with me. He handles these matters for our firm. He can advise you on the possible financial pitfalls and rewards far more accurately than I would be able to. My main job is to advise on the sort of grants you might hope for and the problems you may come up against with the National Park and the conservationists. Part of my job, as you may guess, is getting to know these people and finding where they'll give.'

'Absolutely,' said Alec.

Alvin Hart pulled out a further plan on which certain sections were shaded in dark green. 'It certainly seems,' he said, 'as though a substantial part of the farm will become trees.'

At that moment from outside came the sound of car doors slamming and Sophie's laughter. Alec braced himself for her entry, which proved no less disruptive than he had expected. She stood in the doorway with a puzzled expression, staring at the two strangers who equally stared back at such an unexpected vision. Slowly the happy expression faded from her face.

'Oh,' she said, 'I didn't know . . .'

'Sophie,' Alec said, clearing his throat, 'we're having a meeting about Scarhill's land – what we intend doing with it. Perhaps you'd like to come over here and see the plans.'

So Sophie obligingly came over and sat beside Alec, cupped her chin in her hands and gazed on the plan where Alec pointed.

'We propose to keep these fields in front of the house – for a horse, if you or I should want one. But the rest of the land I'm intending to rent, and the shaded areas are for afforestation.'

Sophie stared at the plans for a few seconds. 'An awful lot's going to be trees, isn't it?' she asked.

'Quite a lot,' admitted Alec, detecting trouble, 'but then timber is becoming more valuable daily and most of this land is useless for farming, there's no depth of soil.' He felt satisfied with himself for this last remark.

'What kind of trees?' asked Sophie.

Alec looked enquiringly at Alvin Hart.

'Japanese larch, Sitka spruce, Douglas fir, western cedar, western hemlock . . .' He broke off. 'I myself would advise the Sitka spruce. It grows anywhere, dead straight – needs virtually no looking after, and you'll see a return in thirty years.'

Sophie stared at him. 'Is that what the Forestry Commission have planted all over the moor in ugly blocks?' she asked.

Alvin Hart chose his words carefully. 'In some cases,' he said. 'Generally they have bordered them with larch or beech, even oak. But of course the hardwoods are very slow growing and not really suited to this altitude. Certainly they are not a commercial proposition.'

Sophie turned on Alec. 'But we came here because we liked the moor. We thought Scarhill's land was beautiful, and now you are going to ruin it with horrible dark trees planted in rows.'

'Only where the land is useless for anything else,' said Alec.

'But what about here and here and here,' Sophie pointed at the plan. 'That's all fields. And this is a beautiful primrose wood under the ashes in spring. I know because Kate Merlin told me.'

Alec looked uncomfortable but was doggedly persistent. 'You don't understand,' he said. 'We can leave woodland – decent woodland – to the children tax free. You get a sizeable concession on trees. The country needs timber.'

Sophie bit her small, eggshell-pink nails. 'I think you'll spoil Scarhill,' she said.

Tim Miller bent forward. 'If I may say so, I think the areas of trees are well concealed and will in no way be detrimental to the general aspect of the land . . .'

Sophie interrupted. 'What about here? They go right up over the skyline.'

Alec looked. 'Well we'll keep them lower, make sure they go round the side of the hill.' He glanced at Sophie's unusually

54

solemn face. 'Anyway,' he said, 'if you don't like them when they get too big we can always cut them down ... But that's years on – we're talking about now.' Never had more devious words been uttered.

Then the telephone rang. Sophie ran to answer and the future of Scarhill's 280 acres, farmed more or less in the same fashion for the last six hundred years, was altered. By the time Sophie returned the plans were put away and everyone was standing on the lawn drinking whisky. Alec had had the foresight to pour Sophie a strong gin and tonic, which he handed her as soon as she came out of the house.

'Who was that?' he asked, hoping to divert her attention from the trees.

'Only Carol. She wondered if we had a field she could rent for her horses – to give their land a chance to recover. I told her I thought we did.'

'We could probably manage something,' said Alec, affably. Sophie glanced at him.

'What did you decide about the trees?'

'We've decided for a mixture using steep and waste ground. We need the cover of the spruce in order to underplant, of course. With oak and beech; grow some ash if that is your preference,' Alvin Hart explained patiently as though to a child.

Sophie twiddled the stem of her glass. Alec sighed. Sophie really was being excessively unreasonable.

'You won't see any difference from your windows,' he said. 'Only the existing scrub. The alternative is ploughing the steep ground, which would be ill-advised and dangerous. You must see that?'

'Can't we just let it go on as it is?' Sophie could feel she was losing the battle. The three men managed to make her feel inadequate, even sentimental – a sort of simpleton to be humoured.

Tim Miller spoke. 'You see, Mrs Deneuve, trees are becoming vital to this country – there are just not enough. Your farm will need stakes and timber in the future. To grow enough trees for your own needs is essential, as I see it.'

'For our needs – yes. But this is on a huge scale, far more than we could ever use on Scarhill. Chestnuts grow very quickly, don't they?' asked Sophie hopefully. Fortunately she had gained some knowledge of trees from her father who before he became involved in archaeology had dabbled in forestry.

The three men looked at each other and smiled. They shook their heads.

'Sophie, you're being quite impracticable,' Alec said. 'I can assure you, softwoods are the crop of the future. They're going to be worth a lot of money.'

'A moment ago,' Sophie said, 'Mr Miller said we were growing trees for our own needs. Now you say it's for the money.'

'Our needs primarily, but naturally the future value of the timber is a consideration.'

Sophie gave up. 'I've said what I think,' she said, 'and now I've got some things to see to, if you'll excuse me.' And she left the room.

Tim Miller turned to Alec. 'You won't forget the two farms I mentioned that are both on the market to private buyers. One has a very considerable acreage of low-lying land that could be put into spruce. The other has extensive land reaching up the side of Barrow Down at the back of Ventnor Farm. All that could be planted up without much problem. The Park wouldn't give you a grant but they couldn't prevent you doing the actual planting; it would pay you hand over foot.'

Alec took out his diary and noted down the names.

'I'll have to consult my partners,' he said, 'but it certainly seems a worthwhile venture.'

'Far and the best way is to sell off the house and buildings with a few adjoining fields – enough for people to keep horses. There's an enormous demand from the hunting fraternity now. More and more people are wanting weekend places. The land you retain will only cost you your temporary interest on the loan.' Tim Miller sat back; he felt he had made himself clear.

Alvin Hart joined in. 'Now is the moment to buy,' he said, 'there's no doubt about that.'

'Why is Ventnor selling?' asked Alec. 'If it had such a big acreage it must have had potential.'

'Oh yes it did. But it's been farmed by a local man with no help but his wife, and completely let go. Then his wife died suddenly.'

Alec looked suitably solemn but couldn't help thinking it sounded a very good buy.

'You'd have to drain the bottom land, but that would really be no problem. You might even get the support of the Park for that – I think they'd be hard put to argue it wasn't suitable tree ground, especially if you agree to dot around a few oaks.'

Alec nodded. 'And this other farm?' he asked, pulling out the particulars.

'That's a good proposition too. I learnt purely by chance, mind you – it consists of an extensive area of moorland stretching the complete length of Lark Down, all of which would be suitable for spruce. It also has a large barn with planning permission that would convert very well for holiday lets.'

'So you feel we should go ahead and purchase?' Alec looked enquiringly at Tim Miller.

'I don't think you could go wrong.'

'Will there be anyone else interested?'

'I think,' said Tim Miller, 'that if we put in an offer immediately, a private offer, it'll never get as far as the open market. I'm sure that's the best way to approach it. The agents are quite a small firm with an office in Meridan. I could go in and see them myself if you'd like me to. I play golf with one of the partners.'

And so it was agreed. It did cross Alec's mind a little guiltily that Sophie knew nothing of his outside venture into forestry on a large scale, but then it was a business proposition. It was to do with his partners in London and really didn't concern her, unlike Scarhill, where he had asked her opinion and listened to what she had to say. Sophie, after all, was beautiful and emotional but not famous for her practicality. He suspected she would lose every penny they had if not well advised, and who better to advise her than himself? Such thoughts passed through Alec's head as he walked Alvin Hart and Tim Miller out to their cars, watched them ease themselves into their seats and fasten their safety belts. One after another they nosed their way over the old cobbles and past the granite entrance, leaving behind them no trace but a small circle of unsightly oil.

'Who was your letter from?' Benjy asked Astra.

'No one,' said Astra. 'I mean, no one in particular.'

'The postmark was Meridan.'

'It's not your business, Benjy, and in future there's no need for you to go looking at postmarks on my letters.'

'Anyone can look at postmarks,' said Benjy stolidly.

'They can *not*.' Astra noticed her mother was staring at her. 'I'm going out,' she said, scraping her chair noisily back over the stone flags.

Kate winced and put her hands over her ears. She frowned at Benjy. 'Did you have to? It really seems unnecessary to pry into Astra's correspondence.'

'I didn't,' Benjy looked injured. 'I looked at the postmark.'

'Well don't.' Kate felt exasperated. She leant across for the apple juice but the carton was unopened and she had to wrestle with it. 'Get me the scissors, Benjy.' But there were no scissors. She struggled with the wax carton and bread-knife while Benjy waited patiently. Eventually an opening was achieved but it was too big and when she attempted to fill his glass the juice slopped over the table.

'Why shouldn't I look at the postmark?' Benjy asked doggedly. He liked getting letters and it seemed unfair that Astra should be unwilling to share even the postmark on hers.

'Oh do shut *up*.' Kate rested her forehead in her hands. She hated it when the children fought – and money was worrying her.

58

Benjy loved Astra. He loved her to the most secret depths of his soul; in fact his love was so much a part of him that he would have been an entirely changed person without it. Astra was a force he couldn't reckon with, a force which was the sum both of himself and his love for her but greater than either. Benjy, although he didn't know it, had had a stormy antenatal life, and had eventually been born in a snowstorm early in February. He had been conceived as the result of a row between his parents in which Kate had torn up Donald's book and he had knocked her flat on the floor. Benjy had commenced during their 'reconciliation' – or that was how Kate liked to think of it. Though this would not logically have convinced most people that Benjy was bound to be an idiot, it did agitate his mother who, in a fashion oddly out of keeping with her normal self, believed she had tempted fate and Benjy being a little bit 'funny' was, justly or unjustly, retribution.

Benjy had adored his mother till he was about five and then for some unfathomable reason his love had transferred itself to Astra, where it wound itself and clung with the strength and force of two stems of wistaria – only Benjy's stem was the weaker, the secondary, the one that wrapped around. Astra, for her part, was as unaware of Benjy's love for her as he was himself. That is to say, it was clear to her that the feeling between them was strong; that she loved Benjy she never doubted, but she never really thought twice whether Benjy loved her back. If anything, probably not, for when she teased him or annoyed him, for the sport of it, which she often did, he would get in a black rage and not speak to her for hours, or even days. Then it was Astra who always made it up for she hated not to speak; but it was from Benjy's heart that a huge burden lifted. When he was not on good terms with Astra then joy had gone from his life and the day was dark as impending thunder. He continued to love his mother, of course, but his love for her was of a different order – it did not contain passion. Astra was his barometer. When 'the

59

woman' came out of her little arch in the wood house, it was Astra and the sun shone; when 'the man' came out it rained. Benjy came to associate the man with his schoolteacher, whom he hated. Man – rain – darkness. Woman – sun – happiness. There it was. The essentials of his life were determined early.

So when Astra came up the rat-gnawed wooden stairs in the stable block in search of him, Benjy was rather pleased. That she had come to bribe him didn't worry him, he was used to it.

Astra stood inside the doorway of the groom's room and looked round, she hadn't been up there since Benjy had taken over. 'Why don't you have curtains?' she asked.

Benjy shrugged. He hadn't curtains, had he? – that was all there was to it.

'Or a carpet?' Astra persisted. For the first time a carpet entered Benjy's head and he looked doubtfully at the offending boards under his feet. Astra sat beside him on the iron bedstead with her hands under her spread thighs.

'It's not bad on the whole,' she said, taking in the entire aspect of the room rather than its individual defects. Perhaps she should have claimed it and not let Benjy reign as king of the stables.

'You'll never do any work now – what about your extra reading? I can't see any books.'

Benjy's heart, which had briefly given a joyful bound, now cowered back into its normal position. He wiped his thumb and put it into his mouth. Astra seized his arm and jerked it out.

'Baby!'

Benjy tried to pull his arm free but she held it fast. He thought he hated Astra. She knew she'd gone too far and let it go.

'Benjy, could you take a letter to the Deneuves for me. To Jude Deneuve? He wants me to go on a moor walk with ... them.'

Benjy leant back on his cushion against the wall and drummed one heel against the side of his orange-crate seat; he

60

watched his sister cautiously. She seemed very fidgety, Benjy thought. She looked at length in the mirror speckled with black spots over the mantelpiece, and he wondered what she was seeing in it. Then she turned round and said, 'Do you think I look all right, Benj? I mean . . . nice.' She was looking at him unusually seriously.

Benjy dragged his finger through the spider's web he'd just seen in the corner by his bed. 'Yes,' he said.

'Honest – cross your heart?'

'Eddie says you're real smart.'

'Smart?' Astra sounded disappointed.

'It means pretty,' Benjy explained, 'when Eddie says it.'

Astra, unlike Benjy, had not been to the local primary so didn't have Benjy's grasp of the dialect.

'Is he in love with me?'

'Yep.'

Astra looked pleased. Benjy wished she wasn't his sister so he could be in love with her.

'Why can't I come on the walk?'

'Because you haven't been asked.'

'Don't they like me?'

'Of course they do, silly, it's only me and Jude going.' She had to be more honest than she'd intended. Benjy still looked dubious and unwilling.

'I'll do something with you if you'll take it,' Astra said. 'Spend the whole afternoon up here. Make it all nice. Pick some flowers for your table.' Benjy still looked doubtful. 'All right then, you say what you want.'

Benjy, unabashed, demanded money. Astra gave in. She'd had a birthday recently and was relatively rich. 'One pound and not a penny more and that's too much,' she said. But the deal was done. Benjy pumped up the tyres on his bike and set off.

It was a perfect afternoon. Bees hummed along the banks and the sky was blue with cotton-wool clouds. Benjy felt happy and rather important. When he got to the Deneuves' he leant his bike against the wall in the front drive and walked

61

down through the yard to the back door. No one answered, so he guessed they were out the front. He was tempted to open the back door and walk through but thought better of it, and instead went round by the old piggeries on the east side of Scarhill yard. They were lean-tos with a corrugated roof over them that leaked badly. On the yard side each section had its own granite trough set behind a small wooden door. Mainly the troughs were full of water from the leaking roof, but in summer they dried out. Benjy opened one of the doors, dragged himself over the trough, and stood upright. The doorway on the far side was almost sealed by elder which grew profusely in the small, sheltered pig yard behind. The Merlins had let it grow because each year it provided them with the first lacy white flowers for white wine, and later the jet berries for red. Benjy carefully pushed past it and made his way down through the pig yard past the wall topped by upended granite, and came to where a lower wall, covered by ivy and an overgrown rose briar, bordered the lawn. Astra had impressed on him that he was to give the letter to Jude and no one else, and Benjy, naturally shy of adult humans, had no wish to confront the Deneuves. He parted the ivy leaves carefully and looked over. On the lawn he saw two ancient beams lying with notches cut along their sides for the joists. Beside them was the old bath unhappily tipped on its side with its vacant outlet hole ringed by rust; next door to the bath was a heap of planks. From inside the house came a shattering thumping and banging, but the Deneuves were not in evidence. Scarlet's 'lounger' lay abandoned, and the cover of the swing-chair flapped in the breeze. Benjy scratched his leg where a horsefly had bitten it and retraced his steps to the back yard.

He was standing uncertain what to do next when the window in the side of the house opposite him opened; Jude's head showed, framed between the two metal bars that protected all the opening lights of the upstairs windows. Jude waved. Benjy hastily withdrew the letter, now extremely crumpled, from his pocket and held it up. Jude beckoned; Benjy approached across the yard, stood on the low wall beneath the window and reached up. Jude stretched his arm as far as it would go through the bars and was just able to take the letter. Once relieved of it, Benjy felt uncertain what to do next – whether to go at once or wait. Jude settled his indecision.

'Wait a mo – there may be an answer.' He grinned at Benjy while ripping open the envelope.

Benjy felt very uncertain of Jude but did as he said. He looked up anxiously at the window; he hated waiting. In a few moments Jude's face showed again looking pleased.

'OK,' he said. 'Thanks. Do you want a drink?'

Benjy shook his head and went.

Kate rang Donald that evening; she had to about money for the pony but was actually pleased to have an excuse. She got his sister.

'He's out – he's gone to see about a boat.'

'Oh I see.'

'Do you?' said his sister coldly. 'I think, though it's none of my business, he's been very reasonable.'

'Actually, I wanted to talk to him about money. Could you get him to ring me, please. When he's got time.'

'Of course.' There was silence.

'Tell him to let me know when he's coming out about his things I've still got.' Kate felt she was prolonging the conversation unnecessarily, as though she was hoping Donald would come in before she finished speaking. Anxious that his sister should get no hint of her real feelings she said goodbye rather abruptly and put the receiver down. To her own surprise she was shaking visibly and when she went upstairs a few moments later it was with relief that she sat down on her bed.

Dread paralysed her – dread of exactly what she was not sure. She got up to wander round the house, stopping in the doorway of each room to stare at the objects within, asking herself if each was in its right place and had, so to speak, found its spiritual home. After some time she sighed and gave up. Often, she had learnt, it took a long time for objects to find their right place. It was a process that couldn't be hurried and had to be arrived at by trial and error. But everything she did or thought led back to herself. Had *she* found the place she exactly fitted? Was it here at Bag Down? Was it to paint? Half unconsciously she wondered what else she could find to do to prevent her reaching her studio, for once in it she must paint or at least draw. To paint was the thing she most wanted to do, and also the thing she most wanted to put off. It would be all right when she had begun, but it was the beginning.

A kind of rage at her own dilly-dallying now impelled her along the passage from which she was only diverted by the toilet half-way along where the cistern was incessantly running. She twisted the handle vigorously and lifted the lid off the top; she bent the ballcock as much as her wrists would allow. To her relief the water stopped trickling and the copper ball floated lightly on its surface. With a certain sense of achievement she entered her newly whitened studio and placed a canvas she had stretched the previous day on the easel. She tipped cobalt pigment into a tin and added the acrylic medium and water. She stirred. The colour thrilled her – she loved colour. Especially blue. Sensuous and splendid. That was one of the frightening things: directly she put it on the canvas, put another colour against it, then it would change. Like people. Each colour changed according to the one it was next to. Add a third and it changed again. Colour, she felt, was everything and yet you had to make order from it. Like life. She dipped her brush deeply down into the cobalt, lifted it, and laid it on the canvas in a bold diagonal, then relaxed in relief. She had begun.

Ten minutes later she put her brush down. She had to see Donald. Had to. Without more ado she almost ran along the passage to her bedroom and started pulling clothes out of her drawers. She put things on and tore them off again, tried out combinations of colours. Finally she turned to look at herself in the mirror and her courage ebbed away. She looked such a peculiarly dressed ordinary woman standing there, a mauve scarf round her head, her longish skirt drooping a little at the back. And slowly but methodically she took them all off again, hung them on hangers, put them in the cupboards or back in her drawers. To go to see Donald would be the worst thing she could possibly do, she was not calm enough, she was bound to make a scene. She must wait, wait till he rang up or came for his things. Her heart gave a small leap of excitement she quickly quelled. She didn't want Donald back – it was too late now. She twisted a strand of hair round her finger, sat on the windowsill and looked down on the water-trough filling incessantly with water that as quickly ran away. Yes, it was too late now.

'It's steep, isn't it?' Astra's face was pink.

'Steep! You can say that again.' Gabe shook his head, surveying the hayfield. In fact it was a piece of cake but he mustn't let the Merlins feel they were giving it him. His eyes came to rest on Astra.

'Still got your pony?' He climbed down and stood beside his tractor, arms folded.

'No. I don't ride any more.'

'Why's that?'

'It takes up too much time and I've outgrown Jessy.' She flushed. 'And I don't like all that horsey set.' She twisted her sandalled foot as though she was doing an ankle exercise and looked at the ground. Gabe didn't seem to consider it necessary to talk, nor did he seem inclined to go on mowing. It was Astra who felt compelled to break the silence.

'Do you want me to fetch you a drink or anything?'

Gabe gave her a curious look; for a moment it appeared he was going to say something, then thought better of it. Instead he said, 'I brought my tea with me, but I could do with a glass of water.'

But Astra didn't move, neither did Gabe. She didn't want to walk away with Gabe watching, she wanted him to get back on the tractor. 'I'll get you the water,' she said, both wishing to be relieved of Gabe Fardon's presence and hoping it might remain. And in due course he obeyed her wish and sat, his hand on the starter, waiting because he saw she wanted to speak.

'I hope,' she said seriously, shading her eyes again because the sun was glinting off the metal on the cab, 'you don't think I'm one of that riding lot, because I'm not.'

His smile mocked her. 'I don't think you're nothing, but I see you've growed up a bit recent.'

Her dress suddenly felt flimsy and tight as though she was bursting out of it – or like sometimes in her dreams when it disappeared and she was naked in front of everyone. She felt both flattered and insulted by the familiarity she had half-consciously invited.

Gabe, as he started up his tractor, thought he would like nothing so much as to strip Astra Merlin and have his way with her in the hay. As this was not practicable, he let his foot off the clutch, Astra stepped back and he twisted away from her, watching the blades as the tractor eased forward.

As soon as Gabe was a little way away, Astra ran down to the house where she stood quivering. She thought she rather hated Gabe Fardon; she wished her mother wouldn't use him all the time, wished she would use a different contractor. But this she knew was unlikely because her mother bartered with Gabe, swapped one thing for another. It wasn't her mother's fault, it was her father's for not giving them more money – or so Astra reasoned. Anxiously she looked at the clock. Jude. At any moment he might arrive to collect her. She both did and didn't want to go but had committed herself by her silly letter she had ever since regretted. Hastily she pressed cucumber on mashed egg and laid a brown slice on top. She made two more sandwiches, put two apples and an orange in a small khaki back-pack and tried it on her shoulders. It felt all right.

An hour later Jude arrived in his car – an almost-new TVR, all navy blue carpeting and navy blue furry seats with the details in red. The dashboard was varnished wood and so was the finish on the doors. Pop was playing from a cassette.

66

Astra put her pack on the back seat beside Jude's pack, which was red. They revved out of the drive and climbed the lane. Out on the road, Jude drove casually with his elbow resting on the lowered window. Astra noticed his shoes – trainers – and his jeans – Wranglers – and his shirt – clean and open necked. His hair seemed longer than when she had first met him. His arms were smooth and hairless, she wondered if his body was hairless too. He opened the sun-roof and a cool breeze blew in; Astra laid her head back on the headrest and decided she was happy. Jude turned up the cassette, forestalling any compulsion to talk.

He stopped sooner than she'd expected, pulled into a gate-way and turned off the engine. Astra sat up.

'Won't you block it?'

'Yes.' He drove the car forward on to the rough grass. Opposite them was an open expanse of moor with a stony track leading up to the skyline. Jude took his pack and helped Astra on with hers. He touched her hair – he couldn't help it, he had to free it from the straps. Neither of them referred to this. Astra had never been alone on the moor with a man before except her cousin flying kites. They strode along side by side with a gap between them. The wind rustled the bent-grass and the minute black dots in the sky above them sang as though their immortality depended on it.

Occasionally one would descend and prove itself a skylark. Jude carried binoculars and a pocket bird book; every now and then they would stop for him to look at a wheeling buzzard or some of the small birds that flittered amongst the tufts of grass. He also studied his map. They were making for a pond, he told Astra. Astra didn't really mind where they were making for.

When they reached it one hour later Jude sat on a rock and Astra near his feet on the turf – it just seemed to happen that way. It made Jude feel dominant and Astra subservient. The pond itself was set in a cleft of hills. Like most of the moor ponds it was an old mining pool. The land rose gradually on every side except from the direction they had come, where it descended with the stream. Little white flags of cotton grass amongst the miles of blond bent-grass marked the area as exceptionally boggy. There was no farm, tree or person in sight; only a few hill sheep and the odd pony. No litter lay on the ground to mark it as a tourist playground; there was no worn grass. They were in virgin country – or as virgin as England can manage.

'How far do you think we've walked?'

'About four miles.' Jude consulted the map.

'It's worth it.' Astra's mouth was full of cucumber and egg. She offered Jude a sandwich but he had his own. He took them out of a polythene box. Smoked salmon and watercress. He offered Astra one and she took it. He held out his flask. Astra hesitated. He poured some brandy into the silver cup and handed it to her. Astra drank. It burned. She drank some more and then some more. She lay back on the turf and watched tufts of white cloud drifting. The whole world seemed to be revolving very slowly – but then it was, wasn't it? Astra felt she was seeing things clearly, feeling things acutely for the first time ... She opened her eyes and Jude was leaning over her, silhouetted blackly between her and the sun. She sat up and Jude sat further back as though he was indeed her shadow.

'What's the time?'

'Not late. I wondered if you wanted to go further or stay here?'

Jude was remarkably close, lying on his stomach pulling up bits of grass.

'You're beautiful, Astra,' he said. He was easing himself up against her; one of his legs was sliding over one of hers.

'You're the most beautiful, exquisite thing I've ever touched.' He kissed her bare neck, his fingers fumbled with the buttons of her blouse.

Astra said faintly, 'Jude.'

'Yes.' His breathing was very loud.

'Jude.'

68

Gradually he moved further over until his body was firmly established on top of hers.

'Astra,' he murmured, 'I want you.'

'Do you?' said Astra because she couldn't think of anything to say, also she couldn't breathe very well.

'I've never wanted anyone so much – ever.' He was kissing her neck while his hands burrowed round her back in an attempt to unfasten her bra. Astra wondered whether she should help or whether he would think it forward. So she just arched her back so he could get at it better, but it didn't seem to help and after a few more attempts he gave up and pushed it up from the front, which wasn't at all comfortable: the elastic cut into her soft flesh. She sat up and unfastened it for him. When she had done so she lay down rather quickly – it seemed better lying down. Jude was undoing his zip. She shut her eyes, she didn't want to see. She was prepared for almost anything except seeing. The next moment he was again on top of her. It was not quite as exciting as she thought it would be but Jude was excited enough for two. He forced his mouth down on hers, forcing her lips against his teeth. Astra freed her arm and pushed his face away.

'What's the matter?'

'You're hurting.'

For a moment Jude looked disconcerted and she thought he might stop, but the urge once aroused seemed difficult to restrain. Astra became silent and Jude began to push and retract and push; a surge of feeling engulfed her. She clung to Jude, who clung to her equally for a few seconds and expired. Astra lay still, uncertain exactly what had happened. Jude started to kiss her face and neck, but without his former passion.

'Jude?'

'What is it?'

'Aren't we going on?'

There was a silence. Jude pushed himself up on his elbow.

'You're much too attractive,' he said, 'that's the trouble. It'll be better the next time – it always is.'

69

So Astra sat up and did up her bra but inside she felt cheated, especially because now it was all over, Jude seemed to have rather lost interest. While she found her hairband Jude took out his binoculars and looked across the pond at some wild mallard swimming amongst the rushes on the far side.

Astra looked longingly at the pond. 'Do you think we could swim?'

'Why not? In our skins.'

Jude was rather thin and brown without his clothes. Astra was much rounder and white. They tried not to show they were looking at each other and got into the freezing water quickly. In the water Jude became interested again and held himself under her. But he pulled her down after a few seconds and they separated.

Afterwards they dried themselves on Jude's shirt because they hadn't any towels and the wind was cold.

'You're even more beautiful with nothing on, Astra,' Jude said.

'Am I?' Astra felt pleased and forgave him everything. But she couldn't decide whether or not she was in love because she had no idea at all what being 'in love' was like.

When Jude lifted his weight off Astra for the second time, she thought she had liked it better but wasn't sure. When she sat up her legs looked white in the grass as though they were not a part of her but odd alien things. She reached for her jeans and Jude reached for his. She noticed there was blood between her thighs, so she sauntered casually behind a mound of ground made by the ancient tinners and wiped herself furtively with a handful of grass. She didn't want Jude to know.

When she returned to Jude he was standing up with his pack on. 'Are you all right?' he asked.

'Yes – perfectly.' She smiled at him to make sure he believed her.

'I love you, Astra.'

She lifted her face as she'd seen actresses do in films. He kissed her and she kissed him back; they pushed their tongues deep into each other's mouths and clung together. Yet she was surprised how little she felt.

'Put your hand down there,' he said, and she did; but she didn't really want to and was glad when he let her take it away.

On the way back they stopped at a pub and sat on a wooden trestle against the wall. Astra had Britvic orange and soda and Jude had lager. The peat in the fire still had heather on the sods. Jude bought a bottle of wine and they took it with them down by a stream in the bracken. They drank it by turns out of the bottle and when they had finished it Jude pushed it down a rabbit burrow and they made love.

The wine on top of the brandy, the Britvic orange and soda; the sun and wind all seemed to combine to work a spell. Astra found that suddenly the whole of her body became soft and sensual and will-less, a pulse started inside her and she clung to Jude with the same intensity as he clung to her. She felt quite awed by the dominance of her own physical being; it had, so to speak, bolted – she had lost control. They fell asleep in each other's arms in the bracken, and when they woke it was dark.

'Is that Alec?'

'Kate? – Yes.' Alec was in the bath.

'I'm terribly sorry to ring so late but Astra and Jude aren't with you, are they?'

'No – no sign. I imagine they've made a day of it – gone out to dinner. It's a good life being young, isn't it?'

'Yes, of course.' Kate didn't feel worried now Alec was on the other end of the line. Even down a wire, Alec exuded confidence.

'Jude'll take care of her – never worry.' He laughed.

'I'm sure he will. I just thought I'd check before I went to bed.'

'Sophie's gone up. Do you want a word with her? I'll give her a call.'

'No, don't.' Kate felt embarrassed; she was making an unnecessary scene.

Alec told her a second-hand version of Sophie's attempt to buy garlic at the village shop. She laughed and he laughed. They put down their receivers that united and separated them. Alec laid his cordless one down beside his bath; Kate put her corded one down on the dining-room sill.

The chill of Alec's bathwater reflected the chill of his spirit. What the hell was Jude up to? What a start to relations in the neighbourhood. He stepped out of the chilly water and wrapped himself in a king-size bath towel.

Astra closed the car door with the faintest click. Far down in the valley a dog barked. All round was a grey haze.

'Will you be all right?' Jude asked.

'Yes,' she whispered. It seemed the time for whispering. Jude leant out and pulled her to him. He rubbed his cheek against hers. It was like sandpaper; Astra winced.

'See you soon – very soon.'

'Yes.'

She watched him reverse up the lane then took off her shoes and made her way down it. When she got to the gate of the field behind Bag Down she climbed it. She felt fairly safe – there were no windows at the back except the bathroom, and that was sunk under the side of the hill so that it was impossible to be seen until you were almost walking on the thatch. She hurried across the field over the lines of hay, only stopping in the middle to put her shoes on because of thistles. She went through the hunting gate and then stopped: there was a light shining from the windows.

Certain her mother must have gone to bed leaving the light on, Astra opened the french windows stealthily and closed them behind her. She turned round to find herself face to face with Kate asleep in front of her painting. Astra stood transfixed while her mother's eyes slowly opened and she blinked, gradually absorbing the fact of Astra's return.

'Why are you so late?'

'We had something to eat and Jude drank . . .' Astra hesitated, 'so we had to wait until he could drive all right.'

Kate looked hard at Astra, who averted her eyes.

'I was worried. It is . . .' Kate looked at her watch, 'nearly two.'

Astra's mouth set sulkily. 'I'm sorry,' she said, her tone full of resentment. 'I'm nearly sixteen and Jude's nineteen.'

'I know.'

Astra began to make for the door.

'Astra . . . tell me about it?' Kate was honestly curious.

Then Astra turned back to her mother, pressed her face on her shoulder. Tears came. Not for long and not many; simply an outlet for pent-up emotion, Kate divined. She slid her arms round Astra, drew her to her. She sensed that the day had altered Astra. So where were they – where, indeed, was she? It was as though the sky had given a jerk and all the constellations were in a slightly different relation to each other. Astra, Kate felt, was very much less hers. Which she didn't mind but had to adjust to. She kissed the side of Astra's cheek; Astra pulled back a little.

'Do you think it's very wrong to . . . to go out with someone you don't love?' she asked.

'No,' said Kate uncertainly. Then qualified herself: 'After all, how can you tell your feelings until you know someone well?'

'I can,' said Astra. 'I mean he doesn't attract me, not properly, so it's wrong, isn't it?'

'It sounds as though it might be.' Kate felt a growing anxiety but from there it seemed difficult to probe further so, by common consent, they started for the door. Before Kate switched out the light she glanced back at her painting as though for help, but it gave none. 'The rector rang,' she said.

'What did he want?'

'You to go to a reading of his pantomime on Thursday. You're to ring him.'

'What on earth does he think he's up to, coming in at that

73

hour?' Alec fished out a piece of thick-cut from Cooper's Oxford marmalade and put it on his toast crust. Sophie drank from a large shallow bowl, bought the previous year at Chartres, and munched her croissant from the Meridan delicatessen.

'I expect they got lost,' she said. 'Everyone does on the moor.'

'Jude shouldn't. They did a lot of that kind of thing at Gordonstoun – Outward Bound with compasses and all that. Didn't he take one?'

'What?'

'A compass.'

'I don't know. Why don't you ask him?'

'Is he awake?'

Alec turned his frown, which until now had been directed at nothing in particular, on Sophie. She wasn't much support on these occasions, he decided, and seemed unaware that lack of responsibility over a small matter could become serious over something more important. He said as much.

'What had you in mind?' asked Sophie.

'If he's going into Gait and Lavalle – handling other people's investments – his attitude is crucial.'

'He doesn't want to. He's more interested in the theatre – or writing.'

'He may be – ' Alec broke his croissant in three like a segmented prawn – 'but that won't make him a living. T. S. Eliot worked in a bank.'

Sophie was silenced. She fell to planning her day, which at present was centred on the swimming pool Gabe Fardon was digging in the walled garden.

Then Jude appeared. He walked into the kitchen looking under the weather. Sophie got up and poured him coffee. Alec waited until Jude had sat before he said, 'It was most unreasonable of you not to have rung us yesterday. Kate Merlin rang me. She was extremely worried. So were we.'

Jude's inner self retracted from his outer, which slid over and protected him like a visor.

74

'We're not children,' he said. 'It's simply not necessary to worry about us.'

'That's a very selfish attitude.'

'Christ,' said Jude, and stood up, knocking the table so the coffee slopped and the cup shuddered in its saucer. 'I'm moving out.'

'Don't talk rubbish.'

'I'll get you some more,' said Sophie, mopping up the pool of coffee with a j-cloth.

'I'm sorry if I worried you – anyone,' Jude said rather loudly, as Scarlet entered '... but I'm not prepared to be ordered around by you all my life. Rather than that I'll rent somewhere for the vacation.' And he walked out, tripping over the corner of the rush matting that had got bent up by his chair.

'Well, well,' said Scarlet.

The front door slammed.

'Now you've done it!'

'He's got to learn,' said Alec. But secretly he was worried.

And when half an hour later he walked the line of the new fence with which he was planning to enclose Scardon, separate it from the Straying Rights used by neighbouring farmers for years, his mind was still filled by the scene with Jude. Jude had brain, everyone knew that, but he didn't apply it. In fact quite the opposite. Even Theobald had admitted to concern for the possible turn Jude's life might take; he had advised Alec very strongly *not* to let Jude live on his own in view of what had happened at Oxford, and now the boy was about to do so. Worst of all, to Alec's sense of shame, he was rather glad. Could it, did it, mean they were not blood relations? Something Jane had once said had made him suspicious, had become the one persisting thought that gnawed away at him, made him suspect his life had been spent providing for a child that wasn't even his. He supposed it happened to others, but that was poor consolation. And it had got on his nerves the way in which recently Jude seemed to have insinuated himself into Sophie's favour, much more so than before they came to the country . . .

Alec tripped over a root of gorse. The sun baked the back of his neck red; certainly the weather was exceptional, not at all what they had been led to expect. If they couldn't, as a family, be happy under these conditions then what would it be like when it rained and they were confined indoors?

In his room Jude stood for a few moments looking round and considering. Then he pulled a large suitcase from under the bed and started to put in his notebooks and cassette tapes. He stopped and thought some more, went downstairs, lifted the telephone to ring Astra, thought better of it and replaced the receiver. Finally he rang Hunters and Dobbs estate agency and asked for a cheap property to rent for ten weeks. He returned to his room and continued packing in a desultory fashion. After all, he couldn't very well move until he had somewhere to go. He was not quite so optimistic as to suppose Astra would move in and live with him but it would at least allow him some freedom to come and go as he pleased, he unreasonably reasoned. His father was a tyrannical old fool, and Scarhill, though pleasant, confining. Sophie was all right; the only thing he couldn't understand was how she could stick his father.

He stopped packing and went out on to the lawn having first made sure his father was not there. Close to the sheep-dip with her head in the shade under the cherry tree he found Scarlet; she was lying with her chin in her hands and a book propped up in front of her, sunbathing.

'I say, aren't you starting rather early?'

'Yes, but then I've only got a few more days to lie around in. I've got a job.'

'Oh?' Jude was curious rather than interested.

'As a PA-cum-secretary. He's a friend of Mummy's and it'll mean I'll get around a bit – travel. And in case you hadn't realised, it's nearly twelve.' She rolled over easily.

'God – is it?' Jude looked at the sun and then down on his

sister. Her almost naked body made him feel uncomfortable, almost incestuous. He averted his eyes. He felt at a loose end; the only thing he wanted was to see Astra Merlin and that, he knew, wasn't going to be easy. He was too proud to be persistent or, in any sense, to pester her.

'You could have let them know yesterday,' Scarlet said.

'I could have but I didn't.'

'I'm glad I shan't be here long. You and Daddy under the same roof is misery.'

'I'm moving out.'

'Ha, ha.' Scarlet didn't even look up.

'I'm serious. I've rung the agents.'

Scarlet did look up. 'Who's going to pay?'

'I am.'

'Good luck.' Scarlet undid the top of her tropical oil and rubbed a bit more on her thighs. Like a seal, Jude thought, who found his eyes inadvertently drawn back to his sister's sleek and gleaming body. He thought of Astra, who was white and soft and unbelievably different. The thought made desire for her mount, made his trousers feel constricting.

'You'd better watch out,' Scarlet said. 'She's under age. And under the auspices of her mother. I wouldn't like to be her.'

Jude swallowed. 'I don't know what you're on about,' he said.

'Good,' said Scarlet, settling herself back on her stomach and putting on her dark glasses.

Jude wandered off down to the pond. He stood staring at it for some time, then baled out the old boat left to them by the Merlins, and drifted round in it, paddling idly. The only possible good thing his father might do, he considered, was to turn the pond into a lake. He watched the Prussian blue and emerald dragonflies dance on the water, then heard the telephone from the house. He paddled vigorously for the nearest bank but long before he reached it, Scarlet had gone to answer.

*

'I think I ought to get back,' Sophie said, 'they're expecting me.'

'Oh dear,' said Oliver Upton. 'Alice has made a cake.'

Oliver Upton was the Poundsford rector and Alice his companion-help. Sophie, who hated making cakes herself, felt for Alice.

'Then I will come – if you'll excuse me only staying for a little.'

She was standing outside the village hall after an audition for a pantomime instigated by the rector. It was intended primarily to collect funds for the repair of Poundsford clocktower and it was no hardship for the rector to find himself the organiser, for he had studied drama with ambitions of becoming a director in his youth, and only when this failed had he turned to the Church. Five years ago he had come to Poundsford and now took services in three other parishes on successive Sundays. He had a thick beard, a small nose, and penetrating eyes under bushy brows. His most endearing quality was eccentricity and, sitting in his dog collar and tweed cap in his old battered 1950s Bentley, he was something of a figure of fun. Just as long as you weren't alone with him, Carol had remarked to Sophie. The village collectively had placed him in his mid-forties, and it was generally acknowledged it would have been more comfortable had he a wife.

Ten minutes later Sophie sat on the rector's brocade sofa eating cake while Alice poured tea from a silver teapot concealed in a cosy. At the rector's insistence Sophie stood to examine his painting of the rectory hung over the mantelpiece. Her voice, the rector meditated, was good, though not as good as Lucy Fardon's, but her looks were invaluable for holding the audience; all kinds of blunders, he reassured himself, could be got over with a beautiful woman in the lead role. And certainly she was exquisite; Oliver Upton studied Sophie's perfect neck with the sun outlining it. Unexpectedly a crumb went down the wrong way; Sophie coughed and turned pink. The rector looked away and Alice refilled Sophie's cup hastily

78

with milky tea and handed it to her. Sophie sat down, balancing it on her knees. It was the kind of house in which a stomach rumble or a fart would be deeply embarrassing, she decided. She wished she hadn't come.

'How's young Jude getting on down here? I met him in the lane yesterday, had a most interesting talk.'

'Oh did you?' said Sophie enthusiastically. 'He's terribly intellectual – and interesting,' she added, sensing that intellect in others might not necessarily appeal to the rector. 'He absolutely loves the country, he studies birds and . . . and wild flowers. He's sort of a natural scientist *manqué* and a great walker too. He's gone off today with Astra Merlin; I really envy them.'

When she stopped there was an unexpected silence as though they were waiting for her to go on. She looked at Alice's large leathery face with two different-coloured eyes and then at Oliver Upton's intent gaze and decided she had said too much. It would be all round the village, Jude would kill her. 'That's why I can't stay long, you see. I'm expecting them back for tea.' She endeavoured to rectify the situation. She picked a further crumb off her knee and put it on the gold-edged saucer.

The rector leant forward, hands clasped between his own broad knees. 'Astra is certainly a most appealing young person,' he said.

'Oh yes, isn't she? She's wonderful. I really love her. She's so unspoilt and beautiful. Like, sort of . . . spring. You know?'

'A Chloë?'

'Oh yes.'

Sophie's Greek mythology was not very strong or she might not have been so quick to agree.

'Kate's a splendid person too,' she said. 'Terribly generous. She's a marvellous friend.'

'Yes indeed.' Oliver Upton coughed. Sophie detected his reservation and wondered what Kate had done to displease him. She had, after all, turned up to the audition. But Oliver Upton's mind was on other things.

79

'I should very much like it if you would play the lead – be Rapunzel. You fit the part admirably.'

'Oh,' said Sophie, taken aback and flattered, 'but that other girl had a much better voice. I'm sure she'd be perfect.'

'As I said, you fit the part,' Oliver Upton repeated.

Sophie put her cup and saucer on the tea trolley and stood up. 'It's very nice of you to ask me,' she said, 'and of course I'll have a try if you're quite sure you oughtn't ask ... er ...'

'Lucy. Lucy Fardon.'

'Yes,' said Sophie, looking at him anxiously.

But the rector, seeing Sophie standing in the bow window, the light coming through her thin dress and clearly revealing the lines of her form beneath, didn't see any necessity for using Lucy Fardon.

'Lucy,' he said, 'is a busy young woman with her work and her home to run. I think it would be placing an undue burden on her to ask her to take such a taxing part. Besides,' he went on, moving up beside Sophie and laying his hand on her arm, 'I don't doubt for one moment that you can do it. If at times I may become a little harsh, it is only to draw out of you more expression, more ... feeling, than you yourself may be aware of.'

His face was rather close. Sophie took a step towards the door, she didn't like his breath. 'I'll do my best,' she said and withdrew her arm, watching the rector's long white fingers with carefully tended nails release her own brown skin. She hurried out through the glass porch, clasping her script.

In the car she heaved a sigh of relief, wound down the window, and waved gaily as one of her wheels rose up and crushed the neat edge of his lawn. Narrowly missing the granite arch at the end of his drive, she drove out into the road and along under the lime trees that bordered the village green.

Carol was sitting on the windowsill in riding clothes with Alec, also in riding clothes, when Sophie got back. She remembered: they had arranged to ride for the second – or was it the third? – time.

'Did you have a good ride?' she asked, dropping her script on the table and pouring herself tea from the already made pot. 'The rector wants me to be the lead,' she went on, 'but I'm just not a soloist. I croaked like a crow in the audition. Why can't he let Lucy Fardon do it, she's got a gorgeous voice?'

'Do you mean to say he isn't?' Carol demanded.

'He wants me to do it,' Sophie repeated, 'though I can't imagine why.' There followed a silence in which she sensed Carol's disapproval.

'You have a very good voice, Soph,' Alec said encouragingly.

'How was our friend Oliver?' Carol asked.

'Peculiar.'

Carol looked at Alec and laughed loudly. She had one foot up on the sill and was clasping her knee; her long mane of hair fell about her shoulders. 'I told you,' she said to Alec, then stood as though it was necessary to stand to make the point she was about to. 'Honestly, Sophie, you don't know what you are letting yourself in for. I should leave it to Lucy Fardon – she actually *wants* to do it.'

'Does she?'

'Yes, she does.'

Sophie put her empty cup on the sink. She had got the message. After Carol had left, she glanced curiously at Alec, who seemed in a very pensive mood. 'Where did you ride?' she asked, as much to dispel the atmosphere caused by Carol's presence as out of particular interest.

'Over Lark Down.' Alec seemed not to want to discuss it. He unfolded the *Financial Times*. Althorpe was discussing a merger with Behtwaters. Was this the moment to sell or hold on? He went through to his makeshift office and dialled his broker.

Sophie, left on her own, looked at the draining-board piled high with dirty glasses. Could they really all have accumulated since yesterday? For a moment she regretted having left London. It had all been so easy with the garbage disposal unit and the central heating; and best of all Peggy, who arrived twice a week from Wandsworth on the 28 bus. Sophie picked a hair grip out of the fruit bowl and fastened her hair back behind her ear. She opened the cupboard under the sink and observed the overflowing rubbish bucket. She stared down on it, wondering whether to tell the rector she would rather not be Rapunzel? Living in the country was in some ways more complicated than London, more involving with other people. She filled the sink with soapy tepid water because the boiler was not yet working properly, and began rinsing the glasses one by one.

When Scarlet had answered the telephone and yelled down to the pond, Jude had come running up breathless and picked up the receiver, expecting Hunters & Dobbs estate agents.

'Hullo,' Jude said, 'Have you got anything?'

'Yes,' Oliver Upton was taken aback. 'If you could come along to see me we could discuss if what I have in mind is the sort of think you could take on.'

'Anything almost will do.'

Oliver Upton thought Jude very keen. It made him hesitate. Perhaps he was more keen than able.

'Well come along and we'll have a chat and I'll put you in the picture,' he said, careful not to say it was a lead role. He could always push him into the chorus if the boy was desperate for a part.

'Where are you – I mean exactly?'

'The rectory.'

There was a vey long silence while Jude's brain ticked over and readjusted itself. 'You mean you want me for the play?'

'I'm interested to involve you if possible.' The rector remained cautious.

'I see.'

He was surprised at the sudden change in Jude's tone. 'If you're interested,' he said.

Jude remembered Astra was in it – had mentioned it. 'Yes, I am.'

'Good. Good. That's good news. When can you come along?'

'God only knows.'

There was a moment's silence during which Jude realised he had taken the Lord's name in vain.

'I'm pretty chaotic at the moment,' he excused himself.

'How about 3 p.m.?'

'Fine.' Jude replaced the receiver.

Gabe Fardon arrived at Bag Down as the sun was reaching the particular point in the west at which it set. Its rays caught the thatch, making it gold; long shadows lay beneath the beeches in the field's corner. Gabe swore under his breath, blamed Carol Granger for detaining him to treat her horse against his better judgement, and thought with anger of his valuable time wasted. If the dew started to come up before he could finish baling it would take the edge off what should have been perfect hay. He propped the gate open and drove in.

Kate in her studio poised with brush loaded, and it was in this moment of hesitation that the baler's powerful rhythm asserted itself. *T-chug, t-chug, t-chug, t-chug.* It was such a peculiarly imperative and demanding rhythm, almost irresistible to a country dweller. The thought of the new round-baler superseding the older type upset Kate, but she put such childishness behind her – anything that saved labour must be good. Or must it? She mused on the point as she slowly lowered her brush. Perhaps she should continue her painting, but would it not be unwise to go on when her mind was not fully concentrated? When the *t-chug, t-chug* was pulling her to another life, a world of the outdoor where things happened and were positive and exterior, were done or not done and there was no doubt or indecision?

She sighed, refocused on her canvas, still unsure whether even the ochre was right. Did it express great slabs of lichened roofs? Should she not perhaps make it warmer, add more cadmium? *T-chug, t-chug.* The baler, she judged, was passing just above the bathroom at the back of the house. She bent a little, strained to catch a glimpse of it through the small window beside the fireplace. A tractor's wheel for a moment blocked the light, followed by red metal. Drawing in a deep breath of pleasure Kate moved towards the french windows, then glanced guiltily back at her vacant, reproving studio. The light's not good, she explained to herself – it's too late in the day with the hedge. Tomorrow would be better. And quickly, as if her guilt might escape the studio and follow her, she shut the doors behind her and let herself up through the hunting gate into the hayfield. *T-chug, t-chug, t-chug* – her heart gave a joyous beat of happiness. It was so lovely just being. She really hated it indoors in perfect weather.

When Kate got up to the field she found Gabe Fardon driving round rather fast, the baler pushing out bales at regular intervals behind it. She saw Astra, Benjy and Eddie but decided not to join them; instead she leant against the hedge amongst the tiny blue scabious and hum of bees. Gabe had stopped; he was walking down the row shifting bales out of the way of the unbaled hay. Kate walked over and started her end of the row, pulling the bales back in the same fashion till she and Gabe met in the middle. Gabe's eyes acknowledged her without the need for speech; his proximity was pleasant. She liked men who made her feel a woman – which as she was one already seemed silly. But she couldn't help her feelings and if Gabe made her feel happy and like singing that was good, it must be, it was good to be happy. And with this agreeable thought Kate started round the headland pulling out any bales likely to impede the progress of Gabe, who was back on the tractor proceeding slowly, pausing, allowing the machine to cope with a heavy patch. Or was it that the hay was already damp where the sun no longer slanted on it? A moment later there was an uncomfortable clang, the rhythm broke, changed from *t-chug* to *t-clunk*; the halted tractor stood shuddering. The baler gave a further few beats and came to a standstill. Gabe climbed down.

'Shearbolt gone.'

Kate looked duly sympathetic. Her years of farming with Donald had given her full knowledge of the standard diseases of machinery. She leant against the baler watching Gabe's hair as he bent in front of her – thick hair caked with dirt and dust. All right when washed, she surmised. Silky. She continued to examine Gabe as a bird might a morsel too large to attack – his thick sunburnt neck, the white shirt covering his shoulders. She thought idly of Carol Granger. Surely not, but it was *just* possible. Kate chewed a piece of hay and frowned. Might not a relationship with someone such as Gabe add a dimension, widen self-knowledge? Kate was still pondering when she noticed Astra coming towards her across the field. Immediately Kate became another person, she positively felt herself alter. She stepped back, folded her arms, became a mother. The light that had been in her eyes for Gabe she now wiped from them as deftly as chalk from a blackboard. Instinctively she buttoned her blouse a hole higher as she advanced to meet her daughter. Astra, she noticed, had that wary and secretive expression she had acquired recently – owing to Jude Deneuve, no doubt.

Kate's bliss sank with the sun which seemed to accelerate its pace as it neared the horizon. She felt no longer herself but insoluably a part of Astra; Astra's anxieties and tensions overwhelmed her even if untold and unspoken. Had she not carried Astra for nine months, influenced her as much before as after birth – or so she read in the magazines – so that in some way any failure of Astra's laid itself at her feet. Kate's shoulders drooped under so heavy and oppressive a weight. Never be a mother, she thought, it's too terrible: the burden, the responsibility, worst of all the guilt. Guilt had a habit of nagging on in a particularly persistent and horrible fashion.

She sighed, lifted her chin a little and pushed back her hair firmly, if unattractively, no longer a self responding to her own ego's imperious demands, but 'a mother', a lone standing column amongst the fallen lintels and rubble of her and Donald's love. *Love*! Kate chewed her thumb, tried to remove a small thorn with her teeth. Was there, after all, much point in being a single column; might not all just as well be flattened? No – a single column presented the impression of grandeur even if only of what was once, of what might have been. Didn't it? Kate argued with herself endlessly and, she often thought, pointlessly, for she generally ended up doing what she felt she had to. Her instinctive feeling, she liked to think, remained true. True to what . . .?

'Jude's coming to dinner.' Astra eyed her mother who she could see was miles away. 'He dropped in.'

Kate took in the full impact of this statement. The cats had managed to get through all the milk; there was no butter. All that immediately came to mind were a few stray vegetables in the garden. Astra observed the alarmed, helpless expression pass across the column that was her mother.

'I'll do the cooking,' she said, 'you needn't worry.'

'Where is he?'

'In the house. He's looking at your paintings – I hope you don't mind.'

'No.' Kate couldn't help but be pleased, though anxious not to show it. Immediately Jude seemed a nicer person, more . . . sympathetic.

'I didn't actually ask him – he just came.'

'I'm glad,' said Kate. Stimulus, after all, was what she needed. The stimulation of somebody interested in her painting. It was such a lonely business. Her walk was quite springy as she followed in Astra's wake down the field. 'What will you cook?' she called, almost shouted, for Astra was drawing away from her, reaching out to another life. She hoped it would be romantic for Astra like it had been for her, but that Astra wouldn't try to cling to it as she had; and just for a moment Kate looked back up the field to where Gabe's tractor was outlined in gold by the last of the sun. You stupid, stupid woman, she told herself, you're much too old. And she followed Astra thinking there were no black peppercorns and they were out of sunflower oil.

Benjy and Eddie had found a viewpoint in the beech hedge.

They sat on a hanging branch, dangling their legs and watching the baler relentlessly munching up rows.

'Your sister's gone in?' Eddie jerked his head towards the point where Astra had disappeared.

'Yes.'

'Heard about her and the Deneuve boy?'

'Who?'

Eddie looked at Benjy patiently. 'Jude Deneuve.'

'Oh.' Benjy was relieved. He'd thought there was someone he hadn't been told about, not Jude, who was a man.

'Heard they was out the moor half the night.'

Benjy took his thumb out. 'No they wasn't. They had dinner. Astra told me.'

Eddie laughed. 'Go on – you'd believe her if she said they hadn't done nothing but walk.'

Benjy looked uncomprehending.

'I knows,' Eddie went on, 'because my cousin who lives out Postridge saw them. He saw 'em having a bit of nooky right out on the grass, didn't even bother to hide 'emselves.'

Benjy had no idea what 'nooky' was but Eddie's voice told him a great deal. He didn't know what to say so he said nothing.

'Wearin' a dress today, I seed.'

Benjy knew where he was again. 'She's going to a rehearsal, I expect,' he said, 'with the rector.'

'Good luck to her,' said Eddie. 'My mum went to one of them and she said it was a put-up job. The rector had made up his mind and it wasn't nothing to do with how good you sing.'

'Astra didn't say she had to sing,' said Benjy, surprised.

'Probably doesn't,' Eddie grinned. 'Not in her case.'

The innuendo passed over Benjy. He slithered down off the branch and saw that his mother had stopped at the very bottom of the field and was standing with one hand on the tractor cab in earnest conversation with Gabe Fardon. As he drew near he heard his mother say to Gabe, 'It'll make a difference, it'll let in so much more light.' Then Benjy knew at

87

once it was the hedge outside her studio they were discussing and guessed his mother had swapped the hay in exchange for Gabe making a gap in the bank beneath it.

He stood beside his mother watching Gabe start his tractor and drive away, baling the headland, stopping at the thick clumps to let the baler gather in the hay without blocking it. His mother laid her hand on the back of his neck but he shook it off.

'I don't want Gabe to take away the hedge.' He beat his head against his mother's groin.

'Benjy – don't!' His mother looked distressed; she walked away from him down the field. Benjy followed slowly, kicking his way through the neat rows, spreading them angrily. He hated things changed, he was afraid for what would never be again, it scared him. Also he loved things, loved them as much as people. When his mother had told him they were leaving Scarhill it was the worst moment in his life. That and his father going away. Benjy didn't like seeing his father any more on those rare occasions when he came: he was a stranger with a voice that might shout. His father made him clumsy and stupid so he upset the milk and tipped over his chair. The last time he had come Benjy had hidden in the loft and not come out till he'd heard him drive off . . .

He let himself into his mother's studio and made his way carefully between her pile of stretchers and canvases. When he got into the passage he ran along it and into the lavatory and bolted the door. He looked out the window while he was peeing and saw Gabe on the tractor precariously crossing the field above him almost as though he was baling the thatch. Another instant and he was out of sight. Benjy did up his zip; he wondered if Eddie had gone.

'It's painting in its own right – emotionally disturbing and exciting.' Jude and Kate were in the studio staring intently at a painting leaning against the wall in front of them.

Kate felt pleasure surge through her and realised to her chagrin that she was waiting on Jude's words with pathetic anxiety, as a dog might its food. When it came to her own work she always lacked certainty.

'Is that how you feel it – really?' She tried to keep the hungry whine out of her tone. It's so debasing, she thought, to be so desperate for interest, for comments, for discussion. Yes, that was it. It was not even praise she needed – well, only in a small way . . .

'It's as near as I can get,' Jude said.

'Yes.' Kate recognised she had been given her biscuit on which to gnaw. She must be content. It was hardly a plateful but there it was: her painting certainly looked better to her now than it had half an hour ago – more impressive. Jude was clearly very intelligent.

'I'm still working on it,' she said, 'but it probably won't change that much.' Was it because Jude liked it that she had decided this? She despised herself for being affected by his comments but praise was the nectar of life even if you didn't believe it. She gave a last savage look at her canvas. She would so much *like* to believe Jude but in the end, in the final count, knew she couldn't. Her painting glared back at her blatantly, crude, unsubtle – no more than a beginning. Certainly it was not a rock on which she would feel safe to stand. She removed it from the easel and stood it face to the wall.

'Can I see any others?'

'There's nothing much,' said Kate modestly, while dragging out some half a dozen more. Jude tactfully halted her on the sixth.

'Mrs Merlin . . .'

'I'd much rather you call me Kate.'

'I was only going to say I think the one we've just been looking at is almost a . . . a great painting.'

'Oh,' said Kate, 'I'd never thought – ' and she broke off. After all, it was rather good. It glowed in what was left of the evening light filtering through the tiny north window. Jude also glowed like a sort of Narcissus, Kate thought. The moment was sublime; she, Jude and the painting wrapped in communion. And somewhere unseen fluttered round the goddess Praise. If I were a poet, Kate thought, I'd write a hymn to Praise. Then the light that there had been, vanished; a cloud must have come before the sun. Kate shuddered and thought of the frightening, the terrible decision to alter something of long standing that everyone had pronounced good . . .

A smell of cooking made her nose twitch. Guilt again caught up. She should be helping.

'I must go and give Astra a hand,' she said, 'Come along when you're ready.'

'You've been ages. Can you lay the table?' Astra looked at Kate resentfully.

'Shall we have wine and candles?' Kate, with a masterpiece under her apron, was feeling generous.

'No,' Astra frowned, 'we don't want to be formal – wine'll be all right but not candles.' Her mother, she thought, had a slightly silly expression on her face, not quite all there. She often had it when she had come out of long sessions with people in the studio. Kate was in fact leaning out of the window drawing in deep breaths instead of getting on with wiping the table, and had been arrested by the transparency of the evening sky with one solo star hovering over the stable roof. The sound of the tractor she had half-consciously been aware of all through her conversation with Jude had now stopped. The field, she presumed, was baled – tomorrow it would be carried.

Kate, Jude and Astra sat on three sides of the dining-room table.

'There's some grit in the leaves.' Kate was edging a piece of grit to the front of her mouth.

Astra blushed scarlet. She had not washed them thoroughly enough. Jude's teeth crunched, a look of consternation crossed his face.

'I should spit it out,' said Kate.

But Jude was extremely chivalrous; he swallowed his

mouthful, grit and all. They ate the quiche carefully, then turned on the blackcurrant fool.

Jude enjoyed it, he said.

Kate added sugar.

Astra thought it thin.

But by this stage they were talking, so what they ate became less important. Kate asked how the Deneuves were settling in. Jude said he thought all right. Then he said,

'My father is building a glass-covered way, a sort of conservatory, a mini-Crystal Palace from the back door to the boiler house. He's got permission from the National Park – God knows how.'

'Won't that alter the house's entire appearance from the back?' Kate asked.

'Yes it will. I've told them so. It's not Sophie, it's my father. I don't think Sophie would change the place at all, basically.'

They ate in silence.

'It may not be as bad as it sounds,' Kate said finally to comfort herself.

'It certainly isn't as bad as his intentions over the land. He's going to plant hundreds of acres of softwoods,' announced Jude. 'I totally disagree with his policy. I'm moving out. But that, unfortunately, will do little to prevent the destruction he seems set on.' His lip lifted bitterly.

'Where will he get the land?' Astra asked.

'He's buying it up. He's planting them here – all round.'

'But he hasn't permission. The National Park will stop him.' Kate clutched at the straw she normally burnt.

'They can't stop him – only withhold a grant. And my father and his partners don't care about that – they'll set it all off against tax. It's all a tax-avoidance ruse in the first place. I find it despicable.'

'Are you really moving out?' Astra was surprised he hadn't said anything about it before.

'Yes I am. I've got a room at the Mill – I'm moving in next week. I shall stay there till I go up in October.'

'Up?' Astra asked.

'To Oxford – that's how they say it,' Jude explained heavily. Astra flushed.

'Isn't it rather ridiculous to have a big place like Scarhill and go elsewhere?' Kate was incredulous.

'If you disapprove of your father's principles and politics, believe him to be a destructive force, then there is no alternative. He's a Thatcherite, you see.' Jude thought this last explained everything.

Kate paused with a spoon of blackcurrant fool to her lips. 'I think you are taking a strong stance,' she said. 'I both admire you and feel afraid for you.'

'Don't lecture, Muma,' Astra said. 'It's not the end of the world. Millions of people leave home for good when they're younger than I am.'

She looked at Jude. 'Do Alec and Sophie know yet?'

'No.'

There was a pause in the conversation while they all visualised how Alec and Sophie Deneuve would take the news.

'Is it definite?' Astra asked.

'Quite. I've paid the rent.' On this conclusive note they left the table and sat in more comfortable chairs.

'Is that why you came round?' Astra clasped her mug of coffee.

'I wanted to see you.'

Astra flushed and Kate looked impressed. Astra could tell she liked Jude; so could Jude, who looked oddly self-satisfied.

'Also,' he went on, 'I wanted to let you know where to find me.'

Kate, in her normal manner, returned to the earlier issue. 'If your father plants trees all over Scarhill land it will ruin it, but hardly the entire area,' she said.

'You don't understand. He's buying up farms to exploit. He's bought one at Lark Down and another at Brent and one right over on the South moor. He's put in for planning permission to convert them for holiday lets, then he'll sell them off for twice the price. The land, of course, he'll keep. He'll make money, don't worry.'

Kate and Astra regarded him in silence. Her mother's face, Astra noticed, was strained as she stood up. 'If you'll both excuse me, I must go and write a letter,' she said. The door closed behind her.

Astra crushed a crumb into the surface of the table with her knife. 'In a way it's our fault – for selling Scarhill to your father. We could have sold it to someone local but my mother needed the money,' she said.

'Did she?'

'To pay back the overdraft,' Astra explained.

Jude's lip lifted, expressing disbelief.

'I imagine what she got for Scarhill must have paid the overdraft ten times over as well as bought this place and a legacy for life.'

'Don't forget my father has his share.'

'That's the rub, isn't it?'

'Yes,' Astra admitted. She hated the way Jude drew the truth out. It would have been so much easier to stand in judgment on the Deneuves, she thought, if her own family weren't in a certain sense implicated.

'Anyway there's no need to share blame,' Jude said. 'It's my father. You couldn't possibly know he was that kind of man.'

'He doesn't *seem* bad – I mean, not really.'

'Don't you believe it,' said Jude. 'He's about as bad as they come.'

Astra was rather shocked by Jude's utter condemnation of his father. 'What does Scarlet think?' she asked.

'Scarlet doesn't think – except about the next party or the price of moisturisers.'

So Scarlet too was condemned.

'Is your mother really writing letters?' he asked.

'Yes – she writes one nearly every day about the divorce. That's another reason she needs the money – for the costs. She's fighting it, you see.'

'Fighting for what?'

'I'm not quite sure. Something to do with the allowance Daddy pays her for us.'

'I'd have thought your mother'd be above arguing over money.'

Astra was mortified. 'You can't be above what you need,' she said.

Jude stood and helped himself to more Brie and biscuits; it helped disguise his curious combination of extreme nerves and confidence. While he munched he studied Astra curled up in the chair, her dark hair almost concealing her face.

'Will you come and live at the Mill?' he said suddenly. Somehow his session in the studio had emboldened him.

Astra felt herself tense with excitement and apprehension. She sat as though frozen for what seemed minutes to Jude, then pushed back her two curtains of hair on either side of her parting.

'I can't,' she said.

'Why not?'

Astra felt uncertain, she fumbled for words. Because I don't love you, she thought but could not bring herself to say, because of the cold hurtfulness of it.

'Because of the implications,' she said.

Jude pushed down his biscuit and took another.

'What implications?'

'I wouldn't want to ... to live with you or anyone,' she added quickly. It was hard to tell what Jude was feeling.

'OK.'

'Do you mind?'

'Why should I?'

They ate celery stalks.

'Christ,' said Jude, 'I must go.' His voice was bright and carefully casual to cover up the intensity of his disappointment.

'It's not late.'

'No, but I've got to call in at Scarhill and collect my things. While it's light.'

Astra went out with him to his car. A bat flitted past them;

it was a still and balmy night for the moor. Besides the gate they kissed. Astra's kiss was particularly passionate to compensate for her inability to wholly love Jude. That and the fear of losing him altogether.

Jude drove like a maniac along the lanes. He thought if he was killed it wouldn't really matter. Ironically, he killed a black tomcat that leaped out of the hedge in front of him. He stopped to make sure it was dead, and flung it over the hedge; then leant against the bank and buried his face in the cool, dew-soaked grass until he regained some sense of reality. Even if Astra wouldn't live with him, life at the present was better than death. Just as long as he could see her. With life, hope remained.

Gradually Jude felt himself grow calmer. He wished he didn't get into such states, he wished he was in control of his emotions and if Astra, or whoever he fastened his passions to, didn't reciprocate them, he could simply switch off. With his mother, for instance; he was apt to feel as though he might sob like a child every time he argued with her – which was nearly every time they met. She irritated him beyond endurance, almost *tried* to rub him up the wrong way. It was the things she said. His father was different; he actually might have been able to like him if he hadn't had such puerile values – or that's how Jude saw them: money, and a voracious and insatiable appetite for gambling on his business deals. Everything he touched turned into profit. Jude both admired and bitterly resented the unquenchable energy that was the hallmark of his father. Only a man with excessive confidence and energy would have left the relative safety of his London business and attempted to turn the country to his advantage. It was as though only a challenge satisfied him.

'I don't see the point,' Sophie said to Alec, pushing the white cabbage and sultana salad across the table to Scarlet. 'I mean when we decided to buy Scarhill it was for us, not as . . . as a business proposition. Now, in a sense, it's become your out-of-town office. So you can buy up the moor.' She stabbed her baked potato with a knife and filled the slit with unsalted Normandy butter.

Scarlet groaned. 'Oh dear,' she said, 'do you have to bring this up now? After all Daddy has to provide money – you're the spender.'

'I am not,' Sophie was indignant, 'and yes I do have to bring it up now.'

Scarlet rested her chin in her hand and looked bored. 'I thought the country was supposed to be peaceful, no rat race, no tension, but all our family has done is argue ever since we've been here. I think it's because there's nothing to do.'

'There's plenty to do here if you're prepared to do it.' Alec was firm, he felt bound to be.

'You mean digging the garden and painting windows and mowing the lawn. All those boring jobs. Honestly, Daddy, those are for middle-aged people. The only social life here is square-dancing in the parish hall once a month.' Scarlet helped herself to a mound of salad. She was dieting.

'Where's Jude?' asked Alec.

'He should be here.' Sophie looked round distractedly, as though Jude might materialise from a shadow. Things, she decided, were getting on top of her. She said, 'We've got off the point. About the moor and you buying it up.'

'My dear child,' Alec said.

'I'm not,' said Sophie, enraged by Alec's patronising manner.

'I'm your dear child,' said Scarlet – and giggled.

'What I am trying to explain is that it is far simpler if I can get some kind of forestry concern going down here. Then I won't need to go up to London nearly as frequently . . . ' He broke off in mid-sentence. Jude was standing in the doorway.

'There you are!' said Sophie, a note of relief in her voice. 'Help yourself to quiche or ham on the side, and come and sit down.' She handed him a plate. Jude forked slices on to his plate and came and sat at the refectory table. Scarlet gave him the salad.

'Well,' said Alec, 'what have you been up to?'

'I've rented myself somewhere to live.' Jude filled his mouth with ham. A silence followed in which knives and forks seemed unduly noisy.

'Where?' Scarlet asked.

'At the Mill.'

'What on earth for?' Sophie felt affronted.

'I just thought it would be better.'

'But we bought Scarhill partly *for* you.' Sophie felt like crying. All at once Scarhill seemed big and empty and pointless. Scarlet, clearly, would only be down when she felt like it once her job started, and now if Jude moved out there would only be herself and Alec. Besides, she liked Jude, looked forward to his company. In some ways he was much easier to talk to than Alec, didn't always make her feel like arguing . . .

'I'm sorry,' Jude said, 'but as you well know, my father and I don't agree on fundamental issues. It seemed better to move out than stay here and row.'

'How much is it?'

'Forty pounds a week.'

'It can't be a palace for that,' said Scarlet.

'It isn't, but it's all I require.'

Jude was talking like a parson, Scarlet thought. He was irritatingly self-righteous at the best of times.

Sophie said at last, 'Jude – what decided you to take this step so . . . so suddenly?'

'Do you really want to know?' He looked from one to another.

'Please,' said Alec, who had pushed his chair out and crossed an ankle over his knee.

Jude cut himself a slice of bread. He buttered it methodically. He became very methodical in times of tension; he found it helped.

'I went into the village shop,' he said. 'I thought I was getting rather peculiar looks; anyway I went round behind the counter looking for the firelighters you'd asked me to get. While I was looking two other people came in – I don't know

97

who they were – women – and one said to the other "I hear those new people at Scarhill are going to fence the whole of Scardon. It's iniquitous – it's been common land for years." And the other said, "He owns it – he's got the money. You can't stop one of them moved-inners – it belongs to Scarhill. He's got the right if he wants to." I got out then, I didn't want to hear any more.' He looked full at his father. 'I imagine it's true, isn't it? That you are going to put an ugly wire fence round Scardon? Impound it for your own capitalistic purpose?'

Alec stood up. 'Look Jude,' he said, 'I shall do what I like. I don't like your insolent, priggish tone. You get out and rent yourself a place, stand on your own two feet. It'll be the best thing that ever happened to you.'

'But Alec,' Sophie said, 'Jude's not being unreasonable. It does seem criminal and unnecessary to fence in that beautiful hill. Why can't we go on sharing the grazing? Are you really going to do it?'

'I plan to – yes.' The force of character, the resolute if ruthless will that made Alec a successful businessman – a man appointed by many boards – came to the fore. 'If we fence it,' he said, 'it will provide us with another fifty-eight acres. We can use it for ourselves if we decide to run some stock, or otherwise let it. Either way it'll make a vast difference to Scarhill as a whole.'

'But Alec, you can afford *not* to?' Sophie was pleading.

'I can't. You and Jude are idealists with your heads in the clouds. You think our money drops from heaven like manna. Well it doesn't. *I* make it.'

Scarlet got up. 'Excuse me will you, everyone,' she said, 'but I have to wash my hair. It's all decided anyway, so why keep on about it? Daddy's going to fence his land and Jude's going to live at the Mill. Neither of them *ever* change their minds so what's there to argue about? They both, presumably, are entitled to the actions they have chosen.' And she crossed to the door. 'I'll come back and help you clear later,' she said, and went out.

'Oh God,' said Sophie, 'I do hate all this. I honestly think it's your fault, Alec.'

'I thought you would.' Alec tried to keep a note of bitterness out of his voice. 'Isn't everything my fault?'

'Oh shut up,' shouted Sophie. And she raised the priceless Crown Derby vegetable dish above her head and smashed it down on the tiles. Then burst into tears. Alec left the room.

Jude came across awkwardly. 'I'm very sorry,' he said. 'It's absolutely nothing to do with you that I'm going.'

'I know,' Sophie could hardly speak, her unhappiness so engulfed her.

'Please don't cry.' He felt anguished.

'Go away – do.'

So he went. Sophie was still sitting in the armchair sobbing when Scarlet found her a quarter of an hour later. She slipped her arm round her; Sophie so rarely cried.

'You mustn't worry,' she said, 'it'll all smooth out.' Then more shrewdly, 'You could probably force my father's hand.'

'I don't think I could. I honestly don't think I could.' Sophie felt as though her trump card, her beauty, had vanished, leaving her in rags like Cinderella.

'You could threaten to leave him,' said Scarlet, and began to clear the table.

When Sophie switched off the lights and went up, Alec was already in his side of the bed, sitting up reading. When she got into bed he laid down his book and drew her towards him.

'What have you been doing?'

'Thinking.'

'My poor little Soph.'

'Can't you stop talking down to me?' Sophie demanded. 'Jude and your fighting upsets me, and what's more I agree with him.'

'So you've said.' Alec withdrew his arm round her, turned away.

'Alec?'

'What?'

'Don't you love me?'

'Yes.'

'Then why don't you ever make love?'

'I do.'

'No you don't. Not properly. Only when you want sex. You don't love me in between.' Alec made no comment so Sophie went on: 'Anyhow if you loved me you wouldn't spend your time doing things I hate, like buying up the moor and planting trees all over it.'

'Actually,' said Alec, 'the last two farms have mining rights with them.'

Sophie sat bolt upright. 'Alec,' she said, 'you haven't bought one of those china clay tips that make the whole landscape look like the moon and pollute the area with white dust?'

'Why not?' said Alec. 'If I hadn't someone else would.'

Sophie detested Alec's logic. Aware it was flawed she still found it impossibly difficult to argue against. 'Next,' she said illogically, but logically to her way of thinking, 'you'll buy up a tract of land and sell it off for a nuclear power station.'

'No,' said Alec, 'I wouldn't do that.' And he switched out the light on his side of their king-size double bed and shut his eyes.

A few moments later Sophie said, 'Do you think we should separate?'

'If you want to,' said Alec.

Sophie was exasperated. 'Don't you care even one little bit about me?' she asked.

'I've said I do.'

'Then why don't you show it?'

So Alec rolled back towards Sophie and took her in his arms; and Sophie laid her soft blonde head in the pit of his shoulder and they fell into an unhappy sleep. In the morning Alec made love to Sophie and afterwards brought her up breakfast in bed. Sophie, who hated rows and atmosphere, decided life with Alec definitely had its advantages and forgave him for the previous evening. But that was the trouble, she thought, she forgave far too easily. It would probably have been better if she'd had a much more unrelenting nature. As it was she pushed the trees and the ugly fence round Scardon to the back of her mind, from which they only emerged at infrequent intervals. Later that day she had another rehearsal that she positively looked forward to – it got her out of the house, if nothing else.

Astra did not see Jude during his first week at the Mill. Jude, offended, left her alone and her pride prevented her visiting without an invitation. Accordingly, she was sitting on the windowseat endeavouring to concentrate on her book when Gabe Fardon came to the house in search of Kate. Kate had gone shopping so Astra answered the door, explained her mother was out and waited for Gabe to go away. Well she couldn't very well shut the door in his face, could she? When he didn't go she asked him in as her mother would have. Gabe sat on the bench and Astra made him tea – as her mother would have. Gabe made occasional comments but on the whole said very little, and Astra felt it incumbent on her to make conversation. She made herself a cup of tea and sat down opposite him – as her mother would have. For some reason she couldn't explain she felt extremely nervous and anxious to please; she even went to the kitchen and found a cake in the cake tin. At Scarhill they had always sat in the kitchen but at Bag Down the kitchen was too small so they sat in the dining room which was also small but smarter, containing dark polished furniture instead of scrubbed pine. Gabe, she observed, didn't look very comfortable on the bench in his work overalls but he seemed unconcerned. He looked round the room and commented on the old painting of a horse hung over the fireplace.

'I haven't seen that one before.'

'No – it was here when we came, so my mother left it. She likes it.'

They both surveyed the remarkably shaped horse with high

withers, deep shoulders, swan neck and tiny head, all supported on unbelievably fragile legs.

'Musta changed a bit since that one were painted. How old is it?' asked Gabe. He left the bench and scrutinised the painting.

'I don't really know.' Astra felt embarrassed by her ignorance but she had never until this moment given the painting any thought.

'Don't know over much, do you?' Gabe turned round and looked at her mock-seriously.

Astra was about to hotly excuse her ignorance when she noticed his expression, and her own changed. It was quite clear Gabe liked the fact that she didn't know much, it put their relations altogether on a better footing. Astra's response was intuitive with no conscious thought behind it. 'No,' she said, 'but I'm learning.' She had come round from her side of the table to view the painting better and now stole a furtive glance up at Gabe Fardon, who looked down on her with apparent amusement. He resumed his position on the bench while Astra perched herself at the far end.

'Back to school afore long, I suppose?' he asked.

'No.' Astra's cheeks burned. She hated to be thought of as a schoolgirl. 'I'm going to the Tech.'

'Where's that then?'

'Allerston.'

'I never knowed they had one.'

'It's new,' she explained, 'it opens next term.'

'Oh.' Gabe stared at her and Astra felt uncomfortable and awkward, as though she'd said the wrong thing and in some way had made herself out to be superior. To mend this misconception she said, 'I don't suppose it'll be much good but my mother wants me to go.'

Gabe made no comment. The silence was complete except for the dripping of water from the roofs and gutter outside. It was late afternoon and the room was growing darker by the moment.

'Getting dark,' observed Gabe astutely.

'Yes.'

Astra thought this meant he was going. But still he sat and the darkness and silence enclosed them.

'No fire?' Gabe regarded the fireless hearth.

'It smokes.'

Gabe again left the bench, went over to the grate and looked up the considerable chimney. He turned after a few moments and faced Astra, who could now only see his face for his darker clothes had merged into the darkness of the chimney corner. He stepped forward, put his cup back on its saucer and moved towards the door.

'Tell your mother I'll drop in again some time.'

'When?' Astra followed him into the small passage before the front door. Again it was dark and only his face glowed from its surround like an old portrait.

'Doesn't this house have lights?'

'Yes,' said Astra and was about to dart to the light switch but Gabe put his arm out and stopped her.

'Don't need them, do us?' he said softly and Astra was aware only of the agreeable mixture of smells that emanated from his clothes. She couldn't have precisely defined them but no one other than a country person could have smelt like Gabe. On Astra, perhaps because of associations with her father, the odd mixture acted as an aphrodisiac and when Gabe's rough skin and sensitive, tentative mouth found her lips in the just discernible oval of her face, she responded to him with a passion that left her blood coursing through her body. The very memory of it sent strange involuntary electric sensations through her for days afterwards.

Gabe, surprised, even a little alarmed, by the response he'd evoked, removed himself from Astra's vibrant body, let himself out of the front door and with a further reminder to tell her mother he'd be back, walked away, a dark shape in the thickening mist.

Astra remained in the porch, her hand up to her hot cheeks, listening to his van start and mount the hill behind the house. Then she went back into the dining room, where she sat in the darkness and relived the entire scene. She felt mortified and ashamed of her behaviour: she simply could not believe it had happened, it was all too incredibly unlikely. It had been Gabe who had freed her, she who had clung to him loath to lose his mouth. How could she have acted so? Yet in those brief moments with Gabe, Astra's self-knowledge had taken a leap forward. She had been aware of an instinctual, primitive leap of response towards his physical being that she had never felt with Jude. It both frightened her at the lack of control over her own feelings, and at the same time removed her further from Jude. If she didn't feel this violent emotion towards him, then surely she wasn't 'in love'?

Yet Gabe Fardon meant nothing to her, it was a great struggle talking to him, she was not sure she even liked him. On the contrary she felt rather afraid of him in his presence, in fact horribly self-conscious. So then what was the appeal of this man? Admittedly he had the glowing good looks, the thick hair, the muscular arms and strong body that youthful workers on the land are inclined to possess. But Astra sensed his attraction lay at a deeper level; it was as if, when the veneer of society and culture were pushed aside, Gabe Fardon came into his own – a Pan figure.

Astra felt afraid, and all at once Jude's sensitive face with the big-lidded eyes seemed infinitely comforting. She shut from her mind the moments when his eyes gazed through her as though she wasn't there, the moments when they stared almost fanatically at his own obsessions, and concentrated on his wide reading and clever brain; those were the things that mattered, those and his obvious adoration of herself. He was full of concern for her, he respected her. Yes, that was it, he made her feel interesting. Gradually she talked her confused feelings into some form of order. She would never succumb again to such a humiliating scene as had just passed – for that's what it had been, a mere nothing – she would not allow herself the chance. And yet a quickly suppressed leap of longing at the memory unsettled her resolve and she was still lost in a confusion of shame and desire when her mother returned, struggling under the weight of a large cardboard box of groceries.

Kate lowered the heavy box with relief on to the kitchen table, then pulled out a newspaper stuck upright in its corner. She spread it out, leant over the table.

'Look at this!'

Astra shifted round until she could see what her mother read:

> 'Mr Alec Deneuve, who has recently acquired further properties on the east slopes of Dartmoor, told the chairman at the board meeting of Deneuve and Benson, his own recently formed company, that he could see no future for the hill farm as it stood. He claimed that major investment in quick-growing coniferous timber would offer financial returns, along with conversion of redundant buildings for holiday lets to promote the tourist industry, with possible ventures into leisure schemes ...'

Kate jerked the paper angrily off the table. 'He's a monster,' she said. 'It's all for his own gain, exactly like Jude told us. It's shameful, yet the Press admires him for it. Or it certainly offers no criticism.'

Astra, who was still on a high as result of her first meeting with her own sexuality, looked at her mother in amazement. How can she get so worked up about the moor? she thought. How can she care that much? Part of her instinctively leant towards the plight of the Fardons and such of the local people to whom any industry, be it forestry, mining, or tourism, was a boon. Her mother, she suspected, would like to keep the moor as a museum piece. She said as much.

'No,' Kate exploded, 'you're entirely wrong and short-sighted. I simply agree with Jude that the exploitation of the moor by private companies – by Alec Deneuves – isn't going to help anyone in the long run except themselves. It's the beginning of privatisation – it's total exploitation, people having to pay to walk on the moor. You'll see.'

'It'll provide work for people,' Astra said stubbornly.

'Very little,' said Kate.

In this she was wrong, but Astra was tired of argument. 'Gabe Fardon called,' she said, peering down into the grocery box. 'He wanted to see you.'

Kate looked at Astra for the first time since she had come in, noticed the high colour of her cheeks, the brilliance of her eyes. 'It's hot in here,' she said, and flung open the window. 'Did he say what for?'

'No,' said Astra truthfully.

II

The bent grass swayed and rustled in the wind; from a distance it covered the moor in pale cream patches with here and there a darker patch denoting gorse and heather. It entirely covered the flattened peat-bog area on the top of Scardon and in some places ran down the sides of the hill to be terminated by short turf or the dark green of the bracken.

Scardon itself was a fine hill for those susceptible to the shape of hills; it was not magnificent like Earndon, did not rise to a peaked summit capped by a tor; rather it blended with the adjacent hills forming a continuous sensuous line, each contour running into the next, open to the sky with its surface only occasionally interrupted by wizened thorn or an upright granite stone that marked the boundary between the parishes.

On this particular day of late August, anyone driving up the road on Scardon's right would have seen not a farmer on his pony searching for hill sheep, nor even a Land Rover bucking over the rough ground to check the welfare of the stock, but a string of three jeep-like open trucks and no less than five men moving between them. One of the trucks now separated from the other two, and drove down from the ridge to within fifteen yards of the road where it turned left-handed and drove along unloading, at twenty-yard intervals, rolls of mesh and barbed wire until it had traversed the entire circumference of the down. Meanwhile the second truck drove to the first roll of wire and dropped beside it a heap of stakes. It then followed the first truck on its circuit, dumping off further stakes by each wire roll. Now came the turn of the third truck, which drove up beside the first pile and let out two men; it then zigzagged on across the bent grass to the far corner and put down two further fencers, for such was their job, and then on over the brow of the hill to let out four more at strategic intervals.

Not long afterwards, Alec's white Land Rover drove up the road and Alec, Alvin Hart and Howard Benson got out. Howard Benson was one of Alec's new partners from the other side of the moor. They strode up to the brow of the hill and stood with the wind inflating their down jackets as they pointed and braced themselves against it. Half an hour later they returned to Scarhill, where they huddled round the stove in the kitchen blowing on their fingers. Sophie, it seemed, was out, so it was Alec who had to heat the kettle and make coffee. Then the three men settled themselves round the table.

'Well, I expect you're glad to have made a start?' Alvin Hart rubbed his mauve fingers. It was exactly six and a half weeks since the Deneuves' arrival in Devon; Alec Deneuve was a fast mover, he'd say that for him.

'Yes . . .' Alec was thoughtful.

'How many seedlings exactly do you anticipate sixty acres will take?' asked Howard Benson.

'That I couldn't say,' Alvin Hart shook his head. 'I'll have to go home and make some calculations.'

'We're going to have beech for a couple of rows on the outside like the Forestry Commission recommend, aren't we?' Alec was surprised to remark the anxious note of his enquiry.

'Of course.'

'How do you think the softwoods will fare up on the brow?' Howard Benson asked.

'They won't be on the brow.' Alvin Hart was quick on to

that. 'We'll keep them back from the brow – leave the rocks and that little patch of sheep turf free. We'll work round the edges, closing into the centre with larch. We want to make it look appealing, if that's what's worrying you.' He looked at Alec.

'It's not worrying me,' said Alec, 'I was just thinking of local criticism. The Park generally likes trees kept back off the brow.'

'Leave it to me,' said Alvin, 'I'll see to it. Never fear.'

So reassured, Alec drank his coffee and discussed the necessary height of the fences to keep out deer, the width of the dividing rides as a fire precaution, and the future of timber on a commercial basis.

'Are you going up again?' Alec asked as Alvin Hart stood up to leave.

'I thought I'd make sure they've got the layout of the fence right.'

'Oh good.' Alec felt embarrassed at fussing but was anxious not to place trees in Sophie's view from her bedroom window. 'Could you ask them to keep right back from this side – the trees, I mean. It doesn't matter about the fence. I know that's got to run along the line of the old wall.'

Howard Benson frowned. 'That'll lose us quite an acreage, won't it?'

'No, almost nothing.' Alec was firm. 'This, after all, is my farm – and my wife's – I don't want in any way to spoil it for her by altering the natural environment.'

'Quite.' Alvin Hart felt it diplomatic to be reasonable. He had never for a moment supposed Alec would agree to plant up half as much of Scardon as he had; it had all come as a most agreeable surprise.

So, outvoted, Howard Benson followed Alvin Hart from the kitchen and by the time Sophie returned everything in the valley was quiet and peaceful and idyllic.

Later, while going for a walk across the fields with Alec, Sophie asked what the hammering noise was, and Alec replied perfectly truthfully that it was someone fencing. And just about the same time, the time of the fence, Sophie was so busy with rehearsals and one thing and another, that the fence round Scardon was a *fait accompli* by the time she saw it.

'Goodness, it's gone up quickly,' was all she said, but inwardly a little shiver of misery ran through her, and only ten days later she found herself in confrontation with Alec over alterations to Scarhill itself.

The builders had been making only moderate headway and Sophie was being driven mad by dust. Dust covered everything. It settled in corners, on ledges and sills, on each step of the stairs, on the top of the stove and on top of jam-jars. Every time they ate Sophie had to wipe a fine layer of dust off the top of the table. She went round shutting doors and imploring for dust sheets to be hung between the area they lived in and the building area, but it was all to no avail. The builders smiled appreciatively at her and promised faithfully to do as she asked, but next time she went to see where the newest layer of dust had come from the doors were all as wide open as before and the dust sheets drooped inadequately, mirroring her own depression.

At lunch she said to Alec, 'I don't think I can bear it much longer. When will they go?' And Alec replied, 'They've still got to put up that ceiling we asked them to raise. Of course if you didn't insist they re-use those ropy old beams, it would make them a lot quicker.'

But Sophie did insist. She liked beams and that was all there was to it. The windows were more of a problem; Alec and the National Park wanted plain, or even plate, glass to fill the areas where the old windows had rotted and had to be renewed. Sophie hated the blind-eyed look of plain glass; she thought they gave an old house a sad, soulless appearance and deter-mined, as far as possible, to renew the pattern of the old windows. Alec thought this an expensive fiddle, and said as much to John Graves, and George Botham from the National Park who had come over specially to sanction the exterior alterations.

'Oh please *don't* have just glass.' Sophie couldn't understand how *they* couldn't understand, but found it difficult to explain her reasons.

Alec was looking at her severely. If she could not give good reasons for her apparent whim then, as far as he was concerned, her ideas were invalid. Certainly it made her exasperating to argue with. He pulled on and off the top of his gold Parker.

'You see, it will bring us up way above the estimate,' John Graves said. Sophie noticed they all spoke to her condescendingly, as though she was a child to be humoured. Even the builders were beginning to look bored and make difficulties.

'The Park will be perfectly happy about it either way,' said George Botham, who was more interested in his position than in the final face of the moor, although he persuaded himself of the contrary. He, after all, lived between the two moors, and regarded the moor itself as a gigantic playground for summer tourists who, by and large, thought all houses pretty as long as they had thatch.

'When was the thatch taken off Scarhill?' he asked.

'About ten years before the Merlins bought it, so I'm told. It was a great collector of rats, I believe.'

John Graves coughed. They all sat suitably silent for a moment as though commemorating the rat-covered thatch.

'I like Scarhill's slate,' said Sophie surprisingly and to Alec's relief.

Then Jude came in. He greeted them all and stood leaning against the stove. Alec was not particularly pleased to see him; Jude felt to him like trouble.

'Did you want anything?' Alec enquired.

'Just to tell you your new fence they've put up round Scardon has been cut.'

'Cut? How do you mean?'

'Someone's taken wire clippers and cut it through in about eight places.'

Alec looked at George Botham as though he must be able to throw light on Jude's announcement.

'Local people, I imagine,' said George, who lacked imagination under pressure if not altogether. 'Villagers, no doubt.' He made them sound like the rats.

'Oh God,' said Sophie, 'I knew it would cause trouble.'

Alec folded the plans up. 'I think we'll call it a day,' he said. 'I'll go up and have a look.'

Jude kept his silence. The Deneuves argued but never rowed in front of other people; they maintained some kind of united front, which was probably to their credit. Nevertheless Jude's face expressed a kind of complacent satisfaction that Alec found intensely aggravating.

'I don't know if you want to come with me, Sophie,' he said. 'I'll take the Land Rover up there now.'

Sophie hesitated. 'No,' she said, 'I think I'll stay here. I've got to make a salad.' Alec concealed his irritation; he knew that the real reason was that she wanted to talk to Jude.

'Do you want to see the damage? George? John?' He looked hopefully at both. But John Graves excused himself, said he wanted to take some further measurements before returning to London, and George Botham had an appointment the other side of Meridan where a barn was being converted.

As soon as they had left and Alec had gone up to inspect the fence, Sophie turned to Jude. 'Is Astra coming over today?'

'No,' said Jude in a tone that told Sophie a great deal. He settled himself on the windowseat and gazed up at the moor.

Sophie pushed cabbage down the Magimix. After a few moments she asked him what was the matter?

'Oh, nothing.' Jude continued to stare into space.

'Yes there is. Tell me.'

'It's no good,' he said at last. 'It doesn't work – Astra and I.'

'Why not, do you think?' She sensed he wanted to talk about it.

He shrugged. 'She doesn't like me enough, I suppose.'

Sophie said in a placating fashion, 'She's very young. She probably doesn't know quite what she wants.' But to herself she thought, she's not young: not in emotions, only in years. Jude's the one who's young. She looked at his almost feminine

112

face beneath his mass of curly hair, his obstinate but sensitive mouth, and something in herself quickened. The whole side of her that Alec shut out quickened and responded to Jude. She felt tears of sympathy prick the backs of her eyes for his unhappiness, she longed to take his head against her body and stroke it. Instead she said, 'She may change – it may just be a bad patch.'

Jude didn't answer. He watched Sophie lick her fingers free of coleslaw with concentrated deliberation.

'I'm going back to the Mill,' he said, and Sophie knew he was telling her this in case Astra came or rang.

'Surely you'll stay to lunch?'

'No thank you. I only came out to tell my father about the fence – it's only what he deserved.'

'He has every right to fence it,' Sophie said staunchly but without conviction.

'Every right – every right,' mocked Jude. 'If everyone did the things they had a right to do where would we be? You put us back in the era of landlords exerting rights over tenants' lives.'

'That's unfair.' Sophie hated being mocked. 'It's not at all a parallel.'

'I think it is.' Jude was nearly at the door.

'Don't go, Jude.'

'I must.' The door closed.

Sophie sniffed. She wiped her nose with the back of her wrist. Everyone seemed so miserable somehow, and she wasn't even sure her own life was going the right way. She and Alec seemed to be much less close than they had been, much less in sympathy since they'd come out to the country. In the country, though everyone knew everyone and outwardly there was more community, under the surface you were isolated, shut up alone in the nucleus of the family. Families lived and fought tragedies that the rest of the neighbourhood never heard about unless violence resulted. Then it came out in the local paper:

Sophie shuddered. In London you could get out, see other people, go to classes, even. There was always *someone* you could ring up, but here it always entailed driving and was much more difficult; people looked at you oddly if you began talking about emotions, they were mainly occupied with more basic problems of birth and survival. Not for the first time she began to have serious doubts as to whether they had made the right choice.

It was late afternoon when Astra went to the Mill for the first time. Since her refusal to live with Jude three weeks had passed, during which time they had hardly seen each other. Jude had seldom emerged from the Mill except for occasional visits to Sophie at Scarhill, and long and lonely moor walks. Astra had sat day after day reading in the windowseat, too proud to contact Jude yet longing every day to hear from him. And as the days passed and still Jude didn't come, her bitten-to-the-quick nails and short temper with Benjy testified to her interest in Jude being greater than she had at first supposed. Or else it was just extremely agreeable being loved, she thought guiltily, as she climbed over the threshold of the pass door, set in the massive mill door, and went up the rickety wooden stairs.

Jude was lying on the floor on his stomach with books all around him. The Mill didn't have proper windows, only narrow slits in the stonework filled in by glass. Through these came shafts of sunlight full of dancing dust, the motes rising and falling unaccountably, each a minute particle of shifting, glittering gold. When Jude had nothing better to do he lay and watched them. Their action seemed to him random, their movement whims of a breath of air; once outside the beam of

114

sun they vanished. Like our lives, he thought. In the stripe of sun where it met the floor he had placed his book to see better.

There was no ceiling to the chapel-shaped interior, the walls, fortified by vertical buttresses, reached to the curved ties where old swallows' nests balanced; beneath each was a heap of droppings. Heat built up from the sun beating on the slate roof, but generally the Mill was a cold place with a bare aspect, Jude's furnishings being minimal. Three orange crates tacked together over which he had stapled a piece of blue material, served as shelves; jackets, jerseys and other of his clothes hung on pegs fixed to a rudimentary board on the wall. Where Jude lay there was a carpet but most of the floor consisted of rough bare boards. Under a light that dangled from a heavy black flex was a table with more books spread on it, and two chairs; against the wall stood a divan with an Indian rug and some cushions.

'Where is the water?' Astra asked for it was a continuous sound, loud when listened to but fading when forgotten.

'It runs directly underneath.' Jude lay on his back, arms beneath his head, looking up at her. Astra, he thought, looked more perfect, more like a dark-haired Eve than on any previous occasion. In the muted light of the barn her lips seemed slightly thicker, her cheeks more subtly rounded. 'I'll show you the stream and the wheel when we go out,' he said.

He crossed his legs and stood up in one movement, plugged in an electric kettle to a large all-purpose plug on the wall, and sniffed a bottle of milk.

'No fridge – I keep a crate down in the water but this one got left out. It's all right – just.' He sniffed again.

Astra sat on his bed while he made tea. She noticed a trunk where she supposed he kept more of his possessions; there was also an electric ring and toaster.

'Do you like it here?' she asked.

'Yes – it's better.'

'Better than Scarhill?'

'Better than being with my family.'

'Don't you think you'll ever get on with them?'

'No.'

The kettle boiled. Jude systematically measured three tea-spoonfuls into a metal pot, which he filled with the boiling water. 'I feel pinioned, inhibited – spaceless,' he went on. 'I'm much better off here. I can begin to find out which are my own thoughts and which those conditioned by my family.'

'Yes,' agreed Astra uncertainly. She thought about it while he handed her tea in a Chinese bowl and set a packet of biscuits between them. She felt content on his carpet in the shaft of sun with the swallows twittering down the far end and the sound of the water; a sort of timelessness. She thought she would like to sit there for ever clutching her Chinese bowl and talking.

'I don't feel like you, not with my mother and Benjy,' she said finally, the thought having floated away and come back to her.

'Obviously not; your mother is not dominant, not always trying to impose her will on others, like Alec does.'

'She *is* quite dominant.'

'No,' said Jude who apparently knew best, 'she's committed to her painting, she's not unduly concerned with you and Benjy. You can get on with your own lives.'

'Perhaps,' said Astra doubtfully. Then, 'I like Sophie.'

'Yes.'

There was a pause in which a swallow dived low and a dropping splattered the floor, narrowly missing the carpet. Both surveyed the impending danger without comment. Deeper thoughts occupied them.

'All the same, she supports Alec, she has to, which is aggravating because half the time you don't feel she's saying what she thinks.' Jude frowned as he spoke.

'I do – when she talks to me. Perhaps she's different with you.'

'Probably,' said Jude airily. Jude, Astra decided, was very certain of knowing all about other people.

'Your father doesn't seem all *that* dominant,' she said.

Jude sat down cross-legged on the carpet in front of her. He took a cigarette, held out the packet. Astra shook her head.

'Not appearing to be is part of his cleverness.' Jude could hardly contain his contempt. 'He's dominant *and* clever. It's a terrible combination – he's a very undesirable man.'

They sipped their tea, silently considering Alec's undesirability. Astra decided Jude more honest than she was – or more intolerant.

'Thank God my mother went off,' he said suddenly. 'I don't blame her a bit.'

Astra was sure he meant the opposite. She felt uncomfortable. 'Are you and Scarlet close?' she asked. 'You seem a lot different.'

'Not really. Scarlet's Daddy's girl. Bound to be.'

'Why "bound to be"?'

'She's like my mother. Exactly.'

'But he married Sophie and she's nothing like Scarlet.'

'It won't last.'

'But that'll be awful. I mean Sophie's sort of . . . special.'

'That's why it won't last.'

Astra felt she was seeing an entirely new side of Jude, quite different to the Jude of the walk and party, or the Jude she had seen at rehearsals and at odd times since. Was this then, the part she had sensed, the part she had recoiled from? Most of what he said was true enough but somehow so full of hate. It frightened her. And as she sat there a feeling of sickness she had noticed in the last few days invaded her, and with it dread. What was left of her contentment vanished.

'Jude – do you think I could be pregnant?'

'I shouldn't have thought so,' he said calmly, taking another biscuit and offering her one. Astra declined.

'But I could be, couldn't I?' she persisted. 'That first time – before we started being careful.'

'You could – but it's very unlikely.'

Astra felt comforted. It seemed the sickness had gone away again, that she had been imagining it. She slid from the divan to the floor and when Jude started to make love to her she didn't stop him; she didn't want to hurt him and cause the inevitable scene. And she did like being with him very much but at the same time half despised herself for giving way, for her lack of honesty. She flushed at the memory of Gabe Fardon and quickly buried it. But undoubtedly it had clarified what before she had only felt – that she was capable of a much more passionate response than Jude was able to arouse. She even began to see it would be quite possible to spend your whole life living out feelings that weren't genuine at all . . .

When it was over and they lay with their bodies close and their souls far apart, her face felt sore where his unshaven face had scratched it. She supposed shaving wasn't very easy at the Mill. She sat up on the edge of the divan and the sick feeling came back; to get rid of it she stood up and walked round looking at things, but it didn't go away.

'I think I *am* pregnant,' she said.

'You could ask your mother,' he suggested.

'No.' Astra was definite: 'if anyone can tell one way or the other, it's me. I'll get one of those home-test kits.'

'I don't think you can be,' Jude repeated obstinately, going on the principle that what you believe makes things true. So they went out and looked round the Mill from outside and the sickness went away so that Astra forgot about it – or, to be more exact, assured herself she had been imagining it.

Kate was painting the down in front of Scarhill as she remembered it. She would paint the bracken as slabs of sienna against the black shape of hill – or what had been hill. Ochre would lighten the umber, raise areas of it, bring it towards her. The birch trunks would be white dragged across the black she had already laid in; she exulted in the thickness of the paint, its cleanness and clarity. Why couldn't painting always be like this, so . . . so direct. To use oils, as she had been lately, was probably the answer.

Half an hour later she laid down her brush and went to the furthest corner of her studio, then looked back at her canvas. Slowly her exhilaration vanished. She bit her lip. Why it was nothing, absolutely nothing! All her feelings about colour and intensity had been an illusion; she could see now the colours were hard and did not work together, it had no depth, no real quality, it was slight, even meretricious.

Kate sat on her wood chair and continued to stare at her painting for a further fifteen minutes. Then she sighed, got up, advanced on it and grasping her palette knife, expertly removed all the thick and luscious paint on to an old slate. She then dipped a rag in white spirit, and scrubbed her canvas vigorously. After this she once again stepped back. What she saw pleased her a great deal more: it was hazy and indistinct; soft colour merged into colour. There were marks on her knife dragged across the paint in her effort to remove it that suggested to her imagination what course to take. She hummed a little, moved closer to her canvas, cleaned her palette and squeezed out fat caterpillars of fresh colour.

Gradually her painting began to grow. She was just getting into it when there came a knock on the door. Kate swore. Why now? Why just when she was really painting? She should have a studio hidden away, a barn in the woods; never, never should she paint where she could be found. She would keep on, ignore the knock, the person would go away. But the knock came twice more and Kate, her concentration gone, flung her brush down and hurried along the passage. She pulled open the heavy front door and was confronted by Gabe Fardon.

'Gabe,' she said in surprise, 'Come in.'

Gabe came. He wiped his boots carefully on the mat and followed her into the dining room, where she left him and went to the kitchen. She put the kettle on to boil, nursing her frustration over her abandoned painting, persuading herself of the importance of personal contact with her neighbours. Minutes later she returned to the dining room with two mugs of coffee. She sat at the table and Gabe sat on the windowseat, his back to the light, his face in darkness. He noticed the paint on her arm.

'Painting?'

'Yes,' said Kate. She enquired after Lucy and Eddie and waited patiently for Gabe to tell her in his own good time exactly why he was there, and eventually, after a second cup of coffee and a discussion of the Deneuves' proposed lake now postponed till the ground was drier the following summer, he did.

'That pony of Carol Granger's – the one Benjy rode – the one was hers,' he looked at Kate to make sure she was following him, 'laid down in its stable and died.'

'Oh God,' said Kate, 'how awful. Why?'

'That's just it.' Gabe folded his arms and leant back, he felt better now the subject he'd come about had been introduced. 'She doesn't know. She's going to send it down to Bill Shaw's for a h'autopsy – have it opened up.'

'Oh dear,' said Kate.

'Trouble is,' Gabe went on, 'she's holding me responsible. Says it was poisoning from the cut.'

'After all this time?' Kate frowned her disbelief. 'And you had the vet.'

There fell a long silence.

'So what you mean,' Kate said carefully, 'is that I should take over the responsibility.'

'No,' Gabe looked injured, 'but if it comes to paying, Lucy and I thought maybe you could help out, like. Depends what they find.'

Through Kate's mind flashed the thought that Carol might have a reason for getting back at Gabe, and that Gabe had more than a reason for getting back at herself. She pushed her hair back from her temples with a nervous gesture. The pony must be worth £120 and where was she to find it? Her overdraft at the bank had already reached the allowed limit and no more substantial settlement could be expected until after the divorce. Her only direct source of income at present was Donald's monthly cheque providing for Astra and Benjy.

Kate felt herself grow hot, she eased her jersey away from her neck. She felt thankful she had a backlog of canvases and stretchers, otherwise even painting would have become a problem; how she could ever have thought of moving the hedge she couldn't imagine. She began to see with depressing clarity why divorce was not, even in the 1980s, to be taken lightly. Either you had to be poor enough to get Legal Aid or rich enough for costs to be immaterial; to be in between, she could see, was a disaster. I could sell some paintings, she thought, have an exhibition, sell at low but realistic prices. But would anyone be prepared to pay for abstract impressionist paintings of the moor? They wanted landscapes with wild ponies and tors in the background – what they saw. She painted what she saw until it became transposed into something else – pure painting, she liked to think, though sometimes doubted. Kate heard herself saying 'You can have that one and that one, but I couldn't part with the blue jug – yes, that's what it was in the beginning – it's my favourite.'

She looked across at Gabe. 'Of course,' she said, 'if Carol feels that unfortunate ride was the cause, I'll pay.'

Gabe was plainly relieved. They sat opposite each other drinking tea and talking of this and that now the pony business was over, and grew quite mellow and happy in each other's company. Right at the end when Gabe got up to leave, Kate boldly asked if he was renting his fields to Carol Granger this winter for her ponies, and Gabe replied that he wasn't. At which news Kate guessed that she had been right, that the affair – or whatever it was – between Carol and Gabe Fardon was dwindling and that she was the pig-in-the-middle taking the brunt of the final vindictive swipe of a woman scorned. Mind you, she didn't really blame Carol; she simply wondered in a mildly inebriated fashion who Gabe would turn his attentions on next, for Lucy, as the village explained, was wrapped up in her home. Which translated into fact meant she was the one left there to look after it.

After she had shut the door behind Gabe, Kate rang Sophie; Sophie had once said that she would like to buy a painting. But the telephone rang and rang and there was no reply, and by the time Kate replaced the receiver her courage had failed.

*

Sophie's days were hectic with last-minute rehearsals. She was also extremely nervous. The entire pantomine succeeded or failed on the strength of her singing, or so it seemed to her, for she was in almost every scene. In fact she sang like a nightingale; her voice floated up and up into the steel rafters of the modern Parish Hall and all the village could hear her practising when they passed. The rector thumped the piano and encouraged her and Sophie struggled to higher and higher notes and held them longer.

If Sophie lacked confidence in her ability to hold an audience, the rector certainly did not – he was happier than he had been in years. He was Pygmalion and Sophie his perfect projection. He had worshipped her from the first; now he both dominated and manipulated her. When she stood up on the stage and sang as he told her to, she became his own frustrated self transposed into a thing of exquisite beauty. He pushed his white fingers over the notes, landing unashamedly on chords that made the tuneful wince, while Sophie's voice wobbled in doubt before miraculously reasserting itself and continuing along its own unsullied path. And Jude, who made an excellent prince in looks if not in voice, was to play opposite her and be, as it were, her prop.

With considerable difficulty Lucy Fardon had been bribed to lead the chorus by learning Rapunzel's part as well as Sophie. The village shook their heads. Though no one actually said so, it was clear that what had set out to be a community pantomime had become almost exclusively middle class. Had Lucy Fardon been given the lead role, others of the indigenous population might have come forward; as it was, they remained in their isolated farms and smallholdings tucked away in the surrounding valleys, and fulminated. Those, they claimed, who had come from up country only a few years ago, now considered themselves local and ran the village. In fact Eddie Fardon, when asked to be part of the chorus, had spat on the ground and said, 'You wouldn't catch me, Jesus no' – which had put the rector's back up and very well expressed the feelings of the villagers.

Astra's part was very small, but she was glad. She was rather afraid of acting and her voice didn't carry; it also meant to her relief that she hadn't had to see much of Oliver Upton. Her most important role was probably that of boosting Sophie's confidence, and it was during rehearsals that she got to know and like her; in fact, considering the eleven years' difference in their age they got on remarkably well. Sophie was fun, young and unshockable; Sophie had no expectations of Astra; Sophie was sophisticated and knew her way around, so it was not altogether surprising when Astra decided to confide in her rather than her mother.

It came about one day at Scarhill when together they were wriggling themselves into tight costumes with difficult access and giggling at themselves in Sophie's free-standing mirror. Its tilt reflected their backs in another mirror opposite, giving Astra, by the fantasy of the situation, a new sense of equality; it was as she peeled her red chorus dress over her head and laid it on Sophie's bed that she said with studied casualness, 'I think I'm pregnant.' She found it difficult to say even to Sophie, but felt a great relief when she had said it.

Sophie pulled her white dress dotted with stuck-on sequins over her head and hung it on a hanger. She was frankly horrified but took care not to show it. She said carefully, 'Will you have an abortion?'

'I suppose.' Astra was fingering a feather fan Sophie used in the last act.

'You could probably have it sucked out if its early enough.'

'I think I've let it go too long.' Astra's voice was flat, without emotion. 'But I don't really want a baby at fifteen, do I?'

'Of course you don't,' said Sophie. 'It'd be madness. Abortions aren't the problem they used to be. How many weeks over do you think you are?'

'Nine' said Astra, 'at least I think so.'

Sophie had spoken with more authority than she felt. She herself had one of those magic rings inserted that didn't worry her and seemed to do the trick. It was pure gold, not plastic, but Alec had paid willingly enough; she did often wonder uneasily if she would end up with cancer of the womb, but there you are – everything to do with sex in a woman's life is a risk. She felt responsible for Astra. She touched her arm gently, 'Don't worry,' she said, 'we'll do something.' She kissed Astra's temple. Astra smiled a desperate, bleak smile.

'I'd prefer not to tell my mother,' she said. 'It'll worry her to death with the divorce coming up – but I suppose I shall have to.'

Sophie looked at her sympathetically. 'I'll ring up someone I know in London, a doctor friend, and ask how to set about it. Unless, of course, you want to go to your own doctor.'

'No,' said Astra in alarm. 'No – I couldn't possibly do that.'

'I'll find out – I'll ring this evening.' Sophie squeezed Astra's shoulders. 'Don't worry,' she said, 'it's nothing to worry about, I promise you. I've got a friend who's had three abortions.' She didn't add that now the friend wanted a baby she didn't seem able to have one. She simply hung up another dress. 'I'll talk to Jude,' she said.

'No. I'd rather you didn't.'

Sophie hung the hanger over the door and looked round at Astra's sharp tone.

'Why?'

'I don't want Jude to have anything to do with it.'

Sophie was about to argue, but changed her mind. 'I won't say a word,' she promised.

After that they went downstairs and had coffee. They said nothing more about the abortion because, in a sense, Jude was between them, but Astra knew Sophie would do as she'd promised. Shortly after that she left.

As Astra pushed her bike up Muddicombe Lane she looked over at the well in crumbled, deserted Muddicombe Yard. Rumour had it that Lucy Fardon's great-aunt had drowned herself in it and the house had not been used for human habitation since but as a shelter for stock. Astra's despair increased as she passed it, and the beauty of the day, the yellowhammers hopping up the hedges singing continually, the foxgloves that nodded their newly opened heads on tall stalks set into the banks, did nothing to dissipate her misery. It wouldn't really matter if she died, she decided, it would all be so much easier, she wasn't much use to anyone and she was about to kill her own child which, according to a television programme she had seen recently, might even let out a cry . . .

She swallowed and forced herself to think of it as a tadpole in lots of blood, a late period. At the top of the hill she got on her bicycle and freewheeled down to Bag Down.

Sophie, left alone, bit off what was left of her fingernails, which wasn't much. Rehearsals had seen to that. Then she dialled an 071 number. When she got through she was told her doctor friend was in Cyprus for a month. She tried another, got an actress friend who she felt was bound to be up in such matters. But her friend told her she was awfully out of date on abortion, surely a family planning clinic would be the place to try. Why not her local one? Sophie felt frustrated at having accomplished nothing, for it was obvious she couldn't ring them till the following morning, so she rang Alec in London. He must have been out to dinner for there was no reply. She rang another friend, an ex-flatmate, who said firmly that she was quite the wrong person to have rung, abortions were still dangerous whatever the Press said, and she disapproved of them on principle.

How odd it is, Sophie thought, that something that sounds so easy when you read about it, seems so difficult in practice. She went to the kitchen and ate some sardines and cucumber and yoghurt, then she took her pantomime part to go over it, and was just going to bed when she had an idea. She rang Scarlet in London. Scarlet was in.

'Do you know much about straightforward, early abortions?' Sophie asked after a few moments of small talk.

There was a moment's silence before Scarlet said, 'It's Jude, isn't it? He's got Astra pregnant.'

'I'm not allowed to say,' said Sophie, which made it clear it was.

'For heaven's sake,' said Scarlet, 'tell him to go shoot himself. Doesn't he have *any* sense?'

Sophie said, 'Shut up, Scarlet.'

Scarlet was silent so that Sophie wondered if she'd hung up. She said, 'Hullo?'

'I'm still here.'

'Please help if you can,' Sophie felt desperate, 'the dress rehearsal's on Thursday.'

'Is it?' said Scarlet. 'Good luck.' She couldn't understand why Sophie of all people should be so worked up over a potty local pantomime. After a moment she said, 'What about the clinic in Allerston?'

'The council censored the last Monty Python film,' said Sophie. 'I doubt they'll be much help.'

Scarlet laughed. 'I'll see what I can fix this end,' she said. 'Tell Jude he's a low shit. Poor Astra.' And Sophie heard the receiver click. She put her own down slowly. On second thoughts she decided she wouldn't go to bed, she'd wash her hair.

At midday the following day, the telephone rang. It rang and rang until Astra finally answered.

'Are you alone?' Sophie asked.

'Yes.'

'It's all fixed. Scarlet has rung her clinic and they'll do it. They say how soon can you go up?'

'Is it one of those suck-outs?'

Sophie hesitated fractionally. 'No,' she said, 'you'll have to go in and have anaesthetic, they say, but you'll be out the next day.' There was a pause. 'I think you should tell Kate.'

'Yes.' Long pause. 'Thanks.'

'Let me know as soon as possible when you'll go and I'll ring Scarlet.'

'Yes,' Astra said again.

When she had put the receiver down, she sat for she didn't know how long wondering what to do. Her feelings for Jude were complex. All her sickness, her misery, was due to him and yet it didn't seem to her to be his fault. It didn't really seem her own either – it had simply happened, it was her body and she had to bear the consequences. It seemed to have an inevitability about it, as though she in some way deserved the situation she was in. She had acted and must suffer. What worried her most, and what she couldn't explain to anyone, was an intuitive certainty that she ought to have the baby and that an abortion was the coward's way out.

The previous night she had woken, dragged the crumpled sheet round her, lain staring into the darkness knowing that she must have it and determined on going through with it; in the morning, the cold light of reason had again taken over and she knew it was madness to saddle herself with a baby at sixteen. She was a modern girl who knew how to cope with her body if things went wrong – or so she persuaded herself. And yet that was not quite how she felt when on her own.

She mooned around the house in the few days before the dress rehearsal, keeping out of her mother's way as much as possible. Every time the telephone went she became very tense in case she had to make a decision. Now as she sat beside the ivory phone the only thing that became any clearer was her next move – she had to tell her mother. She felt dread at the idea, as well as the physical sickness she had come to accept like her shadow.

Her mother was in her studio not actually painting but sitting staring at a largish canvas that Astra hadn't seen before. When she entered through the french windows, Kate looked round.

'Sorry,' Astra said.

'It doesn't matter – I'm stuck anyway.'

'Can I talk to you?'

'Of course – why do you ask? Is it *that* momentous?'

'Yes. I'm pregnant.'

Kate stared, not at Astra, but through her. She didn't see her, she was seeing herself, guilty, horrified; seeing her own failure. She said as though to ward it off, 'You're not serious?'

'I am.'

Kate rose slowly, carefully. She crossed to her easel, took down her canvas and turned it to the wall. She was not quite sure why she did it, perhaps because it was a part of herself, perhaps because it might intervene with what was to come next. She then sat on a chair and Astra on an old trunk; both gazing at the unprepossessing back of the canvas which somehow embodied the ugliness of the predicament.

'How do you know?'

'I just do. I feel sick all the time. I'm sure. I've tried one of those home-kit testers and it was positive. I've missed just on three times.'

'Why ever didn't you tell me before?'

'I didn't think I could be.'

The silence was long and uncomfortable. Kate was adjusting herself to her one but worst dream.

Astra she saw as a black-haired china doll rising in the air in slow motion, cracking into fragments as though by an explosive force, descending, still in slow motion. At her feet lay fragments of her child's life. She must somehow face this new circumstance she had so blithely never believed could happen. It was true she had been against the contraceptive pill but Astra knew about every other method, she had made sure of that years back . . .

'What do you intend doing about it?' She kept all expression out of her voice.

'I'd thought I'd have it.' Astra hadn't known herself what she would answer until she heard herself telling her mother. She hadn't even been clear of her own intention. Or was it her mother's unspoken assumption like the rest that antagonised her, made her react as she did?

Kate only ever smoked in the studio; she said it helped her to distance herself from her work. She lit a cigarette now, inhaled before she spoke, looked at Astra intently. 'What does Jude think?' she asked.

Astra shrugged – as when she had talked to Sophie, she had no wish to include Jude. 'He imagines I'm going to have an abortion.'

'I bet he does.' Kate's lip curled in contempt. Her mother didn't really like men, Astra often thought. As a result men admired her but were mostly afraid of her. She was such a forceful, intense person even in her apparent vagueness. Astra resented her father for leaving her mother but thought she could understand him. He had not been strong enough for her; yet up until the separation her mother had always put his life before hers – or had she merely given the illusion of doing so?

'And if you don't want to, what then?'

Astra could feel her mother's gaze piercing her skin, shining the bright beam of her mind into all the corners that should have remained dark.

'We haven't discussed it.'

'Well you should do. Where is Jude now?'

'At the Mill, I expect' – meaning he had no telephone.

Kate sighed. 'What a mess.'

'Surely,' Astra said hopefully, 'it's nothing these days. I mean everyone has a baby when they feel like it. Unmarried mothers are perfectly acceptable – feminists respect them more.'

'For God's sake, Astra,' Kate lit a further cigarette. 'Has Carol been getting at you?'

'No.' Astra felt resentful of the suggestion. 'She doesn't know anything about it. No one does except Jude and Sophie – and now you.' There was a world of accusation in her final words.

Kate got up and went across to the windows, looked out. Astra could see how worked up she was by the quiver of her hands, the way she smoked. Set against her mother she felt the fragility of her own conviction. Kate came back and sat down again.

'You don't understand,' she said, 'it's not a question of what is or isn't acceptable. I'm not concerned with that. What I am concerned with is your life – and of course the child's – *if* you have it. What you don't and can't understand – no one can till it happens to them – is once you've got a child you're

129

bonded to it. You'll never know the person you are, could become, if you don't spend a period of your life without being attached to someone or another. You'll slide from child to adult without ever knowing your potential. Oh I know most of us never realise anything, but it's better to have a glimpse and not realise than go through life as a slave to the reproductive urge.' She stabbed out her butt viciously. 'That's what a child does to you because you love it more than yourself, you can't help it. And in my opinion that's not a good thing, it's not in keeping with being a thinking person, it's simply to preserve the species. Yet it's so strong that if you oppose it you can never be happy – you walk round for the rest of your life bearing your guilt. Men,' she said, again with a hint of contempt, 'know nothing about it.' She stared at Astra with a curious impersonal intensity, a lack of emotional display that Astra felt grateful for. 'Go and talk to Jude,' she finished.

'I don't really want to.'

'Why not?'

'I don't love him.'

Kate gave a gesture of impatience. 'Whether you love him or not is not the point. The two of you are about to produce a further life. Is it a good idea? Surely you can see that's what you should be considering.'

'I can't see Jude's got much to do with it – it'll be my child.'

'*And* his.'

Astra said nothing. She couldn't really see it would be. It was her body that would grow it, and she who would care for it. It seemed to her slightly unnecessary to enmesh Jude in what she felt to be entirely her decision, she was sure nothing Jude could say would make any difference. She said as much to her mother.

'You certainly think differently to my generation,' was Kate's comment. To which Astra agreed. They seemed to have reached an unfruitful impasse. But Kate had, in a subtle manner, weakened Astra's new-found resolve. She felt her mother's strength, her will. Though she never imposed, never forced, it was difficult, immensely difficult, not to be carried along by her; it was the insidious way it happened that was frightening.

'All right,' said Astra dully, 'I'll go and see Jude.'

'I should.'

Then impulsively Kate stretched out her hand and drew Astra to her. Astra cried with her head against Kate's chest for Kate was taller than she was. When she looked up she saw tears had been running down her mother's face.

'Don't worry,' Kate said, kissing her hair. 'Whatever you decide will be for the best. I'm sure of that. You mustn't let me influence you.'

'I know.' But try as she might Astra could not sort out her own wishes from those of her mother.

Conveniently in time for tea, Alec nosed down the steep drive and into Scarhill yard exactly three hours after leaving his London office. He stepped into a dry and perfect afternoon – an Indian summer that amounted almost to drought – and was greeted effusively by Sophie who had been feeling rather lonely on her own in the house that even the builders seemed to have abandoned. So to cover her lack of self-sufficiency she babbled on to Alec about minor happenings while pouring him tea.

They sat opposite each other across the kitchen table and professed pleasure in having the house to themselves – which was more bravado than genuine because Sophie liked friends. Real friends. Not the kind that used you as an hotel. She had already discovered Scarhill made the ideal stop-over for friends 'breaking' their journey to Cornwall – usually with a nanny and four undesirable children who trampled with footballs and cricket bats over the few brave flowers that poked up their heads amongst the builders' boards, and which Sophie loved all the more for their scarcity.

'Well?' Alec put his cup on the sink for someone else to wash up and settled himself on the windowseat. 'Any more news?'

Sophie glanced at the clock and toyed with the idea of

telling Alec about Astra being pregnant. But she knew the row it would cause, and if Jude was to get through the dress rehearsal that evening it seemed better to wait; that he was her partner possibly influenced Sophie as well. Instead she said, 'The builders have gone.'

'Gone?'

'They've taken out all the windows in the old kitchen and gone. I don't think they're very reliable. I keep ringing them up but it's only Greyman's wife that answers and she says he's been called away on an emergency job the other side of Alsington.'

Alec went through to the old kitchen and stood surveying the demolition. Sophie followed behind. Heaps of old plaster, laths, slates, old windows and new frames, all were blended together in a thick layer of white dust. A jaunty American army cap crowned a stepladder; dust gave it the appearance of having been iced. The rafters were exposed up to the roof.

'Rather fine, isn't it?' said Sophie nervously. She could feel Alec's rage.

'They were due to finish ten days ago. You mean to say they've gone away and left it like this?' Alec could hardly believe it, it was an insult.

'Yes.'

'We must get rid of them. Get someone small and local who cares about his job.'

'But Alec,' implored Sophie, 'that's what I wanted to do in the first place. It's what Kate Merlin suggested. It was you who wanted the place gutted and got on with by a proper firm.'

'How is it you keep ringing Greyman's wife and not the office?'

'The office number is out of order. Actually I think they've had it cut off. Perhaps they've gone into liquidation,' said Sophie hopefully.

'Hell,' said Alec, 'I'll ring him now.'

'You'll only get his wife,' said Sophie.

Greyman's wife was clearly one of those unpaid invaluable

assets without whom the business could not continue, her job being that of buffer between Greyman and all his dissatisfied callers. She was polite and helpful and impenetrable. She took the same message down each morning as though she had never taken it before. Sophie had no doubt it was never given, or if given, ignored. The country, when it came to getting anything done, she decided, made London seem easy. There was always another firm to threaten with, to call in. But here every builder seemed permanently busy with a waiting list of three months.

She could hear Alec dialling vigorously through the door in the room that might one day resemble a study. She took a further glance at the gaping windows, the old stove, the refectory table covered by dust sheets stuck all over with lumps of pink plaster, and withdrew. If it rained she decided she would put a polythene sheet over the table. What more could she do? Alec had got Greyman's wife, she could hear by his polite voice and was impressed that this woman could quell even Alec in a rage. She heard him put down the receiver and dial again. She guessed it would be John Graves, but didn't wait to hear.

She found her handbag, got in the car – not Alec's but her own run-around Fiesta – and let the dust and no-windows blow out of her mind as she sped as fast as possible down the lanes to the Parish Hall. The rector breathed a sigh of relief as he saw Sophie, blonde hair disarrayed, step like a goddess from her vehicle. For a terrible moment he had thought she might not come. As she ran towards the entrance a gust of wind whipped the Parish Hall door free from its stop, propped open for the cast, and heavy spots of thunder-rain began to fall. Oh fuck, thought Sophie, the table. When I get back the kitchen'll be a lake. But the thunder blew over without dropping rain and the weather continued fine. In fact so fine that there was a water shortage and some of the farmers declared it a drought.

It was Astra and Jude who almost failed to turn up to the dress rehearsal. They simply forgot it. Astra had biked down to the Mill, or rather she had wheeled her bike down the steep lane that culminated in a watershoot of slabs of rock, dry now, but treacherously slippery in wet weather, and pushed it over the wooden footbridge. She hurried across, not stopping, as she usually did, to look down into the peat-brown pool beneath for the trout that always lay there, heads into the current, beating occasionally with their tails then drifting back, till another lazy beat would push them forward again. Instead she mounted her bike quickly and pedalled it along the flat valley until the tall ivy-covered Mill rose ahead of her. She propped her bicycle against the wall and pushed open the pass door cut.

'Jude,' she called, before going up the wooden steps. When she got no answer she went up. Jude was asleep, which immediately upset her. How could he sleep when she was in such turmoil? Some of her mother's bitterness rose up in her against men as she watched him stretch then slowly push himself up on his elbow.

'Aren't you coming to the rehearsal?' she asked – which was not at all why she had come.

'It isn't for an hour, is it?' Jude looked at both his watch and his clock as if to restore some order to time; he knew quite well why she had come. He had not fallen asleep from sloth, or insensitivity to the problem that presented itself; rather he had worn himself out considering the insuperable dilemma. The conclusion he had finally reached was, to his mind, the only satisfactory one, the only right one. Unless, of course, Astra wished to get rid of the foetus. Jude recoiled from the brutality of the statement but liked to put it to himself in such language so that he should understand exactly the proposition.

'I've talked to my mother,' Astra said abruptly, 'told her. She told me to talk to you some more.'

Jude sighed. 'Why do you have to do as your mother says? I'd much prefer it if you came to me because you chose to.'

'What does it matter? I've come.' Astra felt this was not the time for Jude to begin altering her. She twiddled a strand of hair nervously. Jude reached for her and pulled her against him, kissing her hair, her cheek, her eyelids; finally he tried for her mouth but she turned her face away and said almost impatiently, 'No, Jude. We've got to talk.'

'I've thought about it. I've been thinking all night. Why don't we get married – or live together if you prefer. Then you can have it.'

Astra looked at him bitterly. 'Don't you realise I'm still at school and you're in the middle of Oxford.'

'You could leave now and go back after to the Tech to do your A's. I'd have finished by then. I could look after it for you.'

'For *me*?' Astra was ironic.

'For us,' said Jude uncomfortably, realising his slip.

Astra's dark eyes stared at him till his own were forced to look away.

'Where would we live? What on?'

'In Oxford. I've got a bit of money and we'd get a child allowance. Thousands do it.'

'I know,' said Astra, 'but isn't it a bit crazy?'

Jude shrugged helplessly. 'I thought that's what you wanted,' he said. 'Last time you said you weren't going to have an abortion.'

Astra's lip quivered. 'You make it all sound so simple,' she said, 'and it's not. And I think it's the worst reason in the world for marrying.'

There was a long silence, during which Astra became aware of the solitary electronic call of a toad rising from beneath the Mill. At last she said, 'That's what I wanted to tell you. I'm not going to get committed to you just because I'm pregnant, but I think I may have it.' She shifted away from him as though the physical dissociation helped her decision.

'Where'll you live?'

'At home, I suppose.'

Jude's eyes narrowed. 'You mean you'll share it with your mother?'

'I don't know yet what I'll do.'

Jude edged forward, placed his hand over hers. She looked down at it without withdrawing her own.

'Astra, I love you. Really love you. Perhaps I didn't at first but I do now.'

'What help's that?' Astra withdrew her hand. 'Don't you see, you are trying to persuade me into something wrong – I don't want to start up a futile relationship that all my instinct tells me is wrong. What good would that do either of us, or the . . . the . . . baby.'

'Wrong? You keep using that word – as though all your world is black and white, right and wrong. What does wrong mean? Wrong in relation to what?'

Astra stared at him. 'Just wrong,' she said.

'Wrong isn't an absolute – it's always relative. It must be.'

Astra felt confused. 'I can only go by what I feel.'

'Why should you feel it about us?'

Astra felt the colour mounting to her face. 'Because I haven't been absolutely honest,' she finally admitted. 'I don't care for you as you do for me – I'm sure of it. If I did it would be different.' She looked at him tragically.

'You mean you can't?'

She picked with her finger at a small frayed hole in the knee of her jeans.

'I don't mind, Astra. It doesn't matter. Perhaps you're just not that sort of person,' said Jude, clutching at a straw of hope. But Astra made no move to indicate a bending of her will. If only she would allow him to touch her he felt everything would be much better, but Astra's ears, metaphorically speaking, were distinctly laid back.

Jude sat, knees apart, his head bowed between his shoulders. He felt himself descending into a chaos where the world around was black and monstrous, where despair and unreason predominated; without Astra he had no desire to live, no will of any sort.

Suddenly he saw with shocking clarity that all he had done in the last few months of the summer vacation, his move to the Mill, his reading, his writing, had all centred round Astra.

She made them possible. Small black and white dots danced in his brain; they formed into lines that were first smooth then violently zigzagged. He wiped his forehead and got up to make tea so that Astra couldn't see his expression; when he handed her the cup he avoided her eyes, when he sat he turned away from her in his 'thinker' position until she could bear it no longer.

'Jude. Talk to me. *Please*? I need to talk.'

Jude lifted and let fall his hands in a helpless gesture. He got up and walked about. Eventually he stopped in front of her. 'If you don't love me,' he said, 'then why have we come this far?'

But Astra was unable to explain that when they made love it was momentarily exciting and gave pleasure to her body, but that she gained none of the emotional satisfaction she craved, and that the gap between them, instead of closing through intimacy, widened. It was this that confused her, made her feel that one moment she loved Jude and the next was alienated from him, and that at times the sexual act disappointed and almost disgusted her. She said doggedly, 'I won't change – I know I won't.'

The zigzags and dots became more intense in Jude's brain. He thought he could perfectly understand people who killed the person they loved, and wondered for a moment if he shouldn't get his gun and shoot first Astra then himself. Instead he stood with his back to her while she washed her cup and glass in his bowl of soapy water and said dully, almost obstinately, 'I don't think it's a good idea for a child not to have a father, and I think it'll ruin your life.'

'That's for me to decide.'

'Yes.' Jude's desolation increased with every moment. He felt so far from Astra, and words only seemed to divide them further.

'I don't think we're getting anywhere,' he said.

'I'll go.' Astra moved towards the steps.

'To the rehearsal?'

Momentarily a look of consternation crossed her face. 'We've missed it,' she said.

'Only the beginning. We could still go.'

'All right,' she said fiercely, so that it seemed to Jude that missing the rehearsal was as much his fault as everything else. They went in Jude's car, both of them concealing their suffering like lead in the hem of a curtain.

Sophie was not actually having quite the evening she had hoped for. To start with, the dress Carol had contrived for her out of two other dresses didn't look right, but far worse had been Oliver Upton's apparent dissatisfaction with her performance. Sophie had enjoyed doing her part, thought her singing all right, and was congratulated by all except the rector, who insisted she stay on for further practice.

So she stood now beside the rector's piano in his living room, sighed, pushed her hair back, and said, 'I don't see what it is I'm doing wrong?' She glanced at the rector then quickly looked away. She had become increasingly conscious that his feelings for her were not quite normal. If it had been straightforward sex, she felt she could have dealt with it, but her instinct told her it was not. It was more . . . she hesitated looking for the word . . . not exactly perverse, but odd. It was as though he wanted to possess her, keep her, have power over her. She sang and he coaxed and forced, demanding always a little more and a little more. Sophie strove. She felt singing was about the only thing she could do and she wanted to do it well. She grew hot and flushed, and tried to avoid the burning, expectant, pale blue eyes of the rector.

It was over a sudden leap down from top A to B flat that he finally halted her. He walked round the room, looked out at the sky translucent from the sun that had just set and which was disturbed only by livid streaks of stormy cloud, stared for a few moments at this or looked inward to his mind, Sophie didn't know which, then came back to face her. This, Sophie had learnt, was the manner he adopted before saying something particularly belittling.

'You're a beginner,' he said, 'not a professional. You have an exquisite voice you don't know how to use.'

'I'm doing what I can,' said Sophie, almost in tears.

Oliver Upton turned to face her.

'I know you try hard,' he said, 'but you've got such a long way to go. You see I chose you, in preference to a reliable experienced singer like Lucy Fardon, for the freshness of your voice; but I had imagined we would cover more ground than we have towards giving it – your voice – the expertise it lacks. I repeat: we've still got a long way to go.'

Sophie flushed. She felt both angry and humiliated. He was a bully, she had realised that a long time back; he had kept a hold over her by continual hints that he could well use Lucy if Sophie did not come up to scratch. She should have walked out immediately, called his bluff, but though she had never allowed a single person to know, not even Alec, she did desperately want to sing the lead if only to prove to herself she could. So once again she pressed her lips together and determined to endure Oliver Upton for what she fervently hoped was her last rehearsal. It had to be – tomorrow was the performance.

'Is that all?' she asked rather abruptly. 'Can I go?'

'You think it's good enough?'

'No.' Sophie was confused. 'I mean, I don't think going over and over it will help. It'll either come on the night or it won't.'

'That is such an unprofessional attitude. A friend of mine who used to do amateur dramatics says that now he will only work with professionals and I can understand what he means. It's the difference in attitude.'

'I think that's terribly unfair of you,' said Sophie indignantly. 'No one could have worked harder than I have.'

'That's what you think, I know,' said Oliver Upton, his shrewd perception having long since told him Sophie was set on doing her part. 'You see, never having been a professional you don't know the standard they set themselves, the sheer work they put into a part like yours.'

Sophie picked up her handbag, but instead of leaving as she had intended, waited. She felt as trapped as a webbed butterfly.

'Don't,' said the rector, 'don't please let the performance tomorrow be spoilt by any suggestion of our problems in working together during the rehearsal period. It won't help you and it would be detrimental to our entire production, make a bad feeling. I can trust you over this, can't I?' He was facing her again.

'Yes,' said Sophie, feeling like a sulky child. But after the performance, she was thinking, I can say what I like. Then felt contemptuous of herself for her own spite. But why shouldn't she expose him, why should everyone believe him eccentric but kindly when in actuality he was a bully who harboured quite an evil nature? He came towards her and placed his hands on her shoulders, kissed her forehead. Sophie stood rigid. 'Good luck tomorrow,' he murmured, 'Very good luck.'

Sophie swallowed. She felt reduced to a puppet in his hands, even contaminated. It's my fault, she thought, I should have refused, insisted the part go to Lucy. And she tried to picture how Lucy would have dealt with Oliver Upton and realised, though only dimly for Sophie was no psychologist, that Lucy would have been all right. Oliver Upton would not have treated her in the same way; Lucy would not have waked in him the same aggression, the need to dominate as a substitute for sex. Sophie backed away from him, holding her music case in front of her as if for protection.

'I hope it'll go well,' she murmured as she slid into her car, sat looking down at her foot on the accelerator and hated Oliver Upton with a dull blind hate. She forced the mask of her face into an attempt at a smile, and drove straight out of his entrance. Only the violent scream of brakes of the baker's van brought her up sharp and trembling. The baker leant out of his window to shout at her but when he saw it was Mrs Deneuve his expression changed. Sophie saw it happen. How terrible, she thought, he's in the same relation to me as I have been to Oliver Upton. I buy his bread, so though I might have killed him, he still smiles. Are we all the same, all living in a great hierarchical power syndrome, all of us smiling only at the right people to get what we want? And she bit her lip with humiliation that she, who thought herself invincible in such matters, could have so easily been corrupted. To the baker she said, 'I'm most terribly sorry. I had something on my mind.'

'Never mind, Mrs Deneuve, we all do sometimes,' he said, cheerfully, 'but I should put your lights on though it isn't what you'd call dark. Better for the lanes.' And he drove off in his white van that itself looked like a bread loaf.

Back at Scarhill, Jude was waiting.

'I have to have a drink – a strong one.' Sophie flopped into the armchair in the kitchen. So absorbed was she in her own state that she didn't immediately notice that Jude was quite as tense as herself.

Jude did as he was told: poured whisky for Sophie and whisky for himself. Sophie drank and felt in some measure restored as the burning whisky slipped down her throat. She was also immensely pleased to see Jude. 'Shall we manage tomorrow, do you think?' she asked.

Jude, whose mind had been somewhere else, blinked. 'Of course,' he said, 'all you have to do is sing.' He laughed. Sophie laughed too. Rather loudly. She pushed her hair back off her forehead nervously. 'Thank God rehearsals are over.'

'Haven't you enjoyed them?'

She shook her head. 'They've got worse and worse – but I mustn't talk about them till it's over. I've promised myself I won't.'

Jude looked slightly mystified. As far as he was concerned the rector was a self-opinionated man of no musical ability who, like everyone, was slightly in love with his stepmother. For all Oliver Upton's theatrical inadequacies he saw him as completely harmless. In any case, what was uppermost in Jude's mind were his own problems. He was the one who needed a listener, even someone who would advise. His only anxiety was that his father might return and deprive him of Sophie's full attention.

'Where's my father?' he asked abruptly.

'Gone out to dinner with his partner.' Sophie lifted her legs up over the arm of the chair, settling herself more comfortably. She held out her glass.

'I say, ought you?' asked Jude, nevertheless refilling her glass. 'Don't forget tomorrow.'

'I've got to get through it somehow. This may be the only way.'

'You could do it on your head,' Jude said, comfortingly.

He stood by the window looking up at Scardon, across which a section of the new fence was plainly visible. 'Couldn't he have kept off the skyline?' he asked.

Sophie pulled herself up a little so that she too could see the line of Scardon with the fence and a low, lopsided moon just above it. 'It hardly shows,' she said. 'Be fair.'

'It's the mentality it represents. Have you been up there?' he asked.

'Yes.'

'So you've seen what he's done?'

'Yes.' Sophie flushed at Jude's incredulous tone.

'You mean you don't mind?' Scorn poured forth from Jude as for a few moments he forgot his own unhappiness. 'My father,' he went on, 'is entirely destroying this environment. Only my father could accomplish so much in such a short space of time. But then I suppose it was to be expected. He destroys everything given time, doesn't he?'

'Jude,' said Sophie, 'if you've just come here to slang Alec I'd rather you went.'

He turned on her then. 'You slang him yourself to yourself, you know it. I say aloud what you're thinking. That's why it's so offensive to you.'

Sophie was rather startled by his perceptiveness. 'That's not true,' she hotly denied. 'I don't agree with a lot Alec does, but I don't kick him on principle like you do.' She paused, watching Jude. His whole body was taut, she could feel a positive vibration in the room from whatever emotion he was containing. 'What is it?' She began to feel anxious.

He put his empty glass down, walked restlessly round the table, up and down before the sink where the washing-up, Sophie noticed, was as usual not done.

'Where's Astra?' she asked, her mind making the logical jump.

'God knows.'

Sophie felt powerless to contact Jude when he was in this sort of mood, which she was familiar with and which she recognised as self-hatred. She yawned. 'I think I'll go up,' she said.

'Don't.'

It was a command. Sophie felt his urgency and stayed where she was, champing up the ice in the bottom of the glass.

'I'm thinking of going back to Oxford early.'

'But you've only just moved into the Mill.'

'I think I ought to get right away from here.'

'Is it Astra? Have you had a row?'

Jude made a helpless gesture of impatience. 'Not just a row. We've separated – more or less.'

'She's still at school . . .'

'For God's sake,' Jude shouted at her, slamming his fist down on the table. Sophie jumped. She felt startled and rather annoyed. She couldn't see that he had any right to come here and shout at her. They remained in a disagreeable silence for some moments. Sophie asked at last, 'When is she going up for the abortion?'

'She is not – that's the whole point.'

'Not?'

'She's not going to have it terminated. She wants to have it.'

Out of the now almost complete darkness in the room, lit only by the moon as neither of them cared to switch on a light, Sophie asked tentatively, expecting to be shouted at, 'Will you . . . get married – or just live together?'

'She won't.'

'Won't what?'

'Won't do either.'

Sophie thought of all the things she could say but said none of them. It seemed better not to. She waited a few moments, then said, 'Is she sure? I mean, don't you think she'll change her mind?'

'No.'

'What about Kate? Can't she persuade her?'

'I hope not.'

'What do you mean?' Sophie frowned.

'I mean it's time Astra made a genuine decision for herself. That's the trouble. I half suspect this is an act of defiance against her mother instead of a thought-out decision.'

'Oh.' Sophie tried to absorb complexities that were not a part of her own nature. 'Is yours a thought-out decision?' she asked.

'It's the only one.'

'Hardly,' said Sophie, 'or it wouldn't necessitate making one.'

'One what?'

'A decision.'

'You mean it's practical for her to have a baby at fifteen?'

'I didn't say it was practical.'

'But you can see that she could?'

Sophie thought, 'Yes – of course she *could*.'

'Well she's going to.'

'So you've said.'

Jude walked round the kitchen, paused by the ceramic hot-plate and switched the knob on and off several times absently, then came to rest on the windowseat.

'There's no way out, is there?' he said at last.

'There never is,' said Sophie philosophically, 'only ways through.'

'I'm the most selfish fool on earth – I've ruined her life.'

Jude's self-pity made Sophie uncomfortable.

'Oh shut up,' she said. 'It's not necessarily true and anyway, kicking yourself won't help.'

'Should I try to persuade her against it?'

With a feeling almost of shock Sophie realised she was being asked to give her opinion on a momentous matter, a matter of life and death. The whole issue assumed a different proportion, became real, ceased to be a matter of clinics and posters up on the side of the Underground, became another life growing inside Astra. She thought of her advice, the 'help' she had offered, and felt herself flush with shame. And yet still it seemed the answer because in an overpopulated world what was the point in an unwanted child?

'What would you do if you were her?'

'Not have it,' said Sophie decidedly, 'but then I'm quite a shallow person, I don't think deeply about things.'

Jude thought his father undeservedly lucky.

'I don't think you're shallow,' he said.

Sophie sighed. 'You look worn out – why don't you sleep here? I'm going up.' She stood, swaying a little. She had had nothing to eat and the whisky had taken effect. 'Help yourself from the fridge if you're hungry,' she said.

She heard Jude move across the room behind her, it appeared he was coming up too. She wondered vaguely which bed he would sleep in, but it didn't seem to matter. She stepped down into her and Alec's room and flung herself on the king-size bed, her head in the wonderfully soft down pillows. A moment later Jude lay down beside her.

'Jude,' she murmured, turning on her side. She drew his head against her, stroked it, kissed his hair, 'Oh Jude,' she sighed.

'She doesn't love me.' He got it out at last, and with it came the alarming muted sobs that shook his body so that the bed itself shuddered. And Sophie clutched him against her, covered him in kisses while her tears joined his and the pillows grew damp to the touch. What else could she have done? His unhappiness struck a chord in her, impinged on her own. Her tears continued to well up from a mutual shared misery that like some subterranean lake lay just under the surface of the entire world.

Kate had been out to see a friend and returned late. Well, late enough. To be exact it was about a quarter to eleven. She felt worked up to an extreme over Astra and had gone out to try to divert her thoughts. In this she had failed, so that now she went along to her studio for solace, but found none, for in the hard electric light her canvases appeared lifeless and jaded. She switched off the light quickly to shut out their disturbing image and walked straight through and out on to the cobbles. There at least she could breathe, calm, herself by the stars . . . She started involuntarily: someone was coming up the yard towards her. Astra?

Kate felt a shiver of apprehension run through her though she could not have said why. She waited. Astra, for indeed it was she, came closer then stopped. Kate could not see her face at all, only her shape, but she sensed that something momentous was happening or had already happened. She hesitated, uncertain what to say, aware of the great spire-like shapes of the dark cedars forming a wind-break for the buildings against the lighter sky. Thank God the thunder had come to nothing . . .

'Astra? Are you all right?'

'Yes' – but Kate knew she wasn't. She wished she could see Astra's face. 'Benjy's in. He's in bed.' Kate announced this commonplace to fill the silence, but listening realised they were surrounded by noise. All the ground seemed full of minute cracklings as though life itself was stirring. She wanted to touch Astra but something in her reticence, her stance, prevented her. She felt worried. Where had she been all day? She was only fifteen and with child, but soon all that would be put right, sorted out. At this stage, so early on, it should all be easy. Even the cervix would not have to be dilated, only a suction tube inserted through the neck of the womb. Kate had read about it often enough in the Sunday papers and magazines. The main thing was not to delay getting on with it. She would ring her own gynaecologist, get something fixed just as soon as Astra could be persuaded to make up her mind. She would probably have to go privately if it was to be done immediately but it couldn't be *that* much for something quick and easy with no anaesthetic ... She stopped herself, shocked by the triviality, the triteness of her own thoughts.

Astra made to pass her. 'Astra,' she said, again.

'I'm going in.'

'Are you all right?'

'Yes – of course.'

'You're not.' She reached out a hand.

'Oh do go away.' Astra turned into the house. An owl hooted from the cedars, it startled Kate, seemed almost to speak to her. She followed Astra in, switched on a wall light and slithered along the bench behind the table, her back to the wall. Astra had gone up without saying goodnight.

Kate sat gazing at the few remaining red embers in the fire, smoothing her hair back from her forehead with a repetitive nervous gesture. She felt humiliated by her lack of certainty, ashamed of her own inadequacy. One simply did not know how to help, what pressures to bring to bear, if any at all. Should she simply keep right out of it? When someone young, someone vulnerable, someone you love more than yourself turns to you for advice, should you withdraw like a snail into your shell? Or if not, what do? Kate felt herself wholly at a loss. Every instinct in her encouraged her to go to Astra, put her arms round her as she had when Astra was a child, offer to absorb her in her own strength, relieve her from the onerous task of making an impossible decision. Why not? From her experience she could see more clearly the course of events, detect the consequences of a move like a skilled chess player. All this and more passed through her mind as she continued to sit and smooth her hair. Should she simply go out? The last she discounted. If she could do nothing to help, the least she could do was stay and share the suffering, as though the sharing in some way lessened it. Perhaps ... Here Kate cut herself off sharply. She had been about to say if she sat willing Astra to take the right course then her will might silently communicate itself to her through the floorboards, rise like incense.

But even Kate at this point regarded with alarm her own

silent desire to guide. That was it really, the crunch of the matter – when to abjure guidance? Prospero had thrown away his wand and she was no Prospero, just a typical mother whose cry stuck in her throat. And intervention, even if apparently beneficial, might be ill-advised. Even dangerous. Her fingers, trembling slightly now, ruffled her smooth hair and scraped it up off her neck in a clasped bunch. And still there was no sound to indicate what Astra might be doing above, and still Kate continued to sit. Even the red, she noticed, had gone from the embers. The room felt positively icy.

In the middle of the night Astra came along to her mother's room, stood beside her bed in her long white nightdress. Kate, as though feeling her presence even in sleep, rolled over and put on the light. Astra's face was white, her eyes swollen and red, her lips thick and quivering. She sat on the edge of the bed, her fingers in her lap, picking urgently at the loose thread of her old-fashioned nightdress, embroidered in the past by deft fingers making a thing of elegance to appeal in the bridal bed. How we deck ourselves to allure, Kate thought, how we endeavour to bring on ourselves the reproduction that divides our lives, splits our soul into fragments of other people.

'What is it?' she asked when Astra continued to sit without speaking, tearing at the thread, unravelling the strange flower it had shaped.

'What should I do?'

'I've said what I thought you should do. If you don't want to do it then you mustn't.'

Kate felt Astra weakening and, in a certain sense, resented it. Go on, she wanted to say, defy me, do what you want regardless.

'What would you do?' Astra was looking at her, imploring her.

'I cannot say,' Kate said, 'what I would do but honestly, Astra, I think it would be better not.'

There, she had said it, said what she really meant. And she

knew it was what Astra wanted to hear and perhaps it was quelling her small inner voice. But what are inner voices, Kate thought, inner voices are not always right. Inner voices took people to fight the Crusades, sent missionaries to convert the heathen, instructed Joan of Arc to lead the French, possibly Hitler and Napoleon to conquer Europe. Might not there be something to be said for the voice of reason? Perhaps because Kate could not think along a totally logical line herself because emotions intervened, she enormously admired people who could. She had been asked her opinion and had given it; it all came back to that. She observed a look of relief flood Astra's face.

'So I don't have to have it?'

'No, of course you don't.'

'You don't think,' she asked, 'it's very evil – wicked, even – to have an abortion?'

'No I don't.' Kate said it with a shade more conviction than she felt. She thought it necessary.

'Afterwards, they say you feel guilty. Regret it.'

'Only if you're silly,' said Kate. 'It's never any good regretting anything. If you want to waste your life regretting that's up to you.'

'So's this.'

'Yes,' said Kate, 'exactly.'

In a sense the ball was back in Astra's court.

'Shall I go to Scarlet's person in London?'

'I can't see the need. You can go here, I expect. We'll find out. I'll ring up Mr McFarlane in the morning, ask him . . .' She stopped. She could hear herself making all the arrangements, taking over Astra's life. She felt quite startled by how easily it had happened. 'On second thoughts,' she said, 'it would probably be better if you did it. If that's what you want I think you should do it consciously, yourself. Not be swept along by me.'

Astra was taken aback. She dreaded what she had to do. 'You'd do it much better,' she said.

'That's not the point,' Kate was almost sharp. 'Don't you

149

understand? You're not a projection of me any longer – you must take responsibility for yourself.'

Astra continued to sit blindly picking at her thread, hating and resenting her mother, while Kate wanted to yell 'Go away' but couldn't for Astra was hers and she was, must be, responsible. Second-hand suffering, Kate decided, is the most terrible of all because the sufferer is impotent, and can in no way alleviate the pain.

Kate's bed was the bed she had shared with Donald; the area beside her proclaimed its emptiness. 'Do you want to get in? she turned back the bedclothes.

Astra slid her body into the cold sheets and curled, cat-like, against the warm back of her mother. Exhaustion made her sleep; and relief that a decision had been made.

Kate, on the contrary, lay awake till dawn, afraid to move in case she disturbed Astra. They had made the only sensible decision, she reassured herself, yet her own inner voice raised its undesired presence to point out that a word from her could have altered the course of Astra's life.

Alec returned from a meeting with Howard Benson in a remarkably congenial frame of mind. Howard had been all for buying the further two farms Alec suggested and had agreed that he and another colleague between them would lend another £200,000, provided always that Alec was in a position to reimburse them should the necessity arise. Alec, as he explained to Howard, felt the risk factor was minimal because he was, after all, acquiring property in the stead of cash, and land value was going up and up, had in fact been continuing to rise at an escalating pace since the late Fifties. To Alec's mind he was on a safe bet – or what is a safe bet to someone with an inclination to gamble.

Gambling had paid off hand over foot in his last five years on the Stock Exchange. One way and another Alec wasn't worried. Neither was Howard – he had no need to be – he was a cautious man and insisted on having the deeds to the farms as surety.

At the end of the evening they shook hands on the deal, fortified by having drunk a certain amount of Armagnac that Howard had brought back with him from his holiday in the Dordogne, and parted with Howard inviting Alec to visit him again, socially, with Sophie.

On his return, Alec put the car away as quietly as possible so as not to wake Sophie, and crept silently and carefully up the stairs. He switched on the light in the passage rather than the bright and wakeful central bedroom light, and was startled and frankly amazed at the sight of two shapes together on his bed.

'Is someone ill?' he asked, standing uncertainly in the bedroom doorway. It was as if his room had been taken over, as if the two already there prevented him, the third, from entering.

Sophie sat up, pulled her arm out from beneath Jude's shoulder, and pushed her hair back. She didn't even look at Jude who got off the bed with one movement and walked out. Alec stood to one side to let him pass. Now that Jude had gone, he felt able to enter; he stepped down into the room.

'You realise it's nearly one o'clock,' he said, looking at the clock on the radio by his bed.

Sophie still didn't answer, she sat on the bed with her back to him unbuttoning her dress.

'What's been going on?' Alec demanded.

'Nothing at all.' Sophie didn't look round.

Alec undressed and heaved himself into bed. He lay with the bedclothes pulled up under his chin, his goodlooking face with the rather thin lips and slightly jutting chin framed by the duvet pulled up round it like a clown's ruff.

'Astra and Jude have bust up.' Sophie got into bed on the opposite side, wriggled her naked body down beneath the duvet and lay on her stomach.

'So what the hell was Jude doing here?'

'I think he's terribly upset. Really.'

151

'So you've been . . . comforting him.' Alec could not keep the sarcasm out of his voice.

'Yes.'

'Good,' said Alec in a tone that meant the opposite. He switched out the light and with a cocoon-like twitch, he jerked himself away from her.

'Alec,' Sophie said, 'don't be cross. Can't you understand him?'

'Very well – the irony was implicit.

'Oh Alec.' Sophie's tone was full of despair, she felt light years away from Alec on these occasions. She would have liked to tell him the truth but the implications for Jude should she do so silenced her.

'Don't be angry with me,' she implored.

Alec didn't answer.

Sophie felt driven. 'Aren't you concerned about him at all?' she demanded.

'He's clearly in good hands.'

'But if I could give him comfort – I mean real comfort – that's all I was doing. Then why not?'

'I didn't say anything. You go ahead,' said Alec. It was his tone that made it meaningless.

'Oh God,' Sophie moaned, 'I'll have to get some sleep or I'll never sing tomorrow. Put your hand on me, Alec, otherwise I can't relax.'

Alec's hand stretched out, touched Sophie's silky body, and lay on it, inert. Sophie sighed. She would have liked Alec to draw her tight up against him, kiss her eyelids, her face and neck, all the spiritual part of her – or what Sophie liked to think of as the spiritual part – forgive her for being nice to Jude and tell her he loved her. But as none of that was to be, indeed almost never happened like that, she turned away from him so they were back to back, his hand slipped off her, and they lay in separate worlds, Sophie wide-eyed thinking of Jude's misery, of their performance the next day; Alec unable to get out of his head the picture of Jude's long slim body lying face down on the bed against Sophie's. And yet they had both been entirely dressed and his knowledge of Sophie made him disinclined to think more had taken place than the 'comfort' Sophie described. But this did little to allay his growing jealousy, his resentment that Sophie seemed in some sense closer to Jude than to him. Alec, who controlled with some success his exterior world, found himself with no means to combat this rage that raised itself within him like some unpleasant parasite that had bored its way into his otherwise regulated brain. So he lay in the darkness maintaining a resentful silence until Sophie's voice broke it.

'Alec?'

'What?'

'Astra's pregnant.'

At first it seemed Alec hadn't heard. Then he turned over.

'Not that idiot Jude?'

'Yes. He's not an idiot.'

'How did it happen?'

'I don't know – I haven't asked.'

'I thought you said they'd bust up?'

'They have.'

'They can't now.'

'Well they have.'

'Shit,' said Alec. 'That boy doesn't know whether he's coming or going. What the hell did he think he was doing?'

'Ask him,' said Sophie.

'Christ.'

Sophie despaired. Alec's reactions were all so predictable, even more so than she had thought they would be.

'Why didn't you tell me before?' Alec was wide awake now.

'I don't seem to have seen you much lately – not on our own. She's only just found out it's definite.'

'Where is he?'

'Gone to the Mill, I expect.'

'I'll go and talk to him.' Alec swung his legs out of bed. He now had righteous ground on which to attack Jude.

Sophie could contain herself no longer, as he moved to the door she reached out and grasped his arm, 'Alec, promise me you won't be horrible – it was an accident – it could happen to anyone.'

Alec's lip curled contemptuously, he freed his arm. 'Go to bed, Sophie – try to grow up.'

Sophie made a last attempt, clung to Alec in an agony of guilt and fear for Jude. 'Please Alec – oh please. I'll do anything for you if only you won't have a terrible row with Jude. He's not strong, Alec – he can't stand much of . . . much of . . .'

'What?'

'Your cruelty.'

'Cruelty?' Alec couldn't believe his ears. He accused openly. 'You have just slept with my son and you dare to talk to me of cruelty.' He pushed Sophie away from him and got out of the door. Sophie ran after him. Leaning over the stair rail she called, 'He wants to marry her – and I *haven't* slept with your son. It's not like you think.'

'Marry her?' Alec was incredulous and even more enraged, 'No one with an ounce of sense would marry him,' he shouted, his feet hastening down the remaining stairs.

'Alec – he's *your son.*'

'So you've said.' The front door closed.

Sophie listened to the car start, pull away until the engine faded and silence closed round her. I'll never sleep now, she thought; why, oh why, did all this have to come up the night before the pantomime – our first performance? For a moment she thought of getting in her car and following Alec to the Mill, but a minute's reflection told her it could only make matters worse. She should never have told Alec about Astra, but was relieved she had for it absolved her from a responsibility that was beginning to frighten her. All her emotions seemed to have suddenly plunged down into dangerous and unplumbed depths.

It was after midnight when Alec reached the Mill. The wind was strong and the trees on the banks either side of the lane leant and bowed before it; their leaves, rustling in agitation, turned up undersides which glinted silver in the headlights.

Alec drove up in front of the big mill door and let himself in through the pass door. He had never been inside before; he waited for his eyes to get used to the darkness, but when it failed to dissipate, called up. Jude was still awake; he had been half expecting his father. He switched on a light that lit the lower floor and watched expressionless as Alec mounted the steps.

At the top Alec gazed round him, as most people did, at the vast shadowy room, the curious irregular lean of the walls, the steep pitch of the slanted roof. He walked about staring at it without speaking, jingling the coins in his pocket. Jude remained equally silent; he sat on the edge of his bed leaving the single wooden chair free for Alec. In a matter of moments Alec returned to it and sat down.

'Isn't there more light in this place?' he asked. For answer Jude turned another switch and a hard bright unshaded bulb gleamed from above, enclosing the father and son in a circle of white light stressing the darkness beyond, so that until their eyes readjusted the barn had vanished, and they could have been seated together in a warehouse or office building, or simply in space. The emboldening effect of drink had worn off Alec and he found it harder than he had imagined to come to the point of his visit, instead he surveyed the furnishings that fell within the circle of light.

'Pretty primitive, isn't it?'

'It suits me very well.' There was no love in Jude's tone. That he had expected his father's intrusion did nothing to mitigate his resentment. He hated his father with the force of hatred initially instigated by love.

'I understand Astra Merlin is pregnant?' Nothing in Alec's outward aspect betrayed the effort he had needed to utter this bald statement.

'Yes.'

'Could it have been avoided?'

'It could – yes.'

'Then why the hell didn't you see it was?' Alec's control

155

left him. Jude gave a faint shrug, remained silent. Alec stood up and paced round.

'What are you going to do about it?' He came to rest with his hand on the back of the chair. 'She's under age, you realise? A child still at school?'

Jude had no answer. The dots and zigzags that had temporarily vanished, came back before his eyes, his brain felt as though it would split in two, he sat with bent head while his father belaboured him with words. And after a while words began to fail Alec. Jude's failure to retaliate, his bowed submission, made an unsatisfactory target. He became silent, and father and son sat with no sound but the whining of the wind round the eaves, the flutter and hum of numerous moths attracted in from outside by the powerful light. Both watched them, their minds elsewhere as the moths fluttered, fell and struggled back to burn themselves again on the bright hot bulb.

'I understand she doesn't want to marry you?' Alec said at last; he felt tired, limp, exhausted. He would like to have dispossessed Jude. There was no love between them, it was silly to pretend there was ... To his surprise Jude suddenly stood up. Apparently his mind had been running along the same lines.

'I may require money from you,' he said, 'it's the only way in which I can help Astra. As you must realise, the last thing I want is to have to ask you for anything. I despise your values, your way of life and your way of procuring it, but just at the moment I have no alternative but to ask your help.'

Alec went visibly white. His knuckles clenched on the back of the chair. Jude's insults, his arrogance, whipped his mellowing spirit up to further fury.

'You won't get money from me,' he said, 'not one single penny. If Astra Merlin needs money then I shall get it to her through Sophie. I very much doubt you are to be trusted with anything.'

'Being your son, probably not.'

Again in the silence both became aware of the ever increasing amount of moths crawling round the floor at their feet, having persisted in their own destruction.

'So be it.' Alec's voice trembled from anger, pent-up emotion, and the knowledge that what had passed between himself and Jude, unlike a row with a woman, was irreconcilable. Too much truth had been uttered, the truth that we ask for so loftily being the most explosive factor we may ever have to face.

So Alec turned and went down the wooden steps and Jude continued to stand motionless, amongst the dropping moths, listening to his father let himself out through the door, start up his car and drive away. He took up his biro and sat tapping his teeth. But the recent scene prevented any coherent thought; he soon closed his book, lowered his head on his arms.

When the first cock crowed Jude was still awake, hunched up on his bed, smoking. Pictures formed and dissolved in the chaos of his imagination, Sophie's face blurred as he caressed it, softened, became Astra's, then again frighteningly changed into the distorted face of his mother.

With the coming of daylight a terrible nervous energy beset him. He reopened his book in a further attempt to study but could assimilate nothing, the words danced elusively before him and a frenzy, that almost amounted to panic, churned round in his brain. He felt a curious lump, a restriction in his throat that prevented him from swallowing, and wondered if it would inhibit his breathing. His panicky feeling increased. He walked round the Mill, tidied up, moved books, shifted things to more organised positions on different shelves. Not much light came into the Mill owing to the darkness of the day, but what little there was cast an unreality over the objects within.

Jude felt detached from everything; all seemed to him value-less, of no interest. He crossed to his bed, picked up some small colour prints of Astra lying by it and was startled by his own indifference. There were some of Sophie and Scarlet too, none of which aroused any response in him. It seemed to him he didn't care whether he ever saw any of them again. Every move he made was an effort but he could not lie down on the bed because the fear would not let him. He sat on the chair for a while, but felt no better. He must get out of the Mill, do something, something that would require all his concentration.

He went over to where his clothes hung to get his cigarettes from his jeans pocket, crossed to the table and after a quick search amongst his papers unearthed a matchbox. He struck a match, held it to the tip of his cigarette and inhaled, letting out the smoke through his nostrils like breath in frosty air; and as he watched it suddenly became perfectly clear what he must do. He plugged the kettle in, made himself a strong cup of black coffee and sat deep in thought. When he had finished the first cup he made himself a second. He blinked and looked round him; miraculously he was able to drink, the lump in his throat seemed less constricting and might even have gone altogether. His actions now were cool and deliberate. He put on his jacket, slipped his cigarettes in his pocket along with the matches and went down the steps. The only thing that worried him was a fear that something might happen to prevent his carrying out the intention that must be pursued to its conclusion at the expense of all else. He felt convinced of its rightness and a little thrill of elation passed through him. He would have liked to run across the footbridge, but made himself walk – it might arouse attention if someone from either of the nearby cottages saw him hurrying, and the last thing he wanted was to imprint himself on anyone's memory.

Benjy woke up and remembered his dream. He had dreamt that Astra was walking away from him over the hill, it was somewhere up on the far side of Barrow Down because he recognised the line of granite stones and the dip where the ground went down at the head of the stream. There was a bog, quite a bad one with cotton grass round the edges and in the centre bright emerald green grass and a weed with tiny white flowers. Astra was being pulled along by a kite she was flying – it was transparent and formed of red and blue and green triangles, it soared and dipped in the wind and shook its long tail of knotted nylon. He was following her, some way behind, hurrying, trying to catch her up. He shouted and she looked back but didn't stop. She was going over the skyline and he knew she was heading straight for the emerald quaking bog.

'Astra,' he called, but the wind was coming from Astra to him and she didn't hear. Then suddenly Eddie was there, and Benjy told him to hurry. Run. Stop Astra. But Eddie didn't seem to understand what Benjy was talking about, he lay on his back like a dog rolling, legs in the air. Benjy looked down on Eddie in despair but couldn't wait, he had to go on to catch Astra. He walked and walked and the skyline moved away from him and the rector said, 'You'll never climb up the tower if you don't wear proper shoes,' – and Benjy looked down on his shoes which were new trainers his mother had bought him the week before and he couldn't see anything wrong with them. He looked round for Astra and she was there in the chorus singing. He felt terribly relieved that she hadn't gone down in the bog, but then he noticed she looked different, not like Astra at all but his teacher at school. So he ran out of the hall and back to the moor and over the brow of Barrow Down. He looked down on the emerald bog and there was a dark brown patch in the centre with bubbles coming up slowly and breaking. He knew Astra had gone down in it and he couldn't save her, and it was the most terrible moment of his life. It was so terrible he woke up.

It took him quite a long time to realise it was a dream and not true, and when he did he lay for a long time feeling relieved. It was not until he went down to breakfast and found his mother and Astra standing around drinking coffee that he realised it was the day of the school performance of the pantomime. Astra's hair was washed; it lay in dark stuck-together ribbons of blackness down to her shoulders. Her face was almost unhealthily white, her eyes and lids pale pink with big mauvy-blue shadows under her eyes. Benjy sat down and ate his muesli and gazed at her stolidly, he was so relieved to see her. It was also an immense relief to find she bore no resemblance to his teacher.

Astra got impatient. 'Can't you stop looking at me like that, Benjy?' She sounded irritable, but then she often did in the early morning. Benjy averted his eyes unwillingly and waited for the egg his mother had put on to boil for him. 'You know what you're doing this afternoon, don't you?' Astra went on rather sharply.

'Yes,' said Benjy.

'Don't be late, Benjy,' his mother said, 'I've told the rector you'll be there at two. I'll leave your tin at the door. You're to collect down the centre – someone else'll take care of the sides.'

Benjy banged the top of his eggshell and listened. It seemed unfair he should be made to go round with a collecting tin while Eddie was helping his father bring down ponies for the autumn sales. He was getting off school for it too, while all the rest of them had to go to the silly old pantomime. He finished his egg and turned the shell upside down in its cup. His mother was looking at the clock.

'The bus'll be here in four minutes – you'd better get a move on.'

Benjy did. He took his satchel and ran. At the top of the hill he was just in time to see the back of the bus receding from him into the distance. He felt rather sick at the thought of the trouble, the trouble if he went home and the trouble if he got to school late. The obvious answer presented itself, he wouldn't go home or to school. At school they'd think he'd had the morning off to help get ready for the pantomime. All he had to do was think where else to spend it. Eddie's was out because he'd be up on the moor and in any case Lucy would tell on him. Benjy was at a loss. Then as he stood whirling his satchel horizontally round him, passing it from one hand to the other, he thought of the Mill. He'd go and see Jude Deneuve who was usually nice to him. It suited him to be, Benjy was a useful go-between.

So Benjy set off without further thought, because he could easily walk there across the fields and he knew Astra wouldn't be going with her wet hair and all the preparations – the cakes and things they were making – so he wasn't worried about that. He climbed a hedge and slipped along beside the bank, ducking well down behind it because the farmer owning the land was friendly with his mother and might report him as truant from school. He hesitated for a moment to wonder whether he really did want to go as far as the Mill, but the morning ahead of him seemed long with nothing in particular to do, so he went on. After midday, if he wanted, he could go home because Astra and his mother would have gone to the Parish Hall. He broke a stick from the hedge and chopped off some bracken; he decided he hated the pantomime though he couldn't have said why. He just felt it, and Benjy's feelings to Benjy were much too strong to ever question. He climbed a gate, went through some woods then along a lane overgrown with brambles and nettles. He stopped to eat blackberries, then tried a sloe and spat it out, running his tongue round his dried-up mouth. Finally he left the comforting protection of the lane and came out on the windy brow of a steep cleave. About two hundred feet beneath him in the valley lay the silver curling river beyond which was the Mill, and beyond that the road.

Benjy stood watching the toy world beneath him to see if anyone was about, but seeing no sign of movement other than a van passing along the road, he sat down in the heather and within a few moments the warmth of the sun and the hum of bees after pollen sent him to sleep.

He was woken by a dog's incessant barking from the valley beneath him. He stood up, sleepy from the sun, and looked to see the cause of its clamour. At first he could see nothing, the valley seemed as empty as before, then, unexpectedly and not so far off, he saw someone moving across the cleave face directly beneath him. And the longer he looked the more

161

certain he became that the walker was Jude Deneuve. Determined to waylay him, he set off down again in bounds and jumps as fast as he dared and was only halted by a wide path set above the one on which he had seen the walker. Benjy set off along it at a jog, pushed along by the searing east wind that blew behind him, increasing his pace down the gradual incline. When he came in sight of the fork where the upper track joined the lower, he stopped; he could not possibly tell whether the walker – who he still felt certain was Jude – was ahead of him or beneath him. In a matter of seconds he knew the answer, for a dark head showed moving purposefully along the lower path. It was undoubtedly Jude's.

Benjy trotted along above him until he reached the fork, then squatted in the bracken and waited. When Jude was very close he planned to leap out to give him a surprise, and until he was only a few feet away this remained his intention. But something in Jude's face, his intense, abstracted expression, changed Benjy's mind, and as he drew abreast of him he kept completely still, flattening himself into the bracken like a hunted hair. Jude passed within inches of him, looking neither to right nor left; had he done so he could not have failed to see Benjy, who was not really hidden and expected at every moment to be accosted. When he was not, he was so surprised that he thought Jude must not *want* to see him, and the rebuff acted as a challenge. Very well, if Jude wouldn't see him then he would stalk him, see where he was going.

Accordingly, as soon as Jude reached and entered the copse in a fold of the hill ahead, Benjy set off in pursuit, stealing from tree to tree, keeping well out of sight. Once or twice he thought he had lost Jude completely but, by a series of lucky chances and a guess that Jude was making for Scarhill, he kept on his tracks. And when, at the other side of the copse, Jude turned right, his guess seemed confirmed and following became relatively easy. It was not until the saddle between Crype Down and Scardon that Jude suddenly did something unexpected: he turned left and took a track that circled up on to Scardon rather than continuing on through the hunting gate and down through the beech woods to Scarhill house itself. So unexpected was this that Benjy was in danger of being seen; he had let himself get too far out on Jude's left flank and once again had to conceal himself in the bracken. By now it had become an exciting game to him, and to be seen would have been an indication of his lack of skill. Jude, again ahead, walked on steadily towards the brow of the moor while Benjy moved from thorn to thorn, trotting along the winding sheep tracks, keeping Jude's dark head always just in sight. When at last he stopped, Benjy for the third time dropped flat on his face. And it was as well he did so because Jude turned and scanned the landscape as though expecting to see someone, then crouched in the dry white bent grass that, along with clumps of creeping gorse, covered the entire top of Scardon. It was in amongst this that single furrows had been ploughed to facilitate the planting of Alec's spruce seedlings and from which thousands of small, stiff, needled spears indicated their presence.

When Benjy next dared to raise his head he could hardly believe his eyes – a patch of dark smoke was blowing vertically across the ground away from himself and Jude, and a small orange flame leapt and flickered. He felt a shiver pass through his entire body and raised himself up in startled curiosity. As he did so the wind, which had been behind him as he followed Jude, blew even more violently. At the same time he saw more flames, and distinctly heard their crackle; the cloud of smoke billowed and thickened. Jude had moved on. At first Benjy couldn't see him, then he picked him out crouched twenty yards further down the hill; as he straightened up a further wisp of smoke made clear his occupation. He continued to move methodically along the new fence, stopping every now and then to set light to a convenient clump. And for the first time Benjy began to feel afraid – if Jude were to catch him watching, what mightn't he do to him? Benjy dreaded to think and lay afraid to move, only daring to raise his head just enough to peer through the bracken fronds at the increasing volume of smoke and the tongues of flame. The noise of their impatient crackle both excited and terrified him. Then suddenly he dropped his head, alerted by a pounding on the ground. A few seconds later, Jude passed him, running, his face flushed, his hair blowing back off his forehead. Benjy held his breath and remained rigid until he calculated that Jude had gone over the brow, then he stood up.

The fence had partially disappeared in the smoke, the fire was moving steadily forward, fanned out sideways by the wind. Benjy gazed and gazed in fascinated horror. The idea crossed his mind that he should tell someone, but hadn't he sat through meals where Astra and his mother had discussed and argued at length the damage caused to Scardon by fencing it, the iniquity of planting trees on the very top of rolling moorland? Now it would be burned and revert to its natural state, and that must be good, Benjy reasoned. But remained doubtful. Time passed.

He did not know how long he stayed watching the tortuous flames but their effect on him was hypnotic – he couldn't tear himself away. It was not until he eventually looked round and realised he was the only person present that he began to grow uneasy. If he was found alone on the moor with the fire, wouldn't it be assumed he had lit it? Benjy turned and ran as fast as his legs would take him after Jude.

The cold east wind, that had driven Benjy before it, whined round Scarhill's eaves and blasted in through the cracks; it was as if the thick walls were permeated with holes through which it found its way. Sophie regarded the newly installed radiator thankfully, but rather wondered if it was big enough. This, after all, was only autumn. She sat before her mirror, forced her face into a smile and her reflection shivered back at her; big blue eyes heavily emphasised with black eyeliner for the stage, a fragile 1920s dress (a whim of Oliver Upton's that Sophie had not chosen to query), pale white net stockings and high-heeled strap white-satin shoes. Round her hair she wore the classic Twenties bandeau. She noticed the high colour in her cheeks and wondered if she was running a temperature from stress. Alec had not told her much about his row with Jude the previous night but her imagination was well able to fill in all that had been left unsaid. She was nervous that Jude simply wouldn't turn up for the performance, he was not known for reliability, and the afternoon was likely to be enough of an ordeal without having to play her part with the unrehearsed understudy – it would be hopeless!

Yet she did *want* to do the performance, she wanted desperately to sing to show people she *could* sing and hadn't been chosen for her looks, which she knew perfectly well was what was being said. Her second and more altruistic concern was a profound sense of uneasiness over Jude. Just to check, she rang Bag Down and got Kate, who told her they hadn't seen him. Kate's voice sounded rather unfriendly, and this depressed her even more. Finally she comforted herself with the thought that more likely than not Jude would turn up, that his conscience would bring him to the hall for the performance at 2.15.

But as time went on and Jude was still untraceable, she became more and more nervous. At 1.15 exactly she took a last look at herself in her long mirror, shivered from nerves or cold, she was uncertain which, wrapped the cloak that was the other part of her costume over her shoulders and went down.

Alec was in the kitchen reading the paper. 'Ah,' he said. 'Ready?'

'Yes.' Sophie's teeth were chattering. 'I think I'd better go. You won't be late, will you? I mean, miss it altogether if you like and come tomorrow – we'll probably be better – but don't come in late because it'll make me go wrong.'

'Have a drink?'

'No – all right, yes.' Alec gave her a gin and martini. She drank it hastily. 'Do I look all right?'

'Marvellous.'

'Wish me luck.'

'I do. I've ordered a big bouquet for the leading lady.'

'Oh Alec!' Sophie kissed him delicately so as not to upset her make-up; he really was being awfully reasonable, considering last night.

'I'm looking forward to it,' he said. And Sophie, dreading that any moment Jude might be mentioned, hastily picked up her make-up bag and hurried out to the car. In the driver's seat she tooted and Alec came to the back door. 'Don't forget there's a seat kept for you – if you decide to come.' She waved, put her foot on the accelerator, failed to adjust the choke and left the yard in a series of jerks.

Alec closed the door, averting his eyes. Sophie's lack of sensitivity towards machines was a source of continual pain to him. He returned to the kitchen and helped himself to the lunch Sophie had left out for him, reading his paper all the while so that the best part of forty minutes must have elapsed before he happened to look out of the window and notice a curious thick yellow-grey cloud curling over the brow of Scardon. He flung open the window, sniffed, then seized his jacket and dashed out of the house; a few minutes later he was driving at break-neck speed up the road to the moor.

Sophie was actually on stage with Jude, who miraculously had arrived early, and was several bars into her first solo when the fire engine came past. Its siren, faint in the distance then gaining in volume as it drew nearer, passed directly outside the hall. Sophie had to stop, she could not hear the piano or her own voice. As it died away Oliver Upton began again at the beginning of the phrase but Sophie had lost her place, dried up, the words would not come. The rector repeated the phrase, the chord. The fire engine caused a stir in the hall, all the children were whispering, fidgeting. Sophie suddenly found the words, tried for the note and sang for a moment unaccompanied until the piano joined in. Her voice floated pleasantly out over the hall with the untrained quality of a songbird. The audience's attention was regained, Sophie's confidence returned, only to evaporate the next moment as a second fire siren was heard approaching up the valley.

This time Sophie stopped before it's whine drowned her voice, shrugged, stood helpless in the centre of the stage, a frail, pathetic and slightly ridiculous figure once the magic of performance was dispelled. The insistent wail of the second siren proved too much for the audience's peace of mind: people began to turn their heads, children scrambled to see out of the window. And when yet another sounded, coming from a different direction, several people got up and made for the exit until only the very front rows remained stolidly seated, including Benjy Merlin who sat with his head screwed round watching the departures behind him with a solemn face. The rector abandoned the piano and went up on to the stage to announce a temporary break, but before he had even begun, a fourth fire siren was heard in the distance.

This had the effect of completely emptying the hall. Kate came out from backstage where she had been helping with the dressing, and the rest of the cast trooped out in their costumes behind her. A crowd had gathered in front of the hall; everyone was talking, pointing across the valley.

'Must be the Common alight if t'isn't a house.' Mrs Bellamy viewed the dense cloud of smoke blowing westwards along the entire crest of the moor. Kate, shading her eyes, kept her silence. She felt fairly certain from the direction of the smoke that it was Scardon that was alight.

'It's Scardon, isn't it?' Sophie was beside her.

Benjy had climbed the wall and was gazing in awe at the ever increasing cloud. Jude, Kate noticed, was standing with Astra only a few feet behind her. She glanced at his face, guessing he was pleased; at the same moment her attention was drawn away by exclamations of excited alarm, for the wind changed revealing the flames leaping and bounding in rapacious joy under the smoke.

''Tis a big fire,' Mrs Bellamy voiced the general opinion.

'I'm going,' Sophie brushed past Kate, 'Alec may need me. I'm sure it's our land.'

'I'll follow you,' Kate said, 'there's no point in hanging around here. We can't go on without you.'

For an instant Sophie appeared to waver, then said bravely, 'There's always tomorrow,' and started to edge her way through the crowd of adults and schoolchildren. The rector caught a glimpse of her fair head making for the car park but by the time he had forged his way through the gathering in pursuit, Sophie had gone.

'It'll be like throwing a bucket on it, mate,' the head fireman shouted to Alec.

'There are more seedlings on the left,' Alec shouted back; the hiss of the hose and pump combined made hearing difficult.

'Not a hope. Us'll have to wait till it dies down a bit.'

'But surely . . .'

'I'm sorry, sir, but I'm not risking my men to save anything except lives. We'll use what water we've got in the tanks, but once that's gone there's no other us can get the hose to – not up here, see.'

Alec turned away bitterly. He found a further supposed chief.

'Can't you at least check it?'

'Oh yes – us'll check it. But it'll run its course just the same. Us'll keep it back from the farm over to your left. The fire itself 'll check anyways at the road.'

'I've 60,000 seedlings recently planted . . .' Alec's voice was lost in a gust of wind that caused an upsurge and roar of flames. A moment later the treacherous wind snatched backwards and Alec found himself coughing and staggering his way from a dense cloud of smoke. Every few moments a new clump would ignite and flames would shoot above the rest to a height of twenty or thirty feet, curling orange and yellow, onion shaped, black smoke rising from the core. The wind took the fire away from him in a long line across the width of Scardon; only a temporary change in its direction had brought the smoke in sight of Scarhill, and now it resumed its westerly course and burnt steadily, almost purposefully, it seemed to him, across the plantation. He gave up his protests and stood in desolation, watching his venture consumed. How much, he wondered, would his insurance brokers pay up? Was it even fully insured?

Inspired by such unhappy thoughts, Alec grasped one of Sophie's brooms he had armed himself with, and set about beating out every small upstart of flame that strayed away from the main body of the fire. On one side of the outer perimeter there were two rows of seedlings that might yet be saved. So busy was he that he did not at first notice the group of watchers who had arrived to see the excitement. One or two advanced to help him, beating out the odd flame with a stick or trampling them with their boots; others simply stood and watched. Alec alone worked on with a mute and futile persistence. In some sense it relieved him.

'But how did it start?' Sophie sat, chin in hand, her elbow resting on the kitchen table, gazing at Alec. They had just returned from an examination of the smoking waste – nothing, absolutely nothing, was left except a few charred fencing-posts and some blackened wire.

'That's precisely what I've asked the police to investigate. They have a suspicion it may have been that idiot Merlin boy. Apparently the park warden saw him walking across the Mill cleave earlier. He should have been at school. If the silly arse warden had had the sense to see what he was up to, none of this might have happened,' Alec said bitterly.

'Oh I'm sure he wouldn't have done it, Alec,' Sophie was shocked at the unproven suspicion.

'Then what was he doing up there?'

'Just walking. I don't see how you can accuse someone like that.'

'Did he tell anyone there was a fire on Scardon when he arrived to do the collection?' Alec looked sharply at her.

'No' – Sophie was definite. On these occasions her wits lagged behind Alec's.

'Then it must have been him – otherwise he'd have told someone.'

There was a silence.

'He mightn't have seen it,' Sophie persisted obstinately, although she could see her defence of Benjy crumbling.

Alec gave a humourless laugh and opened the dishwasher before it had finished. 'We shall see,' he said.

Sophie was thinking of Jude. Where had Jude been that morning? She kept her eyes lowered. Rather to her relief the telephone rang, but relief vanished equally quickly when it turned out to be Oliver Upton. He thought that after the unfortunate forgetting of her lines that afternoon, due understandably to the upset caused by the fire, she ought to go down to the rectory for a quick run-through before the following evening.

'I honestly can't come tonight,' Sophie said. 'Alec needs me here. There's a lot to see to in relation to the fire' – she couldn't think what – 'and I've got to get dinner.' She used Alec as the first excuse that came into her head, she could not bear the thought of another solo session with the rector.

Oliver Upton lowered his voice. 'I think,' he said carefully, 'you may be sorry if you don't come. There's another matter I wanted to mention to you – nothing to do with singing. Come along after your dinner.'

'Can't it keep?'

'I don't know that it will,' Oliver Upton's voice was still low and confidential, full of implied threat, 'it concerns young Jude,' he added.

Sophie felt herself tense. She held the receiver a little away from her, looked round the room as though it might suggest to her an escape from what she felt certain she would rather not hear. Yet if it was about Jude . . .

'All right,' she heard herself say, 'I'll come – but it can't be for long, I hope you understand.'

'Indeed I do,' Oliver Upton said stiffly, 'I think you know me well enough to know I shouldn't bother you at such a difficult time unless I felt it imperative.'

Sophie's heart sank. She replaced the receiver. Should she tell Alec? But the thought of Alec's impatience at being bothered when he was dealing with the consequences of the fire alarmed her too much. Also she had really nothing to tell him. She would get dinner then go, she decided.

She followed Oliver Upton into his study where the piano stood; she couldn't really do anything else. He offered her a drink but she refused, filled by apprehension.

'I think we should sit down and talk first, don't you? Then perhaps a quick run-through of your poor solo that got cut short this afternoon.'

Sophie felt he was mocking her for being a figure of ridicule drowned by fire sirens. She felt beads of sweat on her forehead. She sat down. Oliver Upton crossed his leg, cupped his hands round his knee, looking as though it was only with difficulty that he could bring himself to speak. But Sophie was not taken in, she knew it an act, and that what he was about to say would be particularly unpleasant, and in this she was not wrong.

He began, 'I am assuming you feel a certain fondness for your stepson – though I know these tenuous relationships coming in adolescence are always difficult. Even so, I imagine you would want to do what you could to help him and I think help is exactly what he is going to need.'

'Why?' Sophie was really lost.

'Because at about 10.30 this morning I was out walking – going to see old Mrs Crocker – and as you know I often take my field glasses to look at the birds – well, I happened to look at the side of the Mill cleave where the path joins Crype Down with Scardon and I saw someone walking. It was Jude.'

'So? I don't understand what you're getting at.'

'I think you do, Sophie. You're an intelligent young woman. It must be perfectly obvious to you what I am suggesting.'

'It's not,' Sophie lied, playing for time. Her stomach was fluttering with nervous tension. 'I mean, it doesn't mean a thing, just seeing someone walking on the moor. Benjy Merlin was seen walking on the moor too, someone said.'

'Yes,' said Oliver Upton, his small eyes under his bushy

brows narrowing. 'But I presume none of us would want blame to fall on the wrong person?'

'Why should anyone be blamed? It could easily have been a cigarette from a passing car.'

'I don't think so.' He looked closely at Sophie, watching her reaction. 'The fire started in the centre of the heath, not anywhere near the road. I think we have to face up to the fact that it was deliberately set light to by someone.'

'If you are going to try and accuse Jude on such slight evidence I think it is ridiculous and I don't want to listen.' Sophie stood up.

'Believe me, I am only anxious to help you. I fully understand your very difficult position as stepmother. But as you must know, arson is a serious matter, and the police will take a serious view of it, I'm afraid. But I felt it wise to inform you, allow you and the boy's father to take what steps you may feel necessary.'

Oliver Upton, Sophie observed, shied off using the word 'husband'. 'Yes – I see,' she said. He had moved in closer. She could feel, smell, his moist breath. She kept her eyes down. 'I'll certainly discuss it with Alec,' she said, 'but I can't believe Jude had anything to do with it.' She looked up. 'Can't we sing?' she implored. 'Aren't we going to rehearse?' It would divert him, give her time to think.

'Very well.'

The rector foresaw having the upper hand over Sophie for a while, so felt no need to press his advantage all at once. Instead he sat down at the piano. And Sophie sang, but her voice was unsteady; he reassured her it was probably the shock of the fire and quite soon let her go.

Sophie wasted no time; as soon as she left the oppressive rectory, she drove straight to the Mill. She let herself in quietly, went up the steps and found Jude lying on his back on his bed, almost in darkness.

She took a few steps across the echoing floor, stopped, unsure of herself, and looked down at him. 'I thought perhaps you'd come over to Scarhill – the fire's been a terrible setback to Alec.'

Jude got out of bed, padded across and switched on more light. He poured dregs from a wine bottle into two glasses, handing one to Sophie. He carried his desk chair across for Sophie while he sat on the edge of his bed.

'What does it look like?'

'There's nothing left – nothing of the plantation. Some of the wire is re-usable, Alec says, but most of the posts are burnt too. It's a terrible lot of his money gone.'

'Have all the seedlings gone?'

'Yes.'

'Good.'

In the silence that followed Sophie was certain Jude was aware of her unasked question. She decided to evade it.

'Jude,' she said at last, 'what's going to happen?'

'Happen?' Jude looked at her quizzically.

'I mean it can't go on – this hatred between you and Alec. If you hate him as much as you appear . . .' She faltered under Jude's gaze, which was directed straight at her.

'Why do you stay with him?'

'We're married.'

Jude sighed and his sigh, his contempt, made Sophie feel small and despicable. 'That's not the *only* reason,' she added hastily, 'we care for each other.'

Jude looked down into his glass. His silence implied disbelief and criticism more forcefully than words could have done. Sophie shifted uncomfortably.

'I'm sorry the pantomime was spoilt for you,' he said at last.

'It's not important,' Sophie said, and knew at that moment it wasn't. Her ambition, her desire to prove herself, seemed to have shrivelled away, leaving only a faint smouldering of unrealised achievement and a sense of futility. 'Did you light it?' – the bluntness of her own question was a surprise to her, came out of the darkness to Jude.

He stood up, stretched, gave no outward sign of having

heard. Sophie found herself looking at the gap of bare flesh between his shirt and the top of his jeans that his raised arms revealed – its perfect smoothness, its fineness of texture. When she looked up, met his eyes, she thought she detected mockery in his expression and flushed. Could he possibly be aware of the electric shock of sensation that had passed through her? She dismissed the thought quickly, folding her hands protectively round her knees. Jude walked over to his desk and she looked, now unashamedly, at his back, his wide shoulders and narrow hips in the faded blue jeans. Joy and guilt mingled. How could she, a woman of twenty-eight, desire – yes, that was the word – her stepson? Yet if she was not married to Alec it wouldn't seem impossible . . .

'Did you?' she repeated. The doggedness of her repetition seemed in some way to validate her presence, give her a right to be where she was.

'Yes.' Jude's answer was spoken with a certain complacent satisfaction.

'Benjy's getting blamed for it.'

'Benjy?'

'Yes.'

'Why?'

'Because he was seen up there.'

'I never saw him.'

Silence.

'Did he see me?'

'He says he didn't see anyone – which incriminates him all the more.'

'He must have seen me if he was up there.'

'He's probably lying.'

'Why?'

'Perhaps,' said Sophie at last, 'he doesn't want to get you into trouble.'

'But what about himself?'

'He says he didn't do it.'

Jude came back to the bed and they sat in silence for some

174

while. The moths had begun to enter; Sophie watched them fluttering round the light and felt distress at their plight.

'Can't we shut the windows?' she asked.

'There aren't any windows that open – they come in under the eaves.'

They continued to sit, Sophie's attention in part distracted by the moths. 'What will you do?' she asked at last.

'I'll tell them I did it – as an act of protest against my father's destruction of the environment.'

'You may go to prison. I mean, it *is* arson.' Sophie's alarm grew. Jude grinned; his grin was slightly evil, she thought uncomfortably. 'My father'll have to face up to a son in prison, won't he?' He laughed.

'Jude,' Sophie suddenly burst out, 'Jude you don't *have* to. No one will ever suspect you. Benjy will be all right because no one saw him do anything but walk up there, so they can't possibly prove anything.' She saw the expression on Jude's face and fell silent. He stretched out his hand, laid it on hers. His touch only intensified her misery, her fear for what he was about to do. 'Jude – please apologise. *Please*. I can't bear all this . . . this hate. You've burnt Alec's trees – can't you leave it at that? And there's Astra to think of.' She had meant to keep off the subject of Astra.

'Apologise. For what?'

'For the fire.'

'No. Never.' Jude was passionate. 'I'm pleased. It's the first worthwhile thing I've ever done in my life. You can't let fascists like my father get away with their destruction. Some-one's got to stop him and I intend to be that someone. Going away would be playing into my father's hands. No – I'll stay here and prevent him wherever I can. Prevent him destroying things – people – life. You.' He shot the last word at Sophie to gauge her reaction. She felt the strength in his fanaticism, the truth in much of his argument. Yet it seemed to her he was planning a sort of personal terrorism against Alec that was slightly insane.

'You could have burnt someone in that fire,' she said, 'Benjy, even. Creature's, insects – the very things you imagine you're saving. There was a house quite close.'

'I knew someone would give the alarm, and only a baby left in its cot wouldn't be able to get out of the way. Moor fires don't move fast enough. Besides, this is the legal time of year for moor burning, bar two days,' he justified himself.

'To set going an uncontrolled blaze like that is never legal.' She sighed, started towards the steps. 'I'd better go. We aren't getting anywhere.'

'Don't – don't go.' He came after her, caught her by the shoulders, turned her to face him, and the sweetest imaginable sensation coursed through Sophie, weakening her will. 'Stay here. You can sleep in my bed and I'll sleep on the floor.'

'Jude – there's Alec and Astra. Not just us.'

He let go of her. 'I don't see that has anything to do with it. There's just us now. We need the physical comfort of each other's presence – at least I do.'

'I have to go.' Sophie's statement carried no conviction. She made her way uncertainly down the shadowy steps. In the doorway, as she stumbled over the high threshold, she knew she was running away from herself even more than from Jude. It was this that made her stop and call back, 'Jude – goodbye.' But he didn't answer and she blundered into the dark moonless night as though temporarily blinded.

Back at Scarhill the house seemed full of silence. She glanced at her watch and was startled to see it was after midnight; Alec, she supposed, had gone up early. She helped herself to fruit juice, switched off the light and had started for the stairs when Alec called from his office. Sophie retraced her steps, crossed the living room and pushed wider the office door. 'I thought you'd gone to bed. What are you doing?'

'Writing to the insurance brokers. Trying to get back what we can.'

'Surely you don't have to do it at this hour?' She looked almost fearfully round the immaculate office: the metal files and desk, the swivelling office chair. They seemed incongruous furnishings for the ancient house.

'I was waiting up for you. How did it go?'

'Oh, all right.' Sophie swallowed. Alec must imagine she had been rehearsing all this time; she did not dare admit she had been to see Jude.

'You're very late.' Alec looked at her through his reading glasses.

'Oh several of us got roped in for drinks afterwards – at the rectory,' Sophie was vague. 'You shouldn't have bothered to wait up,' she repeated. That he had done so made her feel more guilty for lying to him. She waited, but Alec was tapping away on his computer. 'Aren't you coming up now?' she asked at last.

'Yes – I'm just finishing this.'

So Sophie went up ahead of him and was in bed with a book by the time he joined her.

'Did you see the dining room?' he asked.

'No' – she hadn't even thought about it. It was typical of Alec to talk about the dining room which most people, in view of the fire and its ramifications, would have forgotten.

'They've done the windows. They're reasonably satisfactory.'

'Oh good,' Sophie replied without enthusiasm or, at this moment, interest. She laid her book down and pulled the duvet up under her chin. Should she, ought she, tell Alec about Jude? Or should she allow Jude to speak for himself? But would he? Hadn't he rather invited her to be the medium between himself and Alec – to take the brunt, the edge off Alec's wrath?

'Do you want the light out?'

'Not if you want to read.'

'I don't.' Alec put down his magazine and clicked off the light. 'I can't see what Oliver Upton needed to rehearse you for this evening at all,' he said, turning on his side and sliding his arm over Sophie's body that was stiffened by the know-

ledge of her own untruthfulness. It had to come out about
Jude, she thought – now.

She took a deep breath, 'I stopped off at the Mill on my
way home,' she said. Her remark was greeted by silence.
'Alec?'

'What?'

'Don't you want to know?'

'Not particularly. Why should I?'

'Alec, I only had coffee with *your son*.' Thinking about it,
they hadn't even had coffee. But it sounded better.

'Only?'

'Yes.' Sophie raised herself on one elbow in righteous indignation. Her guilt, instead of curbing her sense of outrage,
made her more insistent. 'I wanted to ... to help him,' she
said. 'I could see he was in one of his states. You don't – can't
– seem to understand he's very unhappy.'

'So am I,' said Alec without hesitation.

'If you want to know, I think you're cruel and unfeeling.'

'What about Astra Merlin?' Alec flung back. 'Look how he
tramples over people, uses them.'

'He didn't mean to ...'

'Didn't mean to?' Alec rolled on his back jerking most of
the duvet off Sophie. 'Didn't mean to? If you've *done* something, what difference does not-meaning-to make?' He
paused. 'Anyway, what's the matter with you – why do you
have to make excuses for him all the time?'

'I don't.'

'You do.'

They lay in silence, Sophie unable to muster enough courage
to tell Alec that Jude was responsible for the fire, yet aware
sleep was unlikely to come until she did. What would Alec
do? Would he disown Jude – cut him off completely? She
supposed he would be quite entitled to do so. And Jude –
would he go to his mother? No, they didn't get on and she
didn't seem eager for his company. She, like Sophie, had
inherited children from the first wife. Sophie rolled over and
stared at the square of window, dark but lighter than the dark

178

room, and her disordered thoughts went round and round her mind. Finally she slept – dreamt. She was in the Mill, sitting on Jude's bed while he made her tea. He came over to her and then somehow they were lying side by side, and she was kissing Jude's body, their bare flesh was touching and it was exquisite, perfect, the sensation of their flesh melting into one, into each other . . .

Sophie woke. She lay in the dark knowing she was in bed with Alec but still overwhelmed by the sweetness of her dream. She didn't even feel guilt, it was too precious, too . . . she searched for the epithet . . . out of this world. She shut her eyes, tried to allow herself to sink back into the dream where everything was all right and she was supremely, utterly happy, but slowly, bit by bit, the sensation faded as the delicate scent of a flower fades with the midday sun. What did the dream mean? That she desired Jude? Certainly, but it was not just lust. Wasn't it much more? Wasn't it rather love – real love? She had never felt it before, not like in her dream, although . . . although if she was honest she had been aware of it in the Mill that evening. Perhaps right from the beginning there had always been something of it in her response to Jude, but only now had she come to recognise it. She shuddered with a little thrill of happiness and just briefly the exquisite feeling overwhelmed her again. If only she could keep it, Sophie thought, tether it, then she could go on recalling it at will. But, as before, it faded, leaving behind no certain knowledge it could ever again be conjured up. Sophie felt tears trickling down on to her lips, she indulged herself in their sad saltiness.

It was daylight before she again fell asleep and when she woke Alec was making love to her. She clutched him, giving herself in a kind of despair; he was good and kind to her in his own way and her behaviour, her desires, were positively wicked. So shameful in fact, that she could think of no one to whom she would dare confess. She must live alone with her secret. She, who had longed for 'love' all her life, now that she had found it, or supposed that she had, must cover it up, extinguish it. Worst of all, the night had passed without her telling Alec it was Jude who had set fire to his plantation. She felt it to be her final act of cowardice.

Alec dressed and went down ahead of her. When Sophie joined him he was reading his post on the windowseat while he waited for the coffee to simmer. Sophie began disembowelling the newly installed dishwasher, relieving it of its sparkling glasses, storing them away in the newly built cupboards. The novelty of the new kitchen made it mildly pleasurable to work in, but this morning she was all nerves and chipped a glass on the mixer tap which jutted forward aggressively over the double sink.

Alec frowned. 'You're all fingers and thumbs this morning, Soph,' he said.

'Yes,' said Sophie, 'I was going to say last night but it was late and . . .'

The door opened and Scarlet entered. She dropped her carrier bag, unwound her scarf. 'God,' she said, 'I'm famished. Is there anything in the fridge?'

'Not much,' said Sophie. 'You should have said you were coming.'

'I didn't know. I got a lift. Too good to miss although it meant leaving at six. I'll be able to see your panto, won't I?'

'Yes.' Sophie sounded less than enthusiastic. Scarlet moved round, opening cupboards, searching hopefully for food. 'Actually I thought I ought to see the fire-razed common,' she said casually. 'Is Daddy still hysterical? He was when he rang me up.' She looked at Alec, who ignored the remark. 'Also,' she went on, 'I've fixed it all up for little Astra. Thursday.'

Sophie stopped in the act of putting the salad bowl in the lower unit. She had hardly thought of Astra in the last forty-eight hours, but said, 'Kate says she may go into the hospital down here – National Health.'

'Shit,' said Scarlet. 'You could have told me. I've fixed it now. It's a decent private clinic. Is her mother really mean enough to send her on National Health? Why couldn't you have rung and said?'

'Sorry,' said Sophie, 'I really am sorry. It's just with the fire and the performances it didn't occur to me that you'd go ahead and fix it.'

'You told me to. Well, you can do the cancelling. I'm not going to.' Scarlet wedged farmhouse Cheddar between two biscuits, took her cup of coffee and walked out with an offended twitch of her hips, a reproving click of her sharp heels on the slates.

'That wasn't very thoughtful of you,' Alec said, looking over his glasses.

Sophie rounded on him. 'Well *you* do it. You do *something*. They're your children. Why should I do it all?'

'It seems to me,' said Alec, 'it would be better if you'd left well alone. Astra is Kate's child.'

'It wasn't "well" and Astra's child is Jude's child, and Jude is your child.' Sophie shouted.

'My dear Sophie, do calm down. There's been a misunderstanding over arrangements. If it will help anyone I'll certainly cancel the private clinic. But first it seems sensible to contact Kate Merlin and find out their intentions.'

At which Sophie felt ashamed of her outburst and slightly foolish for having meddled where it now seemed it might have been better not to. 'I'll ring Kate,' she said, 'ask her.'

As she went through to the telephone it came back to her that she had still said nothing about Jude.

Eddie Fardon saw fit to torture Benjy. Why not? Torturing was power, torturing was sport – it was an admirably male occupation and now, for the first time, he had a good reason to indulge in such an agreeable task. For had not Benjy set fire to the Deneuves' plantation – was he not a criminal? He needed teaching a lesson, so Eddie took upon himself to teach it: he invited Benjy for the day. He also invited his friend Jack who was large and solid and not normally given to torture unless incited.

Benjy came down on his bike on the morning after the fire. He put it in the shed at Tinners as usual and, blissfully unaware of the day ahead, entered Tinners by way of the lean-to that jutted out like a veranda over the back door and provided shelter for a saw-horse and logs. In Tinners' kitchen Eddie and Jack were leaning over the table, talking. Benjy's heart sank, he had not expected Jack. He knew of old what another friend of Eddie's meant – that the two of them would gang up together and leave him out. Benjy thought wistfully of his bike in the shed and wondered whether he should get on it and go home while he could, but Jack and Eddie were looking friendly enough and his fears dispelled.

'Hi, Benj,' Eddie greeted him jovially.

'Hi.'

'Why do you say "hi" if you ain't a Yank?' Jack wanted to know. Jack was the son of a ganger for the Forestry Commission.

'Because Eddie does.' Benjy's reply was honest and pat.

'Do you always do what Eddie does?'

' 'Course he does,' Eddie was eager to be an example. 'He's a good lad, is Benj.' Benjy smiled happily, apparently he had said the right thing. He wished Jack would go home – perhaps he was just about to.

'Come on out the shed, then, Ed.'

'OK.'

They moved towards the door. Benjy moved too.

'No, not you,' said Jack, 'only Eddie.'

Benjy stopped. His thumb started to go up to his mouth but he arrested it just in time. He was learning *something* at school, if only to keep hand from mouth.

Eddie said nothing.

'Can't I come?' Benjy looked at his best friend.

'It's Jack's bike, see – an' if Jack doesn't want you to see it then I reckon you gotta stay here.' They stared at Benjy, hoping he wouldn't give in too easily and their sport be over.

'Why can't I see it?' Benjy demanded, looking at Jack.

' 'Cos you might burn it up, set light to it – mightn't he, Eddie?' They both laughed. 'What you gone and done it for?' Jack looked genuinely interested. Benjy said nothing. 'Go on, tell us,' Jack pressed.

It now entered Benjy's mind that he'd be thought more of, even one of them, if he said he'd lit the fire. It would prove, he believed, he was not the 'girlie' they repeatedly called him; it would counteract his occupations such as hanging curtains and knitting that he had so unwisely allowed to be known about during a foolish moment of honesty. In short Benjy suddenly saw his way to being accepted, becoming one of 'them'.

'Yeah – I done it,' he said. Oh yes, he knew how to talk like they did – he'd certainly learnt *not* to talk how they didn't. 'I done it with matches,' he went on.

Jack chortled, approached him and tweaked his ear. 'We reckoned you'd done it with *matches*,' he said, grinning at Benjy, 'What us wants to know is what gave you the h'idea? Put it in your mind, like.'

'Everyone says Alec Deneuve shouldn't never have done what he done to the Common.' Benjy got it out. Jack pinched Benjy's ear tighter at this. Benjy's face went scarlet with the effort not to wince or show he was in pain. 'Can I come then?' he asked.

Jack let go of him. 'What do you think, Ed?' he demanded. 'Shall us let 'un see?'

Eddie who was a past master at running with the hare and hunting with the hounds refused to commit himself. 'S'your bike,' he said.

'Tell you what,' Jack said, surveying Benjy's hopeful face, 'set fire to the Forestry's woods next time and us'll show 'ee the bike.'

He and Eddie seemed to find this very funny – they were still laughing as they went out the door.

'Shan't be long, Benj,' said Eddie over his shoulder.

Benjy, left on his own, comforted himself for some moments with his thumb; in fact he was on the table swinging his legs, sucking it and waiting, when Lucy entered.

'On your own then? Where's Eddie?'

'Him and Jack's out with the bike.'

'Oh' – Lucy was only half listening, she was actually thinking what to get for Gabe's lunch.

Getting Gabe's lunch was a chore Lucy had taken upon herself since the day they got married. Either sandwiches or cooked. It was her duty, she had been brought up to believe. He, after all, was a 'working' man and 'working' men must eat. It made sense to Lucy. That she was a 'working' woman, worked from nine till five every day in the Co-op, was simply her choice. Well, she presumed it was. Gabe hadn't forced her into taking the job, she had wanted to, it got her out of the house. So she had come to regard her work almost guiltily as pleasure, whereas Gabe's work was proper work, man's work, hard. The kind of thing you did only for the necessity of earning money. Lucy, on the contrary, earned money and enjoyed it – so in no sense could her toil be compared with Gabe's.

Only sometimes, just sometimes, as she burrowed under the sink for the potato bucket Gabe had omitted to fill, did Lucy question this logic. Like today, Saturday – when Gabe had gone down to the pub and would return in time to eat his cooked meal, and Lucy had got up early and walked up to Joan's to get a lift into Meridan, worked until twelve, then shopped and hurried home, again with Joan because Gabe had to have the van to get down the pub – she did wonder if it was entirely fair that she got the lunch and washed up, and later that evening got the supper which Gabe then, with the expression of a martyr, cleared by shoving the plates in a heap on the draining-board. The trouble was if she didn't make a pleasant home for Gabe he'd be gone off elsewhere – with the Granger woman – about that Lucy was certain. So Lucy toiled and Gabe 'worked' and that was the way things were.

All this and more, in an abbreviated version, passed through Lucy's mind at the same time as she talked to Benjy, so that she was not really registering, but after a few moments, once she had started on the Brussels sprouts, she was better able to concentrate. And immediately the fire came into her mind. Benjy Merlin, it was said, had been responsible, though she didn't think it likely herself, knowing him as she did.

'Terrible about the fire, wasn't it?' she commented.

'Yeah,' said Benjy.

'You was one of the first to see it, Mrs Bellamy said.'

'Yep,' said Benjy.

'What was you doin' up top when you shoulda bin helpin' your mum and sister down the village hall?'

'Nothing.'

Lucy scraped and ripped off the outside leaves. Some of the sprouts she saw to her displeasure were black all the way through, which just went to show she should have known better than to buy Co-op veg.

'You must've been doin' something.'

'I was following Jude Deneuve,' Benjy said, without really thinking.

'Jude Deneuve?' Lucy pricked up her ears. 'What was he doin' up on the Common?'

'Dunno,' said Benjy.

'Was it him lit the fire?' Lucy couldn't see a way to asking other than direct.

'Na-ow,' said Benjy, 'Na-ow. What'd *he* want to set light to his dad's trees for?'

'So then you must've.' Lucy said it as a joke – laughed.

'No I didn't,' said Benjy. 'It's what everyone says, but I didn't. I didn't have matches nor nothing.'

'I'm sure you didn't,' said Lucy, and she impulsively crossed to Benjy and hugged him. Even if the Merlins had gazumped and hadn't paid up for the pony yet, Benjy was a good little chap. Lucy felt herself glow with charity; she kissed him on his cheek and Benjy drew back. Lucy was all right, but he only really liked being kissed by Astra or his mother. He kicked his legs more violently forward and back against the table and looked at the clock – Jack and Eddie had been gone a long time . . .

There was a roar from outside, then the sound of an engine ticking over. Benjy jumped off the table and pulled the door

185

open, but too late. A further roar, a flinging up of grit, and Jack slanted his bike out of the gate with Eddie on the back. They receded swiftly up the long lane. Benjy waited for a bit, but when they didn't come back he put his bike on the roof-rack of the baker's van and got a lift home – or almost home. In this at least he was fortunate, for the way back was nearly all uphill and it had begun to rain.

On the afternoon after the fire the weather broke. Clouds gathered over Poundsford and a general depression settled over the neighbourhood. It seemed to signify the end of summer; only the farmers were pleased with the steady rain.

Jude arrived at Bag Down at 4 p.m. to find Astra on her own; Kate was either out or in her studio. The house looked sad, he thought, under its cloth of glistening, rain-soaked ivy; small rivulets ran down the cobbles past him as he made his way up to the door. He had spent the morning packing his belongings into a crate; what was left over he had put into cardboard boxes and tied round with string. These he had stacked at the top of the stairs. He had then swept the floor so that everything should be in order, put the rubbish out in a polythene bag against the dustbin, and driven himself over. Now he lifted and let fall the heavy iron knocker.

Astra greeted him civilly but just coolly enough to uninten-tionally fan Jude's passion for her. For her part, she felt appre-hension as she looked up at Jude's face in the darkness of the hallway, felt that demands beyond those she normally had to contend with were about to be made. She led the way into the living room, and he followed, sat opposite her across the polished table, recounted his actions and intentions while she listened incredulous, her chin cupped in her hands, even her sickness forgotten. When he had finished she stood up and poked the fire with her toe, it gave her a much-needed moment before she must respond, give her opinion.

'So you'll go to prison?' she asked. 'You'll really go?'

'Yes,' said Jude confidently. 'I don't have much choice, actu-ally. They're blaming Benjy, as you must know ...'

'But he didn't do it,' Astra interrupted, 'Benjy'd never do anything like that in a million years. And how could they prove it? He didn't have matches or a lighter or ... He couldn't have done it. I know he didn't.' Astra felt her proof weakening. After all, other people might not believe in Benjy as she did. 'The worst of it is,' she finished, 'he's gone and told Eddie Fardon he did it – the silly little twit!'

'What on earth for?' Jude was startled.

'Don't ask me. I expect he thought they'd be impressed. You know what those little toughs are like.'

'I don't, actually.'

Astra didn't choose to explain.

'Anyhow,' Jude went on, 'if he's said he did it that really makes things difficult – in fact it gives me no alternative. It would be an act of cowardice *not* to confess. I couldn't possibly allow Benjy to be a suspect even if they couldn't prove it. Besides, prison would give me a chance to make public my stand against my father's exploitation – '

'But who will care about you and your father?' Astra fixed puzzled grey eyes on his face.

Jude looked pained. 'It's not just a private vendetta. It's an individual stand for something of national – even international – importance. It's against the wilful destruction of our environment for individual gain.'

Astra felt herself shrink before Jude's idealism. She was confused because though she agreed with him in principle she couldn't feel sympathetic to his actions.

'Supposing someone stands surety for you?' she asked.

'They won't – and if they did that's only for the weeks before the trial.'

'Sophie might.'

'My father won't let her – and as it was his trees they're hardly likely to let me home.'

Astra said nothing. There seemed nothing to say. 'I go in on Monday,' she said at last. Then smiled ironically. 'It's my act of cowardice.'

187

'Astra – I still love you, you do know that. I'll always love you.'

'Yes,' said Astra dully. Then, 'But what good'll it do us if you're in prison?'

'You'll be able to visit me.'

'Where?'

'I don't know yet. The county gaol, probably.' In fact, like most people, Jude's knowledge of the law was slight – he really had no idea. 'Astra, turn round. Look at me.' He stared at her. 'What's the matter?' he asked.

It seemed to Astra that Jude was always asking what the matter was. She turned away from him and he sensed rather than saw she was crying. His head began to throb again, he could feel the beat of the pulse in his temple.

'Astra?' For answer she took out a tissue from her sleeve and blew her nose. She rounded on him.

'What did you do it for? You're mad – absolutely crazy. It can't possibly do any good. Your father will buy a whole lot more seedlings and plant them again.'

'You can't plant immediately where it's been burnt.'

'So what? He'll still plant them up again. He's that sort.' She gazed at him as though not seeing him but looking far beyond. 'I can't see it benefiting anyone,' she said, 'not even you. Didn't you think of the consequences before you lit it? Or did you hope to get away with it?'

'I knew it had to be done. I don't care about myself, Astra. That's where we differ. You do – I don't. Don't misunderstand me, it's good that you do.'

'Why don't you care?' Astra almost shouted. It seemed the key to Jude, the thing about him she could never understand – that he actually didn't care. He was telling the truth.

He didn't answer.

'Why?' she persisted.

'I don't know,' said Jude helplessly. 'I wish I did.' The pulse was thumping away in his brain again. Thumpety-thump, thumpety-thump. He got out at last what he had been waiting to say from the moment he had arrived. 'If you loved me, it would be different . . .'

But Astra cut him off. *'Don't* say that.' Her voice was low and packed with anger and emotion. 'Don't. Don't ever say that to me again. I will not be blamed for your actions.'

'No one is blaming you. I was simply telling you the reason. You asked why.'

'What you say isn't true.' Astra walked to the window in her agitation, opened it, pushed out the cat that had been miaowing round her legs.

'It's perfectly clear you don't love me.'

'Love? What is love? To me it's a baby I have to abort.' Astra's eyes glistened at him from her flushed face. Even in anger, her beauty held him as though he was a third person observing from the outside. 'And you're complacently going to confess so they'll shut you up,' Astra went on, glared at him. 'You won't even come to visit me in hospital. It may seem heroic to you but I don't care about your trees and principles or you and your father's stupid fights. I care about me. *Me.* If only I'd cared enough I wouldn't be in the position I'm in now.' A sob escaped her. 'I did it for you. I never wanted to fuck – not really. I thought you did, so I gave way. It's so unfair. If I'd been egotistic and selfish none of this would be happening to me – the abortion. All this misery.'

'You could have it.'

'No I couldn't.' But the thought checked Astra. 'Why do you say this now?' she asked him angrily.

'Once I got used to the idea, I wanted you to have it. I wanted us to marry and you to have it. You know I did.'

'Well I'm not going to.' She had to be strong, convince herself, didn't she? She'd decided; it was all arranged for Monday, the day after tomorrow. She would go in on Sunday. She must go through with it.

'Astra . . .'

'Go away.'

'Astra, I didn't mean . . .'

'Go away. *Please*, go away.'

189

Astra's erect back was to him. He took his jacket and put it on, uncertain whether to stay or go.

'If you cared about me – really cared – you could never have done all this.'

'I know. I'm sorry. It just . . . happened.' Jude knew himself that his action had been madness and only the chance to make public his dissociation from his father gave him courage.

She turned to face him. 'Can't you wait – at least till after the abortion?' she pleaded, her eyes tragic.

Jude looked contrite. 'Lucy Martin knows I was up there, Benjy let it out. And if I confess it'll be a shorter sentence – they may even suspend my sentence. But if I wait for them to find out and charge me . . .'

He had moved back to Astra and now slid his arms round her, drew her tightly up against him, his mouth kissing her neck, her ears, trying for her mouth. For a few moments Astra stood passively, neither giving herself nor responding, then she freed herself with a sigh. 'Oh go on then. Go and tell them. What does it matter?' But he saw she was crying.

'Don't, Astra. The last thing in the world I want to do is make you suffer. I'll make them let me out on bail so I'll be with you when you come home.'

Then at last Astra turned her face up and their mouths met in a long kiss mixed with the salty taste of her tears. When Jude finally let her go she murmured, 'Why, oh why have we got ourselves into such a mess? Me having an abortion and you going to prison – we must be terribly stupid. It's the way famous people carry on, not people like us.' Then before Jude could answer she ran away up the stairs.

Jude drove straight into Meridan with a heavy heart; the pace of his life was hotting up, accelerating beyond his control. It was true he had taken action against his father and it had, in some sense, liberated him. He persuaded himself that if the only way to draw attention to your cause was by an act of violence, then he was prepared for it. This he had demonstrated by the fire, and now was the moment to follow it up.

With only the briefest instant of hesitation, he mounted the steps to the police station.

Meridan police were startled, to say the least of it. The moor was regularly burnt by farmers every March, and later in the summer by thoughtless tourists dropping their cigarettes out of car windows, or even the occasional arsonist, but rarely did the culprit arrive in person to explain his reason for choosing to burn down a plantation. Jude was ushered in by the police constable who only manned Meridan two days a week. Jude was lucky to find him there, as was made clear to him. Very lucky.

So Jude sat down opposite the constable at his desk and, after being cautioned that anything he said could be taken as evidence against him, confessed. The caution didn't worry him at all, quite the reverse – he even hoped it might filter through to the Press. He explained his motivation and enquired what charge would be brought against him. This, it was explained, would depend on the result of his trial and before he could ask further questions he was put into a police car and taken down to Taverston where a cell was made available, into which he was firmly locked for the night. He was asked whether he wished his family to be notified but replied that his only adult relative in the area was his father, and as it was his father he had acted against, he saw no point in informing him.

The cell was bare with a hard bed, a single blanket, and a disconcerting slit in the door through which eyes could look. A rather sordid looking chamber-pot with an inner rim of yellow stood in the corner, but Jude, emotionally exhausted underneath his apparent confidence, turned his face to the wall and slept.

'Alec, did you ... have you ever thought it might have been Jude who started the fire?'

Sophie had said it at last.

Alec's eyes narrowed; he was sitting behind her, polishing

his shoes. He watched her as she applied dabs of rouge to her cheeks; his eyes met hers in the mirror. 'No – I hadn't.'

Sophie carefully unscrewed the top of her silver eyeshadow. Tonight would be her second and final attempt at Rapunzel – there were to be no more performances.

'Well it was.'

'Why didn't you tell me before?'

Sophie averted her eyes. 'Alec I . . .'

'What?'

'I tried to this morning but Scarlet came in and then I went to rehearse and when I got back you'd gone out,' Sophie finished feebly.

'When did you know? Who told you?'

Sophie's eyes pricked with guilt, confusion and resentment. 'Jude told me.'

'When?' Alec barked.

'At the Mill.'

'Oh, so you've been down there?' Alec's sarcasm cut through Sophie. She felt enraged.

'No,' she shouted. 'Yes . . . I told you I called in yesterday evening.'

'So everyone knows except me?'

'No. I *don't know*. No, of course not.' Tears of humiliation and rage trickled down her face, smudging her carefully applied stage make-up. 'I hate you, Alec, you're always upsetting me. You never think of me – only you. Why should you shout at me, blame me?'

Alec stabbed at his polish. 'I'm blaming you for not having the decency, the adulthood, to tell me, but behaving like . . . like an idiot schoolgirl.'

'I was going to tell you,' Sophie shouted.

'But you didn't.'

'No.' Sophie got up and ran out of the room. She paused at the top of the stairs, 'I'm going away and I'll never come back. Good riddance I say to you and all your stupid money and mad children.'

And she went downstairs as fast as she possibly could in

her odd, tight Twenties dress that, owing to Carol's sewing, didn't flare as it should have so she had to clutch it up above her knees. She hurried up the yard and into her car. Grit spinning under the wheels, she drove up the drive.

When she looked in her rear view mirror and saw Alec following, she drove even faster. Her car being smaller than Alec's gave her an advantage in the narrow lanes. She squeezed past an oncoming vehicle that he was unable to pass, and drew far enough ahead to take a small turning off down a steep lane barred at the end by a gate.

She sat with her heart beating, listening for Alec's car which a few moments later passed going fast on the road above her. Sophie wound her window up, hastily reversed back up the lane and drove back the way she had come, afraid that at any moment she would see Alec closing up behind her. She was still looking in her rear mirror when she came round a bend and, too late, saw the oncoming car. With a squeal of breaks and a crunch of metal they slid into each other.

For a moment Sophie sat feeling sick with shock and fright. Then the person in the more formidable pick-up she had hit, got out, came along and put his head in through her window.

'In a hurry, weren't you? Are you all right?'

'Yes. I'm sorry,' Sophie muttered.

The man went and looked at the entwined bumpers; Sophie's car had a smashed headlight and buckled wing. His own had escaped more or less unscathed. Sophie got out too.

'If I lift and you reverse, we may be able to get them apart,' he said.

Sophie got in and tried her engine but it wouldn't start. The man hung in her window again; he was clearly a farmer and found Sophie, with her flimsy above-the-knee dress, something of a curiosity. 'Let me try' he said, and Sophie obediently moved across. It was easier to do as she was told than anything else. The farmer tried with no success, lifted the bonnet, tried again.

Time was passing. Sophie began to feel anxious, she had no watch and the car clock seemed to have stopped on impact;

she was sure it must be time for the pantomime. Why had she been so inexcusably stupid, driven so wildly? Just because of a silly scene with Alec! She would be late, everyone would be waiting for her . . . She turned to the farmer, her heavily made-up eyes large and tragic. 'Please, I'm due to sing in a panto-mime. If your car will go, could you drive me there?'

'We best get your car up against the hedge first.'

So between them they pushed and shoved and turned the wheel until Sophie's car was close enough to the hedge to enable others to pass, and then she climbed in the passenger side of the pick-up and the farmer reversed down the lane until he could turn. With torn number-plate fastened up with baler-cord, he drove Sophie to Poundsford village hall and put her down. Sophie thanked him, assured him her insurance would see to it, contact his, apologised yet again, and hurried up to the hall in the gathering darkness.

At the door she unmistakably heard singing, followed by applause. Her heart went cold with disappointment. She couldn't bring herself to enter, she crept along the side of the hall, climbed on a water butt and peered through the window. From the grouping on stage she knew at once they must be about twenty minutes into the performance. Lucy was centre stage. At that moment she stepped forward in a long white dress and Sophie's heart sank. Clearly she was doing her, Sophie's, solo. She pressed her ear to the glass in an endeavour to hear but Lucy's voice was barely audible. What she did hear was the enthusiastic applause at the end. Sophie's misery increased – after all that work, all that rehearsing. Oh, she may have dreaded it but she had still wanted to do it. Would she be allowed to do the second act, she wondered, sing after the interval? But that, she could see, would seem all wrong and besides, her voice would sound thin after Lucy's almost professional one.

Sophie now noticed something that made her press her face even more intently against the glass – Jude's part had been replaced as well as her own. Astra was there, in fact all the others as usual – but not Jude.

Stepping down from the butt as soundlessly as possible, she made her way to the car park. She was searching with her eyes for a sign of Kate's elderly Morris 1000 that she knew was generally left unlocked, when her attention was caught by the sound of voices coming from a van squeezed in between the back of the hall and a high wall. Anxious to speak to anyone, explain her plight, Sophie was too self-absorbed to think as she would have in other circumstances. Predominant in her mind was the idea of getting a lift home. So she moved towards the van, edged along between the wall and the driver's side and tapped on the window. Who owned the van Sophie had no idea and the increasing darkness prevented her having a clear view of it.

At her tap there fell an absolute silence, followed in a few seconds by a further murmur of voices and the van rocked.

'Is there someone I could speak to?' she called, softly because of the performance.

The next moment the window went down and a man's head and shoulders were framed in it. He nodded. 'What is it?' he asked. His voice seemed familiar but, unable to make out his features in the dark, Sophie couldn't place it.

'I'm stuck for a car to take me home,' she said. 'I've had a collision.'

Her statement was greeted by a further silence.

'You wouldn't consider driving me to Scarhill, would you?' she persisted. Then suddenly recognised it was Gabe Fardon. 'Oh,' she said, 'I didn't see it was you. Aren't you listening to Lucy?'

'I come on late – I didn't like to go in, case it upsets her. I'm waitin' to pick her up.'

While he talked, she became aware of a faint but familiar scent; she was also struck by the absolute silence of whoever it was in the back of the van. Slowly her brain shifted from her own plight to the present, and all at once it dawned on her she had disturbed lovers. Gabe had a woman in there with him. Covered in embarrassment at her clumsy intrusion, she edged backwards out of the narrow gap.

'Don't bother,' she said. 'I'll borrow Kate Merlin's car . . .' and she clipped across the car park as fast as her silly shoes would allow her.

Moments later she had found Kate's Morris with the key in the dashboard and was driving herself home. At the same time she pondered on the van and quite suddenly it came to her – it had been Carol in there with Gabe Fardon. It was Carol's scent she had smelt that had been so familiar, but surely, surely, Carol would have wanted to see the performance? Sophie felt oddly forlorn. What passion, she wondered, must Carol experience to make lovemaking in the back of a van assume pride of place? She felt there must be an entire world of sensuality of which she was unaware. Her heart gave a beat of envy most unnatural to it, and her own life by contrast seemed to have failed on all counts. Tonight she was neither singing nor experiencing the nether regions of sexuality . . . It was this thought which made her take a left-hand turn that would take her back past the Mill. Perhaps Jude would be there – her heart thumped in anticipation as she drew nearer along the narrow lane. But the Mill stood in darkness with no lights showing through the slit-like windows; it looked sinister in its height. Sophie stopped, opened the door and called up, but got no response. Where was Jude? With her panic increasing every moment she hurried back into the car and drove on to Scarhill.

Alec, imagining himself in pursuit of Sophie, drove up on to the moor. Only when he reached a fork in the road did he feel at a loss and stop; he sat for a few moments with the engine ticking over, while a group of moor ponies drifted past him, grazing the road banks. He both saw them and did not see them because his thoughts were uppermost, dominating him. It was his inability to suppress his anger that most upset him, it was as if water had seeped through a floodgate and more and more was forcing its way out, widening the crack, against which he could do nothing. But wasn't it reasonable that he should be furious over the fire? Wasn't it deceitful and wrong of Sophie not to have told him Jude was responsible immediately she found out? Was not his anger, his pursuit of Sophie – for what exact purpose he didn't know – only to be expected? But his rationalisation of his irrationality exposed its flaw. Was he, could he, be jealous? Jealous of whom? Of his wife with his son?

Alec pushed the thought from his mind – it was not jealousy, it was common sense to prevent a futile and destructive relationship growing up between them. Reassured of the reasonableness of his actions, he started the engine and drove quickly until he came to the section of road that crossed the western flank of Scardon, where he slowed down to look at the waste of blackened hillside. At this moment the last of the light mercifully faded and Alec was spared the full vision of his burnt seedlings, for, as Jack Bellamy had remarked to Dan Callow in the pub, it was like layin' down pound notes and setting light to them. Whereupon Jack had ordered another pint all round and the locals had shaken their heads mournfully if contentedly, other people's suffering giving a certain shaming satisfaction under the camouflage of sympathy.

Alec continued down the hill over the cattle-grid off the moor, and turned right again into Scarhill. He was surprised to see Kate Merlin's car in the back yard. What could she want? Astra Merlin's abortion immediately sprang to Alec's mind. Or had the pantomime been cancelled, had Sophie not turned up to sing and Kate come in search of her? Alec had not thought of this possibility before, it had simply not entered his head. He went into the kitchen expecting to see Kate and was amazed to find Sophie sitting at the table, nursing a glass of what looked like whisky.

'Aren't you singing?' Alec asked. 'Where's Kate Merlin? Her car's outside.'

'I borrowed it.' And Sophie related the sad events of her evening. 'Lucy's singing instead of me,' she finished.

'Oh.' Alec looked anxiously at Sophie. To be fair to him he had no idea how much it meant to Sophie, because in front of him she had always treated her part as a joke, something she *had* to do, rather than a part she wanted to play. He asked now, 'Do you mind?'

'It's not important,' Sophie said bravely, 'but Jude's gone. I've been to the Mill and he's not there.'

'Is that why you were in such a hurry?' Alec felt his own unjustness but could not prevent it; emotion had taken over at the mention of Jude.

'No, it wasn't,' Sophie said bitterly. 'It was because of you. You ruined my evening for me.' And in spite of biting her lip to prevent herself, tears came. Alec's concern increased, he felt guilty and remorseful.

'Sophie, don't,' he said. He came and put his arms around her, kissed the side of her face. Sophie tried to free herself, she hated Alec, didn't she? She certainly had less than an hour ago. But when you were unhappy and carless in the country, comfort was difficult to resist and Alec was comforting. I'm weak, she thought, weak – I really despise myself. But all the time she could feel herself relenting towards him.

Finally she freed herself to search for a tissue in the cupboard. Alec, feeling vastly better because he knew he had Sophie back – or more or less back – offered to collect her from the hall when she returned Kate's car. Sophie blew her nose and felt relieved. She accepted his offer, then returned to the topic uppermost in her mind.

'Jude could have gone to the police,' she said in a muffled voice, 'confessed.'

'I can't pretend I'd be sorry,' Alec said. 'He was bound to get his come-uppance sooner or later.'

Sophie's eyes opened wide. 'Alec, you're not serious? What about Astra? What about . . . about everything?'

'What about it? Astra Merlin's having an abortion, isn't she? I imagine that little episode will be over.' Alec's tone was contemptuous.

Sophie said nothing. She couldn't. She was thinking about Jude. She simply looked into her goldy-brown whisky and, from time to time, sipped. Eventually she asked, 'Aren't you worried about him? I mean we don't *know* if he's gone to the police.'

Their eyes met sharing the unspoken thought, the possibility that Jude might have done something worse; then Alec, perhaps to hide his anxiety, stood and smashed his fist down on the table so that Sophie jumped. 'I'm not bloody well going to worry myself about him – even if he is my son, which I'm beginning to doubt.'

'Alec!' Sophie was scandalised and frankly fascinated. It was one thought that up until that moment had never occurred to her. 'Have you ever said that to him?'

'No,' Alec felt contrite, 'but I may do if he doesn't stop interfering with my life.'

Sophie was still staring at him. 'Is that why he's like, well, you know. Like he is? Because you *have* told him? You have, haven't you? I'm sure of it.'

'I haven't.'

'Alec, you're lying.'

Alec looked out of the window clearly undecided how to proceed. 'What does it matter anyhow? I'm sure he's just as anxious *not* to be my son as I am to disown him.'

'That's not the point.' Sophie for once had the upper hand. 'He is Jane's, isn't he?'

'Yes of course.'

'Then whose son is he?'

'He could be mine or he could be someone else's. According to Jane it was two successive nights.' Sophie could hardly believe it.

'Couldn't you have had a blood test or . . . or something?'

'I did and it proved nothing – only that I could be. But then so could the other bugger.'

'Why haven't you told me this before?'

Alec shrugged. 'Because I knew you'd react exactly as you are doing – and it doesn't make a bit of difference. To all intents and purposes he's *my* son.'

Alec went out, closing the door firmly, anxious to terminate the conversation he now wished he'd never begun.

Sophie sat for a while without moving, then glanced at the clock. The performance, she calculated, would have just finished; Lucy would be receiving the applause for which she, Sophie, had endured so much at the hands of Oliver Upton. Then her mind reverted to Jude. He *is* Alec's son, she thought. They're even more alike in character than looks, I'd bet thousands on him being Alec's son. There still remained the uncertainty and if Jude knew, as it seemed he did, it would go a long way to account for his hatred of his parents, for always there must be for him the uncertainty, the doubt. Who was the other possible father? she wondered, and as quickly dismissed the thought. Jude was Alec's and that was all there was to it.

Just before the curtain was pulled across the proscenium arch of the village hall stage, Carol slipped in through the double doors and stood at the back. As the applause resounded and the characters came forward to take their bows, she became aware that Oliver Upton was moving down the side aisle pushing aside chairs in order to get to her.

'Do you know what happened to them?' he murmured, low and remarkably close to her ear.

'No, I can't imagine,' Carol lied, for she had heard every word that had passed between Sophie and Gabe from her uncomfortable position in the depths of the van. She hoped fervently that Sophie had not guessed it was her, for after all she had no reason to suppose that it was, and no proof. Carol felt a flush mount her neck at the thought. 'Perhaps their car broke down,' she said.

'It's almost certainly that boy.' Oliver Upton's passion for Sophie made him immediately lay the blame on Jude.

'Why?' asked Carol who found the rector's absurd adoration of Sophie, which had become transparent during rehearsals, extremely aggravating.

'He's unreliable and untrustworthy. I wouldn't put anything past him.'

Carol knew the rector well enough to know he was off on

one of his irrational outbursts. Not, mind you, that she didn't agree with him about not putting anything past Jude. She wouldn't either. He had a funny look about him, she'd always said so to Richard.

'I imagine something must have happened,' she said, and started to edge away. 'I'll simply have to dash – half of them can't get out of their costumes without me.'

'What did you think of it?' Oliver Upton shouted after her.

'Oh excellent,' Carol called back over her shoulder, 'an absolutely super performance. You should have done one more night.'

And the rector was left this balm to cover his very real and smarting wounds.

Kate was helping Astra pack her things for the hospital when Sophie arrived at midday the following day. She leant out the window to see who it was, and on viewing the BMW, quickly withdrew her head.

'It's Sophie.'

Astra, who could feel nothing but liking for Sophie, was surprised at her mother's tone. 'Does that matter?' she asked.

'Well, it's not very convenient, is it?' The car door slammed; clearly Sophie would be calling through the front door at any moment.

Kate glanced round the room. There was an open suitcase on the bed; small piles of folded clothes, mainly nightwear and underclothes, lined its base and all the drawers of the chest were pulled open. Astra's flowered sponge-bag disported itself on the windowsill, her fluffy slippers oozed from beneath a sheet that hung from the unmade bed. The only order was inside the suitcase.

'You go down and see her,' Astra said. 'We've finished this anyhow.' She added her diary and some books and firmly closed the lid.

Kate hesitated fractionally, then went. Seconds later she admitted Sophie radiating her usual scent and immaculate cleanliness, both of which Kate would have like to emulate.

But she was not a tidy person and her clothes, though often beautiful, never had that supreme newness and crispness of Sophie's; her hair never seemed quite as recently washed. All this and more passed through Kate's head in an entirely superficial manner as she told Sophie to sit while she poured them a drink – whisky – there was a drop left in the bottom of the bottle and it seemed the moment for it. Astra was still upstairs.

'I wanted to explain about last night – I even, very briefly, borrowed your car. Did you know?' And Sophie launched into a lengthy explanation, leaving out about Carol and Gabe in the van, and only gradually taking in the hostility in Kate's response. 'I'm sorry,' she finished, 'I know I let everyone down but there was absolutely nothing I could do. And I suppose I gave Lucy a chance to use her wonderful voice?'

She said the last rather wistfully, she would so much have liked Kate to contradict her, say what a loss she had been, but Kate's forehead creased into a frown.

'Of course I understand,' she said. 'I know these things happen – and it must have been disappointing for you after all the work you've put in. Was Jude with you?'

'No.' There was an uncomfortable silence before Sophie said, 'Actually we don't know where he is – not for certain. It's rather worrying. I was going to ask you if you'd seen him? That was one of the reasons I came – and to apologise,' she added hastily.

Kate felt her patience running out. Sophie knew perfectly well Astra was going to hospital today – or could she, in her normal self-centred fashion, have forgotten? 'I'm very sorry, Sophie,' she said, 'but you honestly have come at a bad moment. I'm about to take Astra down to St Stephen's. We were just packing.' She drank the remains of her drink and put her glass firmly on the table. Sophie hadn't even begun hers, but she took the hint and drank it quickly.

'Go back to Astra – don't wait for me,' she said, 'I'd no idea . . .' Kate's rather cold stare made her voice trail away. 'I'll visit her,' she said, 'just as soon as it's over.'

'She shouldn't be in more than a day. She'll be home on Tuesday.'

'Yes – oh good. Could I wish her luck ... or ... or will you give her my love and say I'll keep my fingers crossed for her.' Is Astra angry with me too, Sophie wondered? Why doesn't she come down? Kate was already at the foot of the stairs. 'Goodbye,' Sophie finished lamely.

For heaven's sake, Kate thought, as she started up the stairs, doesn't she realise this is caused by her and Alec and their irresponsible son? No, that's not fair, she reprimanded herself; Sophie really can't be blamed for the actions of an adult stepson. Yet in some obscure way Kate continued to do so; there was something about Sophie's way of walking light-footed over life that was extremely irksome.

One hour later Kate delivered her daughter to the hospital.

Astra, once her mother had gone, breathed a sigh of relief. She was in a ward of ten, partitioned off by curtains into cubicles of two, with everything ultra-modern, fresh, and exuding an air of efficiency; only the faint but distinctive smell of disinfectant that wafted down the corridors acted as a reminder of what went on behind the immaculate façade. Astra undressed as she had been told to do and got into bed. In a few minutes the ward sister came and took notes, while Astra sat against the pillows and gave monosyllabic answers. The ward sister looked at her curiously. 'It's only a very small operation,' she said, 'D & C – a curettage.'

'I know,' said Astra.

'It'll be quite painless. We give you an injection to make you sleepy, followed by the anaesthetic, and when you wake up it'll all be over.' She smiled brightly, reassuringly.

'Yes,' said Astra.

A dull girl, the sister thought, but then it often was the ones with low IQ's that got themselves into trouble. She told Astra to lie on her back and in a moment a nurse would be in to shave her and take some blood tests.

Astra lay on her back and looked at the ceiling while the

young nurse talked and performed her delicate task, which tickled but was otherwise painless. She could not believe all this was happening to her, yet now it was in motion, now her mother had gone she felt relief, as though she was taken over, no longer responsible, and her life was in the hands of others. Yet she was not quite able to dispel the nagging inner voice suggesting to her it was not too late, she could still get up from the bed, leave the hospital, say she had changed her mind. But had she? Would she have got this far had she wanted the baby? That was it – she didn't *want* it but thought she ought to have it ... The nurse came back, tightened a black rubber band round Astra's arm till it hurt, pressed the pump.

'Would you have this operation if you were me?' she asked her. She hadn't exactly meant to, it was as if her voice spoke undirected. The freckled nurse with red hair and a Scottish accent didn't reply, then said: 'You oughtn't to be thinking about that now.' She stared with a troubled expression into Astra's implacable face. Astra didn't answer, so she went on, 'Haven't you had anyone to talk it over with? What about the father, or is he no good?'

Was Jude no good? 'He's going to prison,' Astra said, realising as she said it that it would give quite the wrong impression.

'Oh my goodness,' the nurse said, looking at her in consternation, 'then you are doing the right thing, I should say.' She looked again at Astra and still saw her expression of doubt. As she pushed a syringe into her wrist and withdrew some blood she said, 'If you want to know my opinion, which I've no business to be giving, I think you shouldn't trouble yourself. There're enough babies around without adding one more unless it's wanted. If you ask me the world would be a happier place if the unwanted babies weren't born. When you're working in a hospital like we are, you see things a lot different to what they do outside.' She patted Astra's hand, 'Don't worry yourself – you've got years ahead of you to have babies. You're only a child yourself.'

Astra looked gratefully at this decisive person. It helped her, strengthened her, took away her sense of guilt – whether rightly or wrongly she no longer cared. Sense went with the voice that had spoken; Astra decided to give herself over to it, shut down her tiresome perverse voices which, after all, were most probably archetypal demons of blind instinct.

'All right?' The nurse bent over her.

'Yes.' Astra raised a smile.

'Good girl.' The nurse took up her tray and walked briskly out. She was too deeply into the business of life and death to fuss about qualms of conscience.

Astra tried to read her book, but after a little found she was reading the print without taking in the sense – she simply couldn't concentrate. She got out and went in search of the toilet; when she returned she saw the curtain of the adjoining cubicle had been drawn back to reveal a dark-skinned girl who looked even younger than herself.

'Are you in for the same thing?' she asked, as Astra bent down to take off her slippers, borrowed from Kate for the hospital.

'Abortion, do you mean?'

'Yes.'

'Yes.' Astra climbed back into her bed.

'What happened with you?' The girl was curious but not in an unpleasant way. It was simply the sharing of experience, the acknowledgement that they wouldn't be where they were except by misadventure.

'It was the first time,' Astra said, 'or perhaps the second. It was entirely my fault – I just never thought it could happen so . . . so easily.'

'It couldn't have been entirely your fault,' said the girl. 'It takes two.'

Astra smiled. There was something about this girl's personality that attracted her. 'What about you?' she asked.

'It was after a party. Just a one-off. I'd had too much to drink.'

'You didn't like him, you mean?'

'Oh he was all right, but I hardly knew him. I've never seen him again.'

'Does he know?'

'I wrote to him but I never got a letter back.' She had turned over, she studied Astra, her chin propped up on her elbow. 'You didn't think of marrying – or just having it?'

'Yes – oh yes. But I'm going to a tech next term. It seemed a bit mad.' Astra sat picking at the tassel of her dressing-gown cord. 'I think I might have if my mother hadn't been so dead against it. She saw herself looking after it, I think. She's a painter.'

'What about him. Your friend. What's he like?'

'All right.' Astra felt uncertain. 'He's nice looking,' she said.

'Got any photos?'

'Just small ones.' Astra pulled out of her handbag some that Sophie had taken. She showed them. 'What's your name?' she asked as the girl's dark head bent over the prints.

'Jessica. I'll say, he's a looker!' She thumbed through them and her admiring expressions made Astra feel a certain pride in Jude as her lover.

'Is he as good as he looks?'

'Good?'

'At loving?'

Astra frowned because really Jude was. 'Yes,' she said doubtfully, 'but he's not my type. Not truly. It doesn't mean much when I'm with him – not sex. He's very strange – sort of interesting to talk to, though.'

The girl returned the photos, dropped her head back on the pillow.

'How far are you gone?'

'Coming up to eleven weeks, I think,' Astra said. 'I couldn't believe it till I was five weeks overdue. I tried to get something done but it didn't seem half as easy as they make it sound – not when you live in the country anyway – then I had to wait to come in here . . .' She broke off.

'Stupid, isn't it?' Jessica said. 'If you can just get something done quick enough all this could be avoided.'

206

'What stopped you?' Astra was interested.

'I thought I'd just missed out. He wasn't even properly inside me.' She sighed. 'I'll be glad when it's over, I've never been in hospital before.'

A woman in a white hospital dressing-gown had overheard some of their conversation. She was standing looking out of the window, middle-aged, but in no way old. Now she laughed humourlessly.

'Let me tell you, if I'd never had anything to do with men I'd never have been in hospital. Every single time I've been in's been due to them. This time it's to take out a bit of my cervix. If you want to stay healthy, keep off it – that's what I say.' She lit a cigarette. 'I'm not supposed to smoke in here, but who cares?' She inhaled and let the smoke out through her rather large nostrils. 'In for abortions, are you?' she asked, studying them. They replied in the affirmative but rather wished she would go. Her bitter view of life they instinctively shrank from, but felt the unpalatable truth in what she said.

Perhaps fortunately, further conversation was terminated by the nurse arriving to give Jessica her preliminary injection – in a few moments the trolley would come to fetch her, she would pass out through the double doors of the ward and reappear who knew when? Astra tried not to think about it; at any moment now her own turn would come. It, too, was her first operation. Beside her Jessica was growing drowsy; the nurse came and drew the curtains. 'Good luck,' Astra said, but got no answer and guessed her friend asleep.

They came for her shortly, took her away. Astra, left quite alone, felt like crying. Here she was facing a decision of immense consequence she had taken with no one to give her help but strangers, and even they were now gone. She closed her eyes and must have dozed off because the next thing she knew the nurse was bending over her with a syringe. She tensed against the needle's prick, watched while they stuck the plaster tape in place to stop the bleeding. She didn't sleep, didn't even become drowsy but was wide awake in the operating room until they injected her wrist.

*

When, the day after the fire, Alec had rung Carol to say he could not ride on the Sunday, in fact would not be riding again until further notice, she was both taken aback and distressed financially. For not only had Alec paid high rates in order to be conducted secretly to remote farms selling in the centre of the moor, but she had enjoyed, very much enjoyed, his company. The village had conjectured whether or not there was more to it than cantering over the moor together, but as nothing untoward had surfaced, remained quite in the dark as to any ulterior purpose. So to try and recover, if recovery was possible, from what Carol calculated a drastic loss, she said, 'I'd meant to tell you our cheaper winter rates start in October. Well, right away actually.'

'Thanks,' said Alec, 'but frankly I'm extraordinarily busy. I can't, at present, feel justified to giving the time it needs for a decent ride.'

So it was agreed, rather suddenly, that the rides should end.

Carol said to Richard over their tuna and lettuce salad, 'I got the impression the Deneuves have taken a knock.' To which RIchard answered, 'If that's the case, it's just as well their money's come through for our newtake.' And with this consolation Carol had to content herself, but couldn't refrain from adding, 'Bad luck on Sophie, though, if things don't work out.'

Richard's mind strayed to the pantomime. It had been bad luck on himself, he thought, when Sophie hadn't played Rapunzel. He'd been rather looking forward to it but knew better than to say so to Carol.

'How much did it bring in – the pantomime?' he asked instead.

'Forty-eight pounds after costs. Not much,' Carol said, 'but then it was something of a fiasco, really – owing to the Deneuves. Oliver Upton is a sucker of the worst order to money and status. That's the only reason he used them – or tried to.' She laughed.

Richard pulled a piece of tuna out of his tooth. 'Is the boy really going to prison? Surely they'll stand surety for him?'

'He wants to go anyway, Sophie says. To make his protest. I've always said he's mad, but I have to admit it's brave of him.'

She opened the wood stove, added another log and shut the door sharply. 'We're going to be short of wood,' she said, 'I'll have to get Gabe to bring us a load.' Outside the rain was dropping from the gutters in a depressing, unrelenting patter. 'It's been going round the village,' she said, 'that Alec Deneuve is a plunger – and this time he's plunged too far. In fact they've been saying his money's only paper – he's been forging it.'

'Oh balls!' Richard could not stretch credibility to these lengths.

'We'll see,' said Carol with an element of satisfaction in her voice. For she was not immune to the unconscious – or conscious – desire to see the Deneuves reduced to the level of everyone else.

While everyone else was going about their occupations on that fateful Monday morning, Alec went to London; he had no alternative. There was a rumour going round the City of the banks calling in loans, and as Alec well knew, the fire would undermine his credibility; all he could do was chase up contacts, find others willing to make even small investments to help his venture over its present crises.

To his consternation he met with little success. News from Wall Street wasn't good and the Stock Exchange had taken a knock in the last few weeks; the drop in investments had been substantial. So when two days later he left London for Devon, under his admirably calm exterior he was bearing the chilling possibility of complete financial collapse. Of course he had Scarhill, as well as the flat in London – which was not proving as easy to sell as they had hoped – and some investments of his own, but the sum of money he had recently invested in 'Deneuve and Benson: Forestry' was considerable.

It was while he was sitting in the armchair beside the newly replaced four-ovened shiny white Aga that he picked up the local press. Jude's picture, albeit small, stared at him from the centre of the front page. Alec went white with anger as he read the lines beneath: SON BURNS FATHER'S PLANTATION AS PROTEST AGAINST EXPLOITATION OF ENVIRONMENT FOR COMMERCIAL ENDS. Then beneath, in small print:

'At the Magistrates' Court in Allerston, Jude Deneuve, son of Alec Deneuve, wealthy London stockbroker, shouted across to the Press in the gallery: "I started the fire and I'm happy to have done it. I want to open people's eyes to what is going on under their noses. My father is only one of many greedy people despoiling not only the English countryside, but our entire planet ..." '

Alec read on, his hands shaking with anger. The press had really gone to town, exaggerating and embellishing Jude's hasty courtroom utterance. When Alec had finished, he read it a second time, then went to the stairs and shouted up for Sophie. When he got no answer he opened the back door and shouted again. Sophie, who had guessed what it was, came down the steps from the walled garden slowly. She had seldom seen Alec so angry, his mouth seemed no more than a gash in his face, his lips like thin white scars. He came towards her, thrust the paper in front of her, pointing.

'Did you know about this? Presumably you've seen it.'

Sophie flinched. 'Yes' – her voice was so low as to be hardly audible.

'You connived with him in this ... this lying rubbish. This disgusting ...' Alec, inhibited by anger, was at a loss for words.

'No I didn't. I had nothing to do with it. All I knew was that he started the fire ...'

'Which you didn't tell me about till days later. If you had I might have been able to prevent this.'

'Alec, I explained ...' she began, but Alec interrupted her.

'It's unforgivable. Who does he think he is? He drags our name – the family – in front of the public ...'

'Only Devon.'

'How do you know? The national papers may take up the story. I forbid you to let him into this house again. I disown him. You don't seem to realise the harm he can do us.'

Sophie lowered her eyes in front of his white-hot rage, set her mouth in sullen, dogged obstinacy.

'Anyway, he's gone to prison,' she said.

'Prison?'

So absorbed had Alec been by Jude's statement that he had not taken in the full meaning of Jude's position. 'What's he doing in prison?' Alec was staggered. 'Surely he's been given police bail?'

'He's in the remand wing of the county gaol. You didn't think once he'd told them they'd let him back home, did you?' She could see she had scored. 'Not unless you'd taken his part,' she added.

Alec was silenced. He leant against the wall, hands in pockets, then rubbed his nose. Sophie couldn't help but feel sorry for him. 'We could stand surety for him,' she said hopefully, 'or I could if you didn't want to – if I was living away from you. His mother could, for that matter.'

'Why don't you, then?' Alec shot out. Why indeed, Sophie thought, but remained silent, letting the remark pass. Alec went on, his voice husky with sarcasm, 'Tomorrow's headlines: Father agrees to stand bail for arsonist son who caused him £50,000 worth of damages – and God only knows how much else.'

Sophie felt herself growing increasingly resentful for, all the time, although it was never done openly, she felt that it was herself Alec was attacking.

'He'll have to stay in then, won't he?' she said sullenly. Then suddenly her anger burst out. 'It's not *my* fault. I didn't want you to plant all those fucking silly horrible trees. You did it – wilfully.'

'You aren't exactly much help, are you?' Alec got a fraction nearer to an open accusation. At the same time Sophie's remark reminded him she had only seen the part of the iceberg above water and he couldn't help wondering how she would react if she knew the full extent of his buying up of property.

'Help? What do you mean?'

'I mean you undermine everything I do.'

'I don't.'

They stood on opposite sides of the room, the atmosphere poignant with all that lay unspoken beneath their words but that neither cared to plough. It was the bitterest quarrel in their four years of marriage, and it centred on Jude. Not the fire, not the ruin he was helping to create round Alec, but the unspeakable knowledge that Sophie was attracted to him.

'I'm going to visit Astra,' Sophie said at last, 'I promised I would.' And she took her coat and left him still standing looking at nothing in particular, but suffering in an isolated, mute fashion specific to himself.

It wasn't so much that Alec didn't feel, as that he was incapable of accepting his feelings; his conditioning, his upbringing from his earliest years, allied to other determining factors, made it difficult, if not impossible, for him to give credit to the irrational. He could very well understand that Sophie was attracted to her stepson, but he was no more capable of helping her through such a situation than he was of sustaining himself through the intolerable sensations of jealousy this knowledge aroused. He could only turn back blindly on things he knew about, facts that could be fed into his computer and come out in figures. In short, finance and the tangible, material world.

Sophie, for her part, was in so much of a hurry to get out and away that she banged the door without intending to and bits of old plaster fell of the ceiling. It was perfectly true she had promised to go to see Astra; she had rung Kate earlier to check all had gone well. After all, abortion was nothing these days. They could talk about Jude ... She checked herself. Something of the nature of her own obsession had begun to dawn on her, she realised guiltily the extent to which he preoccupied her. Tomorrow she would visit him, she wasn't allowed to today, she would find out if there was any possibility at all of getting him home before his trial . . .

Thoughts such as these were still in Sophie's mind half an hour later when she arrived at the hospital where, by dint of asking, she found her way to the right ward and settled herself beside Astra's bed. The other bed in the cubicle she saw was empty, and asked about it.

'She's gone home,' Astra said.

'Did she come in before you?'

'No – the same time. She came through it better.'

'You are all right, aren't you?' Sophie looked properly at Astra for the first time and observed the extreme bluish pallor of her skin.

'Yes,' said Astra, 'but I'm still bleeding a bit.'

'Oh I see,' said Sophie, assuming this was normal. She changed the subject to Jude. 'I'm allowed to visit Jude on Friday – I'm hoping they'll allow him out on bail because they say his Crown Court trial won't come up for at least six weeks. It is awfully worrying – I'm sure Jude's got no idea what he's got coming to him. I'm told he'll probably get six months in youth custody – the best we can hope for is that he should get a suspended sentence – his solicitor will appeal, of course . . .' Sophie's voice chattered on.

So he'd have come out when the baby was just born if I'd had it, Astra thought, and a wave of misery swept through her. Her lip quivered. After all, she was lying weak in hospital as a result of Jude who had effectively conjured events so that he could not even visit her, in spite of his professed love. Wasn't her own suffering as bad, if not worse, than his?

'I worry about him altogether,' Sophie interrupted Astra's thoughts. 'You see . . .' She paused as she noticed Astra's distress. She stretched out her hand, laid it over Astra's. 'He'll be all right, don't worry,' she said. 'It's what he wants. I mean getting the publicity and all that' – and she took a copy of the *Western Gazette* out of her bag and laid it on the bed in front of Astra.

Astra tried to concentrate, take an interest, she sat up with difficulty because she was afraid it would increase the bleeding, and studied Jude's photo on the centre front. But looking at it she felt no response, only a faint curiosity. She read the headlines but they simply made her angry. Turning her head away so that Sophie should not be aware of her bitterness, she said, 'How long does he stay on remand?'

'Till his trial,' said Sophie. She, like Jude, had versed herself well in legal matters in the first few days and more or less understood the procedure. 'I hope he's in a shared cell,' she added darkly, 'I think it's safer.'

'Safer?'

'I mean he won't be on his own much.'

'What if he was?' Astra needed to know. Jude's photo with the heavy eyelids and softly rounded chin drew her eyes back to it.

'It could be . . . well, a bad thing,' Sophie said uneasily, then before she could stop herself, 'You see, he tried to burn down his room at Oxford with himself in it.' And then it all came out – the real reason for Jude's 'sabbatical'. She even told Astra about the 'silly psychiatrist's' diagnosis of impotence because surely Astra's pregnancy made nonsense of it – or so it seemed to Sophie's limited understanding of the physical's relation to the psychological. We felt . . .' she finished, 'we knew . . . he desperately needed to make friends and it might have put some people off. Oh I know not you,' she said, squeezing Astra's hand, 'because you're not like that.'

'Like what?' Astra's head ached.

'The sort of person to be put off by a crazy thing done by Jude when he was . . . well, unbalanced.'

'But he's done it again.'

'But this time it was provoked and only did harm to Alec, which is beastly of him, I know' – she paused – 'But actually it's exactly why I thought telling you wouldn't matter any more because you know anyway.'

Astra was incredulous. She was silent for a time absorbing what she had heard, then said, 'Oughtn't I to have known sooner?'

Sophie flushed. 'Yes,' she said. 'Now looking back, you probably ought to have. But I'd promised Alec – sworn – *not* to say anything to anyone. And he's not my son . . .' she ended lamely, only too aware of the accusation in Astra's eyes. 'I couldn't know any of this was going to happen,' she pleaded.

Astra was stunned. She wanted to say, What about me? – but could not find it in herself to do so. She felt too weak, too apathetic. So she let her head sink back into the pillows and watched Sophie's delicate little face as she talked, oblivious of the hurt she unthinkingly caused. And in a way Astra could see the truth in what she said; she personally would have been more . . . reticent, was the only word she could think of, with Jude if she had known. It began to come together, make sense; the vacuum she had sensed in him, seen in his eyes, was actual, not a flight of her imagination. The remarks of Sophie's and Alec's she had heard through the shutters came back to her. What was the point? It was all too late now. She sighed, turned restlessly.

'I'm tiring you,' Sophie said, 'I'd better go. I should think they're bound to let you out tomorrow.'

'I hope so.' Astra smiled wanly.

Sophie gave a nervous glance at the flowers she had brought with her. 'They're not very nice ones, but all I could get.' They were copper and white chrysanthemums, grave flowers, she thought uneasily. She kissed Astra impulsively, squeezed her hand. 'I'll come again tomorrow if they don't let you home,' she said kindly, then made for the door. In the doorway she turned and waved again, then Astra heard her heels clipping along the passage.

'Who is that lovely girl?' asked the middle-aged woman opposite. And it was on the tip of Astra's tongue to answer, 'The stepmother of the father of my dead child', but she didn't because what would have been the point? The nurse had told her firmly it had been no different to any other curettage – a good scrape-out, the foetus undetectable, no better or worse than contraception. Astra doubted but preferred to believe.

Right now she turned her head wearily away from the window, the light hurt her eyes. She shut them.

The telephone had been ringing for some time before Kate heard it. She was not in her studio but out in the garden chopping vigorously at the box hedge. For as the days shortened so, progressively, the light went earlier from her studio. Kate's compromise was to cut the hedge as low as she could but not quite severely enough to kill it; and it was this that kept her out of doors on an otherwise damp and dismal afternoon. As soon as she heard the ringing she dropped her clippers and ran; breathless she picked up the receiver.

'Hullo.'

'Mum.'

'Yes. Do you want fetching?'

The last time she had seen Astra had been on the Monday evening after her operation when she had been sitting up and quite cheerful. She had left on the understanding that Astra would ring on the following day after she had been checked by the surgeon, which was expected to be in the evening. Sophie, Kate knew, had planned to visit Astra that afternoon. Now, however, there was a pause before Astra said, 'I'm not coming out. I've got to go back in the theatre.'

'Whatever for?' Kate was appalled.

'I'm still bleeding. I can't talk now. I just thought I'd better let you know.'

'But Astra . . .'

The merciless pips went. The line cut off. Kate ran upstairs, changed out of her muddy corduroys into a skirt, picked up her bag and ran down the cobbles. Half-way down she remembered she had left no note for Benjy, who would be back any moment off the school bus, so she ran back and scrawled a message and left it in a prominent position on the table.

It was just before the evening visiting hours when she arrived at the ward doors, only to be prevented from entry by a nurse. In no mood to be barred from her daughter, Kate explained her reason and the nurse gave way.

She found Astra with her curtain drawn and the bed next to her empty. The shock at the difference between the healthy girl she had seen on the previous day and the white, wan face that greeted her from the pillow shot Kate through with panic. Worse still, Astra had a blood flask suspended over her bed from which blood was passing along a tube into her arm.

Kate turned almost as white as Astra. She swallowed, endeavoured to show concern rather than panic. She bent over the bed, laid her warm hand over Astra's cold limp one. 'Whatever is all this about?' she asked.

'I haven't stopped bleeding,' Astra said, 'and I've eaten so I can't go back for a further operation yet, and anyway there's no room in the theatre, I'm having this till I can go back in.'

'Have they told you anything else?'

'Not really. The surgeon who did it has gone off. Another's going to have a look at me.'

Kate gazed at Astra, absorbing the full implications. 'I'll go and see if I can get any more out of the ward sister,' she said. 'I'll be back.'

The ward sister reiterated Astra's version of the story, told Kate it was nothing to worry about, this kind of thing did sometimes happen. Kate, slightly reassured, returned and repeated the consoling words to Astra who regarded her with blank eyes. When she tried to question her, Astra murmured she felt terribly sleepy and indeed her eyes closed. Kate looked nervously at the blood which seemed to be moving in jerking motion along the polythene tube. Was she getting enough? she wondered. 'Astra,' she said, 'Astra.' She shook her, gripped her shoulder, but Astra was asleep or unconscious. In a panic Kate ran from the ward. Oh God, she thought, oh God – and it's all my fault for persuading her.

The ward sister had vanished. Kate clattered down the corridor, ran round a corner and almost collided with the theatre trolley. She stood back to let it pass, followed it along to Astra's ward, watched her wheeled away, went back in search of someone, anyone, to ask questions, find out. The ward sister fortunately made a reappearance.

'She seemed terribly weak. How long will it take?' Kate would have liked to scream, shake the bland, pleasant, but mask-like face before her into a human response. As it was, she listened. It depended exactly on what they found, she was told, it could be up to forty-five minutes, even an hour. Perhaps Kate would care to go into the waiting room where there was a television . . .?

Kate had no alternative; she sat before the screen not seeing any of the pictures, going over in her mind what should have been done. Astra should have gone to the London clinic, she should have paid for a private surgeon. Why oh why had she economised, thought the NHS would be all right? But then reason told her the story in London might have been the same and the clinic less well equipped than a large, modern hospital. She sat hunched and tense, clipping and unclipping her handbag, suffering in the timeless fashion of mothers for their offspring, eternally blaming themselves, going back over the steps that had led up to the event and how it could have been prevented. After forty-five minutes she once again went in search of the ward sister – but the one she was used to had gone and a new one had taken her place, well concealed by heavy-rimmed glasses. She was calm and cool, and made Kate feel her panicky unanswerable questioning ridiculous. She went back to the waiting room.

After exactly one hour Astra was returned to her bed, still under the anaesthetic. Kate was informed, but told that Astra would not be fully round for an hour and a half and probably sleepy for a further hour at the least. She learnt to her alarm that Astra was still receiving blood and would probably continue to do so for part of the night. Frightening thoughts of AIDS flashed through her mind but she did not dare voice them. The sister's voice penetrated her consciousness . . .

'I cannot see much point in your waiting here, Mrs Merlin. If you would like to go home and ring us first thing tomorrow morning we can give you a report.'

'But tonight . . .' Kate began, but could see she would get no further.

'The doctor's won't be in until tomorrow so there will be nothing further we can tell you. Try not to worry, and get some sleep yourself.'

Kate thanked the sister, who she felt was doing her best as a cog in a vast machine designed to keep information from all those not involved in its practice, and silently, resentfully, she left the lighted building. She felt deeply uneasy and afraid, suspecting Astra to be in far worse condition than they cared to divulge, probably due to someone's bungle somewhere along the line. It would be hushed up, dusted over, protected by the rest of the massive system as such bungles are throughout the professions, 'Support your colleague till death' being the axiom, in case you yourself may need support for a similar bungle at some later date. And those of us outside suffer in ignorance, Kate thought, impotence and ignorance of the facts – the truth. For truth, of all things, was the most difficult to prise from any history, the most subjective and intangible.

At Bag Down she found Benjy in front of the television; an ice-cream paper and an apple core on a plate described his supper. He stared at her, sucking his thumb, his eyes asking the question.

'Astra's not allowed out for another day or two,' Kate said as casually as she could manage, realising she was herself stepping into the ward sister's mode. 'I saw her for a little while. I'm ringing the hospital in the morning.'

Then she changed the subject to whether he had had enough to eat, and Benjy asked no questions. Why should he? His mother had told him all she considered he needed to know and he accepted. She wanted to say 'Don't trust me. I'm not trustworthy – none of us are. Never trust those who appear to know more – it's a sham, a façade.' She herself was suffering agonies of doubt and mistrust. She sat down beside him now and they watched a programme together until Benjy went to bed. Then Kate rang Donald. She had to speak to someone;

besides, he ought to know. She steeled herself, listening to the dialling tone.

'Donald?'

'Hullo. Oh hullo' – as he recognised her voice.

'It's not very good news, but not terrible.'

'What is it?'

'Astra's had to have a second op.'

A long silence.

'What was the second for?'

'Haemorrhaging – I'm ringing in the morning to try to find out more. They won't tell you anything but I thought you ought to know.'

'Thanks.' Donald's tone was full of icy sarcasm. Kate remained silent. She was fully aware she was entirely in the wrong for not having told him about Astra's abortion until she was in hospital. Now there really was only one move left, which she made.

'Astra could have told you if she had wanted to.'

'Astra's a minor.' Donald's answer came back direct and pat. He was perfectly correct.

Kate saw no point in prolonging the call. 'Anyway you know the situation now,' she said, then added, 'But if you're going to visit her let me know when, then we won't clash.' And with that she put the receiver down, leant her head up against the window recess and wept. It was as though everything was suddenly out of control, her uselessness more than she could bear. She admitted to herself what she dared not admit to anyone – the panicky fear that Astra might die.

Carol Granger rang Kate Merlin. 'How's Astra?' she asked.

'They've made a mess of it, it appears,' Kate said, and Carol could hear the tiredness, the lifelessness in her voice, 'but they think she'll be all right now. They perforated the uterus, I imagine, although they won't tell me a thing.'

'How terrible. Poor Astra.' Carol was sincerely shocked. 'I'm terribly sorry.'

'I've been trying to get hold of Jude Deneuve,' Kate said,

'but he's not at the Mill. I suppose I'll have to ring Sophie. He's not gone to prison yet, has he?'

'He's in on remand. He'll get a second hearing next week. Actually I heard from someone that Sophie's trying to get him out on bail. In a way, though, he'll get a better press if he stays in. It's high time someone put a spoke in Alec Deneuve's wheel. Frankly I admire Jude, though I appreciate it's different for you.'

Kate on the other end felt too exhausted to make any comments but was surprised by Carol who she had thought on very good terms with Alec Deneuve.

'Sophie thinks prison'll bring shame and disgrace on the family, I expect,' Carol went on, 'but then she's got surprisingly old-fashioned attitudes.'

'I'll ring her now,' Kate said.

Richard Granger had been listening as best he could to the one-sided conversation. 'Something gone wrong with the Merlin girl?' he asked.

'The abortion's a cock-up,' said Carol, 'I don't know why they pushed her into it, poor girl.'

'I thought you were in favour of it?' Richard was incredulous, having been pumped for years with Carol's liberated views.

'Me? It's nothing to do with me. It's her mother – she's far too dominant. Astra's never freed herself from the umbilical cord. She's doing what her mother wants, not what *she* wants. That's what I'm criticising – not the abortion. Good God, no.' She paused. 'I'm going out to feed Ladybird,' she said, and left Richard to ponder the significance of her pronouncement.

As she mixed the bran and chaff and added a handful or two of oats she wondered why, when she talked to Richard, she had to be so bitter about everyone, run people down? It had become her way with Richard because he was boring and lifeless and didn't make her happy. Her bitterness, she decided, was mainly a cover-up for her own lack of courage to change her life. She had only one life and was leading it all wrong but didn't seem able to extricate herself from its doomed descent. She tipped the bucket into the manger, slapped Ladybird's flanks and sighed. She thought of Gabe Fardon – it wasn't just lust, although it might seem like it. She really loved him.

When Kate had rung the hospital at 10 p.m. to ask about Astra, she had been informed that her daughter was quite comfortable and sleeping. Yes, she was still having blood, but that was perfectly normal after a haemorrhage – probably at midnight she would be taken off it if her blood pressure was satisfactory. The ward sister was polite but terse. Should she come back to the hospital, Kate asked – might she be able to speak to the surgeon or doctor? No doctors would be on unless called until tomorrow morning, she was told; and it would be better if she stayed at home because she would not be able to go into the ward at night. There was absolutely nothing to worry about . . .

Partially reassured, Kate wandered restlessly round the house unable to settle to anything until finally she braved her studio. She steeled herself inside the door, her hand on the switch, about to turn the dark room into light, about to see her paintings, afraid of her own response. Would they seem vital and living, or dead and lacking soul? She clicked the switch, saw before her her latest canvases leant round the walls of the room. She frowned. Twelve, the gallery in Bristol had said, and only six large – which made it difficult for they were nearly all large. All the ones she liked. Why, oh why had she persuaded the director himself to come all the way down to see her work? But she had and tomorrow afternoon he was coming by car with his co-director – a woman. But of course she would put him off because she would be with Astra. First thing in the morning she must ring him, cancel his visit until Astra was better and she had time to think . . .

She shouldered another canvas across the studio to join the others, propped herself against the wall, arms folded to look at it. The further away the better. Half an hour later she was still in the same position, mesmerised by her work. Only the distant chime of the church clock forced her to move. She made her way back along the passage to the other end of the house where finally, after listening through Benjy's open door to his regular and reassuring breathing, she went to bed.

For a long time she lay awake with agitating thoughts about Astra whirling repetitively and uselessly through her mind. She tried to read but the print meant nothing to her, she simply couldn't concentrate. Finally, worn out with worrying, she switched off the light and fell into a deep sleep.

She was woken by the sound of the telephone. The room was pitch dark except for the grey area that marked the window; Kate was wide awake in an instant, the receiver to her ear.

'Hullo?'

'Mrs Merlin?'

'Yes.'

'I think it might be advisable if you were to come in. Your daughter's in the intensive care unit. Her blood pressure is right down – it may be necessary to put her on the kidney machine.'

'No . . .' Kate's moan was the cry of a stricken animal. In her prophetic unconscious she had gone through everything that was now happening, but the actuality was no less terrible.

'I'm coming now' – she pulled on her skirt and jersey over her nightdress and with only an instant's hesitation, abandoned the sleeping Benjy, stealthily creeping past his room. Once outside she wasted no time, pelting down the cobbles in her socks.

It was after Kate had seen Astra, after she had kissed her still warm face, clutched her fingers, lain with her arms round her body while it grew colder, stood up and shouted and beaten with her fists on the walls of the small, tomb-shaped white room where Astra lay, still on a hospital trolley, that Kate was removed by the nurses, four of them taking her by the arms, half-dragging, half-lifting her between them. In this fashion they got her to the head surgeon's room where she recovered a dull, trance-like composure. As soon as he entered the nurses left, except for one – to protect him in case she attacked him, Kate imagined.

'How did you let her die?' she cried out at once, 'How? How?' Even to herself her voice sounded like a she-wolf's.

'It was a case of the kidneys not being able to take it – they packed up and she lapsed into coma and died before we could get her on the machine. It all happened very suddenly – at midnight her blood pressure was satisfactory, the nurses saw no need to call me. It was one of those unforeseeable occurrences. I was here within ten minutes of the call – we did all we could but I suspect the real trouble was that the blood we gave her wasn't a perfect match. It seemed first she was taking it all right but her blood is not common, in fact doesn't constitute a group. Mrs Merlin, please accept my deepest sympathy – I have a daughter the same age as yours was – I know what you must be suffering. Her death was quite painless – she simply slipped away . . .'

Kate's lips opened but no sound came from them. The nurse bent over her. Dimly Kate was aware of the surgeon discreetly letting himself out through a side-door; the nurse was talking.

'We've rung your husband. He's on his way here. He's going to see his daughter, then take you home.'

'See her?' For a moment Kate's heart leapt. 'You mean she's alive?'

'No, Mrs Merlin, I'm afraid not. Her father just wants to look at her.'

Kate said nothing. She felt dead to all feeling, she thought she would never feel again beyond the threshold of this pain that numbed her. In the same instant Benjy flashed across her mind and fear for his well-being drove her to act.

'Let me out of here.' She took up her handbag and moved unsteadily towards the door. The nurse followed, attempted to press sedatives into her hand. Kate accepted them automatically, then realising what they were, opened her palm and let them drop. A younger nurse picked them up with a frown, accompanied her to the lift, went down with her.

Benjy's alarm clock went off with its usual unpleasant insistence. Benjy rolled over, pulled the sheet up to his ears, kept his eyes shut. After a few minutes he heard his mother's door open and she came along the passage towards his door – which was not unusual, she came every morning to make sure he had heard the alarm, would be up and dressed in time for the school bus. But this morning, instead of just putting her head round the door, she came in, sat on his bed.

She didn't immediately speak; Benjy began to feel uncomfortable with that strange inexplicable embarrassment he always felt when he sensed his mother was going to tell him something she felt emotional about. He never got it with Astra, with her it was different, she could tell him anything just like that. Astra had told him everything about how men put their sperm inside and babies were born and all of that. She had made it sound so good that for a little he wished he was a girl. They had been sitting together in an old quarry on the moor; they'd climbed down there out of the wind to eat their apples, and even now, just remembering it, Benjy smelt the special smell of apples and moor peat as though he was there. It made his stomach turn over with a shiver of excitement. When he and Astra went off on 'moor walks' those were the best days of his life; Astra was with him and no one else was there to interrupt or take her away. Now Jude Deneuve was around it was all different . . . Benjy's mouth assumed a sullen expression as he thought of Jude. He hated the way he had come all last summer, taken Astra off. He'd made her different, like she had secrets, she didn't talk to him now like she'd used to . . .

Benjy's thoughts broke off at the sight of his mother's hands. He'd been looking at them for a while without exactly seeing them; now he realised her fingers were twisting up round a piece of her hair, twisting in and out, in and out. He ventured a glance at her face, saw the redness round her eyes.

'Have you got a cold?' he demanded.

'No' – but her voice was funny too. Thick. The sense of apprehension and embarrassment that had dispersed with Benjy's thoughts swept back over him. 'I'll get up,' he said, sitting up and pushing his white legs that had just recently begun to lengthen, over the side of the bed.

Then his mother clutched him, drew him to her. He smelt her lovely smell of warm flesh and faint scent, yet still he was suspicious. Something was wrong.

'Benjy,' his mother said, 'Astra died. In the hospital.' He knew she was crying because her chest shuddered under his cheek. He fought free of her arms.

'You didn't tell me,' he yelled, 'You didn't tell me she was going to die.'

He started ripping at the open front of his mother's dressing gown, he wanted to hurt her. He tore at her nightdress, then he went over to the corner of the room where his model aeroplane stood on the floor and trod on it. He'd been working on it for weeks, it was ready to paint, his mother had helped him, it was to show his form teacher at school. Benjy stood on it and listened to it crunch up under his feet.

'Benjy – no – *don't*.' His mother's voice seemed a long way off. All he could think of was that Astra would never come back again, she was gone like in his dream, only in the dream she had gone down in the bog. Perhaps this was a dream too, and in a moment he would wake up. He looked at his mother though he couldn't see her properly, only her shape.

'It isn't true, is it?'

'Yes,' she said, 'it is.'

Then the floor came up towards him and the room started whirling round as though he was on a fairground dipper. He clutched at the chest of drawers to save himself, but it was moving too; he didn't feel himself falling but the floor was coming up. After that he couldn't remember any more.

Jude was allowed out on police bail for Astra's funeral, which took place five days after her death. Six weeks later his trial

226

came up in the Crown Court, where he was pronounced by the judge to be guilty of arson with a reckless disregard for life. A farm, it was claimed, could have been damaged and sparks might have endangered the lives of passing motorists. In both cases, as argued by Jude's Defence, an examination of the territory would prove the charges almost impossible.

But his Defence's pleas was overruled, and in spite of an appeal a fortnight later when Jude came up before no less than three judges, he was sentenced to three months in youth custody and the hoped-for suspended sentence was not granted. The social enquiry did little to help by revealing his previous offence of attempted arson; that, with the psychiatric report and his general privileged background, appeared to seal the case against him.

III

Mrs Bellamy put out tins of sardines and mackerel and rearranged the baskets displaying home-grown veg. The fruit was another thing – all imported. She polished up the yellowy, bruised-looking Golden Delicious then took up her broom and swept up the peanuts that two tourists' children had dropped. As she tipped them in the dustbin outside the door waiting for collection, she consoled herself that they had at least been paid for. Nevertheless, she hated to see waste.

She replaced the lid with a feeling clang. It was the way she'd felt about the Merlin girl's death. A waste, terrible for Mrs Merlin – not that the daughter had been easy, mind, but a daughter was a daughter, as she'd said to Jack. It was hard on that poor little Benjy Merlin too – though he wasn't so little any more, he was tall as the doorway, grown something remarkable, due to him being in a bed a lot – all of three months, or was it more? He hadn't been himself since his sister was gone. Mrs Bellamy unbolted the door which shot CLOSED to OPEN and took up her position behind the counter. To keep herself busy she went through the books.

She was still frowning and checking page with page when Sophie Deneuve's car drew up outside. Mrs Bellamy watched through the plate-glass window above the tins of cat food and

228

on-offer Daz, and when a few moments later Sophie entered the shop, she had put her book away and was standing expectantly behind the counter hoping for a considerable order from Mrs Deneuve. It hadn't been a good spring so far. They were already well into April and the two round tin tables and chairs directly outside the shop French-fashion with umbrellas, under which Mrs Bellamy had hoped to serve cream teas, had remained unused. So it was with anticipation born of necessity that Mrs Bellamy eyed up Sophie Deneuve. Indeed rumour that the Deneuves might be leaving had come as a severe blow to the Bellamys, whose small business only just reached the profit margin.

Sophie opened the door and entered in a watery shaft of spring sunlight. She had got thinner, Mrs Bellamy noticed, and something in her face had altered. There was a slight drawn look round the eyes, but then if they were in financial difficulty that would account for it, wouldn't it, she knew what it was like. Sleepless nights wondering how to meet your creditors, there was nothing the Deneuves could teach her about that. Spend like they did, she wondered their money hadn't run out years back.

Sophie wandered round the small shop helping herself to this and that, which she lined up on the counter, then stood in front of it making small talk while Mrs Bellamy totted it up and handed her the bill. Mrs Deneuve had taken to paying cash recently, which might be indicative although she was not quite sure of what. In the past she had always paid by cheque . . . She was smiling now, holding out the money. Mrs Bellamy tucked it in the till and gave out the change. Sophie slipped it in her bag, grasped the cardboard box full of goodies and left, leaving Mrs Bellamy looking wistfully after her. Life, she mistakenly decided, must be of an entirely different order if you were born like Sophie Deneuve. She wondered idly what her maiden name had been.

The shopping accomplished, Sophie drove straight on to the prison. During the six months Jude had been confined, she had increasingly found it necessary to use such excuses as shopping in order to visit him, for Alec was at home a good deal and she knew he disliked her going to see Jude, although he would never have dreamed of preventing her. For Sophie, Jude's prison sentence had been at first immensely distressing, and then gradually developed a side of her life she had secretly come to live for. Towards Alec she felt perpetual guilt, but like most people obsessed she was prepared to live with it.

Now, as she rang and waited she felt the typical nerves of someone in love with another whom they suspect does not return the same degree of sentiment. She looked at herself in a pane of glass, pushed her hair back, unscrewed a tiny bottle and shook a drop of breath-sweetener on her tongue then impatiently rang again. In a few moments she was let in by a prison warder – or 'screw', as Jude referred to them – and conducted along the empty and featureless passages to the high Victorian visiting room. It had a gallery two-thirds the way up its walls on which other warders came and went, or simply stood as though keeping guard. Sophie often wondered if they were armed.

Already visitors had collected, were in groups talking; others sat on their side of the long glass panel which stretched from one end of the room to the other and divided them from the prisoners. A woman warder stood inside the door from the cell block through which the prisoners entered, her hands folded over her navy uniform. Sophie, who knew her quite well by now, smiled, and the warder returned the briefest of smiles.

Sophie sat down on the end seat which she usually tried to get, it being a little more private than a central one, and waited; within a few minutes the prisoners came through, all twenty-four of them, all youths. Every two of them were accompanied by a warder. Jude saw Sophie and, with no expression or indication of pleasure, sat himself opposite her, his hands clasped in front of him, his elbows resting on the table. His hair, she noticed, had been cut yet again. She greeted him with as much vivacity as she could muster before his blank lack of response.

'This is just about my last visit,' Sophie felt herself become tongue-tied, felt the forced hollow note in her voice before Jude's obviously depressive state. 'Think,' she went on, 'you'll be out in ten days.' Jude, for answer, raised his eyes to hers, then looked away.

'What is there to come out for?'

Sophie's heart sank. She made an heroic attempt to remain cheerful, pretend she did not notice his manner. 'How's your writing been going?' she asked.

'All right,' he said, noncommittal and clearly unwilling to discuss it further. Sophie didn't probe. Jude's writing, she had long since learnt, was an activity he pursued in absolute privacy, and intrusion beyond the briefest enquiry was rebuffed unless he was in a mood to be expansive. She searched for another topic. It was up to her, the visitor, to make the running.

'Alec . . .' she began.

'I don't want to know.'

'But Jude . . .'

'I don't want to know.'

Sophie shrugged, put out. 'It makes it difficult to talk if I can't tell you about anything.'

'I'm not interested in gossip.'

'It's not exactly gossip, telling you about the family.'

'Isn't it?'

'Jude!' Sophie felt helpless, there seemed no common ground from which to start. He remained silent, looking at the floor.

'Haven't you liked my coming all these months?'

'Yes.'

'Well you don't show it.'

'How can I?'

She had to admit a certain truth in this. She stretched out her hand and their fingers met under the glass panel; she noticed the warder looking at them and withdrew hers, afraid they might make it an excuse for keeping Jude in longer. He had already lost one month of his mitigation for bad conduct, and in any case seemed indifferent to her touch.

'What's the matter?' she asked unhappily. For answer Jude met her wide eyes with his intense gaze until she lowered hers, wondering what was coming next. Visits to Jude had seemed to follow a random pattern – he could be friendly and pleased to see her or he could be as now, hostile, surly and frankly bloody-minded, she had finally been forced to admit. She wondered how she could persist in caring for him, and knew that when he was in such a mood she should have got up and left. Instead she continued to sit, imprisoned by indescribable feelings. She examined the concrete floor that she knew by heart with its ugly rag-mat, woven, no doubt, by some former inmate. She felt helpless, discouraged and bitterly aware of the futility of her own actions. Yet surely it was she who had kept Jude going? Alec had been persuaded to visit him once only; it had been a complete failure and not to be repeated. Scarlet had been twice, but the onus, the burden as most people thought of it, had fallen on Sophie.

'You'll be out in ten days,' she repeated for want of anything better to say.

Jude turned his expressionless gaze full on her. 'I know. That's what I've been thinking about – planning. You can help me if you want to. Will you?'

'What?'

'When I come out I want the Press waiting for me. I want them to make a final splash, interview me.'

'And then?'

Jude shrugged. 'Who knows. A prison sentence doesn't exactly enhance my future prospects.'

Sophie felt like saying, you should have thought of that nine months ago, but refrained.

'I'd emigrate if I could get a work permit.' He could see this last was like a knife plunged into Sophie – to hurt her gave him a certain relief from his own introverted sufferings.

'What good will running away do?' she asked, sudden anger making her wish to hurt back. 'You *have* changed.'

'Getting out of this country may prove the only way left open to me. In any case, I prefer to be as far from my father as possible.'

Sophie couldn't bear Jude when he talked like that; it seemed a façade – just so much noise. She mustered all her patience, determined to call up the real Jude that she knew lay under the surface. The wounded, hurt person that prison had done nothing to improve, in fact rather the opposite. It was as though Jude's contact with other prisoners, mainly of very different background and sensibilities to himself, had not widened his sympathies as it might have, but had only made him bury the best in his nature even deeper. He had described to Sophie friendships he had made, conversations, fights. Some were funny, some sad, but watching Jude closely as she did on her regular fortnightly visits, she could see the effect had been to coarsen him. He seemed to care less about anything outside himself, be more abrupt and brutal in his conversations with her. She had longed to go to see Kate Merlin, persuade her to visit him. In fact Jude had asked her to. But when she had at last summoned up the courage to visit Kate, so remote and hostile had she seemed that Sophie had not had the courage to ask her, but did not dare admit this to Jude.

She herself could not bear to think of Astra's death, it was the most shocking and shattering thing that had yet ruffled her life. At the beginning she had tried to talk to Jude about it, thinking of the horror of his situation with nothing to do but brood on his own part in it; but he had silenced her brusquely, and it had become a taboo subject between them.

Now she rested her forehead in her hands, her fingers pinching her temples. She felt incapable of helping him, or indeed herself. It was how she felt most of the time in Jude's presence, as though the division between them was increasing and only her passionate, one-sided and impossible love remained.

'You're obsessive about your relations with Alec,' she said.

233

'You project your own self-hate on him' – this last was said with more perception than she credited herself with. 'And anyway,' she went on to excuse Alec, 'his greatest crime to date has been to plant trees.' She laughed boldly, but wondered for the hundredth time if Jude's excessive resentment of his father was due to fear that he was not his son. It was a subject she longed to broach but had never yet dared to do.

'Stop lying to yourself.' Jude was looking at her with displeasure. 'You know and I know exactly what he's like.'

'Well, it's coming to an end.' Sophie's calm was leaving her, her agitation growing. 'He's just about out of money in spite of selling absolutely everything. He's been trying to hang on but he can't meet his huge debts to his creditors.'

Jude looked alert for the first time that afternoon. 'Good,' he said, 'good.'

'What do you mean "good"? Do you think it'll be pleasant to be homeless, live in a bungalow or some dreary place miles out in the suburbs . . .?' Sophie's imagination had been at work and painted a black future for herself, if not Jude. She would have gone on had not the warder come across and spoken to them.

'Would you kindly keep your voices down,' she said, 'there are others who want to talk.'

Sophie and Jude both glared after her as she passed on down the line, checking, always checking, watching out for the cigarettes slipped under the glass to eager fingers.

Sophie, near to tears, blew her nose. Jude, having reduced her to her present misery and gained a psychological advantage, leant forward and said urgently, 'Why don't you leave my father? It's the only way for you. It's not that I want to get at him through you, I'm simply thinking of what's best for you.'

'If I did, what then?'

'It'd be up to you.'

'Why do you think I come to see you – out of charity?' Sophie demanded.

'No – not entirely.'

234

'I come because I love you.'

She had said it at last, after almost eight months. Immediately she regretted it. Jude made no move, no sign he'd even heard, and for a few moments they sat facing each other as though carved in stone. Then Sophie stood. 'Time must be almost up,' she said, making her voice light, as though she had never uttered the previous momentous phrase. It was the name of a Buddy Holly song, she seemed to remember: 'Because I love you' – it rang through her brain.

'Sophie . . .' Jude's voice was urgent, 'you will arrange about the Press? The nationals, if you can get them. If not, the local press will have to do.'

'But what can I say?' Sophie looked at him in despair.

'Say?'

'To Alec.'

'Look Sophie' – the change in Jude was remarkable; his intense gaze seemed to dissolve the glass between them. Sophie felt her whole being become weak and pliant with longing for him. She again stretched her fingers and Jude grasped their tips – 'If you love me then prove it. Do what I ask.'

They sat staring at each other, Sophie taking in the implications of what she was being asked to do.

'But . . .' she began. Then the buzzer rang loud and repeatedly, it was impossible to think or speak for the noise, the restless movement of people standing.

'Time's up.' The warder was coming towards them, seemed to have something personal against them.

'Sophie?' – Jude had never been more urgent. 'What the fuck does my shit of a father matter? Do the one thing I ask – get the Press. It's the only thing that validates my being in here all these months. Either you're with me or with him; you can't be for us both, we stand for opposites. If you can't see that – denounce Alec for what he is – then all your talk about "love" is so much blown air.'

Sophie couldn't help but admit the truth in what he said, but it didn't make it any easier for her to carry out his demands.

The warder was standing impatiently beside Sophie, who also stood.

'Goodbye Jude,' she said forlornly but he seemed not to hear and already he, along with the other prisoners, was being marshalled away from her, back to the cell block. 'Jude,' she called, loudly this time, and the despair in her voice must have got through to Jude, for he glanced back and raised his hand.

Sophie's heart gave a beat of hope. Into that response she tried to read all that had been left unsaid during the previous half hour. Then she was swept away, a part of the troop of visitors whose feet echoed along the passage as they tramped to its end and were let out through the locked and chained doors into the sunlight. Sophie noticed two male warders' eyes on her and flushed. They must gossip about me, the stepmother, she thought, but what did it matter. She lifted her chin fractionally, pushed back her hair from her right cheek, and quickened her step.

As she drove back to Scarhill Sophie's mind whirled cease-lessly and indecisively. What should she do? She desperately wanted to help Jude, she agreed with his protest, admired him for it, yet there was something despicable about her furtively preparing the Press to down Alec. Wasn't he down enough with debts as it was? Should she, could she, leave Alec, go off with Jude? But Jude didn't love her, not as she loved him – she was a mother-substitute and this must colour the nature of his feelings towards her, in fact any form of intimacy with her must seem like incest to him. But if he *wasn't* Alec's son . . .? This thought kept recurring to her however much she pushed it down. They didn't look all that much alike, it was true, although they were not unalike in character – but perhaps that was just Alec's influence.

Sophie avoided a sheep that had chosen to sleep on the tarmac and then accelerated up the twisting hill to the moor. As she swung into the back yard, two grey cars told her Alec's partners were with him. She let herself in quietly and, not anxious to meet them, tiptoed upstairs.

She was in the bath washing away memories of the prison in hot scented bubbles, when she heard the cars leave. She got out, wrapped herself in Alec's towelling bathrobe that hung on the back of the door, and went down. Alec came out of his office when he heard her. He looked old, the lines on his face seemed deeper. For the first time in their four years together the gap in age between them was brought forcibly home to Sophie. Eight years separate me from Jude, she thought; seventeen from Alec. The comparison was ludicrous, she detested herself for even making it, yet its truth remained. Alec seemed as preoccupied as herself. With an effort he brought his mind to bear on the moment.

'Drink?' he enquired, and poured one for himself and one for Sophie, who perched on the soft arm of the sitting room sofa, still clad in his bathrobe.

'What were they doing here?'

'Come for their due – the return of their loans.'

'But wasn't Howard a partner?'

'Yes – but he's been able to pay his share. I haven't.'

'So . . . so . . .' Sophie felt a moment of panic, a constriction in her throat. For some time now she had known this must happen, had even told Jude it would but had never quite believed it could. Alec, she imagined, with his usual financial wizardry, would avoid calamity in the nick of time, step safely from the lion's jaw . . . 'Does that mean we will have to leave here?' she asked.

'Yes.' Alec drank and swilled the remaining whisky round and round his glass.

Alec was so matter of fact, Sophie couldn't believe it. Her fingers fidgeted with the edging of the chair cover.

'I don't understand . . .' she began.

'I don't expect you to.' Alec was justifiably impatient; he spoke as though explaining to a child. 'It's simple, really. The banks are pulling in their loans. The fire, as you know, left me in a financially unstable position – I wasn't fully insured.

237

My colleagues know the situation but they need money them-selves to meet their own debts.'

Sophie swallowed. 'You mean there's nothing else we can do to . . . to . . .'

'There's nothing else we can do. I've already put Scarhill in the hands of two agents – a London one and Hunters . . .' his voice carried on over Sophie's thoughts. Supposing she was to stand up right now, say, 'Alec, I'm leaving you. Jude has shown me what love is – I never knew before'? But she couldn't do it to this suddenly aged man whose life was collapsing round him. Besides, away from Jude, even to her-self, it sounded unreal – a game of make-believe she played on her own. Alec and property and money were the real world, the world in which people lived . . . She heard herself say, 'You mustn't worry or you'll get ill. I'm sure in a case like this it's best if you sit back and just allow things to take their course.' The palms of her hands were clammy.

Alec's lip lifted, the corner curled, the smile was bitter. 'Allow things to take their course is the one thing I can't do if we're not to go under. I have to fight, hang on to every penny I can. You don't seem to realise the implications.'

'I do.' Sophie felt injured. 'What do you want me to do – become hysterical and threaten suicide? Or leave you?' She held her breath, wondering if he would notice what she had said.

He came over to her, slipped his arm round her drooping shoulders. 'Never do that,' he said, 'No, don't do that to me. Anything else, but not that.' He pushed his face close to hers and she put her hand up to touch his smooth-shaved cheek, sickened by her own duplicity. She wanted to cry but was uncertain whether it was for herself or Alec – perhaps both.

She eased herself away. 'Let me get up and I'll get us some-thing to eat.' Alec stood back and she moved, trance-like, through to the kitchen, automatically opened the door of the dishwasher and began unloading it. I've missed my chance, she thought. I should have left Alec when he was on top of the world, when it would have been fair and I wouldn't have felt like a rat. I might have altered the course of my life from a compromise to a sort of truth that almost certainly would have led on to disaster – but possibly life. Whatever life was. Sophie had the feeling always it was 'out there'; only with Jude did she live briefly in the instant, the moment.

She wrenched the drawer open in anger at her own weakness, took out the potato peeler and began methodically to peel, glad of the monotony of the task.

Benjy, lying in bed, eyes closed, had overheard the doctor pronounce to his mother that when he had fallen on the floor after learning of his sister's death, it had been the equivalent of a fit. The foaming at the mouth, the convulsive jerking of his body, all suggested epilepsy. The only contradictory symptom was that epilepsy usually went with high intelligence and Benjy was, the doctor understood, if anything a little retarded.

His mother had argued that as far as she could see, he was in no sense retarded but dyslexic, which had caused the original supposition.

At this stage they had moved out of the bedroom, still talking, while Benjy lay and looked at the white ceiling with strips of black joists appearing at odd places, and spiders making the most of them. He had seen no point in getting up because that would mean he had to go back to school, or so he judged, and to get out of bed required will that Benjy didn't seem to have. Without Astra there was nothing much to do. His mother had held out against the television that he would have loved, so lying in bed seemed as good as anything else. Besides, his mother bought him puzzle books, join-the-dots books, books where you just washed over with a paintbrush and the pictures came up in different colours. Benjy knew they were childish, for five- to seven-year-olds, because it said so on the outside, but he loved them. He knew his mother bought them because the doctor had suggested that for the time being it would be better if he wasn't 'stretched'. And they kept him contented where anything complicated would have required his mother's assistance.

His own brain, it seemed, either couldn't or wouldn't work. He spent a lot of time lying and doing nothing in particular until he found that by looking into a bright light then shutting his eyes, he could see rings of coloured light dissolve, make new colours, then with his lids still closed he could watch the colours as though he was looking down a kaleidoscope – only these were better. Much better.

Then one day he lay in bed feeling hot and sweaty and every time he shut his eyes he saw only black and white – a black line that rippled and jagged up and down in front of his eyes and frightened him so he thought he might die, like Astra. If he could have been sure she would be there when he was dead he wouldn't have minded, but he thought dying was more like when you buried animals or birds: they were limp and floppy, and eventually, he supposed, just disappeared, turned into earth. If you died at exactly the same time he thought it might be all right, but he was sure he was too long after Astra, and that when he got there, in the earth, she would be gone. So Benjy didn't want to die, but he didn't want to get well either. He wanted to lie in bed with his mother coming to see him often.

It was when she was gone one whole day to see the solicitor and Marty was looking after him – Marty was Mrs Bellamy's daughter-in-law – that he got out of bed to sit hunched on the windowsill watching the snow. He loved, loved, watching snowflakes falling. He sat for an hour before Marty found him with the freezing cold coming in through the ill-fitting leaded windows. She hustled him back to bed and switched on the electric fire.

It was the day after that he got a sore throat; it hurt so much he couldn't swallow or drink. After that the black lines came like a humping snake, only thinner, never moving forwards but always trying . . . That was when his nose dripped scarlet blood into the white basin. It was then he started having dreams and Astra was always there like she was real . . .

*

The toe of Kate's shoe caught in the worn matting at the top of Bag Down stairs and she almost went down them headlong. She steadied herself; she must force herself out of the house, make herself buy new matting. Ever since Astra's death she had been reluctant to do anything except attend to Benjy, and now that after a period of over four months he had at last gone back to school, the day had yawned emptily ahead of her.

Benjy's illness had been both a blessing, inasmuch as it had given her a tether, and a torture in that it had isolated her and shut her up with her own suffering. First it had been their doctor who suggested Benjy stay at home because he had thought it would make it easier for Kate; then Benjy had got tonsilitis followed by pneumonia, in fact contrived to be ill for most of the Easter term. He had convalesced lying for days on end on the old sofa, sucking his thumb and kicking the arm until Kate could have screamed – and, on occasion, had. It was such an annoying habit and yet so expressive of what was going on in her own head. *Thud-thud, thud-thud, thud-thud.* Her entire life had seemed to assume the pointless rhythm, the thud had the menace at times of a primitive drumbeat echoing round Kate's brain. She had gone about her tasks with a grim tenacity; intuitively she was aware that if she let go of the habit, the routine of her existence, then she would be lost.

The situation had not been eased by Donald who, she was sure, blamed her for Astra's death. Night after night she had lain sleepless, tossing and turning, switching the light on, attempting to read, then off again only to lie in a blackness of recrimination and despair. It had been unlucky, everyone said. Terribly, terribly unlucky. It was no one's fault – it was one of those things. Kate agreed and yet it didn't seem to make things any better and, unconsciously if not consciously, she continued to blame herself.

Most mornings she had seen the dawn, risen from her bed with relief to welcome the daylight and the coming of spring, only to be overwhelmed by misery that Astra was not there to share the throb of new life Kate could not prevent herself from responding to. She knew she would never get over her child's death, that the pain would never lessen; and gradually she came to realise that the only comfort she could hope for was that, with the passing of time, she might dwell on it less often. She knew that her only way out of the apathy into which she increasingly found herself sinking, was to make herself resume painting, but until now she had been quite unable to summon the will. It was only when she finally realised she was using Astra's absence as an excuse, where before she had used her presence for an excuse, that she forced herself again to face a blank canvas. That and Benjy's return to school. To help herself she had rung Carol, knowing it her half-day, had asked her to sit for her . . .

'So Scarhill's being auctioned next week?' Carol's voice, the subject, jarred unpleasantly.

'Yes.' Kate had never quite got over Scarhill and in the last months it had acquired nostalgic associations – the place, the room, the bed where Astra had been born, where they'd been happy for a time. For a long time. And now was to come its final mutilation – it was to be sold in lots.

'It's the end of Scarhill, really – as a farm.' She voiced her feelings.

'Oh I don't know.' Carol, who had watched the Warren sold off field by field over the years, acre by acre to keep them solvent, had hardened herself to such blows. 'Places come and go,' she said, 'I mean Scarhill's loss will be another farm's gain.'

'I find it difficult to see it that way.' Kate felt embarrassed by the huskiness of her voice. To cover it, she attacked. 'Sophie lets Alec get away with things all the time – although she's dead against just about all he does.'

'Why does she stay with him, then? Why do I stay with Richard?' Carol laughed drily.

'You're very free, aren't you?'

'And Sophie isn't?'

Kate frowned. 'I don't know, she said, 'I can't make it out. Alec seems to have some kind of hold over her – and obviously wants to keep it that way. Though recently it's more as though she's taken her dark glasses off.'

'Recently she's spent all her time visiting young Jude.'

Kate looked at Carol. 'Someone's got to.'

'Yes.' Carol lit another cigarette.

I wish she wouldn't, Kate thought, looking at Carol's nicotined finger, hating her habit of inference, of half imparting information without elaborating on it. She stood abruptly. 'Could you bear to sit for another half-hour, then we'll pack it in?' she said.

Carol took up her position and Kate returned to her canvas. She had posed Carol in front of a piece of heavy prussian blue cloth with great white formal flowers rippling across it. Carol's pale face and neck slithered into their whiteness, creating new and strange shapes held in tension by the eyes and nostrils. Her auburn hair formed a block of sienna, the eyes looked perpetually out. Eyes with acorn-cup lids that were no more or less than any other part, yet in some way the focus. At least so Kate hoped. For the first time in months she felt alive, absorbed, excited, near to something. It was as though all her sufferings, her feelings, had been distilled into this picture. It was an indication of her need to paint; if it could be good, why then she had some excuse for the time given to it, the time taken from her children . . . No, this was not true – or was it? She didn't know.

She checked herself, she must concentrate not let her mind wander. She looked until she no longer saw Carol, or the cloth, or the chair but simply a continuous flow of colour and shapes imbued with life. She squeezed out veridian and orange side by side. She felt almost too nervous to continue; it would be so easy to destroy the spark of life that at present glowed at her from the canvas.

'Will you go to Scarhill's auction?' she asked, taking up her brush, braving herself to dip it in the paint.

'I don't know.' Carol refrained from shifting her head, 'I had planned to have Ladybird shod that afternoon. It's at three, isn't it?'

But Kate wasn't listening; she was painting.

Carol had been gone some time when Sophie arrived, and Kate, exhausted but released, had left the studio. She made herself a further cup of tea and was wondering idly what would have happened if the gallery had ever seen her canvases. Fate had intervened – well, she wouldn't tempt fate again. Once was enough . . . At this moment the iron knocker thudded on the thick door, followed by Sophie's entrance. Before she even spoke Kate knew something momentous was coming, sensed the tension.

She led her through into the warmth of the small kitchen, offered her tea, which Sophie declined and instead pulled out a chair from the table, sat astride it with her chin resting on its back, her jeaned legs sprawled before her, her ankles rolled in.

'Jude's about to come out,' she announced.

'That must be a relief, isn't it?'

'Yes.' But Sophie sounded doubtful, and Kate, looking at Sophie's youth and health, couldn't help but feel resentment. The Deneuves' capacity for self-absorption seemed unlimited. And yet, after Astra's death, no one could have tried to do more for her than Sophie.

'It's been a strain,' Sophie added, then looking up met Kate's gaze before which she visibly quailed.

'Sorry,' she said. 'Sorry. Sorry, Kate.'

'What is it?' Kate asked. She felt tensed, waiting.

'I'm not quite sure how to ask you this – but you know we're selling and going back to London, or Alec is. He's got to. So I wondered if you would consider letting me rent the rooms in the stable block from you. You see, I've decided to leave Alec.'

Kate tried to think clearly, take in all that was implied. Thoughts and emotions whirled round her mind. Could she, could she have Sophie so close, under her roof virtually? Sophie, who was after all a Deneuve, had instigated Astra and Jude's friendship, had been if only indirectly, a party to Astra's death.

'And Jude? What's he going to do?' Kate's eyes were hard as she looked at Sophie.

'I honestly don't know. I wish I did' – the colour mounted up Sophie's neck and face – 'Why – what have you heard?'

'That you have been a dutiful visitor,' Kate could not keep the bitterness, the sarcasm out of her voice.

Sophie's honesty prevented her from denying the implicit accusation.

'We wouldn't be living together or anything,' she said, 'but it does make it all wrong to go on with Alec. And staying with you would be a way of making it clear I want us to separate . . .' Her voice tailed off as she saw Kate's expression. 'Kate,' she asked, 'you're not cross with me, are you?'

Kate couldn't believe her ears. She looked down on Sophie's innocent face gazing up at her, and wondered if she could really be so oblivious to other people's feelings. Rage rose in her; she held on to the stove rail to steady herself.

'You,' she said, '*You* come and tell me this?'

A bewildered, hurt expression came into Sophie's saucer eyes. 'I thought you'd be the best person to ask advice. I mean you're my friend and . . . and wise.'

'Jude,' said Kate, trying to control uncontrollable emotions, '*caused* Astra's death – indirectly. Do you expect me to be pleased when I'm told you and he are carrying on an affair? Can both of you be that shallow?'

'But Kate,' Sophie stammered, overwhelmed by the turn things had taken, 'it was six months ago and Astra never loved Jude. He's told me. He wanted to marry her but she didn't want him. And anyway it's me who loves him, not the other way round. So . . . So you can't *blame* him.'

'Oh can't I?' Kate's eyes blazed. 'I do blame him. I shall always blame him. I blame all you Deneuves for coming here and . . . and messing everyone up with your meddling, your fickle feelings – using people to your own ends.'

Sophie sat for a full moment staring at Kate, the silence

broken only by the refrigerator's hum. Then she stood, slowly, awkwardly. 'I'm sorry,' she said, 'I didn't know you felt like this about us – about me, that is. I knew you were anti-Alec because of . . . of things he's done, but I didn't know you held us responsible for Astra's death – or for that matter, Jude, because Jude was the one who wanted her to have the baby, wanted to marry Astra, wanted them at least to live together –'

'I've heard all this before,' Kate interrupted, beside herself with anger; she couldn't bear her own guilt thrown back in her face. 'The fact remains that without Jude – you Deneuves – Astra would be alive, not dead.' She was shaking from head to foot, she realised now that all this had been bottled up inside her, that she had been waiting to say it, waiting for the moment when she would be unstoppered and it would gush forth, a torrent of pent-up resentment. Against herself not least – a wolf-headed gargoyle.

Sophie was moving towards the door, getting into her jacket. 'I'm sorry,' she repeated, 'I'll go. I'd willingly die if I could make Astra live again. But I can't and . . . and it seemed that caring for Jude, though appearing wrong in most people's eyes, might actually be right. So I came to ask your opinion, because I respect you more than anyone I know.' Sophie's voice tailed away. She fumbled with the door catch.

'You should never ask anyone's advice,' Kate shouted, 'least of all mine.'

Sophie let herself out of the kitchen and would have left through the front door without saying a word had not Kate caught up with her, reached in front of her to prevent her exit. 'Don't go. I haven't finished with you yet. You bought our farm, you've split it up, you're selling it in lots – mutilating it. You and your *husband*.' She spat out the word. 'He's not even content with that – he's destroying the entire area . . .'

'Not any more,' Sophie interrupted. 'He can't – we're broke. Properly broke . . . it's not just Scarhill that's being sold – it's Alec's business – the flat – the lot.'

Even Kate's anger was slightly subdued. 'I see,' she said

icily, 'I suppose that's why you and Jude are leaving him. That would figure.'

Sophie coloured, now angry in turn. 'That's a horrible thing to say. Have you been pretending all this time to like me? It's nothing whatsoever to do with that, and you know it. It's just terribly unfortunate that all this has coincided.'

'It always is, isn't it?' Kate's sarcasm cut Sophie to the quick. 'You may not think you're leaving Alec because he's lost his money, but that's what you're doing. They say money and love are interchangeable . . .' She stopped. 'Oh God,' she said, 'oh God, what am I saying,' and collapsed on the tall-backed, velvet-seated hall chair. Sophie hesitated, uncertain whether to go or help Kate, who looked almost ill.

'Kate . . .' she said, making a tentative move towards her.

'Go away,' Kate summoned all her strength and shouted in Sophie's face, 'go away with Jude for your lover. Why not? It's the kind of thing everyone expected of you. Go, I should. It smacks enough of scandal to keep the village going till Christmas, but don't think you're going to do it under my roof' – Kate listened to herself with horror. Am I jealous, she thought, jealous of Sophie for finding love – because that was what she instinctively knew it to be. Am I a bitter old woman who has never found love, just tried to sublimate the need for it by painting? She covered her face with her hands; a moment later she groped for Sophie, clutched her wrist, her arm, drew Sophie towards her, her other hand still shielding her eyes.

'Forgive me,' she said, 'I know you can't entirely, ever. It's just that I've suffered so much, so much, in these last six months. I haven't been able to accept what's happened, I'm still fighting it, still hating everyone in anyway connected with Astra's death, myself most of all. It was my fault, you see – that's the worst of it.' She withdrew the shielding hand, looked at Sophie with the stricken eyes of a hunted animal, 'I pushed her into it.'

'Oh Kate . . .' Sophie knelt, rested her hands over Kate's which, in turn, rested on the arms of the chair in the dark hall. The fridge whirred and started up in the kitchen, otherwise the house was absolutely still. Kate took the oval face Sophie tilted up to her, like a piece of exquisite sculpture, she thought, and even in the midst of her distress she held it as she might a precious stone.

'Of course you can live here if you like,' she said, 'but please not with Jude. It's not that my reason sees anything wrong with it, it's just that I'm not ready for it yet. I'm not able to ... to cope with myself because it opens the wound. That's what increasingly I realise I have to come to terms with – my own weakness. All that talk about my having strength – it's rubbish. It was arrogance, not strength – as you saw just now.'

'I don't think so.' Sophie continued to kneel in front of Kate; tears welled up, spilled over. Kate too was crying, they cried together. It was as though the sorrow of the world had bubbled up through the two women crouched in the dark hall, fountains taking from the source and splashing out suffering till it gradually dispersed, floated away across a clear surface.

Sophie was the first to move. She stood carefully, dreading that distance should again come between them, aware also that her sorrow had been in part for her own hopeless relationship with Jude. Kate got up stiffly as if the scene had drained her. They went through into the kitchen where Kate plugged in the kettle. With her back still to Sophie she said, 'Can't you leave Alec without going to Jude?'

'I could,' she said without conviction. It was in her next utterance that she became animated. 'I love Jude,' she said, 'really. He's ... absolutely everything to me.' She looked imploringly at Kate, 'Do you think I ought to leave Alec? I feel almost afraid to. Not for myself – for him. He's terribly strong, I know, but I think I am sort of ... important to him.'

'Yes of course.' Kate made the tea, presented Sophie with a mug. 'Why do anything too absolute just at present,' she said comfortingly. 'Why not come and live here for a bit, see how you get on.'

'Could I?' Sophie leaped at the suggestion. 'I'll come alone. I won't make a nuisance of myself.' She sensed the solid mass of Kate, her powerful presence. In her undecided state it came as a boon, gave her a tether. She couldn't live on her own, she knew that, but with Kate . . .

'I'll go now,' she said. 'Come back later this evening. Will that be all right?'

And so it was agreed, Sophie would fetch her things, and return. After she had gone, Kate went up with a Hoover and duster to the room that had used to be Astra's. She took a deep breath, braced herself, and switched on the Hoover. The noise helped her to overcome her total disinclination for the task; Sophie would have to use the room, there was no other. The groom's room was out of the question – in the recent downpour it had sprung a leak.

Alec was marking time. He had been to the head office of his bank, sat for an hour endeavouring to persuade them to allow him to retain sufficient credit to carry him over until he could sell off the recently acquired moor properties, including Scarhill, and put 'Deneuve and Benson: Forestry' into liquidation. This would obviate his need to meet his debts until a later date. It was the way out of a collapsed business and indeed the only way left open to him. He was as trapped in his own 'plunging' as any man could be. If the stock market had been in the ascendant, all might have been saved, but the possibility of an election, a change of leadership, the threatened wealth tax, all had contributed to shake the confidence of investors. They withdrew their money and invested in overseas commodities; the stock market continued to fall; Alec was losing money rapidly and by the hour. Where possible he had sold out, but at an appalling loss, and the strain of recent months had taken its toll. He had developed a twitch in one eyelid that flickered almost continuously; the tense set of his mouth, the greyish pallor of his skin, all conspired to give him a slightly seedy appearance. It was as a tired man that he entered Scarhill kitchen and found Sophie's note on the table: *'Gone to Bag Down to stay with Kate for a while. Sophie.'*

To say that Alec was shattered would be an understatement. He stood holding her note and rereading it as though if he read it enough it would change. Finally he crumpled it up and dropped it in the waste-bin under the sink. He hadn't thought Sophie would leave him because . . . He just hadn't thought that she would. Jane had left him, it was true, but then he had asked for it by having an affair with one of her friends. But in Sophie's case it was inexcusable. His behaviour had been exemplary, she had no reason for complaint – in fact had hardly complained except over the trees. And in any case, now the plantation was burnt, she'd got her way . . . She would be back almost certainly, she wouldn't stay long at Bag Down, it was too small.

Wearily he made himself coffee with whisky, sat at the table and opened as usual his paper. But the words and figures didn't register, were meaningless. They reminded him of properties invested in during the previous autumn that were now unsellable. If he could just afford to sit on them, wait till prices went up again as they must, then all might be saved. As it was, the banks gave no leeway, they were like some robot that proceeded as programmed irrespective of individuals. They were calling in their loans and that was that. Alec's mind reverted to Sophie. The sudden isolation, the loneliness, the uselessness of his life without her overwhelmed him. He must get her back. He could wait till she rang him, which he felt sure she'd do – or he could go over to Bag Down and bring her back.

He debated the best plan of action for some while, then went into his office. He pressed the digits on his computer and figures leaped up, green and flickering on the screen. He pressed other digits that obligingly obeyed his command, but his concentration had gone. He looked round his gadget-strewn office and wished suddenly to be rid of it. It was one more millstone round his neck; he rested his head against the chair-back and for the first time for several days thought seriously about Jude. Sophie had said he was about to come out. How would his sentence have affected him, he wondered, but couldn't find it in himself to care. He was utterly indifferent to his own son, that was the truth of the matter; to pretend to deep feelings of affection would be nothing short of hypocrisy. His mind shifted back to Sophie and with it came the decision to go and get her. Sitting here on his own was intolerable, her card had not been definite ... He went out to the hall and put on his blazer, then ran up to the bathroom for a quick go round his chin with the electric shaver. He clapped his pockets, made sure there was money in them, and went out to the car.

Sophie had already gone to bed when Alec reached Bag Down. Kate, in her dressing-gown, had been about to follow her up and jumped visibly at the sound of the knocker. She guessed at once it would be Alec and didn't at first go to answer but a further imperious knock decided her. Confronted by him, she saw no other way than to ask him into the half-lit room. Alec had to bend his head forward to avoid the beams, he had not been to Bag Down since the fateful day almost a year ago when he and Sophie had been shown over it by Kate and had pressed the invitation to their party on her.

He stood now looking round him, his mind concentrated on his objective – to recover Sophie. Kate observed his haggard face and offered him a drink, which he thankfully accepted. She poured one for herself; she didn't exactly feel at ease with this alien man whose very presence seemed to burst out and beyond the walls of the small room. It was this presence, she surmised, that was more than half of his attraction for women, that and his abounding confidence that even now remained.

But it was not the impression he was making that concerned Alec. He came straight to the point. 'Sophie's here. I've seen her car.'

'Yes.'

There was a sound, a creak on the stairs, and Sophie stood in the doorway behind them. She came down the last step into the room wrapped in a floral and black silk nothingness. 'I had to get away, Alec,' she said, 'I left you a note.'

'I'd like you to come back.' They faced each other, an incongruous couple in their confined surroundings, while Kate sat

251

on the bench beside the table turning her glass stem in her fingers and wishing she was elsewhere.

'I thought . . .' Sophie broke off.

'What did you think?'

'That I had to be honest – make a clean break. I didn't want to live a lie. I don't love you, Alec.'

Kate saw her chance to escape and slid behind Alec to the kitchen, shutting the door behind her.

'So you came here for protection?' Alec couldn't quite keep the contempt out of his tone, Sophie's words had hurt him enough to make him want to hit back.

'No – because I'd nowhere else to go and Kate's a friend.'

'There's London.'

Silence greeted Alec's suggestion.

'You stayed here,' he went on, 'because of Jude. Right?'

'In part. Yes.'

'Sophie,' Alec advanced a step and she backed a step, 'you're making an idiot of yourself – you don't love Jude any more than you do me. Probably less. You're chasing a romantic idea that only exists in your head about love. Jude's not worth one of your gold hairs, though he's my son.'

'I think he is.' Sophie was adamant.

'Believe me, he's not.'

'That's been the whole trouble,' Sophie burst out, 'I've listened to you too much, Alec, and you haven't always told me the truth – just the truth according to you. And now I've got to be separate, be away from you so I can make up *my* mind, find out what's the truth for me. You organise me, organise my whole life and I can't be organised. Not for ever.'

Alec had no answer. He was honest enough to recognise the accuracy of what she said. They had reached an impasse beyond which it seemed they could not progress. Finally he said, 'Sophie, come back with me, at least for tonight. I need you. I wouldn't ask you if I didn't need you. If you don't . . .' His despair communicated itself.

Sophie felt sick with indecision. Alec was playing on her own desperate need for affection, her need of love.

'If I come,' she said at last, 'what'll it be for?'

'For me.'

'Yes. But I've said, I don't love you, Alec. I know now. I've known it for a long time but not done anything – nothing positive – and now I've done something – something definite. I don't want to go back on my decision.'

'Please . . .' Alec's voice broke. He turned his back on her. Sophie felt all the embarrassment and alarm that a strong man weeping can have on someone with a generous nature.

'Don't. Oh please don't. I just want to be truthful. Not . . . not deceive you,' she finished weakly.

'At least come back with me tonight.' The huskiness of Alec's voice prevented him saying any more. He was blinkered and suffering; if Sophie would only come with him now he was sure he could alter everything. He determined not to leave the house without her, became temporarily a child emotionally playing on those closest to him to get his own way. And Sophie was the perfect vehicle, every fibre of her being responded to his plea, only her intelligence held out against what she knew to be ultimate failure.

'What good will going back with you do? It won't alter what I feel.'

'We can talk, get things straight. Please.'

Alec's argument was weakening, but on an emotional level he was winning. Sophie opened her mouth to speak, then shut it again. They stood in silence for a seemingly endless length of time, then she turned and mounted the creaking stairs she had only just descended with such firm intention. Alec waited and in a few moments she returned bringing her bag. She placed it beside him. 'I must go through and tell Kate,' she said, her voice dull and lifeless.

Kate was sitting at the kitchen table. She looked up with anxious eyes as Sophie came in.

'I'm going back for tonight,' Sophie said. 'Sorry, Kate – oh I'm so sorry, but I don't know what else to do.'

Kate stubbed out her cigarette and stood. Sophie came over

to her and they held each other closely for a brief moment, then separated.

'He loves me,' Sophie said, 'he does really. In his own way.'

Kate said nothing. 'You don't think I should go back, do you?' Sophie knew she couldn't expect Kate's approval yet still demanded it, hoped for it.

Kate sighed. 'I don't know what I think and whatever it is, it doesn't matter. You must do what you think. But if you do decide to come back there's always a bed here.'

Yet Kate knew already Sophie had gone back to Alec, would not, perhaps could not, break away from him. She saw an endless succession of attempts of this nature stretching into the future and then, as they got older, Sophie settling for it. It was so odd – she and Donald had got on far better and yet their break had been relatively easy. More final. And her misgivings had slipped away for good now, she was lighter, relieved . . .

Sophie kissed her again quickly. 'Thanks, Kate. I'll come over.' She moved backwards out of the door.

Minutes later Kate heard first one car then another drive out of the gate and up the steep lane. She laid her head down on her arms, drained, emotionally exhausted, beyond thought. A blank.

Benjy, wearing sleeping trunks, stood uncertainly in the doorway regarding his mother, then stepped down into the kitchen; his hair had recently been cut in the same punkish fashion as Eddie Fardon's and stood on end, his head looked rather big on top of his slight body. Undoubtedly he had grown.

'What's the matter?' He surveyed his mother suspiciously. If there was one thing he couldn't bear it was his mother looking depressed when he didn't know the reason why, it worried him, made him feel cross.

Kate pressed her hands against her temples. 'Nothing, really,' she said. 'It's just the thought of Scarhill being sold in lots . . . and one thing and another. The Deneuves, basically.'

'Why the Deneuves?'

'Surely it must be obvious. They're a mess – and as a result destructive to other people.'

'Are they?' Benjy walked past her and helped himself to a bowl of muesli.

'Well, don't you think they are?' Kate found herself saying things to Benjy she would never have dreamed of saying when Astra was alive; he seemed to have grown up suddenly in the succeeding months.

'What have they destroyed?' Benjy shovelled round his plate after a nut.

'Oh Benjy' – Kate felt exasperated.

But Benjy persisted, reminding her of Astra. 'It's not them any more than us,' he said.

'None of this would have happened if they'd never come.' Kate was sure.

Benjy eyed his mother but said nothing. It seemed to him things started to happen the day his father went away, otherwise they'd never have left Scarhill and the Deneuves would not have bought it. They would still be living there and Astra wouldn't have had to go to hospital for her 'miscarriage' because she wouldn't have met Jude Deneuve. So Benjy's mind proceeded backwards logically.

'Who was here?' he asked.

'Sophie and Alec.'

Benjy's teeth stopped crunching for an instant, then went on.

'Are you all right?' Kate asked. He seemed so white-faced.

'Of course I'm all right.' Benjy was aggrieved. His mother was forever asking the same futile question. He finished his cereal, washed up the bowl and spoon, and made to leave.

'Where are you going?'

'Back to bed.'

'Goodnight then, Benjy.'

'Goodnight.' The door closed after him. So uncommunicative, Kate thought, not seeing her own unfairness. It was a bad age, she told herself, but really, just at the present, that

255

was little comfort. 'I'll be up soon,' she called, 'I'm going to have a bath.'

Benjy lay on his bed in the darkness sucking his thumb. He felt unhappy, but then unlike most people he did not *expect* to be happy, rather he slithered into unhappiness like an outsize overcoat. An hour later he switched on his light and put some more brilliant orange gloss on the wing of his latest model plane.

'My dear – I hear you are quite definitely leaving us.' Oliver Upton advanced across Scarhill's lawn and kissed Sophie on the cheek.

'Yes, I'm afraid we are.'

'Can't we persuade you to stay?'

'Alec has to follow his work.' She smiled evasively at Oliver Upton. I'm not going to ask him in, she was thinking. But at that very moment, in the trecherous manner of the English summer, it began to hail and she was forced to do so. Inside, Oliver Upton sat himself in the armchair by the stove while Sophie sat on the far side of the table. For civility she offered him tea, which he declined.

'I really came out,' he began, 'to enquire after young Jude. I have tried on several occasions to visit him, but apparently he prefers not to see anyone.'

'He hasn't told me that,' Sophie replied with honesty. 'But he comes out in ten days' time.'

'I take it he feels his protest, his stance for Conservation, to be complete.'

'Oh not complete,' said Sophie airily, 'but something that was necessary for him, personally, to do.'

'Yes.' There was a difficult silence. Sophie racked her brain for an excuse to terminate the rector's stay; she was uncertain why exactly he had come. But in the next moment it became clear.

'It has come to my ears,' Oliver Upton said as though in answer to her thoughts, 'that you have been his main visitor. Very dutiful.'

Sophie's cheeks burned. Where had he got this 'information'?

'Well naturally,' she said, 'Alec's far too busy so it falls to me, I've got the time.'

'Yes' – Oliver Upton eyed her. He clasped his hands, leant forward, looked at her with a gleam in his small eyes – 'I think,' he went on, 'that you should not put too much faith in that young man. I don't think it was an act of protest as he has led the Press to believe – it was simply an act of uncontrolled revenge against his father.'

'Surely it's all one and the same thing?' – Sophie felt confused.

Oliver Upton sat back. He saw he had scored. 'I don't want to upset you or cause you unnecessary anxiety,' he said, 'but I would suggest the boy is unbalanced. I have had some experience with people of his infirmity, and believe me, they don't change. It goes underground for some years, perhaps, then comes out again under any form of stress. I suggest the stress that prompted his irrational behaviour this time was his passion for Astra Merlin.' He watched Sophie closely, his own absurd jealousy making him believe others equally jealous.

'Perhaps' – Oliver Upton's stab had gone home – 'but I don't agree with you that Jude is in any sense unbalanced – only very sensitive and aware. He is fighting against man destroying life – the environment . . .' she heard herself continuing like a parrot.

Oliver Upton interrupted. 'I hope you don't mind me being a concerned old busybody and worrying about you. But I felt it my duty to make sure you are doing what you intend with your eyes open. It would be unseemly and reprehensible if you should abandon your husband for his son.'

Sophie's breath was taken away. Her indignation flared up. 'What is it to do with you? What right have you to come here and lecture me? Go away. Now.' She couldn't prevent the tremble in her voice.

Oliver Upton moved to the door where he stopped; then

257

said, 'You must understand my only wish, as rector of this parish, is to intervene when I feel it of the utmost importance. I advise you to think carefully before taking what could only be considered a rash and irresponsible action.'

The uncanny truth in his assumptions, the menace she had always felt and now felt again for what he might contrive to do or say to harm Jude and herself, silenced Sophie, kept her standing at the table studying the miniature azalea in the pot in front of her for timeless seconds, waiting for this man, who knew no limits in nastiness, to leave. She refused to look at him, refused to look up or reply, and only by the sound of his footsteps, the closing of the back door, could she tell that Oliver Upton had left. Whereupon she relaxed; her legs felt like straw and she was shaking all over.

Jude stood in the square outside the prison looking round him. He had been discharged at 8 a.m. along with two others, and his own clothes returned to him. The rest of his belongings were clutched under one arm in a brown paper parcel. The others had already departed and Jude alone remained, expecting to be met by Sophie and a press reporter. Better still, several. Ideally he would have liked a story with a photo of himself outside the prison, preferably on the front page.

After another fifteen minutes Jude's patience was exhausted; he began to make his way across to a telephone kiosk by the entrance but before he reached it Sophie drove into the square, caught sight of him and drew up. She wound down the window.

'Sorry,' she said, 'I got held up.'

'Where are the Press?' Jude's voice was level. He didn't smile, only stared straight at her with his pale blue eyes full of accusation. He had counted, absolutely counted, on Sophie bringing the Press.

'Jude – you don't understand – I just couldn't. I agree with you and everything but . . . but I . . .'

Jude undid the door, put his case in the back and got in beside her. 'Drop me at the *Gazette*'s office, will you?'

Sophie put the car into gear and they drove out under the arch in silence. 'What will you tell them?' she finally brought herself to ask.

'I'll simply let them have my story – from the fire up till the present.'

'Yes.' Sophie's voice was small for the thought of Alec's reaction alarmed her more that she dared to admit, and it seemed to her now, as she negotiated the streets towards the local Fleet Street, that ironically, by his act of arson, Jude had achieved far more than he had ever dreamt possible, for indirectly it had led to the financial ruin of his father. Sophie couldn't help thinking this was enough, but glancing at Jude's set jaw beside her, clean-shaven for his release, she understood that it was not. Alec might be ruthless in his fashion but Jude, she suspected – in fact knew – was equally so. And the horror of it was that it was these men that attracted her. Sophie simply couldn't understand this for she hated cruelty, hated force . . . or she did with all her reasoning mind.

'It's too early,' she said; 'No one'll be there. Can't you come home first?'

But Jude remained adamant, accusatory. 'Why didn't you bring the Press to meet me? It's the only thing I've ever asked you to do.'

'Jude I . . . I wanted to. I was going to, and then with Alec not having any money and having such a terrible time, I couldn't do it to him. Jude? Jude? Surely you can understand that?' But Jude refused to look at her, his face was set. 'Please answer?' Sophie felt sick with despair.

When he did his voice was level and cold. 'Yes I understand, only too well. You run with the hare and hunt with the hounds.' He turned his head away from her, looked out of the window.

'Jude I care for you, for . . . for . . . your values. For everything about you. You know I do.'

She pulled up outside the office of the *Western Gazette*. Jude's answer was to get out and slam the door. On the steps he hesitated, went back, leant in the window. 'Don't wait if you don't want to,' he said, 'I'll make my own way home.'

'I'll wait,' Sophie said. And did until half an hour later Jude reappeared apparently well satisfied. Sophie wanted to ask what he had said but refrained and Jude didn't choose to tell her. They talked very little during the remaining miles to Scarhill, and Sophie, acutely aware of the increased difference between them, felt tongue-tied; anything she said seemed dull and inadequate. She let Jude out at the gate and immediately went off to meet Alec's train from London, circumstances having finally reduced them to one car.

Jude, left on his own, drank in a deep breath of the April air, and relaxed fractionally, but not so much that he didn't need to smoke. It was a habit he had acquired in prison where there had been a fair trade in smuggled cigarettes and which he now found impossible to do without.

Prison had been far worse than he cared to admit. The others he had come into contact with, in the main, revolted him; there had been nothing ennobling about the experience only loneliness and humiliation interspersed by Sophie's fortnightly visits. He had both longed for them and been filled with resentment that she could so completely fail to understand his suffering – or so he thought. Her imagination, he believed, was simply not able to fill in what he could never put into words. Secretly he longed and hoped for a visit from Kate Merlin who he believed would know intuitively what he was going through, understand the gradual hardening of his soul. He and she were united in their loss of Astra, and he persuaded himself that he would be able to communicate with Kate in a way he was not able to do with anyone else – other than perhaps Astra. But even Astra had never understood him. That had been the trouble – they had connected at best in an unspoken mode of sensations ... Jude's mind went round in fruitless circles and always centred back on the prison.

He lit a further cigarette. He blinked in the fitful sunlight and endeavoured to close a shutter across the psychological wounds of his time 'in'. If anything his term had increased his egoism, his disregard for people who did not benefit him. The delicacy, the finer side of his nature that had appealed to Astra, had temporarily vanished under a much coarsened manner which was largely born of fear.

Now he entered Scarhill by way of the begun-but-never completed conservatory and went up to what had used to be his bedroom, only to find it no longer existed. The partition had been removed and it had become a long, low double-windowed room with women's clothes on the back of the door and bottles on the dressing-table. He stood for a full minute in the doorway taking it in. It appeared Scarlet must use it on her more and more infrequent visits . . . He sniffed, then looked more closely, observed some of the clothes to be Sophie's from which came a delicate scent. So Sophie slept here. Jude took this in along with the implications that went with it. Only now did he realise how much Sophie and Alec's relations had worsened in his absence. That his room had gone seemed to him in some way final and symbolic; it said uncategorically that he was no longer a part of the family, making a point with which he was totally in accord and yet which still came as a shock. He had only lived in this room for a brief spell of time, but it carried memories, memories of the period he was in love with Astra; from these windows he had stretched to take her letter from Benjy's fingers . . . It seemed years ago rather than months. He backed out, closing the door.

He continued round the house, opening and shutting cupboard doors in search of his belongings. He was still doing so when Sophie returned with his father half an hour later. They met at the bottom of the stairs.

'Hullo.' It was apparent to Jude that it took an immense effort for his father to speak to him; he suspected it was due to Sophie's efforts that he had done so at all. Certainly she could not have told his father about his visit to the Press.

'I shan't be long. I'm collecting my things and going,' Jude answered. Alec nodded and turned his back; he joined Sophie in the kitchen.

'Jude's going, he tells me.'

'Not already?' Panic gripped Sophie.

Alec laid his file on the table; he was sorting it. His frown deepened at Sophie's obvious concern but he made no comment. He took up his papers and went through to his office. Jude was outside the airing cupboard repacking his pack, a heap of left-out clothes beside him.

'Jude?' She was too afraid to approach him, touch him. The world of prison had brought them close, circled them like arms, developed such intimacy between them. Now it seemed all her visiting counted for nothing; in the presence of the home, of his father, their relations were again that of stepmother and step-son. Neither more nor less. Sophie felt desolated and desperate. She swallowed, controlled herself by a superhuman effort, said in as calm a voice a she could manage, 'Aren't you going to stay for even a night?'

'My father hasn't invited me and I don't anticipate he's going to.' He didn't look at Sophie but continued pushing things into his pack, buckling and adjusting the strap.

'What about all your other things?'

'Burn them, if you like. I've taken all I want. I don't want to be lumbered with a lot of stuff.' Jude tried his pack on his shoulders. It seemed to make him feel better; he smiled for the first time.

'So you're going. Now. Just like you are?' Sophie tried not to allow the misery she felt into her voice. Suddenly, overwhelmed at the thought of losing Jude, she said, 'I'm coming with you, Jude. I've decided.'

Jude's eyes lit up for a moment, then he frowned. 'It's got to be your decision.'

'It is.' Sophie looked at him anxiously.

'OK. It's up to you.'

'You want me to, don't you?'

'If it's what you want, then yes.'

'It's what I want more than anything.'

Their eyes met. Sophie wished she could read Jude's expression. Nervously she took a step towards him, and his arms encircled her, he pressed her pliant body against his own hard form dressed in newly laundered home clothes. Sophie's face felt the rough skin of his chin and in that moment she adored him, his physical presence after months of separated visiting overriding all warning voices of her common sense.

In a few seconds Jude released her. 'Could you drive me to the Merlins?' he asked. 'I thought I ought to say goodbye. After that we could go.'

Sophie's eyes lit up with hope and excitement. 'Give me half an hour to pack – and by then Alec'll be having a business meeting here, with the estate agents, so we can take the car . . .' she paused, thought. 'We could leave it at the station – let him know it's there' – her mind leaped ahead.

'Fine.'

'Will you say goodbye to Alec?'

'I've said all that needs saying between us.'

'So I'll go and pack?' Sophie still couldn't quite believe it.

'Yes.' He needed her, didn't he? Needed someone. He felt lost, helpless. All he wanted was to stay where he was, with people he knew and with whom he was safe. But that was the one thing that his father's presence made it impossible for him to do. So he must take Sophie with him, Sophie must be his buffer, shelter him from this sudden panicky fear at the thought of organising himself, facing life outside an institution. 'Yes,' he repeated.

Sophie left him then, went into her bedroom and shut the door. Her heart thumped for what she was about to do, but it was right, she felt certain of that.

The leaves on the trees closed over them in a dark tunnel as they descended the steep lane to Bag Down. Sophie drove with Jude beside her, gleaning happiness from his proximity. Jude hardly spoke and Sophie had given up trying. It was clear to her that Jude's self, his life, was uppermost in his mind but she felt no resentment, caring only that she was allowed to go with him.

'Put me down here,' Jude instructed well before the gate. Sophie applied the brakes, switched off the engine. There was a moment's silence.

'I'll wait here until you've finished.'

'All right.'

'Jude – you won't be too long, will you?'

'No.'

'Jude?' Her tone was full of pleading. She kissed his cheek. He turned his head and their mouths met. Sophie felt she must die from the sweet mingling of happiness and pain; tears ran down her cheeks. He drew his mouth away finally; the window was open and the lush vegetation of the bank intruded its voluptuous growth. After his confinement the scents intoxicated him. He bent over Sophie's head, kissed her neck; her passion for him communicated itself and he kissed her closed lids, returned her ardent kisses. They clung to each other briefly like lovers found entwined in an embrace at the bottom of a dragged lake.

'Jude?' she repeated, 'if you weren't related to Alec ... I mean, it would make a difference, wouldn't it?' She felt Jude stiffen, he disentangled himself from her.

'What difference?'

'It would be more ... more acceptable. Us together.'

'What's he said to you?'

'Only that it's not *absolutely* certain – that you're related.'

Jude didn't answer. He climbed out, opened the back door and dragged out his pack-bag. He leant in the car window, rested his arms on the sill, 'Let's hope we're not, then,' he said. They both laughed. But something about Jude's laugh struck Sophie. She felt uncomfortable – for a moment she wished she hadn't spoken, but almost in the same instant Jude put her mind at rest, he leant further through the window and kissed her at length on her mouth. Then he left her, calling back as he walked away, half turning, 'I won't be long – half an hour at most. Say forty minutes.'

Sophie sat watching him walk away from her down the lane, idly wondering why he had taken his pack with him instead of leaving it with her in the car. As soon as he disappeared from sight, she slithered down in her seat and watched the grasses along the banks wave between her and the blue sky. She felt full of nervous fear but happy – she thought she had never been happier.

Jude knocked on the door and waited. The house was silent; he tried again. Still there was no response. If Kate Merlin was in she was not answering, nor, for that matter, was Benjy. Perhaps they were both out? Jude backed away, looked up at the windows that returned a blank stare. He walked up the cobbles, looked into the studio through the french windows, tried the handle. It turned, opened easily enough. He shouted but got no reply, yet he thought he heard a sound from somewhere inside the house. He closed the french windows, moved away down the cobbles his heart heavy with the finality, the certainty, that he was simply not being answered. His suspicions were confirmed by a glimpse of Kate's car parked down by the stables. He stopped a moment by the water-trough, looked down into the perfect clearness of its depths, the continuous bubbles as the water from the pipe dropped on to its smooth surface; then he swung his pack up on his shoulders, buckled the strap round his waist and left, not through the gate by which he had so recently entered, but by the lane past the stables.

And Benjy, sitting silently on the floor in his bedroom, went to the window when he heard the tread of feet beneath, and watched Jude Deneuve walk down through the yard. He leant forward pressing his face against the old greenish-yellow glass that distorted, blurring Jude's form. He thought of opening the window and calling to him but decided not. Instead, when he could not longer see Jude, he continued to gaze at the whorls in the glass as though at a mandala – except that Benjy had never seen a mandala.

But the sight of Jude's pack had made him restless, restless enough for him to take his bike and set off for Tinners. A short way up the lane to his surprise he saw the Deneuves' car, and as he drew nearer he recognised Sophie in the driving seat. When she saw him she leant out of the window.

'Is Jude indoors with your mother, Benjy?' A small frown creased her normally, smooth brow. Benjy gazed at her soberly.

'He's gone,' he said.

'Where was he going, do you know?' Sophie tried to keep her voice steady.

'I dunno. D'you want to come in and see Mum?'

'No – no thanks. I have to get back. I was to have given Jude a lift to the station but perhaps he's changed his mind,' Sophie lied bravely.

Benjy said nothing. He eyed Sophie because she didn't seem like she normally seemed and it was rather funny her sitting there waiting for Jude who'd gone the other way.

Sophie started the car, ran it down the lane and turned in the gateway. The she drove up past Benjy pressed tightly into the hedge with his bike, waving out of the window at him a she passed. She could see him receding behind her in her driving mirror and was thankful he couldn't see her face – she didn't want to be remembered as a crying woman. She accelerated, the wheels scattered grit, the sun shone on the windscreen so she could not see; she pulled down the sun-shield and drove on. The exuberant vegetation that before had seemed to wave joyously, now lashed the car as it passed.

Benjy reached Tinners only to find Eddie out, in fact all the Fardons out. He hung around hopefully for the best part of an hour before giving up hope, and would have pushed his bike back up the long hill home had he not discovered that his tyre was once again flat. He tried pumping it up but the air hissed out as fast as he pumped, so he decided to abandon it in the Fardons' outhouse and make his way home over the fields.

The tract of land he set out over had once been the Grangers'; it had gappy hedges and gateless gateways, and culminated in the bony enclosure of moor grazing Alec

Deneuve had bought off them, and that was to be sold up again the following week with Scarhill. It occurred to Benjy, as he scrambled up towards a slab of rock at the newtake's top, that new owners might fence it with wire as Alec Deneuve had Scardon, might infringe yet further on his own happy right to wander. A sense of unease that almost amounted to fear hastened him up the last steep bracken-covered yards to the rock he had chosen and on which he settled to study the fast-closing gap between sun and horizon. Dare he, he wondered, wait to watch it set? He would be late for dinner and risk angering his mother, which thought alarmed him more now that Astra was no longer there to divert his mother's displeasure.

But the sun won. He drew up his knees for the air was chill, rested his chin on them and watched the orange ball of sun lower itself steadily towards the horizon. Or so it seemed to Benjy, who could never quite believe that the earth was moving rather than the sun. The river far beneath him curled like a tress of dark hair – Astra's hair, Benjy thought. Light blazed in his eyes from the west; dazzled, he rubbed them. Just in front and beneath him a sallow covered in white flower shone silver in the sun's rays, then a slight breeze came and the flowers lifted and floated about, now rising, now falling; one blew on him and he picked it up to examine it, rubbed it between his thumb and forefinger. When he looked up again the sun had slipped into haze and become a huge transparent red balloon but better than any balloon for more perfectly round. Benjy clasped his knees tighter and rocked, waited, watched the red circle slide, inch by inch, become three-quarters, then half, then a saucepan lid set on earth's range, then it was gone. He felt a quiver of loss and at the same time an intense, almost blissful oneness with his surroundings. The ground on every side was greying in the twilight as the dew rose; a flattened kidney-shaped patch indicated where a cow had recently lain, the acid smell of its dung reached his nostrils, he breathed it in along with the other familiar evening scents. Then a jet tore across the sky, very low, followed by another that seemed set to fly straight into the side of the hill; the noise was so shattering that Benjy instinctively covered his ears while eagerly following the planes with his eyes. Their noise cut off as sharply as it had come, and long after they had gone Benjy continued to scan the pale yellow and violet sky, hoping for their return to terrify him yet again. But only the darkness increased till at last he stood, remembering the previous time, how Astra had gone on ahead, her dark shape above the disappearing white of her legs propelling her away from him, the distance increasing. 'Wait,' he'd shouted – he remembered that.

A maybug passed him now with a loud zoom. Astra was dead. Cremated. Vividly he saw the white petals of the yellow-centred daisies, the orange lilies with stamens in their centres like spears, his sister's coffin sucked inexorably along the conveyor belt to incineration. Benjy didn't believe in afterlife; for him there was no consolation.

The day of the auction dawned warm and mild. On the way there Kate wound down her Morris's window and Alec Deneuve, coming from the opposite direction, slid back his sun-roof. They glimpsed each other in their respective cars but averted their eyes, hastening towards the salesroom by different routes. Kate allowed Alec to get well ahead of her, then entered by a door to the right of the main entrance.

A collection of people had already gathered and were sitting round talking; they were mainly farmers, their arms resting on the backs of their own or adjoining chairs, their gaitered legs incongruous against the modern orange fibre glass seating. Kate made her way across the back row and sat down. From where she was she had a good view, could hear the bidding, study the possible purchasers, then slip out unaccosted. Only curiosity had brought her, for to sell Scarhill in a number of lots seemed to her no less than butchery. As it stood, it had precisely the right amount of arable and rough grazing to make it both viable and self-supporting; in the next half-hour she would see it spoiled as a farm, perhaps for ever, for as well as the division of the land, Alec had applied for and been given, planning permission to convert the barns for holiday tenure – even the buildings, it seemed, were being lost.

She fidgeted forward on her orange seat, crossed one leg over the other, clasped her hands over the skirt she kept for such occasions; she nodded to one or two local people who noticed her, otherwise she kept very much in the background. The Grangers were several rows ahead of her but they, like herself, must have come out of curiosity, for prices were likely to be far above the average farmer's means. She looked around her, wondering who were potential buyers.

When at last the entrance doors ceased to open and shut, the auctioneer looked at his watch, murmured to his assistant and stood up. 'Ladies and gentlemen – farmers or otherwise – this farm I have to auction today is an exceptional property. It's becoming rarer and rarer for a good working concern such as this one to come on the market, and I should like to point out that although I have been instructed to sell it in separate lots – indicated by your maps in front of you – there is no reason, ladies and gentlemen, why anyone caring to farm should not purchase all three lots, house and meadows, arable and afforested . . .' – here the other Hunters' man whispered something – 'I'm sorry, ladies and gentlemen, no afforestation owing to the unfortunate fire Mr Deneuve suffered some six months back, but valuable newtake ground . . .' He paused, found his place, went on.

'So now I am asked by Mr and Mrs Deneuve who, owing to circumstance, have to move up country, to put before you in three separate lots, Scarhill Farm. I shall start with Lot 1, farmhouse and buildings, three adjoining pastures, including pond and fishing stream . . .'

His voice droned on as Kate's mind drifted. The middle classes, of which she was one, had truly invaded the country, brought with them their instability, their impatience and restless desire for change. A way of life was disappearing with every farm sale, every retirement, every farm child who looked for employment in the towns for lack of work on the land . . .

'£165,000 I'm bid. Are you all done at £165,000? Can I say £170 – against you, sir, on my right. Lot 1 – a house such as you'll never find again set in a veritable oasis of twenty acres. £170,000. Thank you, sir. Once,' he brought his hammer down with a rap, 'twice,' he brought it down again, 'three times, and Scarhill farmhouse is sold to Mr . . . er?' he looked enquiringly at the buyer.

'Wykeham-Hurst.'

'Wykeham-Hurst. Thank you, sir.'

Stealthily Kate got up and slipped out.

In the street she drew in several deep breaths, endeavouring to calm herself, contain the sudden homesick misery that had overtaken her inside the sales room. Where was Sophie? She had to know. She waited, hung around trying not to be noticed while the building emptied. At last, at the very end, came Alec with the auctioneer. They were discussing something intently, moving towards their cars. Kate followed, guessing Alec was still endeavouring to sell other of his properties and nervous of butting in with her question. Alec had got in, was closing his car door when he saw her.

'Alec – where's Sophie?'

Alec's face was expressionless, his eyes met hers. 'Gone,' he said, 'I thought she'd have told you.'

'Gone where?'

'I don't know.' Alec's voice was thick, husky. He looked down. Kate was stunned at this tough man broken; she felt embarrassment and at the same time overwhelming compassion. So Alec Deneuve actually felt.

'I'm sorry,' she murmured, 'I'm truly terribly sorry.' And she took a step back as if to enable him to get away from her.

Alec nodded; she suspected he didn't trust himself to speak. He turned his starter key and Kate walked away. She wondered whether she would ever see him again and decided most probably not. So Sophie had at last broken from her cocoon – a metamorphosis of some sort had begun. She didn't know whether to be pleased or cry. It was nothing to do with her any more, she advised herself, the Deneuves had done their destruction and were going. Yet she could feel nothing but loss; it seemed to her at that moment that they were alive and it was she who was dead. Did living and destruction inevitably go hand in hand, or was their 'living' an illusion, hers real? She sighed as she turned into Tesco's. The shopping had to be done, she and Benjy must eat, must continue to exist. She sometimes wondered if there was any more to life than that. For an average person of no particular distinction like herself, did it, could it, have any significance?

'Salted or unsalted?' The assistant behind the cold-storage counter repeated his question, his hand hovering over the butter.

'Salted,' said Kate, then changed her mind, 'No – unsalted, please.' And in this single phrase realised, by implication, that she had chosen life.

Epilogue

The Deneuves had been gone six weeks when the new people moved in. Gabe Fardon, contracted in advance to cut hay, drove up and down, up and down with his new disc mower twirling confidently behind his even newer tractor bought by the bank and for which he paid monthly.

As he drove he looked down thoughtfully on the roofs of Scarhill where an immense horsebox was wedged in the back yard and out of which had descended, so far, no fewer than five horses. He glimpsed women – or was it girls – standing around holding them, examining their bandaged legs for scratches, talking in clear penetrating voices that floated up to him. A few minutes later they appeared in the gateway; they seemed to be watching Gabe, who opened his throttle, delighting in the power of his foreign-built tractor. He looked across the valley to where a faint green was beginning to colour the blackened landscape. Pity, Gabe thought, pity about the plantation – there'd have been money in it all right. That Alec Deneuve had been a shrewd one by all he heard – he'd quit quick enough. Funny that. Some said he'd pushed dud banknotes but you didn't want to believe the stories you heard round – if you did you'd never trust your neighbour. He slowed down to turn, observing the now empty gateway. As he did so a very thoroughbred-looking horse pranced into it and stood trembling, its nostrils distended. It was followed in a few moments by two young women looking hot and anxious.

'Oh God,' said the first, 'Now what?'

The second produced a halter and, hiding it tactfully behind her back, advanced on the horse who pranced elegantly and galloped across the even, shining swaths to the top of the field.

'I'm terribly sorry,' said the first young woman, 'she pulled her halter rope undone.'

Gabe grinned agreeably down from his potent height at her fresh hot face.

'Doesn't look a picnic to catch,' he remarked.

'No,' said Louise, for that was her name, 'poor Nicki.' They watched Nicki advance up the field. When she got near the horse it wheeled round and galloped back to Gabe and Louise. Gabe turned off his tractor and climbed down. When Nicki reached them he offered his help, which they accepted gratefully. He took the halter and with clickings and croons and a soft blowing through his teeth, advanced on the hypnotised horse who stood curiously cowed, allowing Gabe to slide the halter round its neck and over its nose.

'Thanks a million,' said Louise. 'You're obviously wonderful with horses. Do you have your own?'

'Hate 'em,' said Gabe, 'can't abide 'em. Dangerous, they is.' He surveyed the two girls while he rolled a cigarette.

'You're the new owners?' He indicated Scarhill with a nod.

'Oh yes – it's fabulous. We adore it.'

Gabe nodded. He'd always fancied Scarhill himself, and the Warren. Both of them nice farms. Had been.

'Didn't want to farm, then?' Gabe studied them. Delicately plump, long limbed. Of course they didn't.

They shook their heads. 'Daddy's not a farmer,' Nicki said.

'Perhaps you might have some hay we could buy off you?' Nicki's sister – or that's what he took her for – looked hopefully at the juicy swaths.

Gabe altered his stance, a little, folded his arms. 'Hay's scarce, or will be,' he said, looking as though selling hay was not at all in his interest – mentally he totted up what they'd pay – 'I'll have to see,' he said. 'It'll be pricey though, this year, after the dry summer.'

'Oh dear,' said Nicki anxiously, 'Daddy's only paying for the first ton. After that we're on our own.'

'Sisters, is you?' Gabe looked from one to the other. The horse snorted and paced round in a circle.

'Yes,' said Nicki, 'I'm Nicki and she's Louise.'

'I'd better take her in,' said Louise, looking at her horse. She smiled winsomely at Gabe, whose heart melted but only enough to take a couple of pence off every ten bales. 'Thanks for catching Persephone.'

'What do you call 'er?' Gabe couldn't believe his ears.

'Persephone.'

'Where did you get a name like that from?'

'A Greek goddess.' Louise giggled. 'She ate pomegranate seeds in the underworld so she had to spend part of every year down there, her mother couldn't get her up. It's terribly sad,' she explained.

London people, Gabe thought, he wouldn't give them long with their fancy names. One winter'd fix them. He trod the stub of his cigarette into the ground. A car passed on the road and Persephone leaped forward, towing Nicki with her down the field. Louise was about to follow when she seemed to think of something.

'We've had an invitation from your rector,' she said, 'asking us to tea. He's very prompt.'

'Not mine,' said Gabe, 'you wouldn't catch me listening to him on a Sunday. I don't hold with it.'

'Don't you go to church? I thought country people did.' Louise regarded him with curiosity.

'There's people an' people,' said Gabe sagely. To which Louise had no answer. She looked after Nicki, who had reached the gateway.

'We'll see you again, I hope.' She smiled at Gabe, as taken by his dark eyes as others before her.

Gabe nodded and climbed back on his tractor. Moments later he resumed mowing, the spinning discs leaving a wake of pale yellow between the damp green swaths. He thought about the new people. There wasn't anything wrong with them – pity about Scarhill, though – pity about the Merlin girl, a bad business that . . .

Ahead of him a baby hawk fluttered out of a hedge and sat on a fencing-post. Sparrowhawk, Gabe thought to himself, must be.

NORA NAISH

The Butterfly Box

The butterfly box is a small art nouveau cigarette case which has been in Lucy Marshall's family for years. Together with a family portrait allegedly by Klimt, it has been passed down through four generations of mothers and daughters.

But the butterfly box hides a secret, which is revealed when the family come together at Lucy's home in the Cotswolds to celebrate her eightieth birthday. Around her Lucy gathers her daughter Beena, granddaughter Joanna, who is bringing her new boyfriend to meet them for the first time, and, in spirit, her mother Louise. It is Louise's journals, left in Lucy's keeping and long unread, which reveal that the box lies at the centre of a family scandal far darker than anyone suspected.

'An engaging portrait of mothers and daughters who know each other and love each other'
Daily Mail

'Dr Naish knows how to tell a good story ... this is the perfect holiday read'
Evening Standard

SALLY BRAMPTON

Lovesick

Martha's got a secret – pass it on . . .

Harry, Martha, Phil, Jane and David – artist, teacher, lawyer, interior designer and businessman. Five people, all successful and all related in one way or another – a wife, a mother, a friend, a husband, a lover.

Outwardly they are ordinary people with ordinary lives, all their worries buried deep below the surface. But when Martha leaves Harry, launching herself exuberantly on a blazing affair engineered by her sister Jane, she triggers a chain of events that will uncover the most devastating secret of all.

A bitter-sweet, contemporary novel about friendship, love – and the sometimes deadly consequences of both.

'Sally Brampton is an excellent writer'
Literary Review

CAROL BIRCH

Songs of the West

'In Carol Birch's skilful novel, prosperous foreign incomers
to furthest south-west Ireland buy large houses and estab-
lish "affirmation centres", make yoghurt and criticise com-
mercialism. Meanwhile, the local country people get on
with earning a living. Essie, middle-class and English, with
seventeen rings in her ears and a stud in her tongue, makes
earthenware knick-knacks. Rosanna is an anarchic alcoholic.
Their friend Marie is a respectable wife and mother. One
summer Marie falls for a writer from Dublin who passes
through in his yellow caravan . . . Carol Birch writes beauti-
fully about a place she must know and love, and has an
acute ear for dialogue'
Sunday Telegraph

'Full of richly imagined characters, written with a fluent
assurance'
Sunday Times

'*Songs of the West* is extremely hard to put aside . . . it is
good to read the work of a writer who looks and listens so
closely'
Times Literary Supplement

'Bustles with characters . . . a rich, often funny novel'
New Statesman

A Selected List of Fiction Available from Mandarin

While every effort is made to keep prices low, it is sometimes necessary to increase prices at short notice. Mandarin Paperbacks reserves the right to show new retail prices on covers which may differ from those previously advertised in the text or elsewhere.

The prices shown below were correct at the time of going to press.

All these books are available at your bookshop or newsagent, or can be ordered direct from the address below. Just tick the titles you want and fill in the form below.

Cash Sales Department, PO Box 5, Rushden, Northants NN10 6YX.
Fax: 01933 414047 : Phone: 01933 414000.

Please send cheque, payable to 'Reed Book Services Ltd.', or postal order for purchase price quoted and allow the following for postage and packing:

£1.00 for the first book, 50p for the second; **FREE POSTAGE AND PACKING FOR THREE BOOKS OR MORE PER ORDER.**

NAME (Block letters) ....

ADDRESS ....

....

☐ I enclose my remittance for ....

☐ I wish to pay by Access/Visa Card Number

Expiry Date

Signature ....

Please quote our reference: MAND